MONKEYS and MERIT BADGES

Paul Fleming, Jr.

PublishAmerica
Baltimore

© 2004 by Paul Fleming, Jr.
All rights reserved. No part of this book may be reproduced, stored in a retrieval system, or transmitted in any form or by any means without the prior written permission of the publishers, except by a reviewer who may quote brief passages in a review to be printed in a newspaper, magazine, or journal.

First printing

Boy Scout material copyrighted by and property of Boy Scouts of America. Used by permission.

ISBN: 1-59286-658-1
PUBLISHED BY PUBLISHAMERICA, LLLP
www.publishamerica.com
Baltimore

Printed in the United States of America

AUTHOR'S FOREWORD

This story is about a boy growing up during the great depression in the 1930's in a small town in Eastern Arkansas. It is told in the first person using the same style if not the same vocabulary as the boy might have used at the time being presented. I grew up in Eastern Arkansas in such a town, and the settings and events are an accurate representation of the lifestyles and portray plausible happenings for the era and locale. Some of these events are extracted or modified from those of numerous people; some are of my own fiction. It is fairly easy to observe the mannerisms of living people in those described here. However, except for my parents and grandfather, no one should see him or herself in any of the characters presented, because I have tried diligently not to portray any person I have known.

The Boy Scouts are mentioned frequently. I did receive my Eagle Badge; and like I said, it is one of my proudest achievements.

PF
2004

CHARACTER NAMES	ROLL	CHAP. INTRODUCED
GAYLORD THROCKMORTON MONTMORENCY CRAWFORD	MAIN	I
MOTHER, DAD, AND GRAND DAD		I
TIPTON LIGHTWEIGHT CHRISTIAN HAIL COLUMBIA CALVIN JONES	WORKED FOR FAMILY	I
MARYPAMELLA	OLDER SISTER	I
JESSE GAYLORD	MOTHER'S BROTHER	I
JOHN THROCKMORTON	MOTHER'S BROTHER	I
ALBERT MONTMORENCY	MOTHER'S BROTHER	I
MC ADAMS	PARENTS' FRIENDS	I
GAIL LOU MC ADAMS	DAUGHTER OF FRIENDS	I
MR. WORTHING	SUPT OF COUNTY SCHOOLS	II
MRS. COX	FIRST GRADE TEACHER	II
JOHN ANDERSON	DID # 2	II
FRANCIS SMITH	FRIEND IN FIRST GRADE, GOOD SPELLER	II
MAUREEN HODGES	POOR SPELLER, MISSED WORD "A"	II
MISS CALDWELL	TEACHER, GRAMMAR SCHOOL	IV
MRS. SHARP	TEACHER, GRAMMAR SCHOOL	IV
MISS WATSON	TEACHER, GRAMMAR SCHOOL	IV
SUSANNE JONES	GIRL WHO DISCOVERED GAYLORD ON LEDGE	IV
MRS. MCPHERSON	PRINCIPAL O SCHOOL	IV
MR. MOSES	JANITOR, GRAMMAR SCHOOL	IV
JERICHO	TRAIN ENGINEER	V
WILSON GISON	FRIEND	V
CHIEF JOHN HENRY ROBINSON	CHIEF OF POLICE	V
COUSIN ALBERT	RELATIVE, FARMER	V
MISS LUMLEY	ENGLISH TEACHER IN GRAMMAR SCHOOL	V
SHERIFF WILD BILL TAYLOR	SHERIFF OF FRANCIS COUNTY	V
JIM ROPER	STATE TROOPER	V
GEORGE AGENCY	UNDERTAKER	V
Mrs. Swanson	**Kleptomaniac**	V
SOLLIE	DOG	V

CHARACTER NAMES	ROLL	CHAP.
THOMAS JEFFERSON	TERRAPIN	V
AGATHA THOMPSON	DATE AT FIRST DANCE	VI
IDA THOMPSON	MOTHER OF AGATHA	VI
MR. BLACK	OWNER OF DRUG STORE	VI
JOHN ANDERSON	PHOTOGRAPHER	VI
SKINNEY	MEMBER OF SCOUT PATROL	VII
MR. OWENS	SCOUTMASTER	VII
DICK WILLIAMS	OWNER OF POOL HALL	X
MRS. SHOHAN	CALLED POOL HALL	X
JOHNSON TOM	PILOT	XII
BILLY NAIL	SCOUT THAT WAS SHOT	XIV
MONK	CHIMPANZEE	XV
NANNETTE	JOHNSON TOM'S GIRL	XV
SHERIFF	ARRESTING	XV
MRS. ADAMS	HUMANE SOCIETY	XV
MRS. WASSERMAN	HUMANE SOCIETY	XV
JUNE	JOHNSON TOM'S GIRL	XV
MR. JERGENS	HOTEL OWNER	XVI
JOE SMITHSON	HOTEL OWNER	XVI
RACHEL	JOHNSON TOM'S GIRL	XVI
MRS. TAYLOR	ON TELEPHONE	XVII
JOHNNIE	MRS. TAYLOR'S SON	XVII
JIM DODY	FRIEND IN SCOUTS	XVII
MR. FERGUSON	DRUG STORE OWNER	XVII
BIG RED	OWNER OF MODEL "A"	XVII
BULL	CUSTOMER IN BIG RED'S BEER JOINT	XVII
MR. SPOONER	PRESIDENT OF BANK	XVII
MMIE JONES	SCOUT	XVIII
DAVID WORTH	SCOUT	XVIII
MARY AXWORTHY	GIRL WHO DID, MAYBE	XVIII
RUDOLPH MCCRARY	SCOUT GETTING BADGE	XIX
MRS. BROWN	LITERATURE TEACHER IN HIGH SCHOOL	XX
SERGEANT	WITH TELEGRAM	XX

MONKEYS and MERIT BADGES

CHAPTER I

GAYLORD THROCKMORTON MONTMORENCY CRAWFORD

I may as well get the bad part over with, or bad anyway as far as I am concerned. That is my name—all of it—and that was my Mother calling me. Almost anyone will have to admit that is a lot to hang onto a new-born baby, especially at a time when he doesn't know anything yet, and when he can't do anything about it if he did, and when it's done all at once. Except for the Crawford part, which came with me so to speak, I have never liked any part of it. There just is no way you can cut up that appellative collage to make a name for everyday use. Any attempt at abbreviation brings about something that is worse than the whole, if that is possible. Gaylord leads to Gay or to Lord, both impossible if you are trying to be reasonably regular, and of course Throckmorton is hopeless from the start. While Montmorency just might be shortened to Monty, I have never liked that one either, probably from association with the other two. I have known only one other person with a worse name, and that was an old black man who worked for my family for years whose name was Tipton Lightweight Christian Home Hail Columbia Calvin Jones. We called him "Sam". The big difference was that Sam liked his name and had business cards printed to show it off. Not me. Except for my earliest memories, before I knew anything about anything, I have suffered with this millstone all of my life, and I suppose I always will.

These earliest memories precede my second birthday, because I have fleeting recollections of a younger brother who died before I was two. From three on, many events come to mind and these pre-school years passed very pleasantly with the usual pranks and experiments of little kids.

My older sister, Marypamella, about 16 months my senior, started to kindergarten during my third year. Mother took me there one afternoon for a visit and the teacher asked me if I wanted a quarter of an apple. I had never seen an apple cut up like that before and I still think they taste better that way, but she forgot to give me the quarter. Marypamella learned and then taught me how to count up to 100 before I was four. For some reason, I thought she had just made up the number 14 so, when I counted, it was 12,

13, 15, 16... I also found that a tomcat will absolutely scratch you to shreds if you put a spring-type clothespin on his tail, and that your mother gets uncommonly upset when you almost get run over by a truck.

A small creek ran about three blocks from home and this manifested two attractions for me. First, I was forbidden to play there, and second, there were several still pools about the size of a bathtub that provided habitat for a lot of surface water bugs. I used to watch these creatures skim over the surface and ponder about why they didn't sink. I found that with considerable care, occasionally a grain of sand could be deposited on the back of a bug before it scooted away. When this occurred the bug labored some but still could stay atop. As the skill increased but still with a lot of care, the grain of sand became two, then a small cluster, the breakthrough coming for me as well as for the water bugs with a small pebble. I found that any water bug I ever saw can be forced under any time just by dropping a rock on him. I have performed this little test dozens of times, the last being day before yesterday (different creek) and the results are always the same. The bug just goes right down under the rock, and squirms out to one side before he gets trapped. It was astounding to me that after getting free of the rock but while still under the water, a bug had a lot of trouble getting back on top of the surface. He was held down by the surface tension, but I didn't learn the reason until years later. He would dive down and then dart upward and try to break through the surface and if successful flopped on top and then scooted away. If not, he repeated the attempt until he broke out or drowned trying. Most broke out. I also learned along the way that these bugs sink if a small drop of detergent is placed on the water in their midst. You can see the surface tension break into an expanding ring, and the bugs go down, like so many water skiers with broken tow ropes, as the ring passes each one.

At the time, however, I had to endure the wrath of Mother when I got home because skill in dropping rocks on water bugs is gained by lying prone at the water's edge, with your face practically awash. Of course this makes you wet and muddy, and mothers, mine anyway, absolutely like their kids without mud and dry. I guess it all starts when you are a little baby and are never clean or dry. Mothers just never get over it later on.

All of this took place in a little town called Woodton in eastern Arkansas where I was reared in the 1930's. It is difficult for many to appreciate this now, but times were hard —really hard—during all of that decade, and the mere threat of financial trouble was sufficient to mold many personal actions and attributes. A fierce competition existed for every job, and once won, any job was considered to be a prize, and no thoughts were given to raises or promotions. Just holding a job was promotion enough, and many men born around 1900 lived through their own golden thirties in work that did not challenge their capabilities, only to find that with the better times that came with their forties, they no longer were suitable for advancement because the breadths of their experiences did not match those of younger men returning from World War II.

Such was the trap that engulfed my father. His schooling had been interrupted at twelve when his mother died and his father had broken up housekeeping. As a boy he had gotten a job with the utility company in Woodton, and had worked there since. Even though he was considered one of the best and most dependable employees, the chances for advancement were slight, and he always felt that he could have done better under different economic circumstances. I think so, too.

Because of his own limited schooling, Dad was a bear on the benefits of education. He read everything that came his way and possessed a vast amount of knowledge on just about anything. He knew about the details of bird migrations and all about clouds, and about levees, and oil wells and dozens of other things. He had quite a feeling about military tactics and later during World War II predicted correctly several weeks in advance each major offensive of both sides as well as the most likely locale and time for the action. He worked crossword puzzles for years and knocked off the big ones in the Sunday papers about as quickly as most people could do the dailies. Partly because of this and partly because of natural interest, he had a fantastic vocabulary and could give the meaning of almost any word that ever cropped up. This word knowledge was completely passive because he talked very simply, and as he never bothered to check pronunciations, he sometimes had to see unusual ones written down before he would recognize them.

Dad had firm but fair ideas on many subjects. He felt that personal grooming was important, but that it was more a matter of the man than the clothes. "The man makes the clothes, not vice- versa," was his creed. "If a man is shaven and his hair combed, has on a clean white shirt and a tie, and his shoes are shined, then he will look all right no matter how ragged his clothes are. Same way with a woman. If she has her hair and face fixed, and is wearing high heels and silk stockings, she'll look pretty good no matter what she has on." I never heard anyone else express these thoughts quite this way, but I always have found them to be true.

His thoughts on art exemplify some of this. I was in grammar school, the teacher was trying to show us some of the masters and some of the modern examples as well, and having pretty heavy going with all of it. Especially with me. None of it was taking at all and I complained to Dad. He got the whole concept across in a few sentences, "Son, art is just the skillful use of means at your disposal to bring about some desired effect that is more than just making something work. Sometimes the effect is to make a likeness of a tree or some other object, other times it is a pleasant sound like music. It may be arranging the food on a plate so it looks nice. The important concept is skill, so when looking at art look for evidences of skill. You can always admire skill, even if you don't care for the reasons for using it. Same way with art, you don't have to like it to appreciate it." Others may not like this conceptual definition, but it sure did straighten me out in a hurry, and has seen me through ever since.

Dad was a gentleman all the way, and always held his hat in his hand when addressing women, or even little girls only three or four years old. He always stood when a woman entered a room and remained thus until she seated herself or left the room. He would never let it show at the time it happened, but he sometimes would comment that girls should be taught early either to sit down or to leave promptly when men were standing for them. Most did, but occasionally there would be one who never had picked up this little point of etiquette and would stand and yak endlessly while the men shifted from one foot to the other. Of course, none of this means much today in the midst of the women's liberation movements, but it was important then.

Dad always felt that a man should be proud of his work and of workmanship. "If a man will leave a bent-over nail in the middle of a wall where he had plenty of light and a good swing with his hammer, there's no telling what he'll do standing on his head back in some dark corner where he can't get at it." This expressed his feelings on this matter. He felt that it was at least a mild disgrace to be required to do any task a second time. "Do it right, and you won't have to go back," was his motto. He spent a lot of his own time just learning how to do more with his tools and how to keep them in shape; his screwdriver blades were always shaped and filed, and his pliers worked smoothly. A razor blade was as dull as a fork handle compared with his pocketknife. "Don't buy a tool until you need it, then get the very best one made. A good tool will last a hundred years," were his thoughts on how to equip a toolbox or a workshop. I still have some of his tools now, which are more than fifty years old, and only little more than half used up.

X X X X X

It is difficult to discuss my Father without giving a passing salute to **his** Father. These two were exactly alike in some ways, but very different in others. Granddad was, "Damn the torpedoes, full speed ahead." Dad was much more thoughtful in his approach. Both had a wide range of interests, and both read a great deal.

When a young man of about 18, my Grandfather inherited a great deal of property down in the boot heel of Missouri in and around Poplar Bluff. As nearly as I can reconstruct this event, his legacy included a small hotel, two saloons, a drug store and some farmland, and probably represented the equivalency of several million dollars today.

With his usual gusto, Granddad lived it up and wine'd, women'd, and song'd it away in about a year. He worked for others for the rest of his life and never accumulated much although he was never destitute either. When asked if he had any regrets, he always claimed that if he had it to do over again, he would just try to spend it a little faster.

He was a farmer of unquestioned repute, and could grow radishes and carrots the size of footballs. Of course, these were not very good to eat; he would grow a few a year just to show it could be done. "You have to know your ground and your moon," was his explanation, "then you can grow anything, anyway you want to." He certainly knew his ground and his moon, because he consistently grew more cotton, corn, and soybeans per acre than almost anyone around there.

He took us grand kids into the watermelon patch and told us we could have any melon we wanted except a special one that he called his seed melon. Of course, nothing would do but we must eat that particular one, which we did. But he was a lot smarter than we. You see, that was not the seed melon at all, it was over in a corner of the patch, toward the back, kind of hard to get to, and where he said the snakes were.

His attitude toward science represented a true anomaly. He eagerly awaited the development of new fertilizers and insecticides, but he denounced all scientific endeavors in his usual go-no-go way, "Somebody oughta put a stop to them scientific bastards, they're a hundred years ahead of the world now."

Grand dad issued these words about six months before he was run over by a car at the age of 84. He died soon, but not immediately following the accident. Several witnesses reported that he looked at the driver of the car in the eye and said, "I'll wait inside the gates of hell for you."

X X X X X

Dad's courtliness matched Mother's personality very well. She was an unbelievable romanticist and loved names like mine, and of course, she had been responsible for it. Apparently, she had inherited this trait from her Mother, because her's were named respectively and in part, Gaylord, Throckmorton, and of course Montmorency. Fortunately for them, each also had one or two other normal names which made it a little more humane, such as Jesse Gaylord, and John Throckmorton Henry, and Albert Montmorency. I was just lucky she didn't have more brothers because she also liked Beauregard and Lancelot, not to mention Twylagart. Have you ever heard of *anyone* named Twylagart? Mother was completely unaware of the pain my name caused me, and always addressed me by the entire burden. In particular, she never caught on when people asked in disbelief that it be repeated.

I could sense her mood by the way she said it. If everything was all right, it came out GAY-lord Throck<u>mor</u>ton Mont<u>morence-ee</u>. When she had a surprise for me and was about to pop because she couldn't hold it in anymore, the ending trilled up and down two or three times. But when she said it GAYLORD THROCKMORTON MONTMORENCY with all syllables in a row and even like a picket fence, I knew I had had it and she was going to remove the skin. If she added Crawford at the end, hell would be a cave in an iceberg compared to the roasting she was about to give me. From all this, you can tell that at the beginning of the chapter, she was going to remove the hide when she got hold of me.

Actually, Mother didn't whip me too often, two or three times a year, sometimes four or five, six maybe, but those were enough to last for a while. In between, I kept in line because I really didn't want to displease her. Like I said, she didn't give me too many spankings, once a month at most, but when she did the dimensions were adjusted to match the reason. She would send me to get a switch for my own licking, and if she thought it to be too small for the misdemeanor, she would send me back. When she was satisfied with the size, she would lay into me with anywhere from five to fifteen licks, depending upon what I had done. At the end, she would say, "Now here are two (or three, or four, the number varied) extra for having to go back the second time." With that lot signed off, she would add a few more for the next trip and so on. Of course, big switches and a lot of swats went together, so the level of the punishment escalated rapidly for the worse deeds. I supposed this pattern would have continued forever, but I never tested it beyond three trips because ordinarily I could judge the size of the whipping pretty well.

Like the time I painted "This is no bull" on the side of Mrs. Johnson's cow. Generally for something like that, I would have gotten off with a reprimand which we both knew was issued more for form than affect, because her eyes would gleam and I would know she could hardly keep from laughing. But Mrs. Johnson was new in town and she thought most people were vulgar. She was still living in the last century and called legs "limbs", and to her bulls were "gentlemen cows". She put up quite a stir with Mother, who made me apologize in front of her, and all that.

I really hadn't thought about things the way Mrs. Johnson had put them, or anything else for that matter, so when these retribution were over, I genuinely wanted to fix it so she wouldn't be offended so much. So I marked out "bull" and substituted "gentleman cows". Now, my heart was pure, but others saw it differently; someone picked up the spirit and wrote, "RUMP STEAK" across the hind end, right where a cow would sit down if cows sat down. The idea caught on, and within two or three days, about twenty or more words or phrases appeared in various places. Some were pretty steep all right, but most were just plain funny. One pair that always stuck with me was a question on one side of the milk bag, "Where is the milkmaid?" On the other side was the answer written by somebody else, "Cow shed I know?"

Anyway, Mrs. Johnson had seen me making my changes and she complained again; I judged the degree of the offense just right—only six swings with a little switch about the size of a number two knitting needle.

The three-tripper caught me by surprise all the way. I was about seven and airplanes had just exploded into my interests, and nothing would do but I should have an airplane. So I decided to build one.

My knowledge of aircraft design included an appreciation of the general shape only, you know wings, body, tail, wheels, and propeller. The resources and skills of a seven-year-old usually can't be stretched to building items such as these, but again most kids are willing to accept some shortcuts. I found an old baby buggy for the wheels and landing gear, fastened on a 2 x 4 about eight feet long for the body, nailed on a couple of shingles for the tail, a 12-inch plank about six feet long became the wing, and a paper whirligig served as the propeller.

On level ground this thing turned out to be pretty inert, a real lead sled, and displayed no propensity for flying at all. Even at that age I knew an airplane had to go fast to fly, and some sort of hill or slope, seemed the best bet; so I looked around to find a place for my first attempt. Mother drives up from a shopping trip to see me take the plunge in the most literal way, right off the garage roof. I was surprised on two accounts, first, I had expected to go flying off in my airplane, and second, after verifying I was unhurt, Mother picked me up by an ear and set into me with her hand. Right off, she decided that wasn't enough heft, so she sent me after a switch. I didn't satisfy her until the third sample, and then she split me at the seams.

I couldn't understand why she was so mad, and pondered about it off and on for years without finding the hint. Only much later, when a kid of my own pulled a similar stunt did I comprehend her actions, except I wonder now why she stopped so soon.

As time went on my opinions of what is right and wrong began to coincide more and more with hers. When our judgments differed, she would shape me up if it was after the fact, and she would describe the nature of the admonishment if the deed had not yet happened. There was one thing I always knew, and that was if a certain punishment were prescribed for a certain action, that punishment would follow without fail when the act was discovered. By and large I got what was coming to me and only once was I punished for no cause.

A family named McAdams lived near us. Mr. and Mrs. McAdams were about the same ages as my parents, and they all became friends, exchanging social visits and borrowing hammers and cups of sugar from time to time. The McAdams had only one child, a little girl about six months younger than my just barely five years, but this made her an infant as far as I was concerned. Girls were an anathema to boys my age anyway, but this one in particular was really sand in the Grapenuts.

The mothers began to spend a lot of time together, so little Gail Lou always was tagging behind me whenever this occurred. On one such event, Mother and I were at the McAdams' house in the afternoon, and I was told to go play with Gail Lou. So I did, trying to think up games she couldn't play very well, or ones where I could invent new rules when she was about to win.

The McAdams' house had a basement, fairly rare in Woodton, and this was entered from the outside by the traditional sloping doors opening onto some steps that led downstairs. Ordinarily, these doors were closed, and in that case presented a moderately steep surface. It wasn't too comfortable, but it could be sat or stood upon if you wanted to, as we did often.

This time one of the two doors was opened about half way, being propped up on a 2 x 4, and offering a much steeper surface. Mrs. McAdams had been drying some apples or something and had forgotten to close it when she took in the apples, or whatever. I discovered that the greater incline made a pretty good slide. It was almost worth your life to climb up on the skittery slope, but once there one could sit on the rather uncomfortable edge of the door until ready, then with an upward heave, the rump was lifted over the edge, delivering a short but exciting trip that ended in a big sprawl on the ground. Fun! Even with Gail Lou around hogging maybe a quarter of the time on the door.

The surface of the door was not too smooth, so we collected up a rip in our clothing or a scratch or some other injury almost every trip, but none of these were significant enough to halt or even slow down the back and forth cycles. On one trip back up, Gail Lou slipped on the roof surface and skidded down hard on her bottom with a thump and rolled onto the ground. She grabbed herself by the crotch with both hands and began to scream "I'm hurt! I'm hurt!" Of course, I wanted to see and was just experiencing the initial, still unformed, but noticeable titillation's and pleasures of primeval urges with the discovery that things were different down there, when out pops the mothers to investigate. The courses of these two took divergent turns right there. Her mother gathered up Gail Lou and carried her inside to see just what the damage really was—it turned out to be insignificant—but on the way in she tossed a snarl at my mother, "You should paddle him good for being such a bad boy." Well, Mother didn't take that too kindly, because she was sure she knew when I needed to be spanked, and said so letting me think she thought I was innocent. Maybe she did, but she dragged me home and lit into me anyway.

The whole incident was a classic example of punishment being administered for misleading circumstantial evidence as well as being misunderstood by the recipient. **Mother** thought I had taken her instruction to go play with Gail Lou too seriously, and **I** thought she thought I had torn it off and thrown it away.

The storm blew away and Mother and Mrs. McAdams were still friends. So it was a sad day when the McAdams moved to another town two or three months later. In the interim, my views of Gail Lou changed considerably. She never would tell me what she had done with it, but she let me look regularly to see that it was still gone.

CHAPTER II

The day finally arrived when I started to school, but not in the usual way at all. My older sister was in the second six weeks of the second grade, and I was five and underfoot around the house. Mother had been a favorite pupil of, and later had taught under, the present superintendent of county schools. She approached this gentleman who agreed that if Mrs. Cox —who was the first grade teacher in the school at Coldwell— would permit, then I could enroll in the first grade. Mrs. Cox and Mother were good friends, and I am sure there was a bit of prearrangement at work, so it was all signed off and I began the first grade on Monday after Thanksgiving at the tender age of five.

The setting merits a description because only a few examples like it are left anywhere. The facility at Coldwell was a two-room country school, wherein about fifty kids in eight grades were taught by two teachers. The front of the wooden building was painted white, not red, and displayed two sets of double doors symmetrically disposed. Entry through either of these doors was gained by three wooden steps leading into one of the two identical cloak rooms where coats and hats were hung in inclement weather. Every school I have ever attended had a cloak room, but never have I known anyone who owned a cloak, or knew anyone else who owned one. Same thing at Coldwell, not once did a cloak ever hang in either cloak room.

A second large but single door in each cloak room led into the respective classroom proper, with grades 1-4 on the left, 5-8 on the right. Once inside, a stage about a foot high, perhaps ten feet deep extended continuously without break across the entire front of the two rooms.

You might wonder how a stage could extend across two rooms like that, because a wall separated the two rooms just as you might expect. Actually the wall extended only about two-thirds of the way from the back of the room to the front, and there was a ponderous sliding door that normally was closed but could be pushed back into this wall, leaving a huge opening between the two rooms toward the front. When this was done, the entire width of the building was transformed to permit the whole stage to be visible from almost anywhere in either room. When the sliding door was closed, passage between the two rooms was effected by a regular door mounted in the sliding door. We thought it was funny that a door should have a door.

A number of large multi-paned windows admitted light freely, there being no artificial lamps of any kind. When opened, the windows offered the only cooling when the weather was hot. The walls mounted blackboards—real slate, not the painted hard board of later years—in just about any place where there was no window or door. Mrs. Cox and her counterpart in the other room sat at desks on the stage.

The pupils in each room sat in desks arranged in four rows, one for each grade, grade one on the right as seen from the front, number four on the extreme left. All these desks occupied about half of the non-staged area, the remaining part being a recitation area, over toward the internal wall with the sliding door. Incidentally, "recitation" was the first big word that I learned about. I didn't really know what it meant, but we "recited" our lessons because that was what Mrs. Cox said we did. And we did it in the recitation area. Anyway, this area contained two or three benches for the class giving its interpretations of the lessons for the day, and a stove, which was the only source of heat for that room in the winter. Each class was heard three or four times a day for about twenty minutes at a time as the teachers listened to our presentations on arithmetic or reading or spelling.

In our room the recitation area also contained a single pupil's desk, the purpose of which became clear immediately on my first day. Except for this single desk, the other room manifested a mirror image arrangement, the symmetry altered only by individual items such as flowerpots here and there.

I was assigned the last seat in the first row, lowest man on the totem pole and the youngest in the whole student body. Everybody knew my name immediately, even before school started on that Monday. It was two or three weeks before I learned everyone else's name. I thought—and many of the kids helped me think so— that I was really dumb. It was quite a while, a month maybe, before it dawned on me that my job was 50 times harder than theirs.

Each day, Mrs. Cox or the other teacher rang a large hand bell to get all of the kids inside and seated. Mrs. Cox then took up —those were the words we used, "took up"— her half of the school by tapping a little call bell similar to the ones used in hotels to summon bell hops. Everything was rigorously formatted, one tap meant one thing, two something else. I forget the sequences now, but they were firmly implanted in our minds then.

Anyway, the first day, there was a BIG ol' boy, a second grader sitting in that lone seat in the recitation area. As soon as class was in session, Mrs. Cox picked this fellow up by the belt and proceeded to give him a licking, like I had never experienced or seen. He yelled and bellered, and made all kinds of fuss while I sat as still as a mouse and didn't make a sound the rest of the day.

Next morning, school took up on schedule as before and another boy occupied the lone chair. Same scene, first off, Mrs. Cox made a grease spot out of him; he yipped and screeched something awful. Third day. Another boy, same thing. Quickly, I put my counting ability to work on my first practical problem. When all were present, which they were that day, my room contained 23 pupils, although I called it 24 because of that missing 14 number, but I knew how many it was even if I called it wrong. Eleven were boys, three were already used up, plus maybe some others before I had started. By laboriously counting out on my fingers, I determined that—at most— eight more school days would see me in the chair. My embryonic analytical ability left me unsure whether that would happen this or next week, but I went home and told Mother that I didn't want to go to school anymore.

Of course, she just dismissed this as being my reaction to a new lifestyle, so I had to fake being sick the next day and the next. With no symptoms of any consequence, she suspected other things and gradually coaxed it from me. When all the fog finally cleared, I was relieved to learn that some considerable misdemeanor always preceded assignment to that chair. Most miscreants were given the assignment of sweeping the floor after school for one or more days. The serious stuff merited a spanking. In the big scheme of things, most swept, but a few wept. For those who did, today's misdeed was punishable first thing tomorrow so all the spankees had the night to think it over and let it soak in before it was soaked in the morning. That was the usual pace, and ordinarily about a kid a week went through the system.

However, in this particular case, these three boys together had pushed over the girl's outdoor john while Mrs. Cox was indisposed in it. This act merited and received her strongest tactics and all were paddled. The only problem was her system could process only one kid a day, so the three drew straws to determine the order of the punishment.

From this you can see that Mrs. Cox was not the ogre this initial episode might indicate. She was very popular with the kids, and was firm but fair and ran her room by a set of rules that were simple and easy to understand. But sometimes we kids made things a lot more complicated than they needed to be.

Like going to the john. Now Mrs. Cox's rule was that we raise our hand and ask to be excused. However, we kids insisted upon more detail. So, a raised hand with the forefinger extended was a request for "number one". Two fingers meant the other. A raised hand accompanied by a tilt back of the head meant "a drink of water" and so on. A number two excuse could include a little number one and no one would really know, but you were considered mean if you asked for number one and extended it to number two, and beneath contempt if a number one or two requester also took in a drink. Tattling on someone was against the code, but it was considered eminently proper to announce for all to hear, "Mrs. Cox, John Anderson asked for number one and did number two." Of course, Mrs. Cox never did anything about it because these were not her rules, but thinking about it now, she possessed an amazingly large sampling of one and two and drink habits of kids and could have written quite a book about it.

The first grade was a lot of work, but it also was fun. We learned to read from "Baby Ray" books. "Baby Ray has a cat. Baby Ray loves his cat. The cat loves Baby Ray. Do you have a cat? Do you love your cat?..." We learned to count which, like I said, I already knew how to do, except for 14 that is, which Mrs. Cox soon corrected. We learned to add and subtract and also to do long hand writing. Many are astounded to hear long hand was taught in my first grade because some schools today do not teach this until the second or third years. I remember it quite well because when we completed our work at the board, we filled in all our remaining space with our names written over and over again so we could spell them correctly without faltering. I must have written Gaylord Throckmorton Montmorency Crawford a million times before I got it right without first looking at the sample put up for me by Mrs. Cox.

We also learned on the playground at recess. The very first day, some kid found out that I could count and he bet me he could count to a hundred before I could, so I started off with a "One, two, three…," and he lets me get up to about fifty and he rips out, "…ten, ten, double ten, forty-five, fifteen." I didn't really believe that was counting to a hundred, and complained to Mother. She showed that it was, although not the usual way. That made me so mad I learned maybe ten different ways to count to a hundred real fast, but I found that no one really cared including me. It is funny, but I haven't really felt like counting up to a hundred now for a long time.

Another kid taught me to spell "that". He came up and sang out "Rail Road crossing, look out for the cars, can you spell that without any R's?" It took me a while to catch on, but I have never forgotten his spelling lesson.

Except for our names, spelling was taught in the class room in a spelling bee environment. Each day, Mrs. Cox would give us about ten new words which we all copied down in our tablets. We were responsible for any words given out previously, but the thump was particularly hard if we didn't know the words in a given assignment.

At spelling time, the class would line up in a row facing Mrs. Cox. She would select a word from the growing list that had been given out in the past, and offer it to the one at the end of the line on her right. If spelled correctly, she would choose a second word and offer it to number two in the line, and so on. If a word were misspelled by, say number two, then number three would get a shot. Whoever finally spelled the word then moved up in the line, "turning down" everyone who had missed it. The spellers then were ranked pretty well according to ability at the period, and this would be the line-up order for the next day. When you were absent, then in effect all the words were missed that time, so next day you started at the foot of the line. I have never been too much of a speler so I usually hovered in the lower half anyway, so missing a day made little difference. In sharp contrast was Francis Smith, who was my good friend, but I always hated him at spelling time because he could spell anything. He got a whipping at home if he missed a word at school.

One time, Mrs. Cox offered the word "pony" to Francis who naturally was at the head of the line. I had been absent the day before, so I was at the foot. My ears perked up, because incredibly he missed and I could spell it. However, three or four others separated me from the head, and surely someone else would get it right before my turn came. Again, unbelievable, each in turn missed the word, one spelling H-O-R-S-E, another P-O-N-N-Y. My moment finally arrived. Now I would turn down the entire line including Francis at the head! No one had ever done that before. With brave heart born of sublime confidence, loud and clear, I spelled out P-O-N-E-Y.

There was a girl, Maureen Hodges, who was a poor student in general because she was absent a lot, so she missed most of the words anyway. One day, Maureen had missed every single word; Mrs. Cox, in desperation and looking for just any word at all that she might be able to spell, finally gave her the word "a", which she missed or at least said she couldn't spell it. We all agreed that she had to be the absolute worst speller in the whole world.

The first grade coasted to an end in late March for spring farm work. In those times, the older kids were expected to help on the farms when planting and harvesting time came, so the school year was adjusted to accommodate. My memory is vague now, but it seems to me that the third through eighth grade had a six-week session in the summer when the crops were laid by to make up for the short spring session. Anyway, I was out of the first grade before I was six, and passed "on condition", meaning that I could enter the second grade next year, but I would be put back if I couldn't do the work.

With the retrospection of the years, I believe the one and two-room multi-grade school is the finest primary educational medium ever conceived. The various grades can see and hear what is being taught both above and below. One is told what is going to be learned; he/she learns it, and then is they are told what was learned as well. It is unfortunate that this intimate interaction between pupils and teacher and grade, lack the economies of scale necessary to survive today.

CHAPTER III

My first push into aviation came from an air show that was conducted north of Woodton during the summer between first and second grades when I was six. The actual show took place over three or four days, probably including a weekend, but the preparations and clean up required much longer. We still lived in the country at the time and drove right by the site on our trips to town. We stopped as often as circumstances permitted, which was every time, so I remember the whole thing with no problem. The show was advertised for a couple of weeks in advance by displaying a real airplane in the showroom of an automobile dealer. I wondered how they got it through the doors, and was both surprised and disappointed when I learned that the wings were removed first. The surprise came because I didn't know the wings came off, and the disappointment because there was no magic involved.

This event was staged on a field that ordinarily was planted in some crop but this year was lying fallow. Actually, two fields were used because one of the aircraft was a Ford tri-motor conveying no less than Will Rogers to the scene and the one field was not big enough. The second actually was much better for airplanes because it was a pasture and fairly smooth, but it also was much smaller than the plowed one. A fence and a ditch separated these two pieces of land, but this small complication was handled easily, the fence or part of it was removed and a wooden bridge was built over the ditch. A hint of a runway was created by running some trucks up and down until the rows left from last year's crop were mashed down a little. The Ford tri-motor both touched down and started its take offs in one field, rolling into the other by means of the bridge. Other aircraft really didn't need to, but some of them used both fields and the bridge as well. Just showing off, I suspect. These take offs and landings were bumpy experiences because the trucks really didn't do much to level out the plowed rows from all of the past crops. But that was the way it was in those days, and no one seemed to mind too much.

There was an astounding number of aircraft there, perhaps 35 or 40 in all with most staying the entire time. The Ford was the undisputed queen, and all shiny with its aluminum skin. I didn't know what aluminum was at the time, but I recall running my hand over regular rows of crests and valleys in the skin and thinking that it looked like the inner plies of corrugated cardboard only bigger. All of the external metal of the Ford, propellers, the aluminum skin, everything was finished with hundreds of overlapping circular swirls about four inches in diameter, like on the nose of Lindbergh's plane The Spirit of St.Louis. I also remember quite well that the Ford had big aluminum pants over the wheels, not just the mudguards as on most other tri-motors. I have never seen another Ford with wheel pants, but I have seen several pictures of some so equipped. The license number NC 430-H was painted in block characters on both sides of the rudder and on the lower left wing. I couldn't see it but I knew enough about airplanes to know it also was on the upper side of the right wing. That plane was simply beautiful.

There were a lot of biplanes, this being the standard form of the day. One had a big bulging light mounted on the bottom of the lower right wing pointed forward, for night landings, we were told, proving to most of our local town people for certain that the heads of airmen truly were empty. This same airplane had a generator turned by a wind driven propeller about a foot in diameter to energize the lights.

I saw a Sikorsky S-39 single engined amphibian flying boat, the type with the tail assembly mounted on booms extending backwards from the wings. Another one was a Loening amphibian, a big biplane with a huge three bladed metal propeller, with a floatation hull formed under and as an integral part of the body proper and extending out in front under the propeller. The most amazing craft though, was a La Cierva autogiro with its whirling rotor on top. An autogiro, not a helicopter. This machine stayed in the vicinity for two or three weeks, taking passengers for a ride.

Please understand I learned who made all of these planes much later; at the time I was consumed by the wonder and my senses were particularly acute and attuned to it all. I raked it all in and stored it away for analysis later.

Looking back, I wonder what the economic justification could possibly have been. Most of the aircraft were used to hop passengers, so a little money was taken in. Even so, there was a strict limit on how many people could afford to spend two dollars for a trip around the field. I still do not see how that many pilots and airplanes could have found financial succor and sustenance. Another thing of considerable interest is that the entire collection of aircraft came and went without a single accident or mishap.

One firm consequence was that this six-year-old boy had been turned on by airplanes. I had looked at and touched every single one and had rather surreptitiously gotten in four or five, but had ridden in none. That had to wait.

X X X X

I don't remember anything at all about the rest of the summer except that I caught a sparrow just by picking it off of a fence post. Mother was sure that I would die immediately of some yet unheard of pestilence conveyed only by wild birds, or be plagued with mites the rest of my life, a somewhat contradictory set of calamities. Neither happened, and in a wink it was time to start the second grade.

CHAPTER IV

The second grade began slowly while Mrs. Cox diverted our attentions from the playground and redirected them to studies. We kids were wiser this year, however, and with some idea of what was ahead, were not quite as susceptible as in the first grade. There, interest borne of curiosity had helped in getting started, and when time had dulled the keen edge a bit, the habits had already been established. A summer of freedom had severed these fragile ties, making the second grade rougher all around for teacher and pupils alike.

The curriculum was an advanced repetition of the first year, so the tentative skills gained then began to firm up and to become part of the permanent retentivity of our minds. We actually began to remember some of the stuff when at home and when away from the class room, and I was amazed to find some of the words learned in school also appeared on billboard signs and in the comic strips.

About three months after starting the second grade, my parents moved into town and I was enrolled into the consolidated schools of Woodton. Actually, the school at Coldweld and five or six other two-room units scattered around the county were part of this same consolidated system were still functioning as isolated units. But all of the remaining ones and the preponderance of the educational activity were in Woodton itself.

So, other than these few remaining rural schools, the entire county had two grammar schools and two high schools, one of each for whites and one for blacks. In each case, the grammar school was a couple of blocks from its high school. The white high school was a two-story red brick building with perhaps forty class rooms, two large study halls, a library, an auditorium which served no other purpose, a lunch room, and a gymnasium. It had a football field, an actual stadium rather than bleacher seats, and extra buildings for courses in shop and home economics. The black school was similar but had about thirty-five classrooms.

The grammar schools also were generally similar, being two story brick structures with about the same number of class rooms, an auditorium, and a gymnasium. There was no lunch room, and the library was contained in the auditorium, locked in bookcases with glass doors. Grades seven through twelve attended classes in the high school building, and first through sixth had classes in the grammar school. Today, each class has its own building.

Like Coldweld, the other country schools taught eight grades, but later these schools were cut back to six. After that, the seventh through twelfth grades were brought to school in Woodton from all over the county by bus. A lot of kids of all ages living in the country were brought to school in buses, because the rural facilities like Coldweld were not big enough to handle all of those not living in town.

There was quite a fleet of these buses, probably forty or more, usually driven by school teachers who lived out of town and who were looking for additional ways to make money. Finding parking places for this flock of vehicles was and still is a problem, and was solved in part by using space behind the high school building. The problem is almost without solution because during the day a line of yellow buses is an aesthetic monotony with little redeeming social quality, even though a certain pride and resignation is generated when the annual report of the Board of Education lists the capital investment involved, and mentions that yet a few more must be acquired for next year.

The public school system supported no kindergarten or pre-school programs, although two or three were operated privately, and one by the Catholic Church. My sister Marypamella had attended one of these.

School was a little different in town. In Coldweld, we had attended all day in the first and second grades, but in town these two grades met one half day only. You were in the morning or the afternoon session, and if the latter you were not expected to show up until one o'clock. The morning schedule started at the regular time and the kids went home at noon. I guess the school officials thought the small ones would accept schooling more readily if they were eased into it, so to speak. I can't reconcile this with the all-day requirement at the country schools. That is the way it was and I didn't think to question it.

Like I said, in Coldweld we had about fifty kids in eight grades. In town we had a hundred of more in each grade, so many there were at least four sections "A", "B", "C", and "D" in each grade. It was never stated officially but the kids who made "A's" usually were in Section A; "B" students were in Section B, and so on. I was almost always in Section A but the two or three exceptions caused enough concern that the principal sent a note to my parents explaining that a shortage of classrooms or teachers required that I be placed in Section B and that it was not to be interpreted as being evidence of poorer work.

The third grade had classes in reading, arithmetic, music, art and penmanship, as well as "jography", "gym" and "auditorium". I will explain about auditorium later. The next three grades had similar course work, except that the emphasis was placed later on composition and grammar—you know, an adjective modifies a noun or pronoun or other noun equivalency by stating which, what kind of or how many. Reading and history acquired places alongside of geography. Part of all this was a course entitled "Arkansas, Yesterday and Today", which gave the history of the state since the 1700's.

First and second grade pupils stayed in the same room and had the same teacher for all subjects. Starting in the third grade, we moved from room to room, usually remaining for a 45 minute period in each one. We encountered in turn, Miss Watson in Room 3 teaching arithmetic; Miss Caldweld in room 6 teaching reading; Mrs. Sharp in Room 9 pushing art and penmanship, and so on. Of course, Miss Watson and two or three others taught arithmetic to all grades from three through six, shifting from one text to another as Section 3B was replaced by 6A, which in turn was followed by 5C. This general pattern of changing classrooms was followed all the way through the twelfth grade, and I suppose this it the way it was done everywhere.

In town again, each grade in grammar school had a forty-five minute recess in the morning and another in the afternoon. There was some attempt to keep the kids separated by size by letting the first three grades recess together but at a different time than the last three. At noon everyone had a common hour for lunch, so we all managed to play, fight, and scream together.

I remember well the apparent barriers that some courses seemed to offer prior to taking them, and how these impediments to investigative thought wafted away when subjected to a rational and systematic study. In the second grade we were involved in numbers work in which we performed "short" division and I observed the third graders doing something they called "long" division. Of course, the third grade pupils let on how hard long division was, the champion letter-on-er being my own sister.

By the time I reached the third grade I was sure that long division was an un-learnable subject, and said so to Miss Watson early in the year. Well, Miss Watson just smiled, and a few weeks later when we got to division she first reviews us on short division. Then, she said she would show us a little trick and proceeded to demonstrate how to divide a number by a sequence of steps, you know:

```
      56                        56
   7/392    instead of       7/392
     35                         4^
     42
     42
```

So we learned how to do that, and after a few days got pretty good at it, but with me anyway still dreading the next step which I knew was going to be long division. One day, Miss Watson started on a new subject, like simple fractions or something. Somebody asked when we were going to learn long division —it wasn't me, I was hoping she had forgotten all about it and I hated whoever it was. Miss Watson said, "You have been doing it for a week and a half." Then she showed the difference between the two and also that in most cases long division actually was simpler to do because we wrote things down systematically and no longer had to manipulate in our heads that 7 x 5 was 35 and when subtracted from 39 is 4. Well! We were flabbergasted, and we didn't know whether to be happy or not. Here we had gone through all of the agony of dreading the encounter, and then we found it was over before we even knew we were involved. I learned something much more; sometimes people will pretend something they are proficient in is harder than it really is to make themselves look superior or to make you feel inferior, or maybe both together. I've done it myself.

Gym was taught to an entire class of boys or girls, but not both, in a regular period by a teacher who conducted calisthenics, organized competitive games and generally kept everyone moving in reasonably non-destructive ways. It was funny, we had to be told what to do during gym class, but we were never still during recess, or at lunch.

Like I said, the boys and girls had gym at different times twice a week. The girls had to dress in a special gym suit for the occasion, this being a blue short-sleeved affair with bloomer type pants, and sneakers. We boys wore our regular clothes, except we had to change to sneakers when we worked out in the gymnasium rather than out of doors. The school administration was very strict about the gym floor. To preserve the finish for basketball, street shoes were never allowed on the floor under any circumstances, only tennis shoes or stocking feet could touch that floor. Modern finishes may be a little more forgiving but back then in spite of the watchful care it received, the gym floor was refinished on alternate years by sanding down to bare wood and re-varnishing.

I said I would tell you about the course we called "auditorium". That was our name for something with a long forgotten but formal title like Group Social Studies or something, and was taught in grades three through six. All sections in a given grade would meet together daily in the auditorium for a double period with no break, hence the name. Two teachers conducted this class and they alternated in making whatever presentations were necessary. This was a convenient arrangement administratively because one of these teachers also was the girls' gym teacher, which enabled her to attend to her gym class on the days it met during one of the two auditorium periods.

Auditorium was both interesting and unbelievably burdensome. First of all, at the start of each semester, we elected officers —usually a president, vice-president, secretary and treasurer, plus a program chairman. Each day, the meeting would be called to order by the president or vice-president, and the minutes were read, and so on —a regular formal meeting but conducted by grammar school kids. As soon as the new and old businesses were given attention, usually after about fifteen minutes, the meeting would be turned over to one of the teachers. They taught us nature by collecting leaves during the spring and fall, and we learned about clouds, and talked about the Golden Gate Bridge which had just been completed. It was funny, the teacher thought the cars traveled on the suspension cables in some way. All of us boys at least knew there was a roadway suspended down below, but the teacher would have none of that. On a test, the right answer was to say the cars traveled on the cables. All of the boys got it wrong. Most of the girls got it right, on the test that is. That was the first time I ever realized that a teacher might not know everything.

When Washington's birthday was coming up, we sat through a program presented by both of the teachers over a period of two or three days about George and his hatchet. When it snowed outside, we planned an out doors display of some sort using snow as the building material, and then went out and built it more or less, in between the snow ball fights of course.

All of this was not too bad, like I said it was kind of interesting. The bad part was that there was no text as such and we had to keep a detailed notebook of everything we did. We, certainly I at least, didn't know how to keep a notebook so it was a constant struggle to decide what to write down. Squiggles and stick men didn't count, so whatever it was always had to be recopied to make it look neat. Those teachers really wanted everything to be neat.

On Fridays there would be a program conducted by the program chairman. We pretty well knew what it would be because part of the business on each Monday was a reading of the ensuing Friday program by the program chairman. This individual invariably seemed to be a girl, and looking back, I now can recognize the early formations of personal characteristics which ultimately would produce a real bitch. She (the chairman) would read off a list she had prepared with a typical presentation including piano solos, tap dancing, magic tricks or unusual skills, and sometimes a skit. The general rules were that no one would be asked to play the piano or to dance if he or she were not also taking lessons in these arts; everyone had to be assigned the same number of times during the year, but otherwise, just about anything went. You couldn't fake it or sluff off too much because these assignments had the same weight as those made by the teachers and failure to perform meant an "F" for that Friday.

The program chairman always seemed to delight in giving assignments that were difficult for the particular individual. A favorite, involved giving someone who hated to sing the chore of a "new song" or, much worse, "an old song, sung a new way." Only once did this backfire. One girl I recall sang nearly fifty verses of "My Bonnie Lies Over the Ocean". Never before or since have I heard more than seven or eight, but she whined out the lot without any written aids while using up close to twenty minutes of the hour allocated for the entire program. She had a muddy soprano voice pitched about like the howl that sometimes emerges from water faucets when they are opened just a crack (not the water hammering sound, but the howl). The class thought it was a howl anyway, everyone laughed so hard we all hurt and one girl laughed until she got sick and threw up. The songster ignored all of these ongoing critiques of her performance and bayed on and on, every verse and chorus until she used them all. I can't imagine that more could have been composed. Right after that, the rules were changed where they had been silent before so only four verses of any song could be sung unless an encore was requested. In this case, no one asked for an encore, in fact that girl was never asked to sing again. I think she was pretty smart at that.

Usually an hour program used up the talents of about fifteen to twenty kids, so with 75 to 100 total in our classes, each got socked every four to six weeks. The hard part about being on a program lay in the time element. Only three days separated the sentence from the execution, consequently there was a great scurrying through the riddle books in the library so that at least four of the six needed would be reasonably new. A skit was given more time, two weeks as I recall, but that only prolonged the misery of the one responsible for the performance. During the four years that I took the auditorium program, I had to present two skits, but a description of one will suffice for both.

When you were bagged with a skit, you first had to decide what little drama should be portrayed. Most extracted a scene from a book used for a book report. This well-trod ground was good enough for me, so I selected a particular event from a book entitled "Coral Island", or maybe it was "The Coral Island", author unknown to me now, but I hand him or her full credit for a good story, and I recommend it to anybody eight or nine years old. Anyway, it was a pretty good book and that is why I chose it. Several boys were stranded on this island for an extended period and one day their bay was entered by a pirate ship. The pirates came ashore and the boys hid while their camp and belongings were scattered. Everything works out all right, but this crucial moment was to be the scene of my production.

The cast has to be selected, and a check made with the program chairman to ensure that none of these people had other yet-to-be-announced commitments on future programs. Then these persons would be informed by an announcement during the regular session of auditorium. Naturally, there was a regular spot just for this. When the request came for new business, the skit chairman would rise and break the news and give the schedule of skit rehearsals, usually about three in all.

In this way, I lined up four boys to portray the main ones in the story, and four more to be the pirates. There were some administrative problems to be solved, because everyone wanted to be a pirate, and no one wanted to be a main character.

The costumes were minimal; the pirates wore ragged play pants with shirt tails out and handkerchiefs around their heads. The other boys were dressed similarly except they wore no handkerchiefs. A few cap pistols and wooden swords rounded out the props for the pirates. Except for the handkerchiefs and swords, they actually looked just about normal.

We rehearsed two or three times with no noticeable improvement. The trouble was that several important lines, that set up the action in the book, either was ignored completely by my crew or else these were altered in structure so the significance and meaning were lost. On the Friday, the performance itself was a study in chaos and disaster. After the cast had assembled backstage, we were told to pull out the shirt tails and load the pistols. Actually loading the pistols was about all that was needed and most of these already were. With the preparations begun, I stepped in front of the curtain to describe the events which preceded those to be portrayed, the fabric of this speech was punctured two or three times by a cap gun going off backstage, and once by a big bulge in the curtain as someone obviously stumbled or was pushed on the other side.

At last, the curtain was drawn, revealing our hero boys carrying the pistols, whereas in the book they had no arms. When the "ship" was spotted by one, he exclaimed "Look, it's the pirates", but in the book it wasn't known they were pirates until after coming ashore. When the pirates actually appeared on stage, one was dressed as an Indian! A gun battle ensued, during which fifteen cap pistols—most had two apiece—were fired off about a hundred times apiece, whereas in the book, the boys remained carefully hidden from the pirates. Toward the end the boys were overcome by the pirates and each was tied with about 50 feet of rope that I hadn't noticed before, following which each was dragged off the stage, kicking and hollering all the way. Nothing like that happened in the book at all. In fact, there was very little about the skit that resembled the story in any way.

Nevertheless, the class thought it was great and voted that it should be presented during the general assembly before the entire school next time we had to put on the program. Because of the increased stature of the performance, I now had about 20 boys instead of eight. This did not help, because the seasoned players felt they had proprietary rights and the new ones wanted to share in some of the glory. The second portrayal diverged even more from the book than the first, but the virtuosity of the initial acting could not be repeated and no one thought the second performance was good enough even to be rated "bad".

Another incident in the auditorium was my initial lesson in just how little it takes to be an expert. Our assignment for the next day, issued by one of the teachers, was to give a five minute talk on Robert E. Lee. The next day came, and I was seated and waiting for the starting bell when it struck me that I had not even <u>thought</u> about the assignment. Oh, well, not to worry, I could pick up enough from the other talks to fake it and perhaps with luck I might not be called at all. After the business meeting was concluded, the teacher took over and to my horror she selected me to be the very first speaker. Following the philosophy that with the need to talk and with nothing to say one should say it with conviction, I talked for my five minutes draining my brain of every scrap I had ever heard about Lee, which was a fair amount at that because Arkansas had been a Confederate State. At the end of the class a vote was taken to see who would give his or her talk before the general assembly on our next Friday. Guess who won? You got it, good ol' Gaylord Throckmorton Montmorency Crawford.

X X X X X

Like I said, our grammar school building had two stories, but what I didn't say was that it was built at the end of World War I to serve as the high school. It was made of red brick and its architecture was typical of the era, with a certain amount of ornamentation both inside and out. For example, there was a ledge about a foot wide between the two floors that went all the way around the building , and which was clearly visible both from the ground and from the windows of any room on the second floor, if you leaned out some, that is. This ledge served no purpose except to give eye relief to the vertical wall, and to provide safe places for birds to land.

You might challenge the statement about being a safe place for birds, because this feature of the building elicited a fair amount of discussion from time to time, mostly in the form of "Can anyone knock that bird off with a rock without breaking a window?" The school frowned on but had no formal rule about hitting birds with rocks, but it was life imprisonment to break a window. Naturally this kind of adventure was the subject of more talk than action because during school hours there was no feasible way to chunk at a bird without being seen by a teacher, and any teacher automatically would see the worst possible motives and suspect that a window was the target, no matter how many birds were sitting there just asking to be thrown at. Nobody was going to hang around long enough after school to do anything because our day started when school let out, and no time was lost in getting as far away as possible. So we talked a lot, but the birds were spared, not to mention the windows.

One day, Mother was going to attend a meeting of the PTA, and this time the meeting place was to be the auditorium of my building, right after school let out. The meeting usually took about an hour, so she asked me to stick around until it was over and we would go home together. I figured this might be good foran ice cream cone, so I stuck.

PTA meetings are grossly boring to kids in grammar school, and with all due respect, I suspect for the parents and teachers as well. That was one good reason they only lasted an hour, I imagine. Anyway, while the meeting was going on I wandered around the building, inside and out, and looked at a lot of things that we never could look at during regular hours, like in the door of a girls' restroom which was propped open while everything was being cleaned.

Outside, I looked around and happened to notice a strange kind of bird on the ledge. I don't know what kind it was even today, but it looked kind of like a pelican. Pelicans are not normal inhabitants of Eastern Arkansas, so I'm really not an expert in them, but that gives you an idea. This bird was too large to sit comfortably on the ledge, and had to arrange itself to be parallel with the building, at the same time it couldn't seem to get comfortable and with a lot of flapping of the wing away from the building kept reversing itself, pointing first one way and then the other. All the while it would walk along the ledge, but really was not getting anywhere because of its frequent reversals of position. I wanted to get a better look, so I went upstairs to the room nearest its location, and by opening a window, I could look right down at it, only a couple of feet away. So I tried to catch it, but could not quite reach it, although I did manage to touch it several times.

My exertions caused the bird to move away down the ledge, and it soon was beyond my reaching distance as it passed the limits of the last window. I went to the adjacent room, but finding it locked went back into the one I had just left. Suddenly, I wanted to catch that bird pretty badly but it was well beyond my reach by now.

I crawled out onto the ledge with no real plan in mind except to bring it back alive. I inched along the ledge toward the bird, hugging the wall with my face pressed up against the brick. Each time I approached within a few feet, it would move a little farther along, until it reached the corner of the building and hopped around out of sight. I moved on down to the corner and started to turn but found that some of the brickwork of the ledge was loose and misplaced right at the corner, so I got halfway around and couldn't find sure footing to go any farther. Just then, I heard the window of the classroom from whence I came being closed.

I tried to call out to the window closer, but my cries went unheard because my cheek was pressed against the wall and I was facing the wrong way, and who would be expecting anyone to be calling from the ledge anyhow. I tried to change the position of my head to face the other direction, but just moving it away enough to allow the barest clearance for my nose to turn injected me with vertigo, and I stood there in sudden fear that all was not going to come out all right.

It is hard to judge time in circumstances like this, and I hadn't had much practice even under better conditions. So I stood there for some time, and it seemed like a hundred years but actually could have been no more than five or ten minutes. I couldn't go forward because of the unstable and missing bricks, and I wasn't able to back up because I couldn't turn my head around to see where I was going. Anyway, going back didn't offer much promise because the windows had been closed, and for reasons not obvious to this day, these second floor windows always were locked when closed. Besides that, it was beginning to get dark and I was getting cold. So I was stuck half around the corner with my arms outspread on both walls. It occurred to me that bird catching didn't seem important any more.

Suddenly, there was a scream from below, "Gaylord Crawford is on the ledge and ought to be spanked." My benefactor and judge was Susanne Jones, a bitchy girl in my class. She had been program chairman in Auditorium last semester. and naturally, I hated her. She had just proven anew that she had a sadistic trait by wanting me rescued just so I could be punished, or so it seemed to me. She went screaming into the school, and the parents and teachers came boiling out in absolutely zero time. Mother was in the lead, and she immediately took charge, "GAYLORD THROCKMORTEN MONTMORENCY CRAWFORD, you come down here, this INSTANT." Even through the haze of my terror, I recognized her no-nonsense voice tone, and knew she was going to bend me in two when I got down but I would gladly have complied had I been able.

Mrs. McPherson, the principle, was more practical in her approach, even though it took longer. After all, she dealt with these things every day and her experience came through. She went for the janitor.

Now, Mr. Moses was a perfect example of the right person for the job he held. He carefully swept the floors every night, and washed the windows twice a year, and mowed the grass where the kids had not yet trampled it into extinction, changed the light bulbs, cleaned the toilets, and did anything else that needed doing. He was thorough, he was neat, he worked almost completely without supervision, he was prompt and almost never missed a day. He also was set in his ways and did things according to his schedule. When it was time to wash windows they were washed each room in its turn whether any classes were being conducted or not. At this time in the afternoon, Mr. Moses would be ready to start sweeping, a task that he liked to do without interruption starting upstairs at one end and proceeding straight to the other, picking up each room as he passed it, then down the stairs at the end and back on the first floor.

Mr. Moses rarely said anything if interrupted as he was applying his attentions, but one could tell that something would be forthcoming or would be done in sweet time by the way he didn't say anything. Nothing short of disaster changed his course, and Mr. Moses decided what was a disaster.

Something in Mrs. McPherson's voice conveyed to him that this really was one and not the usual erasure in the toilet sort of thing, and that he should come immediately. So Mr. Moses came out and took a look. He stared at me and I stared at him. Nothing in this scene could be covered by past experience, so Mr. Moses carefully took out his pipe and pouch, and just as carefully knocked out the bowl and punched in a handful of tobacco. Then he sat down on the banister of the steps leading into the school and still looking up at me he puffed away at his pipe, re-lighting it a couple of times when it sputtered and went out.

The situation was not as tranquil as my description of Mr. Moses might imply. Susanne Jones from my class kept screaming over and over again, "Gaylord Crawford ought to be spanked", several teachers and a couple of mothers were yelling up to me, "Don't fall", and Mother was dancing back and forth, not saying anything by now but clearly worried. Finally, Mrs. McPherson said, "Mr. Moses, what are you going to do?" He puffed awhile, and said, "I'm thinking."

I guess Mr. Moses must have thought about it for five minutes, but of course, it seemed much longer. Finally, he got up and walked slowly back into the building. Nothing happened for a long time or so it seemed to me. My mother was still walking up and down rapidly, passing in and out of my field of vision and looking very grim. Some of the other mothers and the teachers began to castigate Mr. Moses because he wasn't doing anything. "I think he ought to be fired, this is just disgraceful", offered one of the mothers, and the tone was picked up by one of the teachers. Mrs. McPherson finally stopped some of the acrimonious remarks about Mr. Moses by saying, "I've known Mr. Moses for a long time, I know he is doing whatever can be done."

Sure enough, I could hear a window being opened in front of me, and Mr. Moses leaned out and tossed out the end of a rope which fell to the ground in a disorderly heap. It looked like his end might be tied off to something in the room. His head disappeared from my view, and after a time I heard a window being opened behind me. Mr. Moses issued the longest speech I ever heard from him, "Two of you ladies come up here and catch the rope." Mrs. McPherson quickly volunteered herself and one of the teachers, and they ran inside about the time Mr. Moses came out. Mr. Moses went over to the sprawl of rope and carefully and neatly coiled it up, and disappeared from my view. I couldn't see the action now, but they told me Mr. Moses reformed the rope into a better length and heaved the coil up to the ladies, which unwound as it curved upward, with the end flicking through the window on the first try. Mrs. McPherson and her assistant grabbed it and held while Mr. Moses went back in.

In just moments, it was over. Mr. Moses pulled in on the rope and popped it up over the ledge and up my back, holding it there with tension applied from his end. Quickly, he tied it to a desk—desks were screwed to the floor in those days—and said to Mrs. McPherson, "Now, call the fire department, I ain't got a ladder long enough to reach 'im." So Mr. Moses returned to his sweeping while the fire department was summoned and I leaned back against the security of a strong rope stretched tightly across my back and rested my aching arms and fingers.

The fire troops arrived with sirens going and lights flashing. They unlatched a ladder and laid it along side of me and somebody came up and helped me onto the rungs. Susanne Jones down below was still screaming, "Gaylord ought to be spanked," even as I made it to the ground, but she hugged me tightly and had tears in her eyes as she said, "Oh, Gaylord, I thought you were going to be killed." Mother hugged me too but I could tell that more was coming.

Mother piled me into the car, and we went straight home without even stopping for the ice cream cone. The closer we got, the madder she got, and I guess it was plain luck that Dad arrived home just as we did, because Mother was almost incoherent by this time. He sensed that this was one of the times when he would be the dispenser of the discipline, and he quietly questioned me about the entire sequence. When the whole story was out, he delivered one of the most devastating punishments I have ever received. Without raising his voice, he said, "Gaylord, that was really dumb."

CHAPTER V

During the years that I am talking about, Woodton was of little interest to anyone fifty miles away, and if you lived more than a hundred miles from there, chances were that you had never heard of it at all.

Woodton was and still is similar to about 5,000 or more other towns all over the country with populations in the low thousands. The main observable differences are that some are built up on either side of the railroad tracks, while others face a river or perhaps have been arranged around a square. These distinctions aside, it is a safe bet that if any one of them is selected out of a hat, the main street will be named Main Street, and there also will be an Oak Street, and probably a Pine, and a Chestnut as well.

All towns and cities seem to have a particular spot where one is as far into town as one can get. This location is the middle of town as far as mental orientation is concerned, although it frequently is not at the geographical center. In New York, this place probably is at Times Square, in Chicago, it is near State and Madison in the Loop, and in Little Rock it is at Fifth and Main Streets. In Woodton, this particular place was at the intersection of Broadway and Main, about which the town lies in an irregular pattern that extends a mile and a half to the north, a mile to the south, and about three fourths of a mile both east and west. All of this area was not built up, there being a fair number of vacant lots, but all of it was laid out in blocks so that nowhere would anyone think they were in the open rural places. Within this area you were in town, outside you were in the country.

There wasn't too much to the business district or "downtown" as it was called. Even today, downtown is not a lot bigger than it was at that time, but then as now there was enough to cater to most of the needs of the people thereabouts, and I suppose that is all that really is needed.

The main business section occupied an area equivalent to about seven square blocks, arrayed fairly uniformly around the corner of Broadway and Main. Within this perimeter were five drug stores, six clothing stores, a women's dress shop, two jewelry stores, five restaurants, at least five service stations, two banks, two furniture stores, two liquor stores, three or four grocery stores, two hardware stores, a hotel, an IOOF meeting hall, two movie theaters (with one closed), a cleaning shop, four barber shops, two wholesale houses, five churches, the telephone office, the post office, and a pool hall. There were a number of offices on the second floors of these buildings, these being used by six doctors, four dentists; maybe a dozen lawyers; the county agent; an engineering and drafting group, from the state highway department and several "buyers" who bought and sold agricultural products that they never saw.

The tallest building was three stories high, and only one of these. The single passenger elevator in town was in this salient of the skyline, although a lot of buildings had freight elevators.

Removed from this nucleus but still not far away, were two more hotels, a newspaper office, an undertaker, a blacksmith shop, the office of a junk dealer, two lumber yards, the national guard armory, a farmer's market, two more wholesale houses, the court house, the train station, a farm implement dealer, two car dealers, the combined police and fire station, the bus station and the train station. Five churches found permanent congregations; two or more came and went as the particular fervor waxed and waned.

Farther out yet, appearing here and there interspersed among and surrounded by the residential areas were another laundry, the city owned electric power and water plant, a couple or three drive-in hamburger stands, a pair of florists, and a radio repair shop. There also were a scattering of small manufacturing plants such as a mattress factory, a wooden box factory, a gunsmith with a national reputation who furnished finished gunstocks and blanks for those who felt that no gun worth owning could be left with the factory stock, a dress factory, and two or three others small manufactories, as well as two cemeteries.

Completely beyond the edges of town were several beer joints and taverns. These generally had tough reputations, usually were called "honky-tonks", and were the subjects of many a sermon from the local pastorages.

To me, living in town proved to be much more fun than the country because there was so much of interest compressed into a relatively compact area. Like the railroads.

A hundred years before, or even as recently as fifty, good transportation for a small town meant that it had to be on the bank of a navigable water. The railroads had changed all that, and Woodton benefited from the presence of two railroads, the Rock Island and the Missouri Pacific, the first a main line running east and west, and the other a little less important going north-south. A lot of trains used these tracks, perhaps every 20-30 minutes east and west, and every hour or so north and south.

The east-west line has been placed first, sometime in the 1870's. The route had been surveyed by a former Confederate general who had camped on the future town site of Woodton while doing some of the work. Being first, the east-west tracks had the right-of-way, so the north-south trains often had to wait until an east-west cleared the crossing. The north-south tracks had an S-curve and a slight grade so that a south bound freight, when stopped, had to back up at least four or five miles and get a running start if it were to get around the curves and up the hill. Fairly often, another east-west train would arrive by then and the south bound would have to stop and do it all over again. Sometimes the southbound would try a jerk-start to avoid the long back up and run process. To do this, the crewmen would set the brakes on the last three or four cars by hand, then the engineer would slowly back the train into these cars so that all of the slack and play in the couplers were removed and the train was compressed into its shortest length. Usually there were several feet of slack like that in a long train. The brakes then were released on the last cars, and the engineer would open the throttle abruptly but not too much as to make the wheels spin. If he did it right he would jerk the first car into rolling motion, just barely you understand, but unstuck and rolling. The first car would jerk the second and so on. This wave of jerks along with a loud grinding slamming noise would propagate backwards from car to car until the entire train was moving. Meanwhile, of course the engineer had really opened up and the front was going pretty good by the time the last car started. They really started, I should say, because the tail end cars of a train were yanked from a dead stop to several miles per hour in just about zero time. It was a high energy version of pop the whip, and sometimes couplers would break and then everything would be held up until the repair crews got there and fixed it, which sometimes could take all day.

One time, when the train was all backed up and compressed and ready for the start, I ran up and put a rock in front of one of the wheels. It started with no trouble at all and made dust out of the rock. Come to think of it, that train was subjected to two jerks at a time.

The jerk-start worked maybe a fourth of the time, but it almost always was tried first, because it saved a lot of time when it did. This trick isn't used much any more because the diesel locomotives of today have more traction, and I have seen a diesel start a train on that same grade with hardly a grunt. But that is the way it was done then.

Despite this constriction placed upon south going trains, these two railroads carried most of the products used by or emanating from the entire area. There were a lot of trucks too, but the heavy stuff and the big numbers were carried by the rails. The trains also carried many passengers. The east-west tracks bore a passenger train one-way or the other every hour or so. Some of them were expresses that made no stops between Little Rock and Memphis, but most stopped at Woodton.

North-south passenger trains were fewer in number and were less ostentatious than those going east-west. Most made all stops, only one a day each way ran express schedules. That just meant that flag stops would be ignored. Usually, no one wanted on or off at one anyway, so the express runs really weren't much different from the regular ones. With all this traffic, no difficulty was experienced in traveling to or from Woodton in any direction by rail, by day or night.

As a boy, I often rode this line about five miles to the north to Coldwell to visit with my uncle for the day. There always were two or three others making the same trip, to Coldwell that is, not to see my uncle. I have forgotten the fare, but it seems now it was a nickel, and certainly no more than a dime. For this grand sum the station agent duly made out a ticket in all the necessary copies, with stubs. The conductor in turn punched all segments and left me with one copy as a receipt. Incidentally, the efficiency of this transaction was equally low for the adults in my family. The train station in Woodton was about a mile and a half to the SOUTH of our house, and the station where my uncle lived was a full mile to the NORTH of his, so the distance between the actual houses was about two and a half or three miles. I suspect that Mother and Dad just wanted me to have the experience of riding alone on a train in circumstances where I couldn't get into too much trouble.

This was long before the time when almost everyone was well traveled, but becoming train wise was important because trains were the links with exotic places as New York City, and San Francisco, not to mention Cincinnati. In keeping with this mystique, the entire aura of the better trains was that of pomp and style. "Our" locomotives always were trim and impeccable and shiny black, and the wheels of one of them always were painted silver. These wheels must have been repainted after each run, and if so represented an enormous amount of maintenance effort. The gain in public relations also was enormous, because the Crack Eagle could be recognized as far as it could be seen from the glint and flash of light on these wheels.

Moving or stopped, these mechanical behemoths were terrifying from the size alone but even more so from the noise. The fireboxes always emitted roars, particularly when under forced draft, and they seemed to expunge steam at unpredictable times, also emitting gorgeous black smoke as well as a distinctive wholesome odor from the coal burning in the fireboxes. Today, we would call this pollution, and somebody would get sued but it was just lovely then.

Typically, these beasts were 4-8-2 types, weighing more than 218,000 pounds, not including the tender, and bore upon the eight drivers with a weight of 199,000 pounds. Steam at a pressure of 350 pounds per square inch was admitted into the two cylinders where it expanded against pistons 17-1/2 inches in diameter, moving these through a 28 inch stroke, and turning the 84 inch drive wheels, thereby generating a draw bar pull of 28,000 pounds.

I learned these facts from the engineer, who repeated them daily to anyone who would listen. I listened often because the engineer was a giant among men, at least to us kids, and to a lot of adults too, I suspect. At each stop, he descended from his cab with a huge oil can with a spout about a mile long and squirted oil on the crank pins of the drive wheels, and the eccentrics as well as the yokes, guides, and crossheads. Most of this was pure show, because he also oiled a lot of things that didn't move, or move fast enough, like the hip pockets of us kids who got in his way.

Other railroads undoubtedly had larger locomotives, but these examples were all that I needed. Anything bigger or noisier or grander would have been more than I could have taken.

The first cars behind the locomotive were baggage and mail cars. Before the train arrived, the station master always rolled up 8 or 10 hand-drawn baggage wagons, each piled up with the luggage of those departing, or with the packages and boxes being sent by railway express, or with mail sacks. Two or three empty wagons would be placed along side the loaded ones. As soon as the train stopped, some of the sacks and boxes destined for Woodton would be placed on the empties, clearing some space on board. Some of the outbound things then were moved onto the train thereby clearing a wagon, which then received more materials for Woodton. The entire exchange was made in five or six minutes, always with two or three persons running up to mail a letter on the mail coach.

Almost all mail moved between towns by rail then, and it was a great treat to post a letter on the train itself. The side of the mail cars contained slots over which were stenciled the imposing words "U. S. Mail". A great satisfaction always welled inside when the train puffed off, bearing your letter. In contrast, nothing happened when a letter was dropped into a mail BOX, the feeling sometimes arose, then and now as well, that perhaps this particular box no longer is used and has been forgotten by the Post Office. However, when a letter was placed on a train, you knew it was on its way, because no one could forget the existence of a train. Even so, the mailboxes are still around, as unsatisfactory as ever, while the few remaining passenger trains may not be around as long as tomorrow morning.

The conductor and brakemen alighted as the train came to a stop, and immediately placed down their little step stools to narrow the space between the ground and the first step on the train. Usually these portable steps were placed at the first and last cars of the ten to fifteen passenger coaches which followed the baggage section; but once in a while, there would be a third one somewhere in the middle if the train were unusually long. After helping down each passenger who was leaving the train, those departing were assisted in boarding one of the ten to fifteen passenger coaches that followed the baggage section. Some of these were Pullmans, which carried such elegant names as Winnewautuk, Western Star, Mist of the Morning, and the like.

Some of us used to think it was great fun to steal a step stool. One or two of us would distract the conductor while another would race up and try to snatch the stool. We then would go streaking up the steps and through the train to the last car and jump down there and scamper away. We did this three or four times, gleefully evading the efforts of the train crew to catch us.

On or about the fourth day, a particularly long train pulled up with maybe 20 passenger coaches. We went zipping up the front steps and ran to the rear, pushing our way through the de-training passengers in the aisles. We got to the last car and were about to jump down when we found the entrance door closed! The conductor was right there with another guy and we were locked in the lavatory until the train pulled out. It puffed slowly up the tracks for about three miles. There it stopped and we were handed down to the ground and the train left. We didn't do that any more.

Most passenger trains had dining cars as well, with the waiters in white jackets bearing trays of food, and manifesting the same atmosphere of circumstance that oozed from all the rest. There is something about seeing a hot dish being uncovered when this action takes place on the other side of a dining car window. Everything looks good, and you just know it smells good too, although of course, the windows effectively bar all permeations of aromas. Also, its funny, but the same food served at home just wouldn't have been as tasty, or so it seemed to me then. Of course, we kids tried to spoil it for the eaters.

We sometimes would stand just outside a dining car window as the clientele was being served. We tried to distract the diners by looking forlorn and hungry but we never got any reaction from any of the diners. We hit on the idea of pretending to throw up. We got pretty good at this because once one of those eating threw up on the table.

The most remarkable car was the last, this having an "observation platform" with about four seats where passengers could sit and watch the rails recede. Not too many did, and it never occurred to me that this platform was a sooty, noisy and swaying place, looking much better than it really was. It was a real disappointment when I found this out much later for myself. Embellishing the rear of the train was an illuminated sign identifying the railroad and also proclaiming that the train, which had just passed, was the

Crack Eagle. No one had to tell us kids, we knew that all along.

As you can see, the railroad tracks were a powerful attraction to me and to many other boys in Woodton. We played around them whenever we could, and knew by sight anyway most of the train crewmen. In my case, the interest was abetted by my paternal grandfather. As I said, he had grown up in Poplar Bluff, Missouri, and Poplar Bluff was and is a railroad town. It was the location of the repair facilities for the Missouri Pacific railroad, and was host to such interesting things as the roundhouse for working on the locomotives, with a turntable to place each into the proper working stall. Not only that, there was a large marshaling yard where the trains were made up or rearranged to be sent out in one direction or another. We visited these wonderful places whenever we went to Poplar Bluff, which we did every year or so, and Grand Dad would fill me with tales of railroading. This was particularly interesting to me and I thought he had spent his life on the rails. I was about ten I guess when I learned that he had never worked for any railroad for so much as a day. He was just interested, and infected me with the same interest.

X X X X X

Somewhere along about the third or fourth grade, I found a piece of metal on the railroad track. It was thin, like a calling card, and was maybe three inches long by a half wide and with a bulge at one end. I puzzled over this treasure and showed it around to all my friends. My wonder was put in its place by a classmate, "That's only a nail. A train will squash one flat." I determined to find out for myself, and did. A train will smash a nail without even a grunt. Artistic temperament now began to emerge. By bending the nails slightly, a curve would result in the product. Two nails lying crossed on the rail are merged —sometimes even cold welded—into a thing which resembles a pair of scissors, if you look at it long enough and pretend a little, that is.

The north-south line did not have as advanced a signaling system as the other railroad. When a north-south train stopped for the east-west a crewman would walk back a mile and place several "torpedoes" on the rails. If another train should come up while the first one was stopped, it would run over the torpedoes which would explode loudly enough to be heard over the noise of the train, and at some distance from the tracks as well. the engineer of the train coming up then knew to stop or to proceed more slowly according to the number of explosions he had heard. Of course, I just had to experiment.

I had four or five 22-caliber cartridges and laid these on the tracks like I had seen the torpedoes. The big difference was that the torpedoes were held in place on the rails by a couple of metal ears that were bent under and up close to the underside of the steel rail. My cartridges were just placed on the rails, with me hoping that the train would not shake them off. I sat down to wait.

After a few minutes, I heard a whistle in the distance, and I began to get hiked up as it approached. Suddenly, it occurred to me that the train might be blown off the track. I really didn't think so, but it certainly seemed possible. Not wanting to be associated with such a disaster, if it happened, I got on my bicycle and rode slowly away, very slowly like so as not to attract attention. When I was a half mile away, the train was almost at the spot, and I carefully conquered all urges to turn around and look. I pedaled along, and the train kept on going—so did I.

Soon the last car passed, and I decided the danger had passed also. Back I went to the scene and by careful inspection I found the remains of each cartridge, smashed as thin as paper. Not only was the train spared, but the noise of the explosions was so insignificant as to be unheard by anyone.

In school, from grade three on, we had to read at least one book each six-weeks and make a book report about it, using a format that was pretty well standardized because the teachers had to read all those things. The best ones in a class were given special recognition, and a committee sent the best of the lot to a newspaper in Little Rock. Again, after being poured over by an editor who wished he had more interesting work, the very best from all over the state would be published several times a year in the Sunday edition in the section on education. One of my book reports was about trains, and I relied on a little information that was not really in the book but it should have been there if the author had just done his job. My report survived all the way to the newspaper, and was published in due time. That hadn't happened to anyone in Woodton before, so I was instantly famous. I was in a sweat, that somebody would want to read the book and would find where I had enhanced it. But I needn't have worried, none of the boys would have been caught dead reading it now because that would have added to the recognition that I had already received and no one was going to do that because I was hated for setting such a bad example for the parents to point out. None of the girls were going to read it because trains were dirty and smelly and made a lot of noise, and who cared anyway.

Like I said, the teachers had read most of the books the kids reported on, but a few kids were always bringing in some out of the way example that had never been seen before. The train book was in this category, and it was approved by my teacher, Miss Lumley, who checked to see that it was about the right length and not too easy. After the newspaper had published my report, Miss Lumley called me in and said, "Gaylord, I read the book you reported on, and I found it interesting how you —er, ah improved upon it. I am not going to do anything about it because you did do a good piece of creative writing, and that is one thing we are trying to teach, but Gaylord, you aren't going to do that anymore, are you?" I answered simply, "No, Ma'am." And I didn't.

x x x x x

So I watched many trains and inspected most of those that stopped anywhere near. When a train stopped in Woodton, there usually would be a considerable number of motor vehicles backed up because Woodton was fortunate in having two highways as well as two railroads, with the highways and the rails running parallel to each other for at least thirty-five or forty miles in all four directions from town. The two highways crossed at the spot known as downtown, that is to say Broadway and Main, this location being a half block north and a block and half east of the commonus of the rails. As with the rails, the more important highway was US 70 which lies east-west. An anomaly in names existed here, our own Broadway Street crossed highway 70 which was known locally anyway as "the Broadway of America." As far as I know, this never caused any problems, although at first glance you would think it might.

During the 1920's, the country had engaged in tremendous endeavors to convert its muddy roads into highways. The first phase was to prepare drainage and to build good graveled roads, the second was to place hard-surfaced pavements. Highway 70 had been graveled in the 20's, and had been rebuilt completely and paved in the early 1930's. The north-south road was part of the state system and had been paved by the mid-30's. Both highways had a growing traffic in automobiles as well as in tractor trucks and motor busses.

Using the rails or the highways or both, much freight and many travelers "made a right" or "took a left" in Woodton, although some "just kept on going". Few of those who turned or continued could recollect later the name of the town giving host to the event.

With no air terminal or even an airport, Woodton was not served by an airline. However, an east-west air route connecting Memphis and Little Rock lay just south of town, and an airway's beacon was installed a couple of miles away. Other similar beacons could be found at intervals of 25 to 30 miles in a generally east-west line, thereby identifying the location of the airway at night if the weather was good. Each beacon mounted two powerful lights, shining in opposite directions, and rotating on a vertical axis, making one turn in 60 seconds. When viewed from a distance, two flashes of light were visible from each turn. On a clear night, the beacons some 25 miles on either side of Woodton could be seen, but more faintly of course. On some occasions, I can recall seeing the next beacon beyond that, and rarely —very rarely— the one beyond that.

In the early 30's, the airlines flew Ford tri-motors, and changed to Douglas DC-3's by 1936 or so. Several flights were made each way each day, and for some reason the airplanes always were called "mail planes". Once, a DC-3 crashed a few miles west of town, killing all on board. My father received a bronze award from the utility company for outstanding service in assisting the airline during the cleanup operation. Two or three years later, another one made a "wheels up" landing in a pasture when one engine failed. A couple of mechanics came over from Memphis, jacked up the plane and lowered the landing gear, and changed both engines and propellers. All of this took about a week, and two or three hundred people including me were on hand to see it take off again.

However, for the most part, the airlines existed but did not interface with us on the ground below. Virually no one in town had flown anywhere on an airline, and almost no one had any thoughts of doing so. Those who might have did not say much about it because they would have been considered equally dumb and brave.

Even so, there always were one or two airplaines owned by someone locally. These flew from the most elementary of fields and were housed in sheds or "hangars" built for the purpose. The owners, being local people, were not considered to be daring particularly, and because they had a good deal of money, no one would say they were dumb. But they were apart, many feeling that if God meant for man to fly, it would be in heaven and we shouldn't be looking for previws here on Earth.

All of the surface transportation facilities presented some disadvantages. The merchants of Woodton suffered somewhat from being in the shadow of Memphis which lay but 40 easy miles to the east. Those selling work clothes or farm tools, or food or lumber did not have to worry too much about the competition from the big city. However, anyone who was looking for dress clothing, or furniture, or household appliances likely would go to Memphis to enjoy a larger selection. Of course, the local merchants resented this exodus of money, and the chamber of commerce championed such phrases as "Shop Woodton first". Such a circumstance prevails today in the suburbs of large metropolitan areas. In Ramsey, New Jersey, which lies 20 miles from downtown Manhattan, one can find only one or two stores selling men's suits, but food stores and hardware stores abound.

Even with this drain upon its cash, Woodton was slightly more fortunate than most of its 5,000 sisters across the nation. It was and is the county seat of Francis County, and in consequence is the scene for legal transactions that originate anywhere within the County. Sales of land and live stock are registered by the county recorder, not to mention countless other documents of great personal value to the owners, such as school diplomas, wedding or birth certificates, military discharges, and the like. All disagreements that were negotiated out of court were handled by the dozen lawyers who practiced in town, as were all litigation's arising within the county that were tried in the courthouse. There was a mild buzz which was created by the activities that evolved from all the people in the county and which were completed in Woodton.

The county surrounded the city limits, which lay centrally in an overall dimension of about 25 miles north and south and about 30 east west. Of course there were numerous farms upon which grew cotton, corn, and vegetables. It was a common feeling among the adults at least that life in the country was better than in town and infinitely better than in any city. In the country, a man could move about and if times were hard he always could grow a few beans and potatoes in the right of way of the highway, or he could shoot a rabbit or lacking cartridges, he could make a trap. In contrast, in the city if the money gave out a man would starve if he couldn't find a bread line. In the country, he could get rid of the mice by getting a few cats, but in the city the buildings were so close that the rats and mice just moved over if a cat lived in one of them.

Each farm had its expected collection of animals: horses, cows, pigs, ducks, chickens, guineas, cats and dogs. Although, the cats and dogs offered and received the normal affections; relatively few enjoyed the position of being just a pet. Cats caught mice and in recompense were given a little milk once a day when the cow wasn't dry. If the cats did a good job and cleaned out all the mice and began to go for the rabbits and birds, one or more cats would be given away or put to sleep. The ideal balance was found with slightly scrawny cats, just a vestige of mice, and enough milk to keep the birds safe.

Dogs were kept for protection against prowlers, or to kill rats. They were fed table scraps and a very small quantity of scrap meats and bones. Dogs and cats alike slept outside in the shed or under the house next to the chimney. When they were sick, they either got well or they died; no money was spent taking them to the veterinarian. Except for administering rabies shots, the vet had little time for dogs and cats, anyway. He was kept busy nursing along the ailing horses and cows and pigs. These were important animals, costing sizable sums and worth the fees. Dogs and cats, except for a few pedigreed examples, were plentiful, cheap and expendable. I don't want you to think no one had a dog just for the sake of having a dog. Lots of people did, including us, but these did not get too much money spent on them when they got sick, including ours. I'll tell you about one of our dogs, but first a little more about the country side near Woodton.

So, the country life was preferred by the great majority of those who lived there. These feelings were shared by most of my family, which was fortunate because all of them were agriculturists of one kind or another, except for my father who, like I said, worked for the utility company. Both of my grandfathers were farmers and both were successful and respected. Two blood uncles, the husbands of a couple of aunts, and several cousins all wrought livings from the soil, but with unequal displays of skills and effectiveness. The poorest, by a considerable margin was Mother's cousin Albert, who worked a large plantation that barely paid the interest on the mortgage. He had been wealthy when no one used efficient methods, but as tractors began to replace mules and then became common, and as crop rotation became recognized as being better than one-land-one-crop, and as intrinsic betterments of scientific techniques began to be recognized, his methodology began to lose in the competitive struggle for survival. The death came slowly, with about fifteen or twenty years transpiring between the first tottering and the final fall, during which time he failed to recognize that a change was dawning and that those blind to the new light must stumble and go down.

On the opposite extreme was Uncle John Throckmorton, who had attended agricultural college just after World War I and who always was tinkering with the mechanics of farming. He stirred continuously the mix of acreage allocated to cotton, corn, soy beans and later, to rice. He loved cattle and raised horses for profit and later for the pride of developing a strain of stock that was named for him. After a few years, he became comfortable, then well off, and eventually mildly wealthy.

The rest of my family lay somewhere between these two in comfort and in status. Virtually everyone on both sides was a high school graduate, and a few had some college. Dad's feelings about education were held in common, the benefits of learning were hammered into each head as it matured so that it was understood that each child, if possible, should have more schooling than the ones before. It is a fair statement that all members of the family manifested a true interest in the doings of the school system.

The big money in town was made in cotton. The fields grew practically up to the city limits and provided work and income for most of those who lived in town. There were a dozen or more cotton buyers who knew at all times the prices of middlin or fair-to-middlin cotton as well as of all other grades, both in long and short staple. There were at least a dozen cotton gins in the county and in the fall these converted the freshly picked cotton into bales, it being a popular fiction that an acre of ground produced a bale of cotton and that a bale weighed 500 pounds.

If the price was not right at pickin' time, the cotton could be stored at the "compress", this being a company with the facilities for compressing bales to a much smaller size and then for storing these until the owner decided that he was ready to sell. The cotton seed could be sold to an "oil mill" which extracted the oil from the seed and also manufactured cotton seed meal, cotton hulls and similar items which then were shipped elsewhere for conversion into mayonnaise or fertilizer. That is the way it always was stated, but the frequent repetition locally had dulled any sensitivity to the diversity of the products.

Rich or poor, a man's standing in the community derived from two or three manifestations of performance. First, he had to own real property. The fact meant more than the form; the amount or the splendor being unimportant, those who rented houses were looked down upon even if all the other evidences were present. Second, he must work hard, pay his bills promptly, and even if poor not be on public relief. A man down and out was expected to obtain succor and substance within his own family and only if infirm could a man accept relief and still retain the respect of the town. And third, he must demonstrate a respect and regard for the properties of others. Hell raisers and drunks were not in with anyone; the police, sheriff, and the courts were lenient and tolerant of almost any violation that involved only the offender, but all were tough and quick in handling those who abused either public or private belongings.

There was an incident when I was about 12, which was illustrative of these feelings. Members of the high school football team tended to hang around together and one Saturday night, the group in a spirit of mischief turned over four or five brick barbecue fireplaces in a small city park. Apparently they were noisy enough to attract attention because the police investigated and arrested all. By Monday evening all had been before the municipal court and had received sentence which drew the accolades of the town, because it fit the crime perfectly. "Put them back just like they were", was the order of the judge, so the boys reported each day after school to a designate of the court and laboriously broke up each barbecue fireplace into its component bricks, chipped off the mortar which still adhered. Under the supervision of a local mason, the team mixed new mortar and rebuilt each unit. Several weeks were consumed in these acts. Penologists may argue whether or not punishment deters crime, but in this case this particular brand of desolation has not occurred since.

This bit of vandalism was not typical of the behavior in general, but one should not infer that the community was without criminal acts. A half dozen or so houses would be entered and robbed during a year's time, these intrusions being aided by the casual habit of never locking doors. Houses were left unlocked for years on end, even when the occupants were absent on trips. Consequently, the wonder is that house robberies were not more common.

Similarly, every year or so someone would be shot or a store window would be broken and merchandise would be stolen with about the same frequency. Once in a great while, an automobile or a bicycle would disappear. Some of the transgressions were against society rather than individuals, there being the usual drunkards and occasionally other acts of public nuisance. In general however, the town was quiet and Chief of Police John Henry Robinson tried to keep it that way.

Chief Robinson policed the town with five men besides himself. During the day, one man remained in the police station to keep records and to receive calls. The chief and two others covered the town in two patrol cars and on foot. There was no radio, but scattered over town and also at Broadway and Main were a dozen or more loud ringing electric gongs and about four telephone call boxes. If a call came in which required the attention of a patrol car, the desk man would energize all of his gongs. When a man in a patrol car heard one of these, he drove to a convenient telephone or to one of the call boxes and reported in. The gongs then were turned off and the reasons for the call were given.

Except on Saturdays, there was no desk man at night, and a single officer patrolled the town and the night telephone operator handled the few calls that did materialize. The gongs were not used unless a real emergency arose, so the patrolling officer had to cruise by one of the call boxes two or three times an hour to see if he had any business. Whenever he stopped for a cup of coffee, which was at least three or four times during his shift, he first checked in with the night operator.

MONKEYS AND MERIT BADGES

In similar fashion, Sheriff William (Wild Bill) Smith and his one deputy sheriff patrolled the rural areas. He conducted only a few nightly patrols, these being made at irregular intervals so that a pattern could not be discerned. The main highways within the county were covered by a single trooper from the state police. His chief mission was to apprehend speeders, although once in a while he set up road blocks (with assistance from the Sheriff or from Chief Robinson) to warn that the Fish River was flooding and the water was over the road surface, or to catch car thieves and others fleeing from the law.

Actually, few arrests resulted from the activities of these three operations. About once a week, Chief Robinson drove to the home of Mrs. Frank Wilson and politely confiscated the small articles she had stolen while shopping, and returned them to the proper stores. Mrs. Wilson was a known kleptomaniac and everyone was happy if the goods merely were returned undamaged or paid for if they were not. About once a month the state trooper looked the other way while George Agency, the owner of the funeral parlor and of the only ambulance in town, gave this vehicle a high-speed test on the highway. He exceeded the speed limit by twenty-five or thirty miles an hour at these times, but he was listening for strange sounds and feeling for abnormal handling characteristics. The ambulance did not get much use and he was always afraid that something would fail through unintentional neglect.

X X X X X

I said I would tell you about our pets, so this is as good a place as any. Even though times were tough, we always had pets while I was growing up, usually a dog and a cat. Occasionally, we might have two dogs for awhile, but ordinarily we just had one of each. Once we had a monkey. We only had the monkey for a short time. I never knew how we got him or what happened to him. But I liked him and always wanted another one.

One dog was named Sollie, after a fox in the old Barney Google cartoon strip. We got Sollie when he and I were just pups, he about three months old and I about five years. Sollie's entire reason for being was that Dad thought a boy ought to have a dog, I was a boy and Sollie was a dog, and was free. The reason he was free was he was half German shepherd and half Airedale, his German shepherd mother having papers back to Adam and Eve. His father was well known about town, but his documentation was skimpy.

Sollie was solid black with a long pointed tail and nose, a pair of floppy ears, and weighed about 55 pounds. Sollie was my constant companion from the time we got him until he died. And he lasted ten years, not too long today when dogs have every care lavished upon them, but it was a good stretch then for an ornamental pet. For the times, Sollie received very good care, but today's mutts would consider his life to be a hardship case. He was licensed by the town by a very simple system that municipalities today would do well to copy. According to the law, a dog living in town or the county had to have rabies shots and those in town had to be licensed, but a lot of people sort of ignored that, and as long as the unlicensed dog didn't cause any trouble, then no one complained. But to be legally compliant, a dog was licensed and to be licensed the dog must have rabies shots. These shots were taxed a quarter or maybe fifty cents by the town and the rabies tag then became the license tag also. The vets collected the fees and generally administered the system, and it worked quite well. Today my dogs rattle around with two and sometimes three tags, one for the license, one for rabies, and one for identification.

So a dog without a collar was chased by the dogcatcher on sight, and got a one-way trip to the pound. A dog with a collar obviously was owned so was not chased until it caused some trouble, like if he howled or committed too many public nuisances in inconvenient places, or bit anyone. A dog with a collar but no rabies tag was advertised in the public notices column of the local paper, and if claimed then the owner would be reminded, "There is the little matter of it being unlicensed, you know, and the fine for that is..." When an owned dog was caught, the rabies tag immediately identified the owner, who paid a small dog catching fee to get it back and a scolding from the police as well. Sometimes the tag had become detached and lost, and upon proof of being immunized then the dog was given back for the catcher's fee. Incidentally, the rabies tag we had then could be embossed on the back with the owner's name and address, and some were, but most depended on the rabies record to establish identity. Besides, most owned dogs were known by almost everyone anyway.

Now Sollie was the smartest dog that ever lived, I want you to know that. To show you just how smart he was, we still lived in the country when he was new and we kept a rooster or two and a few chickens for eggs as well as for fryers and baking hens. Everybody did. When Sollie was about 10 or 11 months old, he chased down a chicken and killed it. Dad saw him do it and really lit into him with a paddle and when he finished with that he locked him up in the shed out back for a couple of days. Maybe you think this was a little harsh, but dogs simply must not be allowed to kill and in particular eat domestic animals of any kind, because sometimes a dog so conditioned will revert to some of its wild instincts and will become a stock killer after that. It happened often enough on the farms that everyone knew that a dog must be broken of that habit before it ever became fixed in its mind. So Sollie was punished according to the crime as it was viewed at the time Well, it must have worked because Sollie didn't bother any chickens after that and time rolled along for a year, until just before we were about to move into town. One of the roosters we had was pretty aggressive, and he would jump on you and claw you at almost any pretense. He had done it both to Mother and Dad when they happened to be feeding the chickens, so it was a well-known trait of this rooster. One evening, my older sister went into the chicken yard to feed the chickens, and she carried a dishpan of corn for the food. The rooster jumped up and clawed her on the arms and legs. My sister got a big scratch on her arm and went squalling back into the house, leaving Sollie with the rooster. This was the first time Sollie had seen this act and he immediately chased it away and ran it up a fence post.

Now, Sollie knew not to harm the rooster, but one of his people had been harmed by it, so Sollie had to do something. Staying strictly within the rules, and without ever touching it, Sollie killed the rooster. He walked it to death. It required about three days, during all this time Sollie was never more than three feet from the rooster, and when he flew up on a post for a little respite, Sollie sat down and waited. Like I said, in three days, the rooster just keeled over and died, completely exhausted, and Sollie was pretty far gone too, but he got him. Sollie went to the back porch and scratched until Mother came out and fed him, the first thing he had eaten in the entire while. Sollie then crawled up under the house and slept for a whole day. I remember this little drama well, and Dad talked about it often.

When Sollie was about five years old, he suddenly discovered terrapins. He probably knew about them all along, but this is when he started to collect them. There was no shortage of them around our house, almost any time you wanted one you could go out in the fields and find one. Not too many people did, so that is why there were enough for someone who might just decides to have a look at a terrapin. Anyway, Sollie always was bounding across the fields chasing a rabbit or something, when suddenly one day he practically turned end over end as he tried to stop and turn around while still in the air. He disappeared in the weeds for a few seconds and then here he came, jumping over the weeds in big leaps with a terrapin in his mouth. After that, he picked them up often.

The first few times he did this, he just brought it back to the house and played with it, tossing it in the air and catching it in his mouth, or sometimes missing, it then would go crunching onto the ground with a roll of a foot or two. Sollie then would recover his terrapin and do it again until after a few repetitions, he would tire of this and lie down to nap, but with his prize still held in his paws. The terrapin would lie low in his shell for a few minutes, then he would start peeking out, and then he would go for the deep grass a few feet away. Sometimes he would make it and Sollie would have to find himself another one, but sometimes the terrapin would be missed by whatever terrapin sensors that Sollie had deployed while sleeping. When this happened Sollie would get up and go pick up the escapee, and bring him back, and then he would continue his snooze.

One time the terrapin was slow coming out of his shell. Sollie waked up, and after checking the security of his property walked away and out into the weeds. Next thing he is bounding along again just scaring up whatever was to be flushed, when he does his flipping stop again. Down into the weeds he goes and up he comes, and he has a new terrapin in his mouth which he brings home. For the first time in his life, he now owns two terrapins. Something in his brain assembled into a critical thought mass, quickly, he pawed the two terrapins together, and went zipping back into the field. Within a few minutes, he was back again with his third terrapin, which goes down with the other two. One of the initial pair had emerged while Sollie was gone and was trying for freedom about the time he returned with number three, but Sollie made short work out of arranging his triad into a small pile, and back to the weeds. Within about fifteen minutes, Sollie had eight or nine examples, all piled up neatly in front of him as he lay down to survey his riches. Soon he fell asleep and after a bit some of the terrapins began to extend their heads and legs and to beat it out of there. A couple almost made it when he aroused, quickly got up and put each one back on the pile. Of course a dog has a lot of other things to do besides watching a bunch of land turtles, so when he attended his other interests some of them would truly escape. Sollie then would go out and fill his quota, and put them on the pile.

This went on for several weeks, and some of the terrapins began to look familiar. One in particular I began to recognize and I named him Thomas Jefferson. TJ seemed unusually susceptible to being caught by Sollie, sometimes he would get away for maybe a day, then Sollie would find him again and bring him back. For no other reason than I was a boy, I carved my initials on his back and the date, and let him go, but Sollie kept him pretty well rounded up most of that summer.

Sollie turned his interests to other hobbies after a while and all of the terrapins got away. Thomas Jefferson stayed around in the edges of the yard or in the flowerbeds or somewhere close to the house for years. I often took him with me when the family took short trips, and later I took him with me on lots of hikes when I became a Boy Scout.

X X X X X

One other dog approached Sollie for the rank of super dog. That was Freddie, but he came around after I was an adult. Freddie was a small black poodle, weighing about 7 pounds. Freddie was a dominant dog, and he immediately established his dominance over other dogs, many of these being fully grown German shepherds and dogs of similar size. Being dominant, Freddie never backed down from anything, but there were times when it was clear Freddie wished he didn't have to make the stand. When he knew he could handle the situation, he would bark "Wulf". When he was making a stand where he was not sure about this, but was not backing down anyway, he barked "Wulf-wu". When about 14 months old and little more than grown, he encountered a snake that had gotten into the house someway. Through all the screams and shouts and scurrying for weapons, Freddie stood there nose to nose with the snake, with his head thrust forward, the snake's head and neck pushed well back, Freddie trembling all over, going "Wulf-wu". If snakes could bark, I imagine this one would have gone "Wulf-wu" also. With the armory of a modern household arrayed against it, the snake silently slithered out through the door held wide with a broom extended at arm's length. Having protected his people and his house, Freddie stopped going

"Wulf-wu" and threw up.

Freddie was too small to be a guard dog, but he would have died trying, but you might have mistaken him for an enraged powder puff while he was doing it. He made up for that by being a good watch dog. When anyone came up on the porch to ring the door bell, Freddie always beat the bell with "Wulf" Bing Bong. When in his prime, he was chagrined if it went Bing "Wulf" Bong. It was truly sad as Freddie got older to see his senses deteriorate so that in time it became Bing Bong "Wulf", and finally one day just Bing Bong.

Freddie never backed down from anything, not even once.

X X X X X

I caught the whooping cough when I was in the fifth grade. I don't remember a lot about it except that I missed almost two weeks of school. That in itself would have been all right, but in Woodton there was an incentive system for attendance and scholarship. If one had a "B+" in a particular course at the time of the final examinations and with no individual grade in any other course lower than "B", and if one had no more than three excused absences or three excused tardies in that particular course, then the teacher could excuse one from taking the final examination with the final grade being the mark earned up until that time. A pupil with a "B+" could choose to take the final to try and raise it to an "A". Since the grade also might be lowered, no one in a position to make that decision ever chose to be examined. No one. So the pupil was in contention for being excused from one or more examinations, or he or she had to take the entire lot. Being excused from all of the finals was a prize really worth working for, because it meant that you could relax during all the reviewing in the last few days. Even having to take only one or two exams was an honor, and we tried hard to be worthy. In this case, because of the long absence with the whooping cough, I had to make up the work and take all the exams even though my grades otherwise met the tests. Like Dad always said, life is not always easy or fair.

A younger sister was born about that same time. Although my values ultimately changed, the whooping cough made more of an impression at the time.

CHAPTER VI

The social swirl started the summer between the sixth and seventh grades when I was invited to a dance. This happened fairly often after that, the format was the same in each case, so I will describe the first I ever attended and this will do for the rest of them.

Some girl who considered herself to be quite a scion of society in our local scene would decide she would have a dance. To even consider such attainments, the girls parents had to have some substance because these little affairs were costly. Most girls could count on no more than one in her life, two if extremely lucky. One measure of success was the amount of space captured in the society column of the local daily, so choosing the age when she made the effort was important. If too young, the hostess could not count on much from those in the higher grades, and if too late, her smoke would have been blown away by her contemporaries, and not as newsworthy. As you can see, the natural competitive spirit caused these little shindigs to get bigger and bigger as time went on.

Well, the telephone would ring, and the girl would be on the other end and she would deliver her little spiel, "Gaylord, I'm having a dance on Saturday night, July—and I really want you to come and bring Agatha Thompson. It will start at seven and will be over at eleven. Bye now." The first time this happened I didn't even know who was calling, it being characteristic of these young queens that each assumed that you would know her voice. This of course led to some flaps, so most hostesses learned to be a little more careful. It also was a characteristic that none of these girls ever dreamed that anyone would refuse an invitation. Once when I did because I already had something else in the works, like an appendicitis operation on the morning of the evening, my hostess got real mad and accused me of upsetting all her arrangements.

Actually, the arrangements were a bit complex. First, it was necessary to invite the same number of boys and girls because each had to have a date. Absolutely no unescorted girls, a girl would rather die than be without a date. To hear them tell it, some of them did, but they seemed to get over it by

Monday morning. Also there were no stags ordinarily, but if one or the other just had to happen, then an extra boy or two was all right, but not too many.

Usually, the hostess-to-be would pair up those who were dating one another, but this was far from simple because those who were "going steady" were not likely to be by the time the dance was held if it was more than a few days off. That was about the size of it anyway, because usually the invitation preceded the event by maybe ten days, sometimes less. After accommodating the steadies, the hostess then would try to match up those who she knew liked one another but for some reason, shyness most likely, had not been able to make the first move. With these potential if not impending pairsomes paired, she then would let her attention play where her matchmakers heart desired, that is those that SHE would like to see dating one another if she the hostess had it her way. With her cupidity for being Cupid assuaged, some would show real bitchiness and would assign an unsuitable partner to some one to get even for some past offense. She then would assign any boys and girls left over to enjoy or endure the other's company for one evening. Since this was the tail end of the pickings, it was mostly endure.

Somewhere along the line she had to decide just where the dance was going to be held, and I suspect that the parents' assistance was needed here. A number of these little gatherings had over a hundred kids of all ages in attendance, so it was necessary to get it out of the house. A popular spot was the community center, the same place used for the meetings of the Boy Scout Troop, and the arrangements at the scene were almost the same. Clear floor, with no obstructtions, but for the dance the walls were lined with chairs for the sitters-out to use, not to mention the chaperons.

A band was scrounged from somewhere. There always seemed to be bands hiding in the woodwork. The same group played on at least two of these occasions, and it was called a band by the first hostess, but she was topped by the second who referred to it as an orchestra. The same songs were played both times, and they sounded about the same to me. but it sounded better to have an orchestra even if it didn't sound any better itself, so after that the classier and tonier dances all had orchestras.

One big difference in the arrangements (from those for the Boy Scouts) was that there was the punch bowl at the dances, with the punch being served by the lady chaperons. I never have understood just why women get such a kick out of ladling up punch, or pouring coffee, or making sure everyone has a little napkin, but it seems to be one of those things that women do and enjoy that cannot ever be explained to men. Whatever the reason, no real harm ever seems to come of it, which is not true of some of the things women like to do. Men, too I hasten to add. But back to the preliminaries.

Now, the hostesses played the game two ways; some of them also would invite the girl, so she at least knew you were going to call her. Others invited the boy only and told him whom he was expected to bring. The first way was the better, because, with the second, every once in a while a boy would show up with a girl not intended to be invited, and with the one who was supposed to be left at home. In either case, he was supposed to call the girl assigned to him and somehow determine if she knew about the dance and also find out when to pick her up. Usually this was about thirty minutes before the official start, so that you could get there pretty close to the initial dance, but not so early as to be the very first ones there. Being first showed that one was too eager, and that would never do because one must be very suave and do every thing just right. On the other hand, you didn't want to get there too late either, because it was considered a disgrace to the girl if she didn't dance every single dance, or at least have a chance to refuse.

It was necessary to get the girl a corsage. To do it right, you had to know the color of her dress, but it was considered improper for a boy to ask what color she was going to wear, in fact it was a little risqué, for a boy to show any interest in girls' clothing at all. There was a clear lock-up of moral and practical objectives in force here, because the corsage simply must match else the young man was not properly "attentive", and inattentivity was an insult to the young lady. As you can see, girls could spend a lot of time being insulted if they worked at it at all, and a lot of them did.

Solving this little dilemma required a bit of back stage work by the mother, or a sister or an aunt (in that order of preference), of the young man. If this female relative knew the mother of the girl, she would call up and ask the important question and that was that. If the two mothers had never met, then protocol dictated that the boy's mother must find a way to be introduced to the mother of the girl. Notice that males always were introduced to females, even if she were only three and he were ninety, so by extrapolation, the mother of a male would be introduced to the mother of the female. All of this was very important, and to violate any of it marked you as not being from a good family, or if the family was impeccable, then a black sheep had gotten out.

A socially conscience mother could arrange these little things easily, and part of the daytime activities of women was setting up and attending little teas and coffees and brunches so that so-and-so could be introduced to such-and-such. I want you to understand, most of these little functions were not expensive to lay on, the times would not allow much of that, but they were proper. A simple little tea, no more than thirty minutes, served in good implements without chips or cracks, and accompanied by linen or good cloth napkins, with little sugar cookies was all that was needed. The tea and coffee services then were carefully stored away for other similar functions in the future, and never mixed with the everyday dinnerware.

The simplest third party arrangement was where *Mrs. A* wanted to be introduced to *Mrs. B*, and where *Mrs. C* knew both. *Mrs. C* would hold a little half hour tea, and invite *A* and *B*, and simply say "Ida (that was *Mrs. B*), I want you to meet Joyce (*Mrs. A*)", and that was that. After a short time of chit chat, *Mrs. A* would leave first, followed by *Mrs. B* a minute or so later. If *Mrs. A* and *Mrs. B* had no common friends, then it was a little more complicated, but if *A* still wanted to be introduced to *B*, and if *A* knew *C* and *B* knew *D*, and *C* knew *D*, then a larger function was necessary so that *A* could be introduced to *D* by way of *C*, (whose participation now was ended) and then *D* would introduce *A* to *B*. Of course, *C* could have been the surviving intermediary, and there were rules about when *C* or *D* did it. Got all that? It was important that the introductions be made in the right direction, to flub up on this showed no breeding or background. Women, some of them anyway, really got their happiness shots from figuring out how to get people introduced, this was where the brunches and luncheons came in, sometimes it was necessary to have eight or nine people present in the proper sequence to pull one of these things off. When something got up to this level, several women would go in together and have a group to-do so that just about everyone alive got introduced to everyone else, and all in the proper order.

It was truly great fun for the ladies, and like pouring punch no harm came of it, except that a complicated introduction sometimes could be overtaken by events. Like if a girl was pregnant. The father took over then and addressed the young man with a simple, "Get you ass in the car, we're going to see the preacher."

In almost every case involving me, mother was able to set up the necessary function, then with the introductions out of the way, a delicately phrased question was offered, nothing so crude as "What color dress is Agatha going to wear to the dance?", but something like "These young girls are so pretty these days, aren't they Mrs. B, and they have so many colors to choose from in making their clothing. What is Agatha's favorite color?" Now, if *Mrs. B* has half a brain, she knows why she is here in the first place, and she will have the answer all ready. If she has a whole brain, she will say, "Oh her favorite color is Federal blue, (or what ever) in fact she is making a new dress right now and I just happen to have a little snip of it right here in my purse", and with that she whips out her little snip about two inches wide and eight long. It now is Mother's turn, "Why, that is the most beautiful piece of goods I have ever seen, where on earth did she get it, I would just love to make a blouse (skirt, pillow case) out of that". "Why, she got it at Goldsmith's, why don't you just take this along so you will be sure you get the right thing." Now, all of this is in the little white lie category, Mother can't stand the color and is thinking, "My God, poor Gaylord Throckmorton Montmorency is going to have to be seen with this abomination all evening, and *Mrs. B* is thinking, "She can't wear this color, it would accent the bags under her eyes." But the deed is done, now Mother knows exactly what color to match the flowers to and is in charge of a sample, and shortly thereafter the little get together breaks up with each assuring the other two that we must do this again soon, knowing full well no one intends to.

The only time these little occasions misfired was when one set of parents had moved in shortly before from some other part of the country and didn't know the rules. If it were the girl's parents who were the newcomers, then the particular *Mrs. B* of the moment would not respond to the cue and would turn the conversation into a discussion of HER favorite colors, or something equally off track. The hostess then would swap glances with *Mrs. A* indicating "I tried". In such a case, next day *Mrs. C* would ask *Mrs. B* about the color and would relay to *Mrs. A*. If everything failed, as it did sometimes when not enough women were in the household, the young gentleman would simply send or bring white carnations. White carnations were respectable, not a black mark exactly but somehow were not considered to be as thoughtful in some way. If he were from a proper family, this was chalked up against her; if her credentials were in order, then his family was remiss. It happened on several occasions when both were from impeccable backgrounds that a girl purposefully wore a white dress to match the flowers she knew were coming because this little protocol train had derailed somewhere, and she didn't want to embarrass the boy or his family. These were gentle times, economically very hard, but the little things that represented tradition and breeding and good family were held dear. Ragged clothes were forgivable if they were clean, but ragged manners were not.

Now that we had the color of the flowers all lined up, ordering the corsage must be attended to. Florists know just how to handle these things, "Why, yes, MR. Crawford," speaking to me, who is all of almost eleven and a half but going on twelve, "we will take care of everything and do you want this put on your account?" Well, yes, of course, not knowing just what it meant, but not wanting to let on either. When I found out later, I really felt ten feet tall, but I found all my male classmates had grown with me because all of them now had accounts too.

These details taken care of, I thought I was about ready, but Mother didn't, and naturally she got her way. I really hadn't thought too much about what I would wear, I deemed some short pants and my tennis shoes would be about right. I can hear the scream to this day. "TENNIS shoes! No son of mine is going to wear tennis shoes to a DANCE." So we go into my room and I try on that suit that she had bought me just last year, "My goodness, the pants don't even come to your ankles, I didn't realize you had grown so, now let me see if I can let them out?" She thought she could, then we looked at the coat, it was tight but with a little attention to the sleeves maybe it would do, now let's see about a shirt, don't you have one without a frayed collar, maybe I can turn this one —let me see, no I turned it already— I will just have to buy you another one...make me a note right there. Where is that tie I got for you, here it is all knotted up in the corner of the closet, oh dear I wonder if it can be pressed out...Now let's look at your socks, don't you have any color but white, my goodness look at the hole in the heel, both heels, and one toe too, Gaylord Throckmorton Montmorencee, why don't you tell me when your things are like this so I can fix them up, I'll just have to get you some socks make another note right there, what did you do with that piece of paper it was here only a second ago, oh here it is now where is the pencil, oh I stuck it in my hair, now let's look at your shoes GAYLORD THROCKMORTON MONT<u>MOR</u>ENCY (that was close to her exasperation tone, however, she had stressed one syllable in Montmorency, so I was still all right)) when did you shine them last and just look at those run over heels, don't you know to use a shoe spoon and not to bend over the heels like that when you put them on, let's see if a little polish oh dear me this one has a hole in the sole, and all the way through..." On and on, but she really wasn't mad or even upset, Mothers just aren't happy unless they are clucking away being a mother. They always claim otherwise, but they are miserable if everything is all mended and hung up in its place, because then they would figure no one needs them anymore.

So Mother was in her glory getting me ready, which she did, and I looked halfway respectable and debonair when she got through. Uncomfortable as a fish swimming in mud, but I looked pretty good.

While Mother was doing her thing, it was necessary to see about transportation. None of the kids below the eleventh grade could drive legally, and I was a year younger than others in my own grade, so I either had to walk or Dad had to drive me and my "date" to the dance. First off, I didn't consider her as being a date, I was just going to the dance with her. Second, walking was out if either of you lived more than five or six blocks away from the dance site, and both of us lived more than a mile. No schoolmates were going to drive, so Dad was it.

First, I had to wash the car, and clean it thoroughly inside. Dad opened up on his principles here, "Son, don't ever let me hear that you went for a young lady in a dirty car. If she is worth taking out, she is worth cleaning the car for." I couldn't disagree with that, it made a lot of sense, and I still subscribe to it. "The car may get muddy on the way to get her because it is raining or snowing outside, but it started out clean, just like you did." Dad still speaking of course, but I agree.

I thought I had done a pretty good job and Dad came to inspect. Our car was a '36 Ford V-8 with an integral trunk and an external spare tire. He opened the trunk. Oops! It was tiny by today's standards, but it was just as unkempt. "Straighten up the trunk, you never know when you might have a flat, and you want everything to be neat." Dad speaking again. Finally, the car passed his inspection.

It had been agreed that I would pick up Agatha at 6:45, this would give fifteen minutes to go through the routine of meeting her parents, and then driving to the dance. The entire distance from our home to Agatha's house to the dance was about two miles so we should arrive just after seven, being neither first nor last. The first dance shouldn't start until about ten after so everything should be just about right. Stay tuned.

So Dad put on his suit to drive me for Agatha, on the way he fills me in some more, "Son, when you say you will pick up a young lady at 6:45, that means you ring the doorbell at 6:45, never earlier, and at most no more than a minute late. If something should happen that you just can't make it, then you must call and set another time later in the evening, then you must be right on the dot the second time. If they don't have a phone, then you must send a small gift —it doesn't have to be much— the next day as an apology for being late. Remember, when you make an appointment, you are dealing with other people's time as well as you own, so it is not polite to waste theirs." I never had thought about any of this before, but it all made sense so I accepted all of it without question.

We arrived at the address. I ascended the steps, and as near the second as I could judge without a watch, I rang the bell. No answer. I rang again, same result, complete silence broken only by the bark of a dog inside. Rang again. I stood there, and after a few seconds the dog stopped barking and substituted growls instead. Clearly, no one was home.

I went back to the car and conferred with Dad. "Are you sure you got the right girl, what was her name again? Agatha Thompson...now I know where just about everyone in town lives, what is her father's name?" I didn't know. "How about her mother?" I didn't know. We went back home and Mother offered the information that Agatha's mother's name was Ida. No help. Mother called *Mrs. C*, who had arranged the introductions and found that these Thompsons lived at a different address than the one where we went. Dad talked to *Mrs. C* and thought he knew the place, meanwhile Mother tried to make the necessary call that we would be there at twenty after, but they had no phone. She relayed this as we were getting into the car. We took off, with

Dad driving pretty fast, because we were about fifteen minutes late already. Nothing to do but tough it out.

Well, we got there, late like I said, and I was received coolly by Mrs. Thompson with a crisp comment about being prompt, and that Agatha would be ready in a minute. That was all right, because the girl was not _ever_ supposed to be ready when the boy arrived. So, I sat down on the couch, and Mrs. Thompson began to pump me for information. What did my father do, is that so? How interesting, but you knew she didn't think so at all. Does your mother knit? She is such a nice person, I enjoyed so much meeting her, do you have any brothers or sisters, yes ma'am an older sister and one younger too. How interesting. What are your hobbies? I didn't really know exactly, I liked to ride my bicycle, and to throw rocks at birds. Oh, my how horrible, did you ever hit any, why yes ma'am I got one last winter and another one a couple of years ago, OOOO-o-hh, did you really, what else do you do? Well, I had started a live bug collection that Mother doesn't know about, I knew immediately that was too much information, and regretted it instantly. Is that so, why doesn't she know, well she might not like for me to keep it under my bed. Wrong answer, I knew at once. I was right, Mother _didn't_ like for me to keep it under my bed, and somehow she knew about it the very next day. It was the six live roaches that really ticked her off, but she didn't like the woolly spider either.

This one-way exchange of information went on and on, and there was no sign of Agatha. After maybe ten minutes, Mrs. Thompson decided to check, these girls sometimes forget the time you know, yes ma'am I know. So she left with the absence being a definite improvement. After about five minutes she comes back and says, "Agatha will be down in a minute, I must help her with her dress."

Mrs. Thompson left the room again, and I sat there and wondered what the humming noise was that I could hear at more or less regular intervals. It would go "HHHH-MMMM" for maybe ten seconds, then there would be a few seconds of silence, then H-H- HHHHH-M-MMMM" again. It suddenly registered, that was a sewing machine. This continued for about thirty minutes, with me staring at the living room wall and Dad sitting in the car wondering what the hell? They both emerged at about 8:20, with Agatha's eyes all red where she obviously had been crying. Mrs. Thompson smoothed it all over with a casual "There was a tear in Agatha's dress that we had to repair." Considering all the sewing I heard, the tear must have been a couple hundred feet long.

Agatha accepted the corsage with a weak smile because obviously I had done my part matching the dress, but all that sewing changed the color some because it didn't seem to go with the flowers at all. In fact, her dress wasn't even close to the color I was supposed to expect. I was all tuned up to say "What a nice Federal Blue dress." With her mother there, that was considered proper for a boy my age, but this one was a color I really couldn't name, like burp green or something, so I thought it better not to say any thing, and didn't.

We left, and Mrs. Thompson just couldn't resist one final little dig, "You must learn to be prompt when picking up your date, Gaylord." I decided when I got around to picking up dates, I would be prompt. Somehow, this didn't count.

Dad was asleep when we got to the car, but he came to with good grace and drove us to the community hall. There were a lot of cars there ahead of us but we got to the door without any problem and let us out. We all agreed he should come for us at eleven. I suppose Dad went home to sit it out, but he never said.

We went in and because we were so late, almost every one was dancing, I guess. The band —I believe this one was a band— was kicking up a fast number which I don't remember, but everyone was doing the latest thing called "The Stomp". It's kind of hard to describe, but to a beat that would support a Lindy type of dance, the dancers rise slightly on one toe, he on the right say and she on the left. Then in time to the music, his left heel (right for her) is sort of kicked outward twice, while the right (left) heel is brought down twice with a resounding thump each time. Then everything is repeated with the other foot, or feet I should say because both of you are supposed to be doing it together. When everyone gets it going good to a jumpy tune, these stomps all in unison will crack the foundation of any building. That was what they were doing and doing a good job too so nothing would do but we should join in with the stompers.

I can't imagine how this got by Mother, but it became clear right then I had received no instructions at all about dancing. None. She had been so busy with all the little details this very significant item fell through. Looking around me I could see how to hold the girl, and I suppose she could see how to be held, but as you know, the footwork is a little more complicated then the holding. I don't think she had ever danced before either, so it was pretty bad, but we were able to create a stumble that kept time, and looking around at others, we seemed to be doing as well as most.

I soon learned an inexorable fact of ballroom dancing, If you have mastered only one step, it becomes a little boring to continue through a long dance and another and another and another, all to the same step. But that is what we did. There absolutely was no relief, there being no stags and no boys with dates standing one out, because every girl was determined not to sit out a single dance. When dancing with someone not of your choice, and who really doesn't turn you on in any way, the conversation soon dwindles away to the perfunctory "Would you like some more punch?" and the equally mechanical "Why yes that would be very nice." She drank about a gallon of punch and we stompled through dance after dance, grimly determined that this was really having a good time.

During the intermission, I didn't even know they had intermissions or why, we exchanged inane comments with the other couples, the girls just adoring each other's dresses, and the boys saying in a knowing way "I see you holding her pretty close there", or "why don't you hold her closer, she won't bite you know" I didn't know, I only knew this was misery in an outgrown suit.

Finally, it was over, and we strolled, you always strolled at a dance, toward the door and out to the car, or so we intended. If everything went smoothly at one of these things, your car would drive up just as you got to the curb outside, and that is the way it worked for some. In our case, Dad had gotten boxed in by a couple of cars and couldn't get out, so after standing at the front for five minutes or so, we decided to walk (by now I at least was walking) through the cars and locate him. This we did, but we couldn't leave the area until the road blockers moved, which took quite a few more minutes while we sat like dummies in the back seat and Dad sat in the front, not a word being said. At last we moved out, and started toward her home, I thought, when Dad said, "Where would you like to go for a coke?" I had forgotten all about this bit of etiquette, it was absolutely necessary to buy her a coke before taking her home. Mother HAD briefed me on that.

All of the drug stores downtown offered curb service for fountain drinks, so all you had to do was drive up to the curb in front and toot the horn and some one, often the owner, would come out and take your order. Almost anything simple, coke, limeade, root beer was a nickel, fancier stuff like banana splits ran more. Some things cost as much as twenty-five cents.

We picked a drugstore, parked and tooted, and sure enough Mr. Black, the owner, came out and Agatha asked for a banana split! That was a heavy-duty order, and I sensed I couldn't embarrass her by getting a coke, so I will have one too. Dad sees what is happening so he will have one also. The owner goes back inside and Dad gets out and goes inside for a few minutes and returns. The splits came and we sat there eating them, without a word, just the silent scraping and occasional clinking of the spoons on the dishes. You were served in real dishes then, none of this disposable stuff. She was a pretty slow eater, and I noticed that Dad was eating slowly too, and it penetrated my skull that I should slow down and finish at the same time as she did. So I stretched out the last ten per cent of mine to match her progress through the remaining 90 percent of hers, and did pretty well too.

At last, all banana splits were consumed, the serving tray picked up from the car window, and Dad said to put it on the account. Mr. Black thanked us for the business and asked us to come back. We drove to Agatha's house, and I got out to escort her to the door, where we were met by her mother in her house robe and curlers. Mrs. Thompson was furious, the dance was supposed to be over at 11:00 pm and here it was 11:45 and where had we been, etc, etc., not only was I late in arriving but I was late in returning and what kind of girl did I think her little Agatha was anyway? Agatha was whisked in with the closing door almost cutting off her words, "Thank you for taking me Gaylord, I really had a good time." Girls have good times for different reasons than boys, I have noticed it often.

I climbed into the car exhausted. Dad added to the load, "I knew you didn't have enough with you to pay for the banana splits, so I fixed it with Mr. Black for you to come in tomorrow and pay him. Have you got enough money?" I was short a dime when I counted it out at home, Dad loaned me the final amount and I went in and paid off. I commented to Dad that it didn't seem fair that I had to pay for all three banana splits when I was expecting only three cokes, with his coke being a token payment of appreciation. "Look son, I know you were bagged there, but it wouldn't be fair to me if I paid it, would it?" I had to agree, it wouldn't. "Life is not always fair," he added.

I went to one or two dances a year after that. Until I could drive legally, about the best I can say is that they were ordeals for me, and couldn't have been much better for any of the girls. I imagine it was the same for Dad. Generally if he could say nothing good about somebody or something he just said nothing, so it is significant that Dad never commented about driving me to the dances at all.

X X X X X

Time moved on and at age eleven, right after that first dance, I moved into the seventh grade. This, along with grades eight through 12 were taught in the high school building, it said so right over the main entrance, and once again I was the youngest in the entire school.

An entirely new and different flavor attended the academia in the high school building. First off, there were two well-organized sports, namely football and basketball. During either season, the weekly general assembly in the auditorium was used as a pep rally. The cheerleaders would try out the new cheers that one of them had just made up with the hope and intention that everything would go pretty good at a regular game. Sometimes it did.

We always sang the school song.

"On the city's northern border,
Reared against the sky,
Stands our dear old alma mater,
As the years roll by.

Forward ever be our watchword,
Conquer and prevail,
Here's to thee our alma mater,

Wood-ton <u>High</u>, all hail!"

The tune was the same as in a famous college fight song, and I was probably a senior before I stopped believing that <u>they</u> had stolen <u>our</u> song.

Other more subtle changes showed that we were growing up. Not so fast as we thought, but much more rapidly than our parents wished. In grammar school, we had written in tablets, now we used loose leaf notebooks with two rings, only two rings were acceptable, the three ringers had to wait until college. Previously we had art courses, so each year we had to buy a box of "colors" or crayons. Only Crayolas would do, any other brand was unworthy of recognition. The art teacher and the rich kids had the big boxes with the double or triple rows of sticks, most of us made do with the simple box of eight. Now, there was no more art.

We now studied "mathematics" instead of "arithmetic" and it took no more than 30 minutes to climb to the ultimate sophistication of referring to it in an off hand way as "math". It was difficult not to act as superior as we felt when taking such an exotic course. Also no more recess, although we did have an hour for lunch. The activities at lunch were much more sedate, it being considered kid stuff to play marbles, or shoot cap pistols. The older kids began to pair up, some of them by the ninth grade were even dating.

And we had lockers for our books and coats which meant that only those things used for the next class needed to be lugged about all day. We had to buy combination locks, all alike except for the combination of course. That was recorded in the principle's office so the lockers could be entered in an emergency. Two or three times a year the lockers would be searched for forbidden items. It may seem fairly tame today, but cigarettes or bottles of beer were about as tough as it went. Drugs and hard liquor were unknown, or at least to me and my crowd.

We also had study halls. Two whole periods each day when we could study. The best of all worlds was to have a first and a last period study hall, because you could study first thing after reaching school, and if you really needed to for a test maybe, you could go a little early and get some extra time. If the grades were good enough, one was excused from the last period hall, so that meant going home early.

The physical load carried to and from home also diminished dramatically because of these features. This was heaven. I now began to have time to think about things other than school, so I started my first business.

XX X X X

Somebody in my family always has taken a lot of pictures, This is not to say that these individuals necessarily were expert photographers, rather that at least one person in any particular era always was looked to as the recorder of family happenings in pictures. As a result, there literally are hundreds of photographs of members of the family, some long ago forgotten or never known by anyone still living. Even at an early age, I knew one should take a picture so the heads were not cut off, and so the photographer's shadow would not be in the picture. In time, when eleven and in the seventh grade, I was given a camera. This was a 127-size camera, one that is difficult to supply with film today, but I still think it was one of the best sizes ever made. It provided 8, 12, or 16 exposures to the roll, depending upon whether the camera was arranged for full-size, square or half-sized negatives. Although later I had examples of the smaller two, this first one was a full size, and wasn't much, but it was all mine. All I had to do was find a way to buy the film.

Somehow, I was able to scrounge enough to buy the first roll or two, then I found out about the other half of the financial commitment, the development. At that time, we took film to the drug store, and they sent it away somewhere, and about ten days later it would come back to be picked up. Not too different from the way it is today, except there were no promotional gimmicks of a free roll of film for each one developed and that sort of thing.

Well, in spite of all the accrued knowledge of a family of amateur photographers, my first photographic efforts all on my own were not too swift. A lot of the pictures did not materialize at all, either being too dark or too bright. In others, the compositional value was near zero; the dog, which was the center and hopefully the focus of my interest, turned out to be a small blob surrounded by a large expanse of yard, with a few distracting bicycles along one edge. What I thought was a hot shot of a parade formation produced only part of the front line, and this was blurred because the motion was too fast for the shutter speed. On and on. In particular, I found it annoying to pay out the developing money and get back an entire roll with nothing on it at all.

I determined to do better, but the mechanics of the process were elusive. There was a long article in the Encyclopedia Britannica's in the library, but much of it was completely beyond me, because I was not ready for emulsion speed, circles of confusion, and other technical details of equal rank. Off and on I tried another roll of film and got better, because I couldn't have gotten worse.

One day while thumbing through a new issue of the Sears Roebuck catalog, I discovered a couple of pages with cameras and accessories. There were some film developing chemicals with exciting names like "developer" and "fixer" and "hypo". A tube of PQ developer was a nickel, and it said right there that it would develop up to a dozen rolls of film. Fixer was even cheaper, because it was good until it was exhausted, whatever that meant.

The trouble was, I had not the slightest idea of how this stuff was used. Again I tried the library, and found there was not a single book on the subject. There <u>was</u> a professional photographer in town named John Anderson who had a small "studio", who eked out a living by photographing brides in their wedding gowns and all of the kids for class graduations, and that sort of thing. I went to him and asked how you developed film, but he wasn't too friendly. He didn't like the idea of anyone invading his professional space, even though the amount of business I would drain away was zero. But I persisted, and asked him to explain emulsion speed for me. That did it, he lived in a world with no one to talk to, and what discussions he had were with his clients while defending the photograph of the matron who thought it made her look too fat. No one gave a damn about the work and artistry behind the scenes. "OK Gaylord, come in back and I will show you how to develop film."

He led me into his darkroom, a mysterious place mentioned in the few articles I had found, but not described by any. The room contained some heavy odors which were rather pleasant in a pungent sort of way. There, with the lights on, I saw he had some tanks on one side maybe 12 inches square, and about as deep. The last one on the end was considerably bigger than the others. He explained that the first contained the developer, the next the shortstop, and the third the fixer. The big one on the end was the washing tank. He had a couple of rolls of film to develop for some customer, which really surprised me because I thought film had to be sent away. It had never occurred to me that anyone in Woodton would know how to develop film even if he happened to be the photographer. It did not seem inconsistent to me that I should have these thoughts at the same time I was asking him about developing film.

He turned out the regular light and the room was illuminated by a red bulb. After a minute of two for the eyes to adjust, he explained that the film was insensitive to red light, then he broke open a roll of exposed film and unrolled it off the spool. Actually, there was the film itself, and the paper that you normally saw that separated the layers of film on the spool. He let the paper curl up on one side while he captured the film in his hand, and at the inside near the spool end where the paper was attached to the film, he separated the paper and let it fall to the floor. He then stretched out the roll of film so that each hand held one end of it, a pretty good stretch even for him, because this was a big size roll. He then curled the film against the natural curling direction so that when he held the ends in his hands held about six inches apart, the film descended downward in two parallel strips with the curled turn at the bottom. This he lowered in the tank with the developer, and quickly moved his two hands alternately up and down so that the entire length of film was immersed uniformly in the developer. He continued this seesawing motion and gradually in the dim light, one could see the outlines of the exposures beginning to form, and a few seconds later it was possible to see that some of the images were distinguishable, but in negative form. He held the film strip up to the red light, inspected several of the negative areas, put the film back and developed it some more, inspected, developed for a few more seconds, inspected, then quickly immersed it in the second tank. "This is the shortstop," he said. "You don't really have to have it, but it stops the development and saves the fixer from being depleted so fast."

About fifteen seconds in the shortstop, and he placed the film in the fixer. He repeated the back and forth motion of the film for about a minute, then bending the film completely back on itself so the two ends met to form a loop, he fastened them together with a little wooden clothespin, and lowered the roll gently into the tank. He let me unroll the second roll, and start the developing. As this proceeded, he relieved me and after several inspections under the red light, he let me put it in the shortstop and then the fixer. When the second roll was pinned at the ends and placed in the tank, he said, "Now that is all there is to it as far as procedure is concerned. When the film fixes for about 15 minutes, I'll take it out and wash in the cold running water in that big tank on the end for about thirty minutes. Then I'll wipe it off gently with this chamois skin, and hang it up to dry, like those over there. When they're dry, they'll be ready to print. We'll print some of those that are dry in just a minute, let me see if anyone is in the front." No one was, so he came back and took down one of the films that were hanging by one end. "We're gonna make some contact prints, that means the customer wants them the same size as the negative, or at least doesn't want to pay for enlargements."

He cut the long strip of film into shorter pieces a couple of feet long, being careful to trim between the negatives and not to cut into the picture part of the negative area itself. "You just make this some convenient length, it doesn't matter. It looks a little better to the customer if it all comes out even, so I cut a 12 exposure role into three sections with four exposures on each, a 16 exposure one into four equal sections, but it really doesn't matter. Then you look at the negative you are going to print, if it is real contrasty like this one, you use a soft grade of printing paper. If it's kinda average, like this one, you use medium, for a flat one like this, you use a hard grade. The grades are marked right on the boxes of paper. Sometimes if the whole roll is taken at the same time and in a short time, all of the shots will use the same grade of paper, but most rolls are in the camera a year and people can't even remember what is on 'em, and in that case every negative will be different. Now, what you do is you place the negative against the printing paper and turn on the white light for a few seconds, you judge it by experience, and then under the red light you put the paper in developer just like you did the film. When the picture comes up —er you can see it right there in the tray— then you take it out and put it in the short stop, just like before, and then in the fixer. After ten minutes of fixin', you wash the b'jesus out of 'em otherwise they'll stain or fade and the customer'll come back two years later and complain."

He showed me a cabinet he called his "paper safe". It was arranged so the white light went out when he opened the door, and the red or "safe" light came on at the same time. So he picked up the first section of film, arranged it on what he called his "printing frame", although it looked just like a piece of glass to me. He looked at the first negative on the glass, decided it needed medium paper, opened the door to the paper safe and the light went off. Leaving the door open he carefully aligned the printing paper on the negative, and when he thought he was ready, he closed the door and the white light went on. He counted off "one-thousand-and-one, one-thousand-and-two, ..." when he got to one-thousand-and-eight, he opened the door to the safe and the white light went off. He put the exposed piece of paper in a box inside the safe marked "exposed" and went on to the second negative. With the white light on, he decided it needed hard paper, and he opened the door to the paper safe and repeated the process. When he had printed the entire roll, he again opened the door to the safe to kill the white light, and took the entire lot of exposed paper to the developer, and put in about four of them and stirred then around while inspecting each one, transferring each to the successive baths when he thought each was ready. He did this over and over again until the roll was processed, including fixing. He placed all of the prints in his wash tank and turned on the water, while he went back to roll two. I didn't know anything about it, but I could see several ways to speed up and simplify the procedure considerably.

When the first batch had washed enough, he then rolled them out on some very shiny plates with a rubber roller. "That gives the prints the glossy look that everybody likes. They'll pop right off when they dry enough." Sure enough, after about thirty or forty minutes, they did start popping off but it took ten additional minutes or so for any given print to peel off the plate completely.

It was getting late and I had to go. I thanked him profusely, and he said I could come back anytime I wanted. I couldn't wait to go into the photography business.

I had enough money to order a bare minimum of the chemicals, namely the developer and fixer. I had learned that the shortstop was not absolutely necessary, so I skipped that to the detriment of the life of the fixer. I needed some trays, and somehow was able to persuade Mother that several large soup bowls would not be harmed. The big expense was the printing paper. He said I needed three kinds for each size of film. By careful reading and calculation of costs, I found I could buy packages of large paper and cut them down more cheaply than buying the packages of the precut, however it cost more initially. That would have to wait, I decided I would specialize in 127 size contact prints only, and would gamble that most of the negatives would be normal or contrasty, so I got two grades of paper.

I sent off my order. It came to 76 cents, including the return postage. Sears Roebuck got a lot of orders in those days for less than a dollar. I waited. Sure enough, in about five days, here she came, and I could hardly wait. I let it be known in school that I was in the film developing business. My stock rose considerably, because none of my school chums had ever dreamed of developing film, but then not too many of them took any pictures either. But some did, and they were to be my customers. After a few days, I got my first order, a roll of 127 film, full size, eight exposures. You could get this done at the drug store for 40 cents, which made photography a pretty expensive hobby for the times, so I figured I could do it for 30 cents and make a killing, because the paper was about a penny a sheet. So I took my business home. Long before this first order, I had started to arrange my dark room.

Now, if you have never done it, it is amazing just how hard it is to find a room in an ordinary house that can be made pitch dark. Even at night there still will be stray rays of light that somehow meander into the room. The articles that I had managed to find all said that the bathroom was the ideal place for a temporary darkroom, but this was in the day before homes had two or more bathrooms, in fact a lot didn't have bathrooms at all. A darkroom would interfere with the normal traffic to the bathroom to be sure, but since I needed water for washing the prints, I thought this made a lot of sense, but Mother thought otherwise. I could wash the prints on the back porch in the laundry tub with a hose. Well, OK, if you insist, which she did. That still left the selection of the dark room itself. I finally settled on my clothes closet, a cell about 30 by 40 inches, placing a little stand along one wall and arranging my bowls thereon, and rigging up a white and a red light. I almost forgot to mention, I found a red Christmas tree bulb for the safe light.

I mixed up my chemicals, placing them in quart jars and labeling them very carefully. All the articles said do that. I set up my bowls and retired within the closet to develop the film. I cracked the seal on the roll, spooled it off, detached the paper and let it fall on the floor, feeling very professional like. Grasping the two ends of the film I slushed it back and forth like I had done before and waited for the outline of the negatives to appear, because I had to start inspecting right after that, although I was not too sure just what it was that I would be looking for. I slooped the film back and forth for what seemed to be a pretty long time, and nothing seemed to be happening, except that it kind of looked like it was turning clear! Upon closer inspection under the red light it indeed was almost clear. Quickly, I transferred it to the fixer, and allowing a short fix of five minutes, as near as I could estimate, I took it outside to the laundry tub and water hose. While the water was running I gave it a good look under full daylight and was horrified to see only the faintest outlines of what probably were the negative images of something.

From a background of an almost clear negative, and with a long look, fueled by a little desperation, I was able to discern that some of the exposures were of people, in the usual uninspired poses standing in front of a bush, and with one —maybe two— seeming to be an animal of some sort. After a lengthy and close examination, I deemed it to be a dog, this conclusion being aided considerably by the knowledge that my school chum had a dog and his folks didn't have a cow or a horse.

With the roll hanging up by one end to dry, I went back to my dark room to develop a roll of my own. I repeated the procedure, and with the same result. This time I knew what the pictures were supposed to be, so I was able to pick out the almost invisible images on the almost clear film. I began to suspect that I was doing something wrong. This feeling was reinforced when I discovered that the bottom of the developer bowl contained a very dark colored, almost black stuff that could be flattened out into a thin sheet. Nothing like that was in the bottom of the tank downtown at the photographer's studio.

I recovered the glass vial that had contained the powdered developer before mixing, and read the instructions more carefully. A key sentence caught my eye again, "Mix thoroughly in warm water of about 100°," which I had done. In fact, I had to ask a lot of questions to find out just how hot 100° was. It had been Dad who had provided the clue, "It will feel barely warm, not hot at all, in fact you could leave your hand in it all day." The instructions continued, "Develop for five minutes at 68°." Oops, that had gotten by me, I had mixed the developer and had started developing the film right away, and I really didn't know how hot it was, or how long I had developed it for that matter.

My instructions downtown had not included either of these details. Although I wasn't supposed to use the phone except in an emergency, I made a call to the photographer, figuring this might be one, seeing as how I could be on the way to a bloody nose. I phrased the question very carefully, the vial said to develop at 68°. Just what would happen if the temperature was too low. "Oh, it just takes longer, but usually it will come out all right if it isn't too cold." What about too hot? "It develops faster, and sometimes you might not have time to inspect the film before it passes the point of best results. Of course, you don't want to get it too hot, (my ears really tuned up at this) because the emulsion will melt off of the film." That was it. My developer had been too warm, and the emulsion had melted off, and had fallen into the bottom of the bowl.

Now I knew what the problem was, and how to correct it, but I still had to face my customer. Very carefully, I cut the film into two equal lengths of what should be four exposures each, placed these in a business sized envelop and approached him at school. I showed him the negatives, and pointed out the outline of the dog, I had decided it definitely was a dog, and was about to show him the people when he broke in "Why, that's just great, I didn't expect anything to come out at all." With that reprieve, I was able to negotiate from relative strength, so we agreed that, since I couldn't print the pictures from these "thin" negatives, I thought that term would show just how much I knew, then all he owed me was a dime. He took his negatives, and showed them all around, pointing out to anyone who cared and not surprisingly few did that here was Spot his dog, and this was Aunt Mary, and etc. He got so many jollies from these almost non-negatives, he probably couldn't have stood it if real prints had been the result. Anyway, he talked it up and sang my praises, and first thing I knew, I was doing a roll or two of film a week for somebody. At a glacial pace I pulled up my capital position by my own bootstraps, such that I was able to acquire all three grades of paper, and in the large dimension which I trimmed to any size I needed. That allowed me to accept all sizes of film, as long as they were satisfied with contact prints.

Mother put a stop to it. First, her bowls were being used just about all of the time, and once in a while she wanted to serve soup in them. She discovered that they were acquiring a stain that did not come off with washing. Developing chemicals possess a powerful odor, like I said before, and Mother was sure that remnants of this odor stayed with the bowls even after thorough scrubbing, and to her no soup ever tasted right in these dishes again, although guests just thought she was using some secret ingredient that she didn't want to talk about. There was more to this odor thing, my closet began to have a set as far as smell was concerned, and this began to attach itself to my clothing, and I began to have an air about me that others began to notice. At first, I passed it off with an off-hand "It's just photographic chemicals from my studio" (notice that I had acquired a studio.) So, after a time, five or six weeks as I recall, Mother closed me down. She took all my clothes and hung them on the clothes line for a couple of days, during which she placed an opened box of baking soda in the closet, and left the door to the closet as well as the windows to my room open and the door to the rest of the house shut. The odors gradually decayed away so that in time they were barely noticeable except in the very corners of the closet. These persistent spots remained so for months.

That was my first business venture, it failed because of the usual reasons, inadequate capital, poor managerial talent, and something that would become more meaningful in later years, pollution of the environment which caused difficulties with the authorities.

CHAPTER VII

Dad was a veteran of the first World War, or THE World War as it was called then because the second one had not yet happened, and he was active in the American Legion. The Legion was the sponsor of Boy Scout Troop 11 in Woodton which was the only troop we had then but we got another one later on. In time, he was elected to the committee which oversaw the affairs of Troop 11, and ultimately he obtained placement on the sub-committee which served as the Court of Honor before and to which the Scouts addressed themselves when aspiring to higher ranks. After a year or so, he became chairman of the Court and retained this post for 15 years. I came of scouting age a couple of years after Dad became chairman, and he was determined that I was going to be an example for other boys to follow. Dad's urgings really were not necessary because I was naturally interested anyway. I had seen the older boys in their uniforms, and had heard about swimming, tracking, firebuilding, and knot tying. Also, I always had an interest in Indians and had vague thoughts that Indians and Scouts were similar if not identical. So, on the next scout meeting after my twelfth birthday, I joined Troop 11.

"Upon my honor, I will do my best to do my duty to God and my country, and to obey the Scout law, to help other people at all times, to keep myself physically strong, mentally awake, and morally straight."

That is the Scout's oath, and all who become Scouts must take it. The Scout Law says, *"A Scout is trustworthy, loyal, helpful, friendly, courteous, kind, obedient, cheerful, thrifty, brave, clean and reverent."* There are some more words to pump it up a little, but the whole concept is very straightforward, simple and just about says it. We all felt taller and bigger both inside and out just by repeating the words, being quite impressed that it was an OATH. We knew we were not supposed to swear, but an oath was different, mainly because the Boy Scouts said so.

We were soon put in our place because in Troop 11 anyway the very next thing on the agenda was the initiation. This lasted about an hour and was intended to show each of us just how low we were and how much we had to learn. We had to eat some "rotten chicken" that really was raw oysters, which didn't improve the acceptability any when we were told what it really was. We had to walk blindfolded up a plank that was held up on one end by three or four of the bigger Scouts, who then would rock and swing the plank so that we could hardly stand. We were required to walk the entire length and jump off. There was a big tank of water to land in, and while in the air we were swatted on the rump. Somebody chipped a tooth falling in the tank of water, so the initiation was stopped right there by the Scoutmaster. Some of us had been initiated all the way by that time, three or four only partly. We felt superior and said we were all-in, and considered the others to be only half-ins. We tried to make them feel sub-standard, but somehow we couldn't pull it off. After a couple of meetings, only the individuals themselves could remember who was half-in and who was all-in. Except for the guy with the chipped tooth, that is. His parents decided we were a bunch of roughnecks, and wouldn't let him stay in at all.

The troop met once a week, Monday night usually, from 7:00 until 10:00 pm. Maybe you think that was a little late for a school night, but that was the time. The meeting was conducted by the Scoutmaster, Assistant Scoutmaster, and two or three Junior Assistant Scoutmasters. The first two were adult men, the Junior Assistants were older boys, usually Eagles. It was quite an honor to be selected as a Junior Assistant Scoutmaster. From the ranks of the troop, we elected a combination role keeper and treasurer. He had to take the role at each meeting, collect the dues and generally account for the money in the treasury, which usually was a fair little sum. The troop always was receiving small donations, particularly at Christmas, and it all mounted up. Keeping up with all of it was a thankless job, and was not considered an honor at all, so it was used as a prerequisite to being a Junior Assistant.

We were organized into patrols, each having its own patrol leader and assistant patrol leader, and each being named —usually that is— for a wild animal like Beaver patrol, or Fox Patrol, and so on. The exceptions in Troop 11 anyway were the Flaming Arrows, and once there was a Pine Tree Patrol. Each patrol had its own call, which supposedly mimicked the namesake, with the Flaming Arrows going "Wsssss". The Pine Trees had a tough time coming up with a call, so the name was changed right after that.

There were eight "men" to a patrol. It was all right to be short one or two men, but for some reason, it was unthinkable to have more than eight. Usually, there were enough boys to form four patrols, but sometimes there would be a couple left over. In that case, a fifth patrol was created by taking one Scout from the other four and adding the two or three extras that made the fifth one necessary in the first place.

On meeting nights, the entire troop would assemble at the meeting place. Sometimes this was in the basement of a church, sometimes in the school gymnasium, but most often in the community center building. Like I said before when I talked about the dances, this contained a large but austere assembly room, about the size of a basketball court, but with a bare stage at one end. The large floor was ideal for our purposes, there being no permanent chairs or obstructions, and that was handy for the various activities of the evening.

At 7:00 pm, we would "fall in", which meant we would line up by patrols, four or five patrols across, with four Scouts in the front row and four in the back of each one. Some wore uniforms, most not, but almost everyone wore at least one piece of the uniform. The most common element was the neckerchief, followed by the hat. The Scoutmaster or one of the assistants would call us to "ten-hut" and we would listen to a spiel from the Scoutmaster about developing leadership in the community. A fair amount of circularity attended the logic of these talks, similar to "we're here because we're here because we're here..." No one really paid much attention anyway, just waiting for the better stuff later. Don't get the wrong idea, we liked the Scoutmaster all right, our minds just were not on the subjects of these little lectures.

On some nights, we would play shinny, which is dry land hockey. We always brought our shinny sticks, which could be anything from a select tree branch with just the right amount of crook on the lower end, to a store bought one if your parents were rich. The puck always was a small tin can, the three-ounce size such as potted meat comes in, or used to anyway. The cans were battered quite a bit and one night of action was about all that could be expected from one can. There was no shortage of these cans, so I suppose people ate a lot of potted meat.

A significant number of injuries resulted from these shinny games, mostly turned ankles and cracked wrists from trying to stop before running into walls. There was a significant amount of noise too, just imagine a game with

15 or more boys on a side and no rule of consequence other then "keep your shinny stick touching the floor."

We also played "Capture the Flag", which is a super game for thirty or so boys after it gets dark. It has to be dark because the whole object is to capture the flag of the enemy, and you have to do a lot of sneaking up on things to do it. It is hard to do any good sneaking in the daytime. Anyway, this game is best played on rolling ground with a lot of trees and bushes, also with crests of hills about a quarter of a mile apart. Golf courses often have this combination of features, and we usually played on the golf course at Woodton.

The ground was divided up into the territory assigned to each side and a strip in the middle maybe a hundred feet wide that was no-man's-land.

Each side set up its Headquarters on the top of a hill, if one was available. It was important that the headquarters of the two sides be equal distant from no-man's-land, and a lot of arguing established when the two locations were located "fair and square". Each headquarters then was marked with a flag, usually just a handkerchief. The flag was draped over a flagpole, it being against the rules to tie it on. The pole almost always was just a stick maybe six or seven feet long, but we always called it a flagpole, anyway. Just a few feet from the flagpole was the jail, this usually was a square about 10 feet on a side marked off with some ropes strung on sticks jabbed into the earth. If the dirt was too hard, we would just lay the ropes on the ground.

Each side divided its men up according to the strategy that emerged from a joint shouting session in which the leaders would try to assign duties over the objections of those being assigned. The duties really were only two, either you were a guard or you were a runner, with most people wanting to be runners. A guard had the duty of guarding the flag and capturing anyone from the other side. The runners had the job of trying to penetrate the guard lines of the other side and capturing its flag. There usually were about three layers of guards, the first being two or three Scouts right in the vicinity of the flag, five or six more in a ragged line maybe halfway to no-man's-land, and another five or six patrolling just inside your own territory and maybe just a little inside no-man's-land. Every one else, three or four at most, was a runner, and it was the runners who sneaked through no-man's land, avoiding any contact with the opposing guards until just a few feet from the flag. Then with a loud shout and a sprint, the runner would race for the flag and snatch it from its pole and take off for home. You had captured the flag if you could regain your own territory before being intercepted and captured yourself by a guard. All a guard had to do to capture anyone was to grab him and hang on long enough to shout "Caught! Caught! Caught!". It had to be three shouts, if the runner could squirm free before the third "Caught", he could try to make it home again. Of course, it was important to capture someone from the other side, and this was one of the problems, just remembering who was on your side, and recognizing them in the dark.

Once caught, a prisoner was put into the jail, and several guards kept him from escaping and from being rescued. Escaping or being rescued was very important because the flag could not be captured as long as a prisoner was held in the jail. To release a prisoner, a runner on the prisoner's team would have to get close enough to the prisoner to grab him and shout "Free! Free! Free!" then the rescuer and the rescued would streak for home trying to avoid being captured before crossing no-man's-land.

As you can see, a good game of Capture the Flag would take maybe two hours before a flag would be stolen, during which time there would be two or three caught on both sides, along with the attempts to rescue, and the ensuing chases. It was all great fun, and popular with the boys if not the parents. About half of the trouser knees would be torn out from falls, and shirtsleeves sometimes got ripped off from being caught. Of course, the handkerchiefs used for the flags never made it home again.

Sometimes we would practice marching for several meetings in a row, usually starting about six weeks before some parade that was coming up. This was not too popular, but was tolerated by the boys because the Scoutmaster would intone that doing things we didn't want to do built character. The results were turbid at best, and often pathetic. Apparently, other troops to this day do little better. My thoughts then and now are that there is nothing quite so scruffy as a Boy Scout troop in a parade.

Three or four times a year, the Court of Honor would meet and would hear each Scout who had completed the requirements for another rank or merit badge. Each applicant already had been judged ready for the Court by his patrol leader and the Scoutmaster, but on the big night those waiting to be heard would have their work reviewed again by the Scoutmaster or a designate to be sure everything was in order. If not, the Scoutmaster would withhold his recommendation to the Court and the Scout would be forced to wait until the next session.

The Court consisted of five or six men from the community selected because they personally portrayed the image of being fair and honest. During a Court, the Scouts would be arranged into a number of groups equal to the number present on the Court that night. Care was exercised that a reviewer had no family ties or special interests in a particular Scout. It never came up, but if a Scout had ties to everyone on the Court, then arrangements would be made so that Scout could present himself to a Court in a nearby town. A Scout from another town presented to our Court one time, but none of ours ever had to go anywhere else.

Each member of the Court would hear the Scouts assigned to him individually and would approve any work that clearly had been done properly. Anything that was thought to be marginal was reviewed by two or three of the Court. The consensus of the several reviewers then decided whether the questionable work was good enough, and the action needed if it was not. Those passing outright would get the stamp of approval of the entire Court, those on thin ice would be handled as seemed appropriate. If the discrepancies were minor, the Scout would be given a reasonable time like a week or two to conform and to present himself to a designated member of the Court. Usually, in these cases, the applicant would be required to do part of the work over, or to present it a little more neatly. If all was well at that time, then his advancement was effective from the time of the original presentment. Sometimes, because of conflicts in schedules of those involved, the new review would be deferred until the next Court. Rarely, actually not very often, someone would be failed completely, mainly because those who probably could not pass were not allowed to stand before the Court. When considering all this work, it was understood that the work, whatever the nature, had to be done as well as could be expected of a boy in his age group. An older boy was expected to perform better than a younger one if both were presenting for the same rank at the same time, so the youngest set the standards that had to be surpassed by the older ones. If work were failed, it had to be better the second time. No claim is made that personal opinions and personalities did not influence the outcome of some of these deliberations, but great emphasis was placed upon fairness and reasonableness, and in the main I think the Court did itself proud. I'll stand up for it anytime.

Actually, most of the work had to be taken on faith, and that of course was the reason it was called the Court of HONOR. Each Scout was on his honor to tell it like it was, and not to claim work not done. Failures before the Court usually were the results of workmanship going awry, or a misunderstanding of what was wanted. There never was a suggestion that anyone had not done what was claimed. Honor, duty, country, and respect may sound a little corny and naive today, but it was solid stuff then, and will be again.

All of this I learned in due time, aided quite a bit by the fact that Dad was the Chairman of the Court. All I knew after initiation was that I had to get started on my Tenderfoot badge.

X X X X X

The Tenderfoot rank wasn't too hard to pass, and purposefully so I suspect, and it was all spelled out starting on page 28 of the Handbook for Boys, published by the Boy Scouts of America, price 50 cents. The Scout had to be active in his troop for at least two months, know the composition of and customs relating to the United States flag and the forms of respect due it, tie the square knot and eight more from a list of 18, repeat by heart the Scout Oath and Law and be able to explain what each part meant. The most interesting part for almost all of us was the knot tying.

The most basic knot of Scouting is the square knot, so named because it looks kind of square shaped if you insist upon it. With two ends of rope held in the two hands, the left end is laid over the right, then both ends around and turned back, the new left end goes <u>under</u> the new right and each now is passed through the bend made by the other. Simple to do, and hard to describe unless we both have a piece of rope. If done correctly, and if the two ends being tied are the same size rope, the square knot will hold. It is not, the Scout Handbook statements to the contrary, always easy to undo, particularly if the rope is wet and has held a pretty good load on the knot. Now, the Handbook never did come right out and say it was easy to untie. That was something we just knew was so. When our wet knots were set up solid, it was because we had not tied them right, even though the knot itself looked all right. There I have set that matter straight, and I don't want you to think the Handbook was wrong in anything it said. Once in awhile, it didn't tell the whole story, but it always was right as far as it went. However, I have strayed a little, back to the knot. If, in the tying, the left over the rights become mixed up, the Scout or anyone else for that matter ties a disgraceful "Granny" instead of a square knot, displaying to all that this neophyte is not yet mature enough to be even a lowly Tenderfoot.

The knot skills were developed constantly. Each Scout supplied himself with a length of finger-sized rope, maybe three feet long, usually of cotton braid, but a few used manila. The raveled ends had to be "served" just so by winding button thread around the last half inch, catching the ends in a disappearing knot that is easy to do but difficult to describe without a diagram. It said in the book that the serving thread would hold better if it was rubbed with bees' wax before winding it to the rope, We never had any actual bees' wax so we used paraffin instead, feeling a little guilty about it because that was not the official way.

We always carried our knot ropes with us, the accepted and approved way being to wrap it around our waists with the ends tucked under. Lumpy, but the thing to do. All of the knot ropes of the entire troop, tied end to end wouldn't have made a good grazing rope for a cow, but that didn't matter a whit. We were walking examples of the Boy Scout motto "Be Prepared". We were prepared to demonstrate any knot at any time, any place. We had to be able to tie ropes into knots, and to get them undone. It was not necessary to use the knots for anything, although four or five were handy at times.

Usefulness aside, knot tying was a lot of fun. An older Scout instructed a group of four or five of us new comers about knots in general, but he leaned into the best ones for the Tenderfoot test. As soon as we got reasonably good at tying each one, we began to have competitions, first among ourselves and then as a peer group with the troop as a whole.

We would line up with our ropes, and a leader would state the knot to be tied, and everyone would indicate they understood. We would hold out the ends of our rope in our hands, with the excess length hanging down. When the leader was satisfied that everyone was ready and no head starts were already in progress, he would shout "Go" and we then would tie the knot as quickly as we could, throw down the rope and hold up our hand. A good knots man could whip out a square knot in about a second, probably less. It was hard to measure, because reaction time of the timekeeper entered into the result too much for accuracy. The last one down was eliminated, all other knots inspected for correctness, being eliminated if not, and the process repeated with increasingly more difficult knots. In less than ten minutes, much less usually, the champ was revealed. It was hard to be champ, and it was even harder to retain the title for any time at all. We always tried very hard not to be eliminated, particularly on the first six or seven knots. So we were pretty good at tying knots, not so hot sometimes in untying them.

I passed Tenderfoot at the first Court after joining, and I began working on Second Class right away, but I had other things to occupy my time so it actually took about eight months before I passed, with two being minimum. Not record breaking, by any means, but respectable enough considering that a goodly number of Scouts never got beyond Tenderfoot. I finally made it to Eagle, but like I said, a lot of things kept getting in the way. Like aviation.

CHAPTER VIII

This aviation thing was just hard to suppress, and like I said, Scouting conflicted heavily with my interests in aviation both in demands upon time as well as in financial resources. I read anything I could find about airplanes and I soon had exhausted the resources of the town library, as well as the libraries both in grade and high school. Even with these restrictions on my learning, I found quickly that even my own limited knowledge far exceeded that of just about anyone I knew or met, and in fact almost no one showed any enthusiasm for the subject at all. I longed for any avenue to expand my meager knowledge and I learned a great deal from a rather unusual source.

One hot day in the summer when I was twelve, I saw a housefly that somehow had become stuck to a piece of thread about a foot long. In spite of this impediment, he actually could fly a little, and it was quite interesting to observe that he didn't apply power continuously, but did so in spurts, maybe ten seconds on followed by several of rest. Although clearly having a hard time of it, the fly could gain a little altitude during the power-on intervals. He went down more than he went up so this created an irregular flight pattern of slow ascent followed by steep descent. Actually, his flights were fairly short, so he always was on the floor fairly quickly. I say flights, because naturally, I encouraged the fly to repeat the experience a number of times. I would toss him up and at the top of his trajectory he would come on and delay but not halt the inevitable trip back to the floor. After a half-hour of this, the fly checked out and I began to wonder if other flies could be made to do the same thing.

A length of number sixty thread attached to the belly of a fly with a tiny dab of model airplane cement showed the performance was not unique, and was reasonably reproducible from fly to fly. A few days later, the thought materialized that if a fly could almost fly tugging a piece of thread, it should be able to soar if used to power an airplane. A small airplane, of course.

A fair amount of experimentation produced a working model. The wings and tail were cut from thin tissue paper, the kind that comes with ladies' scarves, and things. Most of this around the house was wrinkled too much for immediate use, but it was not too difficult to get Mother to press a piece for me. Her curiosity about my need was parried with a vague comment about "a flying experiment". She was reminded daily about my interest in aviation, so this was accepted without further inquiry.

The body was a toothpick-sized piece of balsa wood, with a slightly widened flat place in front for the fly to sit. The wings were about four inches long, carefully folded up slightly at the center to form a dihedral angle for stability. A gentle curvature was bent into the wing to form an airfoil section, and the entire thing was attached to the body with minute amounts of model airplane cement. After gluing on a tail that was about half the dimensions of the wing, it was necessary to test glide the craft to get it flying pretty well before adding power. To do this, you had to balance the plane at about the mid-point of the wings, and this needed a fly to counter balance the weight of the tail. At first, I tried a dead fly, then I found that a 1/8th inch cube of balsa wet with saliva weighed about as much as a fly, and was easily stuck in place by the spit. After six or seven test glides, and adjustments to the wing and tail after each one, the plane was gliding with a slight turn, maybe three feet in diameter (Remember, these little airplanes only had a four-inch wingspread.) Just about right for a living room.

It now was time for the power plant. But, like they say, first you have to catch a fly. Not too hard in the big middle of a hot summer, or so you would think. Ordinarily, when you didn't really care, but would rather not have one around, flies seemed to be just about everywhere. But when you want one, all the flies anywhere near get the message and disappear. But that wasn't the end of it of course. Once a fly is found, you still have to catch him. I have caught a lot of flies, and a good technique for me at least is to let him land on the left hand, and then come up slowly very slowly with the right hand until about three or four inches away and then ZIP move the hand forward as fast as you can and scoop up the fly. This works for me about 8 times out of 10, and once I caught 37 straight this way.

With a kicking house fly in hand, carefully held between two fingers, a pinhead size drop of cement is squeezed onto the flat spot of the airplane body and the fly is placed as straight as possible on the glue, careful like so as not to squash him too much. Now, this excites the fly considerably, and he will begin to buzz and kick, but you must hold him securely until the cement sets, maybe three minutes. It is very important that all of the legs are free, a fly just refuses to do anything for you if one of his legs is glued up under him.

With the cement dry, the plane is launched by carefully gliding it forward toward the center of the room. It may be necessary to move some of the chairs to get the space, and if so it is best to do it while your Mother is downtown at the hairdresser, or at a church circle. You want two or three hours of unsupervised time to complete a good experiment.

No matter how much test gliding is done, each fly affects the plane differently, so almost always you must make a couple of test flights with the fly on board. When everything is right, the fly usually will start buzzing right off, and will circle around three of four times and will gain a couple of feet of altitude before shutting off and resting for a few seconds. A good airplane, powered by a good fly, will gain more than is lost and will wind up at the ceiling, buzzing along and bumping into it as he tries to climb higher. Several flies on several occasions succeeded in landing ON the ceiling, with the airplane hanging straight down, and the fly apparently grasping the ceiling with his foremost feet. I never did see exactly how this was done, but I can say that no fly in my group executed a half roll or a half loop to get on the ceiling. I really don't know how they did it, but a lot of them did.

After a few minutes, even the best flies begin to tire and lose their grip on the ceiling, or otherwise begin to glide downward more than they can power back up. As the floor, or maybe a tabletop approaches, most flies will give a little burst of power, trying not to hit the bottom so hard I guess. Each spurt resulted in a little zoom gaining six or eight inches of altitude before cutting off and starting back down. Some flies will do this four or five times before they give up and let the plane land. Most flies have just about had it by that time, requiring an engine change if the experiment is to continue.

Just so the record is complete, be advised that some flies are powerful enough to take off dragging the airplane with them. This is when they are fresh, not after a trip to the ceiling. Sometimes when skimming the ceiling, the planes will suddenly spiral down sharply or otherwise show a sudden loss of control. This rather mysterious behavior finally was traced to the plane collecting minute amounts of lint, or spider webs, or other miniscule trash that adheres to the walls and ceilings but is not noticed even by a fastidious housekeeper like my Mother. Also, for the record, multi-engined fly powered airplanes are dismal failures, mostly because one fly can't power the bigger craft all by himself and it is hard to get two or more flies going together. They seem to go on and off alternately. Also, big flies seem not to have as much excess power as small ones. And a small design detail —it is important that the body of the plane protrude in front of the fly's head about a sixteenth of an inch. This is to prevent knocking his brains out if he flies into a wall, which a lot of them will do. When this is about to happen, the fly produces a lot of turgid buzzing, the equivalency of backpedaling in the fly world, I suppose.

As you can see, I used up a lot of flies, and the supply became a problem if the main work was not to be held up. A good afternoon will require about 25 or more flies, because not all of them are powerful enough, and other mishaps reduce the effective number from the actual count. I began going around with a quart jar with a perforated lid to hold any flies that I might catch. Not too bad a scheme if you only want six or seven, but it is difficult to the point of being impossible to add a fly to a jar with a dozen already in there without a net loss.

Catching flies is not the easiest subject to become well informed about and I will guarantee that your library won't have a word about it. So I struggled along with a shortage of engines until rescued by a farm magazine that published an article and a plan for a flytrap. This was the type where the flies ascend from a bowl of sugar water inside an inverted cone with a small hole at the top and exit into a closed container. I had never heard of a flytrap before, but I had me one within an hour, with mine emptying the flies right into my quart jar.

I now had all the flies I could use, but one problem remained, and that related to extracting just one fly from a jar full. Each removal of the top allowed at least a dozen out, and since these little airplanes must be flown indoors where there is no wind, Mother began to wonder how all of the flies were getting into the house. I knew, but went out of my way to ensure that I closed the screen door tightly and called attention to the fact each time I went through, and otherwise distracting her attention from the real source.

Once, during all of this, I was holding a capped jar of flies and looking in the refrigerator for sandwich material or something when the phone rang. Quickly, just for the moment and not really thinking about it at all, I put the jar of flies inside the refrigerator and answered the call. It was Mother, downtown, wanting me to do some little special chore before she got home. I forgot all about the flies for an hour or two and when I finally did, I found them very quiet and sedated. I screwed off the jar top and removed a couple with no trouble at all. I left the jar open on the counter for a few minutes and went to the john or something, and when I returned about 50 flies were out of the jar and zooming around the kitchen. I got out the fly swatter and made fast work of most of them before Mother got home, but there were still too many left. I took it on the chin for being careless and leaving the screen door open again, knowing that the technical inaccuracy was insignificant compared with the general truth of the statement.

After that, I would operate the flytrap, get me fifty or sixty flies, and with Mother out of the house, put the jar in the refrigerator for an hour before starting to work. I was able to do this on three or four different days and really learned a lot, when one day I forgot to remove the jar of flies from the refrigerator before she got home. There were only a dozen left, but Mother absolutely exploded. She took out everything and made me scrub out the refrigerator with Lysol, and fearing that was not enough, she repeated the job herself, but with real lye this time. It took two full days of scrubbing and airing before she, with misgivings and doubts about exposing her family to unknown diseases borne only by houseflies, allowed food to be placed back in. A bunch of stuff spoiled while we were making the refrigerator whole again, and this triggered a new series of admonishments. It was a week before everything was normal again, and Mother was relieved, but perhaps a little disappointed as well, that the entire crew had not contracted some dreadful and incurable sickness, as she had predicted.

X X X X X

I turned again to a literature search to increase my meager knowledge about aircraft. I had combed through every promising book and one day I was listlessly thumbing through others just to see what they might contain, and was amazed and delighted to find that our set of World Book Encyclopedias had several sections about aviation, but under different headings. This gave me a new start, because from my photographic experience I knew the town library had several editions of the Encyclopedia Britannica, which offered even better treatment.

One of these contained a treatise which described how to make a hot air balloon out of tissue paper. These are available in kits today, but then one had to collect up enough tissue paper to make several panels, or "gores" as the article called them, about five feet long, and maybe a foot and a half wide. That is quite a passel of tissue paper in case you haven't tried it. These panels were stuck together along the edges with about a half-inch overlap using flour and water paste. We used flour and water paste for just about anything that needed gluing in those days, and it has a lot to commend it. Like cheap. On the bad side, it also spoils if it sits around too long, and smells pretty rank. Anyway, considerable care was required to make sure all of the cracks and slits were sealed up. At the bottom, because of the shape of the gores, an opening was left that was about a foot in diameter. Following the instructions, this opening was reinforced with a hoop of small iron wire.

A cross then was fashioned out of two pieces of the wire each about 15 inches long, held together by a couple turns of scrap wire. A small ball of cotton was fastened at the intersection of the crossed wires, and the whole thing was attached to the bottom of the balloon with the cotton ball in the middle of the opening. To effect flight, the cotton ball was soaked in kerosene and ignited, out of doors of course. Hot air from the flame fills the cavity formed by the tissue paper, and hot air being lighter than the surrounding air, the balloon rises. Actually, this took a little doing because the balloon was limp as a rag, and it was difficult to get kerosene on the cotton without dousing everything else. I finally hit on using an eye dropper which worked fine, and even though I rinsed it out carefully, it did add a sting to the eye drops after that.

After igniting the cotton ball, it took a few minutes to heat up enough air for the balloon to hold its shape. When completely inflated it, the balloon that is, looked like a big light bulb. Well, a lop-sided bulb, if the truth must be told, and a Scout is truthful. It said so right in the book. But when it filled up, man, I am telling you, that thing took off. And that is the truth.

It was fairly breezy on the day of flight, and in just a few seconds the balloon was far and away, much beyond any hope of recovery. I was thinking that I should have put my name and address on the balloon somewhere. These thoughts soon were reversed and exchanged with thankfulness for forgetfulness. The cotton suddenly blazed up, and ignited the entire balloon, which fell into a field of dried up corn stalks. These erupted instantly it seemed to me into the most spectacular fire. Half the county turned out to beat out the flames, but fortunately no one was hurt, and other than a few fence posts that caught fire and were soon extinguished, no property damage resulted.

A lot of people talked about the fire and wondered just how it started. One interesting hypothesis which received immediate acceptance was that the morning dew formed drops of water that focused the sun's rays like a magnifying glass, setting the blaze. The clinching part of the argument was, "Everybody knows that is the way forest fires start". I didn't see any reason to offer any corrections, because no one would have believed me anyway. I know, a Scout is truthful, but it doesn't say you have to tell the truth if everyone is going to think it is a lie. It is better to say nothing, and that is what I did. And, on balance I suppose since the beginning of time more fires have been started that way than from tissue hot air balloons catching fire and falling out of the sky.

X X X X X

One of the biggest differences between the society of today and that of the 1930's is found in entertainment. Nowadays, there is so much to attract the mental process that you can be rather selective in how to spend unstructured time. The cosmos of choice both is fed by and helps to produce more leisure time, so that one of the rewards of success is three or four weeks off with pay each year, not to mention the money to make the free time into a vacation. It really was different then. Almost anything we did required a great deal of participation by the one being entertained, and one could be comfortable knowing that if the event of the weekend was a fishing contest, that one was not missing out on the fun of a horse race, because the resources of production and those of consumption usually could not support more than one such transpiration of time.

A pretty good event was the county fair, and on a more noble scale the state fair. Practically everyone has been to one of these so there really is no profit in a description, but we looked forward to them and talked about the prizes and fine hogs for a long time afterward. Every year, there was something new to attract the populace, once there was a ghost story telling contest, another time a turtle race which became more or less a permanent part, another year a dog jumping contest to see which dog could jump the highest and the farthermost. It turns out good jumping dogs often tend to be dominant examples, so this spectacular wound up in the most rampageous dog fight I ever saw. The next year they cut it back to a frog-jumping contest, but all the frogs that were displayed were lazy louts and none of them would move. I suspect some of them wound up on the tables of the owners that night.

Even though we talked a lot about it, I never really thought much about the fair as a conscious thing. It was something that happened every year, but I would have thought if I had ever stopped to think about it that the fair was a natural consequence of the world being round and everyone dressing up on Sunday. Which is to say that I wouldn't have had a cohesive concept about it at all. It happened, I went along with everyone else and we had fun and there was never an idea that I might participate in any of the competitions.

The year I was thirteen, they announced a kite-flying contest for the next fair. When I first heard of it, I thought it was kind of funny, I couldn't imagine just how one kite could enter in a contest with another. But then as the rules became known, I began to develop more interest. All kites had to be constructed by the entrants, and all had to fly to win anything. There was to be a prize for the largest kite, and for the smallest, the most decorated, the most original, and so on. There were a lot of prizes, and since I had always liked to fly kites and had developed a box design of my own that was pretty good, I decided to enter. Three categories interested me from the start, the smallest, the largest, and the one flown farthest out on the longest string. I won all three prizes, two with clear conscience, the third a little iffy. Let me tell you about it.

First, I made several examples of ever smaller kites of standard architecture, using smaller and more delicate materials until I was able to produce one that was about three inches long and restrained on about 15 feet of the finest silk thread that Mother could find. I flew it at the fair and had a clear-cut win, no questions asked. No one else even came close.

I also won the biggest, but this took more doing. This was a winged box of conventional design and construction, six feet tall and with a wingspread of six feet. It was made of pine scantlings about one half-inch square and of whatever length needed. It was covered with oilcloth, and ready to fly weighed about eight pounds. Finding a suitable tether exercised my ingenuity because it turned out that in a good breeze, and it took a good breeze to fly it, it could break a 75-pound test line without much trouble. I couldn't find anything stronger than wasn't actually a rope, so I tried to use two 75-pound lines doubled. This does not produce a 150 pound strand at all, but something more like a 75 pound line that is twice as heavy. What happens is that the kite draws each line taut separately, but somewhat unevenly because it is difficult to equalize the pull exactly. A good gust comes along and tightens the tighter line, which often as not breaks. The entire load then is transferred to the remaining one which breaks immediately. When this occurs, the kite comes tumbling out of the sky and regular as daybreak lands in somebody's back yard. A bit of surreptitious trespassing usually recovered it all right, but there was an instance now and then of voices being raised.

At last I got about 150 feet of line that was supposed to be "over 100 pounds test" that would hold the kite, so Dad and I flew it several times before the fair. It was absolutely brutal to fly. Like I said, it took a pretty stiff wind to put it up in the first place, and then it pulled continuously at better than fifty pounds and with peaks up to 80 or 90 pounds. That may not sound like much maybe, but after thirty minutes even a grown man was worn out. Most people couldn't hold the line up against their body very long at all, but stood leaning back against their heels and with their arms outstretched forward, the two hands grasping the wooden piece about the size of a hammer handle with the line securely attached. It was a hammer handle, that is the reason for the size being what it was. After ten or fifteen minutes of this, most people couldn't even pull their arms in at all, so one person usually couldn't take the kite in alone, unless it was by letting go. The usual procedure was for one person to pull in about six feet of line, and then hold the kite with the shortened amount while a second person wound up the loose end. With sufficient repetitions, the kite would be drawn down and recovered. Like I said, it was brutal to fly, and it won the largest kite prize with no real competition. I had it for several years after that, but we never flew it again, it was just too much work.

I also won with the kite flown on the longest string, and at the time I had a clear conscience. Later on I was not so sure. To win that I knew I had to come up with a weight lifter to pick up a lot of string, so this was a kite a little larger than the ones you normally would buy in the dime stores, but I lightened the sticks and braced them with fine wire I got from the edge of a piece of door screen. For no good reason, I decided to cover it with cellophane, I guess because a store down town gave me a piece of it that was about a yard square. It turned out this machine flew pretty good and because of its transparent cover it became almost invisible when let out only a few hundred feet. The tail could be seen wriggling back and forth and the sticks could be made out if you knew what to look for, but the kite itself was vanished. I thought it would be great to make the tail of cellophane also so it would fade from sight too and this turned out to be no trick at all. The tail was visible a little farther than the kite proper, but a little more string lost everything, particularly if it was overcast or hazy.

On the big day with two wins already packed away, I was feeling pretty good and figured I would let out about a mile and see who would challenge that. This would take about ten and a half balls of string, not allowing anything for the stretch which we couldn't measure anyway. I had 15 balls of string and thought I would hold off the competition easily. That was the plan, but it didn't work out that way.

The moment came and another boy in town who also flew kites and knew what he was doing entered and I could see that this might be more of a contest than I had thought. Right off, we both let out about eight balls and it became obvious to everyone there that no one else had a chance because no other kite owner even had that much string. With eight balls out his kite was visible in the sky but pretty small of course. Mine long since had become invisible.

The judge says to us, "Let out three more balls." Well, we did that and his kite was just the tiniest of dots that sometimes passed out of sight. The judge had us let out three more balls, and then the final one that I had. My competitor just had fourteen balls with him so the judge asked if we wanted to call it a tie of if we wanted to continue. Of course, we wanted to go on, but each of us had to have more string. So his dad and mine went into town and bought ten more balls each and just about cleaned out the ready supply and came back.

The judge verified that all were identical and contained the same amount of string.

By this time, we had begun to attract a little crowd and each of us found we had our own group of supporters. It was kind of nice having people urge you on, but it was a little annoying too because some people I thought might root for me were cheering for him. Maybe he felt the same way about my followers, but he never said. Come to think of it, neither did I, this is the first time I ever brought it up.

Well, we tied on some more string and let out and tied on some more and let out, with the judge being careful that he had the exact count for each of us. We both had out twenty balls and each kite was pulling away and it looked like each of us could go some more. The judge had us run out all the string we had so that we both were flying twenty-four balls and there was one ball left over. The tugs on the strings were still there, steady like with the string jerks all smoothed out because the erratic motions of the kites dipping this way and that were attenuated by the long travel down the string.

When you let out a lot of string like that, it starts out leaving the hand angling upward toward the kite, but of course with a lot of sag. As more and more string is released the upward angle diminishes until, if you keep this up, the string will leave the hand horizontally for a while before it arcs upward toward the kite. It is difficult to tell when this point is reached precisely, but when it is the kite is as high up as it is going to go. It can go farther horizontally, but no higher. With still more string let out, it sags away from the hand and angles downward toward the low point and then starts upward toward the kite again. Sooner or later, the string actually will touch the ground before it starts upward. More string beyond that, we will see the string laying along the ground for an increasing distance as more and more is released. That was the situation for both of us. About the time his kite was no longer visible, and long after that point for me, the strings were descending from our hands to the ground about twenty five feet or so in front of us and then lying on the ground for some distance before ascending upward again. As we let out more and more, it got so we couldn't see where the string left the ground again at all and just took it for granted and on faith that the kites were still up there somewhere.

Sooner or later, in a contest of this sort one of the strings will break, and of course the kite will come tumbling down with the event being signaled by the string going slack in the hand. Well, the string of my competitor broke first, so I was declared the winner. He reeled in his string, and as luck would have it, his break occurred about five or six balls out, so he wound-up with a pretty good lump of string when he got through. Somehow we had the idea about the same time that he should tie his string onto mine, and we would really see how far out a kite could be flown. So we did and we let out every bit that he had wound in on top of all that I had already let out. I stood there just holding one end of the string, feeling kind of silly, when suddenly it broke somewhere and it went slack in my hand. I reeled it in and recovered maybe two or three balls in all. There was no doubt about it, my kite was the clear winner.

A year later, at the next county fair, they repeated the kite flying contest. I didn't enter that year for some reason that escapes me now, but I was there to watch it. For the farthest out contest, here comes a guy about 80 years old, and he enters a kite that looked familiar. Closer inspection verified the thought, it was my kite of last year. I didn't say anything, but I wondered how he had gotten it. While wondering about it, he opens up this big sack with a huge ball of string in it, I had never seen so much string at one time in one place, but of course I had when spread over time a little. "Last year this kite" he says, meaning mine, "came by my front porch kinda low like, draggin' this here string after it, so I jest gits down off my porch and catches that there string and reeled her in. Musta took two hours to wind it all up." When he read about the kite-flying contest, he figured he must have enough string to win the long distance event this year. He did too, no one else even came close, and he didn't even use half of his string.

X X X X X

In all these activities I just talked about, the particular project was cut short for one reason or other, but no great clamp was put on me because there really isn't enough excitement in fly powered airplanes, or tissue hot air balloons, or kites to contain an expanding interest very long. So I continued to read and to try to find new events in aviation. Things were slow for maybe six months during which time I wouldn't say I didn't rile Mother a time or two, but not about airplanes, when I saw an article in the Memphis Commercial

Appeal newspaper about model airplanes. The coals of interest burst into flame again, and I began to search for reading material anew.

I suddenly became aware that there were aviation magazines, a fact that had eluded me up until then. I soon found that a good way to become informed about almost anything is to find a good magazine on the subject and read it regularly, the only trouble being that there is no beginning or end to the subject material. You sort of jump into the middle of the written stream and swim among the chunks and pieces of information until after a time you have begun to amass a body of knowledge that sooner or later begins to coalesce into a meaningful understanding.

So I haunted the several newsstands and discovered a model airplane magazine. By today's standards, it was practically free, but it was a whole fifteen cents an issue, especially when you consider that the Boy Scouts and a couple of dances a year were competing for my resources, and very little was contributing to them. It didn't take long for this to develop to the point where I wanted to build model airplanes, and I could tell from the prices of the supplies in the advertisements that this would be a fairly expensive hobby. I could see a dollar a month disappearing without a ripple if I really got into model airplanes.

Several alternatives presented themselves to solve some of the problem. First, Christmas was coming up in a couple of months and I might be able to swing a subscription as a present. One magazine, not my favorite but not bad, offered a free kit as a bonus if the subscription was ordered before a certain day. I felt enough time had elapsed since the flies, so I approached Mother and suggested that the subscription would be real nice, particularly since the kit was included. She smiled and said, "We'll see," and I knew it had taken, so now all I had to do was wait for Christmas.

While waiting, I could buy one of the kits sold at the dime store and satisfy some of my urges with it. The dime store had quite a selection of these, ranging in price from a dime to thirty-five cents. By my own observation the thirty-five center had been on the shelf for almost two years, but the ten cent ones sold fairly briskly. I bought a Nieuport Scout, a replica of a World War fighter plane used by the French and the United States. Everything had to be cut out and glued together, and the tissue covering applied. My first effort was not a very good job, but I could see where I could do better if I built another one, which I did. After that I built a couple more kits and got the bigger one at Christmas, each one looking and flying a little better than the one before. There was not too much kick in building a kit, for me anyway. The magazines all talked about original designs. It looked like much more fun would result in seeing an original design that flew well, or even badly for that matter.

So I began to think about and then to sketch out and later to lay out a series of original designs that were not intended to be models of any full sized airplane, but were to be free flying miniature aircraft with a three to four foot wing spread, and rubber powered. There is quite a difference between a model airplane and a miniature airplane, and over the years, I suppose I have built over a hundred miniatures, both rubber powered and with gasoline engines, but no more than a dozen models. I learned a tremendous amount from building and flying these aircraft, and I believe that anyone who is going to fly airplanes should be required to design and fly a miniature. Many phenomena such as wind shear and gust effects are demonstrated dramatically, as are many principles of structures, such as accumulating fatigue.

All of this made demands on my time. There just wasn't enough time to pursue all of the things I thought I needed to do. In particular, Scouting was lagging and I had to get that Second Class Badge.

CHAPTER IX

The tests for Second class were a lot harder than for Tenderfoot. There were twelve requirements in all, the first to have been a Tenderfoot for at least a month and knowing how and when to wear the Scout uniform. We also had to show proficiency in first aid, this being the van courier of more extensive skills needed later in this subject when going for First Class. We had to be familiar with elementary signaling, using semaphore (wig wag) flags or international Morse code, or Indian sign language. Most of us chose the signaling flags and much time and effort went into in learning the code and in practicing signaling. We had to show that we could track a person for a distance of half a mile within 25 minutes, that we could employ the Scout's pace of 50 steps walking and 50 running to travel a mile in 12 minutes. No tolerance was given on this time, so we had to finish practically on the second to qualify. We had to demonstrate how to use a knife and a hatchet and how to build a fire in the open using no more than two matches and no other man-made materials. We had to cook a quarter pound of meat and two potatoes in the open without utensils of any kind, and we had to earn and deposit at least one dollar in a public bank or savings institution. We had to know the 16 principle points of the compass (north, north-north-east, north-east, east-north-east, etc), to exhibit at least five rules of safety for use at home or at school, and we had to furnish satisfactory evidence that we had practiced the principles of the Scout oath and law.

Almost everyone was well past the month by the time all of these things were done, but few of us had had much opportunity to wear the uniform. The entire outfit was moderately expensive, so few parents wanted to put much money into such a specialty item until a growing son had demonstrated that Scouting was not just a fad. So, except for the few rich kids who got a full uniform right off and who were hated for it, our knowledge of the uniform was almost entirely second hand, and from the book. From this, we knew when to wear it but again few of us had had the opportunity to show how. So we described how with drawings and pictures.

The most significant part of these items was that most of them represented a fair level of skill or knowledge in subjects that the boy probably had never even thought about before, and it is not surprising that almost nobody took less than three or four months to pass all of them. And like I said, I took eight.

Meanwhile, being a Tenderfoot was not a very comfortable place to be in our pecking order, because not only did we not know anything, most of us did not even suspect anything, and we were reminded of it daily. Most of us wanted to get on to Second Class just so we could lord it over someone below us. Also it was particularly humiliating to see a Scout who signed up after you did make it to Second Class first. So we tried, and most of us made it in respectable if not record breaking times. Even my eight months was not too bad, because a lot took more.

With Second Class put away, we next turned to First Class. Again, there were 12 requirements, some with options, but in most cases these were extensions to and refinements of the skills begun when passing Second Class. We had to have two months of satisfactory service as a Second Class, and to be able to explain the meaning of all of the badges of rank, to swim fifty yards, to earn and deposit at least two dollars, to send and receive a message in semaphore, Morse code or Indian sign language at the rate of 30 letters a minute, make a 14 mile hike, know some much more advanced first aid, to cook in the open with utensils at least one food selected from several different ones in a list, to read a map correctly and to make a map of a local area, to use the ax for felling a small tree, to judge the sizes of several objects and distances within 25%, be able to identify in the field several species of trees, or birds or stars, and to furnish evidence of practicing the principles of Scouting.

Again, not too many of us completed all of this in the minimum time. For one thing, if one happened to be initiated at the end of the summer, then it would be the next summer before swimming skills could be demonstrated. There were no indoor pools then. Woodton was fortunate in having a good municipal pool; lots —in fact most—towns didn't have that. Also, the winter time was not suitable for some of the outdoor work because all of it had to be completed on weekends and the weather was not always suitable. Maybe the Indians and pioneers lived outside in rain and snow, but our mothers saw it differently. If you ever did it once, you agreed with your mother.

The fourteen mile hike separated many from attainment of the First Class rank. This was seven miles out and seven miles back, carrying enough gear for the time on the hike. Although it might appear that this could be completed in less than five hours, in actual fact it always was a long all day event. Usually two or three would take this hike together, so with our packs made ready the night before, we got up with or even before the sun, and struck out after a good breakfast prepared by mothers who knew what they were doing. We would walk at a leisurely pace, resting every hour as closely as we could estimate the time. All the books said we should do that.

Outbound at least we wasted a lot of time with such things as throwing rocks at suitable targets. These targets no longer were birds, because some of the concepts of conservation were beginning to sink in. But bottles, tin cans, and insulators on telephone poles, all were there to be hit. And they were.

Dawdling along like we did it, the leg out usually took about three and a half hours, and by then it was time to eat lunch. Sometimes a Scout would try to get the cooking requirement out of the way while on this hike, but the smart way was to eat the sandwiches prepared by the mothers who knew what they were doing. You really would rather be taking a nice snooze out there during the lunch period, or wrestling, or almost anything rather than trying to make a fire and then cooking something. You can blow the entire respite of the lunch break cooking two potatoes while on a fourteen mile hike.

The trip back tended to be a little slower even than the outbound because everyone now was a little tired, and we knew just how much more we still had to go, and it always was a lot farther than we wanted to think about. Some of the feet became a little touchy about the middle of the afternoon, and occasionally someone would develop one or more blisters. That was pure misery, because the first aid that was prescribed was to paint around the blisters with iodine and to place some sort of bandage over the affected area. Regardless of intent, some of the iodine always got onto and into the blistered spot, this lead to a lot of hopping about on the good foot until things cooled off enough to apply the bandage which usually was about as uncomfortable as the affliction. Most of us preferred to risk infection than to endure the treatment.

The lifeblood of Scouting was and still is camping, and certain camping achievements were mandatory for advancement at almost every level, so we camped a lot. We did this with great and genuine enthusiasm, these excursions being organized by the patrols, or among two or three who might be in different patrols, or sometimes by someone alone. Usually the loners were trying to qualify for the Camping merit badge, which stacked in among a number of other requirements, stated that a Scout had to spend at least 50 nights camping out. This is quite a pile of nights, in case you haven't done it and might be inclined to think nothing of it. The first eight or ten go pretty fast and are the usual fun. By that time, those who were not going for the badge, at least not at that time, would have worn off the immediate shine of camping for a while, so the number whose schedule coincided with yours and who could be persuaded to go along dwindled and shrank, and finally vanished. The seeker of the Camping merit badge was almost sure to spend at least half of these nights alone in the woods somewhere. I slept out alone more than 30 times.

A lot failed to complete the camping requirement, and I suspect that fear might have been a part of it for reasons without comprehension to adults, or to anyone who has never slept alone out of doors. Although we never discussed it openly, some of the younger boys, say thirteen and younger, were a little afraid to spend a night alone in a camp. The fourteen year olds were a little afraid too maybe but of course would never admit it, so some of these always were making the stab at the requirement. I suffered my share of being afraid.

Whether you go alone or with others, the campsite should have been selected in advance, one of the worst things to happen in camping is to use a strange site so that you don't know the lay of the land, and which way the wind is likely to blow, and a lot of other things.

Even a teen-aged boy is likely to be a little bushed after walking about four or five miles with his camp kit, so you want to "make camp" as quickly as possible, a euphemism meaning that after unpacking the gear, you sort of make a bed out of the blanket and lie down to relax, and maybe take a little snooze. It is best not to succumb too much to this need and desire, because it is necessary to get on with setting up the camp and gathering up the firewood. This takes a little while, an hour sometimes, so one should not wait until it gets too late. On a couple of occasions, I napped until after dark and I can tell you it is hard to do some of these things in the dark.

Some make the bed and pitch the tent first, others find wood and build a fire. I have done it both ways, and can offer no particular advice except that both have to be done. If pushed about it, I guess I prefer to get the fire going first because you have to get started cooking, if you want to eat that night that is. Except for the 14-mile hike, we were honor bound to cook when camping, and we would have been drummed out if we had brought a sandwich or even the makings of one. The results of this adherence to honor were amazing.

Some of this trail cooking was really gross, even by the junk food standards of teen-agers. I mean it was bad. Take potatoes. The manual told just how to do it. You dig a hole in the ground maybe 18 inches in diameter and close to a foot deep, using a spade that none of us ever acquired. That's not quite right, I did get a collapsible belt spade, but that was much later. Anyway, we used knives to break up the ground and removed the dirt with our hands. Then, you build yourself a fire pit by lining that rascal with stones. In the manual, these looked liked brickwork, they are so carefully laid in. Our stones never looked even at all, mainly because it was hard to find very many the same size.

Then you build yourself a good old campfire, using no more than two matches, and no paper or other man-made combustibles to help it along. When that camp fire has burned down to just coals in the fire pit, it then is ready to receive the components of the camp cuisine, the first being the potatoes, which have been prepared while the good old campfire has been burning itself down to coals. Preparation is simple. After washing it "to remove all dirt", the eyes are scooped out skillfully with the knife tip, it says, and the potato is covered with mud about an inch thick. Why it was necessary to wash a potato before covering with mud has never been made clear, even to this day. This globby mess then is inserted in the coals, putting out about half of them, covered carefully, and if enough fire survived it will be done in maybe an hour. An hour! It took an hour to build the pit and get the fire to this point. Hunger to the point of perceived starvation would advance the moment of consumption, whether done or not, which frequently they were not.

With the potatoes on the way, the meat is stuck on a sharpened stick, and the bread dough is mixed up and this also is wrapped around the stick. Only the simplest of bread was ever attempted because it was too much to lug milk or butter or anything like that. You have not lived until you have eaten bread cooked over a campfire after the dough is wrapped around a stick. According to the book, the stick is rotated slowly so the bread comes out all nice and fluffy. In reality, rotating the stick loosens the tenuous remaining grasp the bread may have and it usually falls into the fire, collecting ashes like a wet paintbrush.

The final product offered no competition to any serious maker of fine bread. With these simple ingredients, and simple recipes, and even more simple cooks, one gets simple results. Burned or raw, usually covered with ashes either way. Of course we were having so much fun we didn't notice, anything "cooked on the trail" was good eating, by definition.

But back to the potatoes. The big thrill in cooking potatoes in the coals is the explosion. Potatoes don't explode, but rocks do when placed in a fire pit that way. You can get hurt two ways —three, if you count eating the potatoes— the first being from the jagged pieces that go zooming by, the other is from the fire and coals that are scattered all around. The first time this happened to me, I was scared silly, but I recovered my senses enough to put out all the little fires that were starting.

It took awhile to find out just what was happening, the quest being held back by scornful remarks like "Rocks explode? You have a few in your head." It turns out that we always got our rocks from the bottom of a creek nearby and rocks that have been in water for a long time absorb a lot of moisture into the tiny cracks and interstices that penetrate all stone. When heated rapidly and sufficiently, this water turns to steam and in lots of cases the pressure simply splits the rock, always with a loud noise, and often with a dangerous flyby of pieces. So the solution was fairly simple, just use rocks that have not been in water a long time. This meant that the rocks had to be dug out of the ground, which is a tad harder to do than picking them off the creek bottom. But let me tell you, rocks dug up like that will explode too, because there is a lot of moisture in the ground. So it came down to identifying rocks that had no water entrapped in the cracks. I never learned the secret of this selection, and no one else did either, so after several of us were nearly brained two or three times, it became the accepted lore in our camps that fire pits would be unlined, or else the rocks would have to be "seasoned" by heating them up slowly to a moderate temperature and holding it for several hours to drive out the water gently. That was all right if you were going to be there for several days, but not too much with it for an overnight camp out. So mostly we used an unlined pit.

In time the realization matured that the mud coating on the potato didn't do much for it, so I began to leave it off. Now, either of two consequences follow, on the one hand if the spud is enveloped in coals, it will be burned to a very small crisp that has no remnant of food value even to a Scout on the trail who is ready to eat anything. On the other hand, if the potato is covered with ashes not coals, and then if the ashes are covered with coals, a nicely cooked potato will form inside a burned black crust about a quarter inch thick. It at least is edible, but it needs to be a good-sized example to have anything left to eat. It also takes a pretty good number of potatoes to make it through a week end of camping, because precious little else prepared out there has any esculent qualities at all, making the potatoes the main and sometimes the only dish. For the record, these black crusts removed the need to cut out the eyes before cooking them, and the incinerator methods sterilized everything so that potatoes need not even be washed.

Somewhere from our tribal lore about camp cooking we were made aware that eggs make good eating when consumed under the open skies, away from the noise of the town, at peace with oneself and in communion with nature. From personal experience, I will say this is largely true, I found I could fry a half way decent egg, but it took two or three trips before I learned that the eggs must be preceded in the pan by the frying of bacon of some other source of oil or grease. I think the structural cement and adhesive industries could learn a lot by trying to remove the remnants of fried eggs from a Scout skillet, when this is the initial cooking venture for the meal.

Although eggs did produce the most palatable of the comestibles, eggs themselves are not good hiking foods. Again, it takes several trips before one learns to pack an egg to survive a hike where one is tripped by one's best friend two or three times a mile, and returns the favor with shoves that result in spills and rolls downhill. Little advice can be offered by this veteran of the hike, other that the toe of the spare pair of socks is not a good place to carry an egg on a hike.

These hiking trips did lead some of us into a form of experimental cookery. On one trip, I discovered the sassafras tree, which has three distinct leaf shapes even on the same branch. These leaves are very aromatic, so we used to wrap our potatoes in sassafras leaves before covering them with mud or burying them in the ashes. In either case, the results were exactly the same, there absolutely was no difference in the final product. We tried several other things, but our camp food always was as dismal as ever, no matter what we did to brace it up.

The trouble was that most of us had no experience or interest in cooking of any sort, not even knowing enough to carry salt, or to use it if we did. Off hand, I don't know why the mothers didn't take a more intensive interest in all this cooking, but I don't recall that any of them did. In any case, we were doing the absolute minimum for one cooking test or another, and we had no standards to go by. Everyone turned out crap like that, we simply didn't know it could be any better, so no one had any pricks of conscience whatsoever when standing before the Court of Honor and claiming that indeed meat, bread and potatoes had been cooked and eaten in the field. I am sure the members of the Court had no idea just how incredibly bad it all was, had they known none of us I know would have passed a cooking test of any sort. They had no reason to doubt us, we had no reason to think there might be a reason. So it was very honest duplicity.

The Scout law stated plainly that we were supposed to be clean and this of course included eating from clean implements of all kinds, but there really wasn't much emphasis on technique. We did wash them, or went through the motions, but again we didn't know what to do. The accepted practice was to wash out the mess kits in water and to scrub them with sand or dirt and then to rinse and wash them again. The water always was cold, and any grease that remained from our meat congealed instantly if it was not already that way. Scrubbing with dirt was a skill learned from the older Scouts, everyone knew that a little dirt wasn't going to hurt you. Actually, dirt does a good job of scouring so that if done aggressively, almost any metal utensil will look fairly clean and this is the misleading part. Cooking in the metal skillets of our mess kits probably did in most of the bacteria, but the forks, knives, and such were used again with no qualms about sanitation. It never occurred to me that any of these things should be boiled, and there was no feasible way to do it if we had wanted to. I am surprised to this day that we did not contract dysentery from the dirty utensils. In actual fact, I can not remember a single case in all those camping trips, although surely someone must have suffered. Probably the bacteria that cause dysentery were all killed by the food.

With the evening meal taken care of, or at least in progress, attention next was offered to the camp bed. All the books talked about gathering boughs from trees and making a mattress by laying them side by side in profusion and in such thickness as to make a fine soft inviting place on which to slumber, again at peace with the world and in communion with nature. Don't you believe one word of it. I have tried to make a bed of boughs dozens of times, and didn't succeed even once.

Maybe it didn't turn out so good because I am not too sure just when a knobby limb becomes a bough. Most of the branches I could find had an assortment of short stems and sprits about as stiff as screwdrivers always — mine anyway— numbering in the thousands per branch. The manual says you should cut off these offending elements with the Boy Scout hatchet, carried in the regulation sheath on the regulation belt. The manual even had a picture —an ink drawing, not a photograph— of the Scout neatly trimming off the small twigs and suckers of a limb, the detached pieces all in a neat pile just at his feet. I guess it must be the official hatchet, I never had one, I had to make do with a hatchet my grandfather gave me. It actually was a little heavier than the official item, but it lacked the Scout logo stamped on the side of the head, and that was what made the difference.

Based on my experience, yours may be different, I would say that a hatchet is not much of a tool around camp, except to drive tent stakes with, or maybe to sharpen them first before driving. Other people did just fine or said they did, but I never really chopped off a limb, or even trimmed off much of the little stuff with a hatchet. Full sized ax yes, hatchet no. I was fairly advanced in Scouting before I learned the ax is a good implement, but I had private reservations about the hatchet early on. I pass this on to you as my good turn for the day.

The result of all this was that the bed of boughs never approached the neat rectangular squared cornered sleeping place called for in the specifications. Mine always was kind of blobby, no real form or shape, except longer than wide but with the long dimension seeming to have the orientation that was desired for the short. The visual affront was not the end, the physical experience was one of being poked and stuck by parts of the brush pile all night long.

Now, all the books about trappers and Indians told how ol' Trapper Joe, or Chief Eagle Wing would sleep "rolled up in his blanket" with his feet "pointed toward the fire". This was in direct contradiction to our training and experience about camp fires. Never, I mean never, let a fire burn when someone is not right there gazing right at it with the eyeballs wide open. A sudden breeze or gust can cause sparks to fly out into the woods, and under ideal conditions or un-ideal I think everyone really meant, the camp fire could be the source of a forest fire. No one ever said so, but it is common wisdom and a good bet that a Scout setting a forest fire would not make it by the Court of Honor when going for his Camping merit badge.

All of these things happened whether with a group or alone, but any calamity always was harder to handle when alone. Camping alone merely pointed up and emphasized that hazards always were present in anything you do, and some of these were greater when alone than when with a group. Lots of sports and activities are like that. So when camping out by oneself, in particular it is necessary to extinguish every trace of the fire before going to sleep. Dousing it with water is the official way, but it takes a fair amount to kill a good camp fire, which always is going good by the time you want to put it out. Water always was in short supply unless camping right on a body of water which few liked to do because the rumors were that the snakes would bite there. Camping farther back requires that the water be carried to the campfire, but in what? Whatever it was must be carried first to the camp, and as always on the Scout's back. The book never said so, but when all this is taken into account, and evaluated properly, the best way to put out a camp fire is to urinate on it.

With the fire out, the chill of the evening descends quickly, even in the middle of the summer, as does the solemnity of the night. Rolling up in a blanket may have been all right for Chief Eagle Wing, but it is the first step to freezing within an hour or so, not just because of the chill, but because it is difficult to bend and flex at the knees when rolled up tightly like that and the legs become cramped. Two or three bends and unbends pretty well loosens the blanket at the feet, one of which always is able to find its way out from under. A few nights like that and you learn that you have to roll up loosely just so you can bend and shift a little.

It's funny how you never notice any of this at home, but in the woods, there are all sorts of bugs and insects that do two things; some chirp and all of them crawl all night. A fair share of the crawlers also manage to take a bite, so that by morning, most people, me anyway, are covered with red spots where the itching was suppressed by several good rounds of scratching. I often wondered just how all of these creatures would manage to survive if someone like me didn't happen to camp in that very spot every once in a while.

In some ways, the chirping bugs are worse than the crawlers. For one thing, the noise seems to taper away an hour or so after dusk, and for a time after that, it is really quiet, and it would be a relief to hear anything at all, even the chirpers. As though in response to this desire, at intervals all through the night, there would be little rustlings in the brush all around. Every once in a while there would be a frantic cry as if something were being eaten alive, and I imagine something was. One never really knew what made these sounds, but in the day time when night noises were discussed, everyone knew that these came from mice and small animals, which made their livings running around in the woods after dark. No one I have ever known has ever seen any of this, but every one knows it to be a fact. The mystery about the source amplifies any uneasiness you might have already, so the first few nights alone tended to be long and scary. In time you got used to it.

Rain. Rain is a pain, and not just on the plains of Spain. When time is running out on a merit badge, Scouts sometimes had to hike and camp even when it looked like it might rain. No one I knew ever started on a hike when it already was raining, and most would return home if the rain began before reaching the camp spot, but there was little to do except wait it out if it started during the night. There are several wisdoms that I shall pass along, won by the honored method of having gotten wet.

The first is that one never ever camps right along side of an innocent looking little creek trickling along in a channel a couple of feet wide but confined in a deep natural ditch say fifty feet wide. There is a reason for it being that wide, and that is the flash flood. A rain several miles away that you never see drains a large area into these creeks and a creek can go from two feet to fifty feet wide in just minutes. Of course, the current is pretty stout in a fifty foot stream that is emptying a large area, so many things get washed away. A lot of camp gear can be lost in five minutes this way, and it will be absolutely gone. It may be washed down stream for several miles, or it may get caught behind a rock or stump and then become buried in the silt and sand that is rolled along with the flood. Either way it is gone. The unbelievable part is that the water will be back to normal in just a few hours, like the next morning, and it will be hard to convince anyone not there at the time that the event actually happened. Parents in particular are likely to think that the equipment was just left lying around in the woods somewhere. There was some truth to that from time to time, but no one leaves *everything* back in the woods.

We usually camped in the open if we thought the weather was going to be good, and sometimes we carried a pup tent if we thought otherwise. At that time, pup tents came in halves, with a Scout being the owner of just one half. It was necessary to buddy up with someone who had the other half, so that a complete tent sheltering two Scouts would result. These two pieces were joined at the ridge by a number of buttons, and one end was buttoned similarly to form a housing that was closed on one end and open on the other. The open end also had a number of buttons to which could be fastened some unidentified and unavailable piece of canvas to form a door. We never had this, and I often wondered if it really existed. So three choices were available, either the opening could be left open —not too bad if it didn't rain— or two tents could be pitched end to end to provide shelter for four rather than two but with no convenient door, or an extra shelter half could be borrowed from someone not on the hike and this could be sort of draped over the end. Usually, we draped something over the end if we needed the protection.

Our forecasts were off now and then, so part of the play when sleeping out like that was waking up with the well developed feeling that you now are soaking wet. The answer to this is to get up and build a roaring fire, assuming that anything dry can be found. According to the books, dry tinder and kindling always can be found by the good woodsman by looking under pieces of bark or by whittling off the bark of a dead branch. Maybe so, but in the cases I know about first hand, getting that fire going was a major undertaking, and an exercise in brute force and awkwardness. Undertaking is an appropriate description, because the flames died often and regularly, and it was just plain luck with no identifiable skill in evidence that we ever got a fire to burn at all. In case you wondered, we used a lot more than two matches.

Occasionally, we hit it right, I started to say "lucky", and we would find we had brought pup tents when it actually did rain. When pitched correctly, a pup tent affords a protection against the wet that is indescribably cozy. One lies there, nice and warm and dry listening to the pit and the pat of the rain drops on the fabric only four or five inches from the face. The restfulness produces a drowsiness that cannot be conquered so one sleeps in peace and with clear conscience, knowing that nothing that needs doing can be done anyway.

This feeling of well being and laziness always yields in time to first a gentle, then a more pronounced and finally urgent need to take a leak. There is no short cut, one must get out of the shelter and go somewhere. In dry weather, somewhere would be twenty five feet or so away, but this distance was shortened dramatically as the intensity of the rain increased. If it were really pouring, there always was the feeling that the integrity of the tent, once breached for an exit and reentrance could never be established again. Besides you would get wet and bring at least some water back with you. The unofficial, unapproved, but practical and often practiced method for handling this was to uncover the flap a mite, point outside and let go.

A pup tent is supposed to be pitched so that the open end is pointed downwind. I agree, that is the way it ought to be, because then a sudden gust of wind will not catch it in the open end and balloon out the sides. This is the precursor to being blown away, unless the tent is really anchored down. We always tried to determine the direction of the wind for just this reason, also we wanted to build the fire down wind so the smoke would blow away from and not into the tents. It always seemed to me that just before the rain came, the wind would suddenly gust to about a thousand miles an hour, puffing out the sides of my tent anyway just before ripping it from its stakes and hurling it away to be chased frantically as the rain fell like pouring water on a flat rock. It is like helicopters in the television programs. No matter which way they are pointing when sitting on the ground, following a takeoff, and while hovering just over the ground, they always turn right around 180° and fly off in that direction. The wind was the same way. No matter which way the tent was pitched, the wind gust always shifted so it was straight into the open end just as it gusted.

When this happened, you could just bet that it was not going to be a halcyon night of snug contentment. It is impossible to set up a tent when it is pouring so that anything inside will remain dry. So, an estimate must be made of when to stop trying to repitch the tent and make it more water tight, and getting so wet that it makes no difference. Once wet and once inside, there was no feasible way to dry anything out.

I have mentioned the Scout manual several times, but none of this is a put down for the manual. That is a great book and if done properly, the methods found there would work just fine. Part of the problem was that we often didn't read what it had to say until after the initial need for the information. And like any instruction guide, it is quite impossible to give directions for every imaginable situation. We were supposed to be developing initiative and character and all those good traits, so the manual often left us so we had to invent our way out. In this respect, the book was superb, and we did a lot of inventing. And as anybody knows, not all inventions are successful.

Also, don't be mislead by these descriptions that ill events were the rule, most of the time we had a good time, and nothing more serious than bruises, torn pants, and an occasional broken tooth accompanied these excursions. When it was a group, the meals were a little better, because then we cooked a lot of potatoes, and a lot of bread, and the chances were better that some examples of it might be good than when all rose and fell on just one sample. Same way with the meat and other stuff, somehow we could elevate the quality minutely through larger selections.

If it was a group, after the meal was finished some of us would go swimming if the weather was warm and if the water was deep enough in the creek, which varied considerably depending upon the weather during the past few days. When swimming, we were careful to see that no one swam alone and that someone with a lifesaving badge was on hand to see that no one drowned.

Actually most of us were pretty good swimmers. Like I said, Woodton had a municipal swimming pool, and during the summer most of us went swimming once a week. If you had a season ticket, you could swim as often and as long as desired, from the moment the pool opened at 11:00 am until it closed at 12:00 pm. I had a season ticket once, just once, and that was just about what I did. You became a pool rat, continually water logged, sun browned and with hair that acquired a squeaky clean fly-in-the-wind appearance that was offset by a peculiar odor attributed to the water purification chemicals. One firm result of all this immersion was that most of us were thoroughly at home in the water, and under it and jumping into it and later diving into it from a board.

So, most of us had no problems with the swimming merit badge. About all we had to do was practice swimming until we could swim the required distances and show proficiencies in simple dives, floating and the like. The pool director and the life guards were qualified to sign off on our tests when we passed them so swimming was a matter of staying at it, and practically no one needed any encouragement.

Lifesaving was another matter. Being at home in the water is absolutely essential if one is going after another who is drowning. However, merely being familiar does not improve techniques of form or develop life saving skills. Here you had to demonstrate ability to break several holds that a drowning person might clamp on the would-be rescuer, and also to tow the one in trouble by several different techniques. These skills were physically difficult for the younger hence smaller Scouts. Some were held up in their advancement because they were not able to do some of these things until they had grown a little. So it was something to earn the lifesaving badge, but all of us who did felt a little guilty about it, not knowing whether we actually could save anyone or not. None of us ever let on, so our untested skills were put on the line often because those with the badge were asked to serve as life guards whenever the others swam. Fortunately, none of us ever had to produce, I don't really know if I could have pulled anyone out or not.

Perhaps others have shared these thoughts, because the emphasis today is to reach for people in distress with a stick, or to throw them something to grab, or to go after them in a boat. Going into the water for them is the last thing a rescuer is supposed to do today, but then the stress was placed on water rescue by swimming for them. I know that was not the intent, but it certainly was the interpretation and the practice. Fortunately we didn't get any real practice.

First aid also was in the untested category for most of us. Again the thrust of the Boy Scouts was and is to be prepared and to do whatever you do with judgment and good sense. If, in spite of all precautions, people sometimes got hurt, then skill in first aid supplied the knowledge and techniques by which these mishaps were attended. Each of us always carried a first aid kit on our hikes, there sometimes being more compresses and iodine capsules than anything else if the inventory were taken, which it wasn't. We knew not to move anyone with any real injuries, we knew the symptoms of shock but few of us had ever seen anyone in shock. I haven't to this day. We talked about applying tourniquets to stop bleeding and demonstrated just how we would do it, and we showed how a splint would be improvised out of broom handles, boards, or even tree limbs. We jokingly referred to these administrations as being "last aid" because some of the attempts at bandaging and tourniquets were pretty sloppy.

One night we were learning the "finger lift", I can't find a single reference to it now, but I recall it as being a required skill then. Someone has been injured, and needs moving. People stand shoulder to shoulder as closely as possible around the injured person, who is laid out on his or her back. Upon a signal, all the movers stoop and insert the index finger of each hand under the victim, again on signal everyone merely stands up and walks the injured party to the location desired, which hopefully is only a few feet away. Its value lie in the fact that no one has to exert much to lift a very large person. Maybe the reason it isn't stressed anymore is that you can kill someone this way. Easy. Not from picking them up, because if it is done right it is a very smooth lift and the patient hardly knows what is happening. The danger comes from dropping him. Once we were carrying some one in practice or were about to, and had just gotten the signal to stand up. We all started up all right, but when we had lifted about 18 inches, somebody lost his balance and fell over backwards. Instinctively, he grabbed for anything and caught his neighbor who also fell and grabbed. The fall propagated around the group in nothing flat, and the simulated victim was dropped without warning. I know that 18 inches doesn't sound like very far to fall, but to one not expecting it, it is bone breaking or almost anyway. We still practiced the finger lift fairly often, but we tried to be more careful, because it is a true teamwork effort.

The big problem with first aid training, both then and now, is that the practitioner is in no way prepared for an accident of any consequence. By that I mean most first aid is taught in neat and clean and calm surroundings. An accident is a bloody mess, with people screaming and lights flashing and lookers-on asking "Are you hurt?" which has a redeeming value, but others ask "How did it happen?" which has no relevance to the problem of first aid. No one ever seems to ask, " Can I help?" or not very many anyway. Nowhere did I learn at that time that minor head injuries often bleed profusely whereas very serious injuries in other parts may have almost no symptoms at all. It was stressed over and over that someone should go for a doctor, and that is super advice, and that is one thing that I am real good at. But going for a doctor can be a lengthy excursion. At that time, most telephones were manually operated and about all you had to do was tell the operator you had a problem and she would notify the proper authorities, and get them there. Today it is much harder to do, because phones are automatic, and dialing up the operator may give you someone who is a hundred miles away and doesn't know the territory. The worst of all such experiences is to be trying to make an emergency call from a pay telephone along side the road where half the dial has been broken off, no directory is to be found, the number tag is long gone, you are standing where someone has defecated on the floor, and then have the operator insist that she —sometimes he—can do nothing for you because you don't know the area code of the telephone where you are talking.

These things aside, we did our best to be good at first aid, and most acquired a fair appreciation of the need to know more about the subject. Other than putting iodine around cuts and scrapes, none of us ever had to use any of it, and for that I am grateful.

I think snakes provided the single greatest fear for me in all this camping and hiking. I never was really comfortable stomping off through the woods or high grass because I was sure that sooner or later one would zip out and get me. We often talked about snake bites, and as part of first aid we studied how to open a bite with a sharp knife and to draw out the venom by sucking on it. We didn't want to have to do it because the book said that we would be poisoned if we had any sores in our mouths. So the approved and much more popular alternative was to draw out the poison with a heated bottle. No one ever tried any of this because none of us were ever bitten by a snake, and no one wanted to volunteer to provide an actual case even for instruction.

Now, we saw our share of snakes, almost every hike in the summer half of the year would turn up at least one. But somehow we never succeeded in surprising any of them enough that they struck at any of us. I think most of the others shared my feelings about them, and this common but unanimated qualm was the source of our reactions when a snake was seen.

Immediately there would be a shriek, the book said we should "cry out", but we shrieked "SNAKE, SNAKE!" Instantly, the group would surround the creature and we would beat it to death, unless it was fortunate enough to go slithering off into the brush. Once in the high grass, the snake definitely acquired the upper hand, difficult for a snake to do I guess, but the snake certainly gained the advantage, so the pursuit stopped at the edge of the weeds. I know and we knew that most snakes are harmless and provide useful roles in the environment, but snakes were reprehensible to most of us and elicited little sympathy.

Of course, every group will have someone in it who gets some sort of kicks out of handling snakes, and we always had one or two Scouts who were snake handlers. These individuals earned our profound respect and revulsion at the same time. I was sure that anyone who actually touched a snake would be contaminated for life, and this irrational feeling persists to this day. I don't like snakes, but today I am willing to let them go their way if they will leave me alone while doing it.

I think spiders are as much of a hazard in the woods as snakes. There certainly are a lot more of them, so the simple chances of exposure indicate that you will be spider bitten every now and then. Now no spider just comes up and bites, none that I ever saw anyway. Most spiders just sit there behind a web of some sort and wait for something to come along and hit the web. When the web is jiggled, the spider comes rushing over and bites the jiggler until it is subdued enough to be wrapped up for a meal later. So when you are looking for firewood and picking up those nice dry limbs to chop up, there likely is going to be some spiders under or around nearly every one and it is their natural instinct plug a tooth into you because you shook their web. The golden rule of picking up something in the woods is —don't put the hands anywhere you can't see— in particular don't go reaching into a hole in a tree trunk or reaching under a rock and things like that. Failure to observe this advice will guarantee being bitten by something sooner or later. I know, because I received a number of spider bites. Most got well after a time, all were painful, some took a very long time to heal.

Like I said, I took my terrapin, actually Sollie's terrapin, Thomas Jefferson along on most of these hikes, and Sollie occasionally went along too. TJ didn't weigh very much and didn't eat anything at all that I had to carry, and he seemed to enjoy it, or so I thought. Sollie didn't though. After a few hikes where he came home foot sore and sick because he was so tired, he got so he would go to the edge of town with me and then he would quietly just disappear and go back home.

I made First Class three months after becoming a Second Class, only a month more than minimum. That was pretty respectable, and not too many did it any faster. Of course, not too many Scouts were being urged along by a father who was Chairman of the Court of Honor either.

My next goals were Star, Life, and Eagle in that order, each with an increasing number of merit badges in various subjects. But the financial pressure on me was increasing and I looked for a job, any job to add to my modest income. I stumbled into it really; I found one in the local pool hall, right down town.

CHAPTER X

He felt like a snob when he talked about it, but Dad was not happy about the job in the pool hall. The work was honest enough, consequently no objection could be offered on that account. The hours were about what were to be expected for a boy in school and so was the pay. So that was not it.

It was the flavor of the surroundings, the aura of the clientele that created the dissatisfaction. Any man worth his salt was too judicious with his money to blow it playing pool. Also, a few of the town gamblers hung out there and a friendly game of cards —no money showing— was in play at almost any time. Of course, there was a beer bar there, and some of the customers brought in their own bottles of real stuff in paper sacks, and for them the pool room sold Seven-Ups and Cokes for set-ups but did not encourage drinking. It was widely, although not universally, held by the town's people that drinking in moderation was all right IF a man had the money. During times such as these, few did, therefore most who drank were condemned for economic rather than moral reasons.

Although hardly a chamber for moralistic thought, these local mores invaded even the pool hall. Dad did not want me to associate with drunks or heavy drinkers, still he felt that I should see life as it sometimes was rather than as it ought to be. In any event, Chief Robinson, or one of his designates, dropped by about once an hour to ensure that the drinking was done discretely and that no one got too drunk or even high.

Even though he could not express himself adequately, Dad still was quite uncomfortable about letting me take the job. Uncle John Throckmorton was more succinct: "Show me a man who is a good pool shot and I'll show you a man who's not worth a good god damned because he hasn't enough time to do anything else". Other members of the family commented less forcefully, but in general none approved, even though none other than Uncle John Throckmorton offered open objections. So I went to work but with a feeling all around that it just wasn't right.

I started for work as soon as I got out of school. Since my grades were good enough, I was allowed to skip the last period study hall, so I usually left school at 3:30 pm and rode my bicycle the mile and a half that separated school and the center of town, where the highways crossed. The pool hall was just four stores from this point.

I had to find a place to leave my bicycle. The first two or three days, I just parked it on its rear wheel stand on the sidewalk in front of the pool hall. It was knocked over daily when the sales people emanated from the stores at six o'clock and the walks overflowed momentarily with tired people going home from work. Chief Robinson observed this aberrant to his sidewalk traffic and on the fourth day he was waiting for me as I rode up. "Hi, Gaylord," the Chief began, "your wheel has caused me a little trouble. Mrs. Williams says she broke her purse strap on the handle bars. Wonder if I could ask ye— t' park it some where's else?" My heart leaped. I knew that the Chief was telling me and not asking, at all. "Sure, Chief, sure. Only place is in the alley, and somebody might steal it.

I know just about every wheel in town an' if I spotted somebody behind the wrong handlebars, I'd stop 'im. As far as I know, there hasn't been a bicycle stolen in town here for three years, more mebbe.

There was no room, really, for argument, So I moved my bicycle into the back alley while the chief looked on. I stood it on its stand in between two garbage cans and started around to the front. "When d'ya get yer first pay?" Chief Williams asked suddenly. "Saturday, I guess," I stammered, "Why?"

"Jes curious," he answered. Then as we reached the front door of the pool hall, the Chief added, "Noticed ya don't have a light, boy. Speck ya'd better not ride too much after dark 'til ya get one. The rear reflector is a mite loose, too. Well, tell your Mom and Dad I send my respects."

I emitted a weak "Bye", and entered the pool room. The Chief had me boxed in and he knew it. I had until Saturday to get a light and to fix the rear reflector, other wise I wouldn't dare ride my bicycle after dark. Dad would know that some sort of mix-up had occurred because the Chief had sent his respects. The Chief would ensure the message was delivered because some time during the next day or so he certainly would encounter one parent or the other and would remark, "Saw your boy the other day. Nice kid." My parents then would know that something had happened and would ask why they had not been informed. "You get into trouble with the law and you're in real trouble with me," was the axiom that Dad had voiced but once, but once was plenty. The only thing to do was to tell everything and explain that I had to use some of my first pay to buy a light. But back to now.

"You're late," was Mr. Williams' greeting as I entered the door.
"Yessir, Chief Robinson wanted me to move my bicycle."
"You start at four, don't let me have to mention it again."
"Yessir." There was no point in reminding Mr. Williams that I had stayed late the night before.

The job itself was simple enough. I racked the balls for the next game, straightened up the cue chalks and swept the floor, and generally made myself handy until nine o'clock. At the moment I had to bring in ice from the back and put beer bottles in the cooler. After that, nothing much remained to be done for a while so I sat down in a chair and looked at the wall.

The wall was dirty and the paint was cracked and peeling. Several arrays of hooks were prominent, each issuing an invitation for something to be hung there. One invitation had been accepted, and a jacket hung shapelessly near the door. A row of square mirrors were mounted about head high, each turned forty five degrees so that a pair of diagonal corners represented the tops and bottoms of each of them. One mirror had its bottom corner broken off and all should have been washed years ago and regularly since. The front wall ended by abutting a plate glass window which had been painted on the outside so that only a square section —upended like the mirrors— was left transparent to let in light and the gazes of whoever might care to look. Few did. A green neon sign burned in this area that proclaimed this to be Dick's Pool Parlor. The transformer which energized the sign sputtered at the top of the window and created interference in radios for fifty feet around.

The front door separated this window from its twin, the only difference being that the sign in the second window didn't work. Dick—Mr. Williams to me when I spoke to him or about him—sat at a small counter near this window, facing the interior of his parlor, and armed with a cash register and a telephone. The telephone rang at sporadic intervals, and Dick would pick it up and say, "Dick's pool hall," and then after having listened a few seconds,

"Why, no ma'am, Mrs. Shohan, I ain't seen Joe all week." If Joe happened to be there at the time, he squared up his pool or card game right away and left. Dick never admitted anybody was present, or had even been seen in less than a week. He truthfully could say that he had not spoken to Joe either, at least the last five minutes, because Dick always carefully mentioned the last name of the wife that was calling so that the husband got the message without personal conversation. If Joe really wasn't there, there was no need to call the wife by her last name, so the customers could tell by the way Dick talked into the phone whether further attention was in order.

The long wall on Dick's side mounted cue racks, as well as more hooks for coats. No mirrors were found here, because at some time in the distant past, Dick's predecessor had placed mirrors on both walls, but the multiple reflections of ever decreasing size proved distracting to the players, so Dick had removed them. You could still see the scars on the wall where the mirrors had been pulled off. In case my description has not conveyed the idea, the place was a dump.

My first week at the pool hall ended on Saturday, this being a big day for all merchants in Woodton. Most stores were open during the rest of the week but were just marking time for the sales on Saturday. You either made it or you didn't on Saturdays.

Those who resided in the country did not ordinarily come into town during the week because the trip was time consuming. The age of the horse-drawn wagon was not yet over. The number of people who depended solely upon wagons for transport declined steadily during the decade, and was nearing the end by the start of World War II, but the actual demise was deferred because of shortages during the war. Even though the main highways were good, some of the side roads were not, and wagons have advantages now long forgotten. Wagons can move over roads that will founder automobiles and trucks, but its pace is that of a walk. Even a five mile trip in a wagon must have more than a casual justification. There always is plenty to do around a farm anyway, something to be plowed or planted, or fertilized or hoed or picked, or fed or watered or repaired. During the week these endless tasks take up almost all of every day, consequently the justification came on Saturdays when the need for shopping for supplies could be combined with a day off from the hard work.

So, except during inclement weather or during certain critical periods when crops required immediate or continuous attention, those in the country came into town on Saturday. They started early, arriving in town by mid-morning, and stayed late. It was the unwritten courtesy that people in town should do their shopping during the week so the people who came in on Saturday could do theirs without competing for the same sales people. Thus, on Saturdays, the barber shops would have few customers who lived in town, but during the week it was the other way around.

The number of people involved in this influx was remarkable. At the time Woodton had a population of about 5000, and the county about 30,000, including Woodton. On a pleasant Saturday, anywhere from a third to a half of the county would be in town concentrated mostly in the immediate downtown section. Individually, most of these people were poor, some desperately so, but collectively they represented an enormous amount of business. The interaction between a lot of those who wanted to buy a little, and a few of those who wanted to make a lot of little sales, made Saturday a big day all around.

After the main business had been conducted during the day, the men and women would collect on the sidewalks in small groups of two, three or four, and swap gossip and yarns and crop information. These groups would mill and merge with others and dissolve and more would form until about ten or eleven at night, when the first ones began to leave to go home. On pleasant nights, the last would not leave until twelve or one o'clock, and some would not arrive home until three or four in the morning.

On Saturdays, the opening of the stores was deferred by thirty minutes or an hour, because most of the crowd would not arrive before mid-morning anyway, and also because no one closed until the last customer was served and absolutely no one else wanted in. For the dime stores and drug stores, this usually was around one in the morning unless it was raining in which case things might fold at nine or ten. The restaurants stayed open until the movie crowd was served and then waited to get any business that was generated when all the store clerks got off.

Saturdays were rough and rugged days for business people serving the general public, because no one would give up any reasonable opportunity to make one more ten cent sale. Thus, the typical employee in these small concerns worked about ten hours a day from Monday through Friday, and as much as fifteen hours on Saturdays. No one received overtime, and no one complained because of its lack. The 40 and 48 hour week and time and a half for overtime were won by the large labor unions in the 1930's, but the idea did not permeate the small town at any time during this decade.

Like I said, people worked hard, and did not have much leisure time. Even finding entertainment required and still requires to this day a certain contribution from the participant. In a city such as New York, one can find entertainment of endless variety merely by spending money. In Woodton, in common with most small towns, no amount of money would reveal the social activity if one were not "in".

Of course there were the movie theaters to which admission was gained with 25 cents for adults and 10 cents for children. The weekly schedule began on Sunday, when one feature, a cartoon comedy, news reel and short subject would be shown in the afternoon at 2:00 o'clock and again that evening at 7:00 and 10:00 o'clock. The twice nightly schedule was repeated Monday though Friday except a new offering would show on Wednesday through Friday. The week ended with a long Saturday, there being a matinee and two evening shows of a shoot-em-up western starring Tom Mix, Buck Jones, Tim McCoy or Hopalong Cassidy. Then after the comedy, news reel and short subject, there was an installment of a twelve-part serial in which Kit Carson, Flash Gordon, or Jungle Jim would be decimated at the end of each part only to find next time that he had conveniently gotten away again.

Some of these movies were produced for no money at all. The same ranch house was used in countless films starring Tim McCoy, and one serial which aspired to be an aviation epic actually used Tootsie Toy airplanes suspended by wires. One scene in which a barn was used for a hangar, actually was a model constructed on a table. I know it was a table because the edges and just a whiff of the legs were visible.

This complex of concepts and conditions also were applicable in the pool hall. ordinarily, during the week, the hall was open at eight in the morning, and closed around midnight, and I worked from four until nine. We opened at nine on Saturdays, like so many of the others, and supposedly closed at midnight because it was illegal for most businesses and certainly pool halls to operate on Sundays, or at least to accept new business. The pool hall got around this as did other establishments by locking the doors at midnight to new customers. Those already inside could stay as long as the money flowed, usually around three or so in the morning. Of course, my Saturday hours matched those of the hall, such that I dragged home after closing dreading the morrow, because it being Sunday, I would be expected to go to Church with the family, and I really needed the sleep.

CHAPTER XI

Since my boyhood, I have lived in eleven states and visited in all of them, and from my experience, no matter where you are in this country, the local people will claim that right here in this very spot will be found the finest churches, the best schools, the dirtiest politics and also this is where the true tongue is spoken, everybody else having an accent. If there is a local hospital, the people will state also that there is no better hospital for its size to be found anywhere. For some reason, hospitals always seem to be qualified as being excellent for their size, but the other characteristics are the best or the worst without regard to physical magnitude. Woodton folks were very normal in this respect, and their claims were just as defensible as those made in other towns.

At the time we did not have a hospital, but the region supplied congregations for about 10 churches in town, and probably sixty or more in the country. The largest faith by far was composed of the Baptists, accounting for about 50% of the total. The Methodists were next, representing something like 25%, and in lesser proportions were the Presbyterians, Episcopalians, Christian Church members, and the Catholics. The few Jewish families were non-resident members of synagogues located in Memphis or Little Rock. For the most part, their beliefs were both respected and suspect, and not understood. Any other denomination would have been considered as being some brand of Holy Rollers. The Negro population virtually without exception was Baptist or Methodist, there being a common saying that if one ever came across a Negro who was not a Baptist or a Methodist, then some white man had been fooling around with his religion.

Nearly all of the churches in the country were built of wood, but those in town were of cut stone or brick construction. Typically, those in town also were equipped with stained glass windows, maroon carpeting, unremitting wooden seats, a choir loft, and a piano. Most in town also had pipe organs and a bell in the belfry. Those which baptized rather than sprinkled had baptismal fonts under the pulpits, these being uncovered when needed by lifting out or hinging back sections of the floor.

It was practically a sure bet that a church would be heated by a stove placed at one side of the sanctuary, but a few had furnaces fueled by coal or oil. In the summer time, the interiors of those in town were cooled by large four-bladed electric fans suspended from the ceiling, aided by whatever movement of air could be encouraged by opening the stained glass windows and all of the doors. Those in the country were cooled by opening all the windows and doors, there not being electricity in the rural areas until late in the 30's, and not all places then.

The churches were led by men of the cloth addressed as "Reverend Smith", or often as "Brother Smith". When not in the presence of the man himself, the title of the post was "the Preacher", "the Pastor", or "the Reverend", this last often being used in a lighter or slightly facetious connotation when describing an embarrassing or awkward situation such as "and there we were drinking beer and playing poker, when in walks the Reverend...."

Ministers were not paid much in cash and sometimes they had to wait quite a while to get that. In recompense, they were accorded a good many privileges by the town. For example, ministers and their families were given access to the movie theaters without charge and some stores allowed discounts for their purchases. Part of his job was visiting people in their homes so the minister himself, if not his entire family, received a great many free meals because he was sure to be invited to dine at the home of some members of his congregation several times a week. Of course, he could not refuse these requests except for unusual circumstances, and more often than not, fried chicken was offered as the main dish, backed up by mashed potatoes, English peas, and homemade rolls. He did his penitence on Earth if he didn't care for fried chicken, because like I said before, just about everybody raised a few in their own back yards, and this was cheap and eminently respectable.

A large amount of social activity emanated from the churches. The women were organized into numerous little "circles", there being the Tuesday Circle, Wednesday Circle, and so. Of course the Tuesday Circle met on Tuesday so there was a group for just about any day of the week except Sunday. The place of meeting was passed around from one home to another.

The avowed goal of the Tuesday coterie was to convert all the heathen in China. On Wednesday they took on the job of getting all those who drank in the big cities to see the light and swear off, The Thursday group would make spiritual war on Mohammedism, and so on. A lot of women belonged to two or more circles, and the minister's wife was a member of all of them. She would rotate through all these groups and would attend the doings of each one about 8 or 10 times a year. Even so, she was criticized because she only attended 65 or 70 of these meetings a year.

Even as a child, I viewed these activities as being endeavors in sustained futility. A group of eight or ten women would meet every week, year in and year out, and go through the motions of casting their weight against their problem of record. These meetings would convene at 2:00 pm with an opening prayer and the pledge of allegiance. The minutes of the meeting before were read and invariably the motion was given and seconded and the vote taken that the minutes be approved as read, but always in defiance of the rules of order, there would be some nitpicking change after the vote.

The report of the treasurer would be read and the chairwoman would ask a motion to authorize the treasurer to buy 24 cents worth of stamps and a ten-cent package of envelopes. With this important business out of the way, inquiries would be made of any other old business outstanding. Mrs. Jefferson would then introduce the fact that the doughnut committee, of which she was chairwoman, was supposed to visit the wholesale houses on next Monday to seek donations of ingredients for the doughnuts which were to be sold locally on Friday so the proceeds could be sent to "our" foreign mission in Upper China where the heathen were unusually thick but where success was impending. However, Mrs. Jefferson's little Millie had tried to open a pop bottle with her teeth and had broken two —for which I spanked her good, believe me— and now had temporary caps but had to go to the dentist on Monday for the permanent repair. Consequently, the begging mission would have to be put off until Wednesday, and maybe the doughnut making and selling too, not to mention the funds for the heathen, but she knew that on Wednesday Mrs. Jones, her co-chairwoman on the doughnut committee and also chairwoman of the handkerchief committee of the Wednesday circle, was supposed to make a report on the proceeds obtained from selling the handkerchiefs which had been donated by the ten cent store, so could Mrs. Jones make an adjustment in her schedule so that——"This exercise in minutiae and trivia would consume thirty or forty minutes, Mrs. Jefferson proclaiming all the while that she didn't want to take up too much time, following which the collection plate would be passed, the yield of forty-two cents being counted in the presence of all and recorded in ink by the treasurer.

The program chairwoman then would present her program. Perhaps the main feature would be Mrs. McCullough, a visiting speaker from the Thursday Circle of another church in town, or if luck were really good, she might even be from another town. Mrs. McCullough would talk about the projects of her group, perhaps one of which might be setting up a mission in Mexico. These endeavors were always some thousands of miles away, never within town limits or even the state, you understand.

When the last participant in the program had finished, the program chairman would thank everybody for the wonderful presentations and the generous cooperation and then would announce, "This concludes the program for today and I now turn the meeting back to the President."

The president or chairwoman then would determine that nothing more needed to be discussed and no announcements had been left unsaid, and with a clear conscience, she would adjourn the meeting until 2:00 o'clock next Tuesday at Mrs. Wilkins' house. The hostess then would serve coffee and little cookies and after an hour of gossip, all would leave and rush home and toss together a meal for the husband and kids.

I remember well one such meeting at our home. I was about five and was playing in an adjacent room, both visible to and within earshot of the Circle. Part of the procedure was introducing the kids of the hostess. After all the ladies O-o-o-h-ed and ah-ed and exclaimed how much they had grown, the kids then were to disappear. This time I was duly presented and Mother asked me to reveal any new words I had learned, because she was a bear on building vocabularies. I learned quickly the vocabulary is not be built with, "I'll be a son of a bitch".

I should add that no obscenities of any sort were used around my mother or any of the other women in my family. "There are at least thirty thousand good talking words in the English language, and those foul words count up to a few dozen at most. You restrict your ability to express yourself if everything you say must be funneled through one of them." Those were her thoughts, and I agree. However, all those foul words bottled up inside sort of need release, so once in a while I have to rip out a couple from the few dozen. When done in moderation and for good cause, it cleanses the heart of unpure thoughts. I've noticed it often enough.

Once or twice a year our congregation, and I suppose others as well, would hold a picnic somewhere in the country under the shade of a nice grove of oak or maple trees. The women would prepare in advance baked hams, fried chickens, cole slaw, and potato salad by the ton, as well as iced tea, a jillion kinds of pie and cake, and all the stuff that makes up a picnic. In addition, the church would buy two Dixie cups of ice cream for each youngun twelve or under, and one for each teenager. The church also would furnish one bottle of Coca Cola or other soft drink to each person. These free comestibles necessitated that a fairly fool-proof system be evolved to prevent all the emerging young Christians from getting more than their share. None of the systems ever passed this test, and one that did not work at all was to have each applicant for ice cream declare how many already had been consumed. It was amazing how many would affirm that this was the first requisition while standing there with chocolate on his or her face. In one scheme that worked reasonably well, each person who was eligible for one of the handouts was given a small piece of paper, which was exchanged for a particular ration. A green slip would be good for one ice cream, and a red one would bring a soft drink. Sometimes these colors were changed for each social function because there always was someone who would collect and save the unused tickets from this outing to cash in at the next one, not to mention the little counterfeiters who would make up a batch as soon as the colors were announced. Later, someone hit on the idea of stamping the date on valid examples and this worked fairly well.

A few times when I was quite young, the church picnics took the form of a fish fry. These were generally similar to the picnics in that the women prepared all the things described, but cut back on the ham and chicken. The group would gather on the bank of one of the rivers or small lakes that were found in the vicinity, and while most of the men and a few of the women went out in boats all morning fishing, the rest of the women and men laid out the tablecloths and got the big fires going. Somewhere around eleven o'clock, sometimes as late as twelve, someone on shore would ring a bell or would beat on a dish pan as a signal to those still fishing to return with the catch. These usually were pretty good, each man or woman bringing in from four to twenty fish, crappie, and bass mostly. A lot would hook more than the legal limit, but the game warden never bothered a church fish fry, because when compared against all the baited hooks the average number of fish taken came out all right. The fish were cleaned and fried in big pans of oil and eaten hot, the gaps in the appetite being filled in with some chicken and the ice cream and pie.

Regardless of the type of picnic, after everyone was stuffed and comfortably uncomfortable around the stomach, things would be quiet for a while with a lot of people dozing off. Then, after an hour or so, the kids would start running around and falling over everyone who was still trying to snooze, so after a little of this all would be gathered up and the sack races, egg-in-a-spoon races and similar competitions would begin. After that, around three o'clock, a baseball game would start. Usually, these would be between two teams organized on the spot by the men. Before the day was over, everyone, even little kids four or five years old, would play "move-up".

In move-up, everyone played for him or herself, and everyone not batting was "working" in the field. Only one base was used other than home plate, and everyone was a fielder except the pitcher, catcher, and the one baseman. Thus, there might be fifty or sixty people in the field of all ages and skills. The batter remained at bat as long as home runs could be made. A single or a walk wouldn't do because there was no one to bat you in from the base.

The batter was allowed three swings or four passed balls, including fouls on strike three, so a maximum of seven pitches gained another run or the batter was out. The batter went to last place in the field and worked up again until becoming baseman, catcher and pitcher in that order, after which a time at bat had been earned again. Things usually moved along pretty fast so when everyone had been at bat, say three times, depending on how late it was getting, prizes would be awarded to the four year old with the most runs, as well as to the teen-aged girl, or the man or woman with three children with the most runs, not to mention the winners of all the races.

Just about everyone went home with a prize, these ranging from hand lettered bookmarks with a verse of scripture, to a 1/16th or a 1/8th part of a Bible. Other competitions staged from time to time also would award fractions of a Bible so that when one possessed enough eighths, quarters, and halves, a complete Bible could be claimed which then would be presented at one of the honors ceremonies held several times a year. Keep in mind these were depression times, and these little schemes allowed the church to award prizes liberally, without much outlay of cash. Additionally and perhaps most important, the winners must persevere in the good work and win some more in order to get clear title to any of it. It was expected that three-fourths of the winnings would never be used, so this was an eminently respectable rip-off conducted by the Church. It would have been considered un-Christian to complain or comment adversely, and I suppose that most never even thought about it.

This was not the only example of cutting corners. Because of the hard times, the churches made do with the most parsimonious budgets that the members could get away with, and still hold claim to being good Christians. The interiors of the Churches were clean, austere, and absolutely without non-essentials. Not one had an amplified speaker system to boost the voice of the minister. I doubt that any had a telephone in the church building, although the minister usually had one in his home, paid for by the church. Few if any at all had water fountains, only one or two had rest rooms. Indeed for most, the only water connection led into the baptismal font.

This single connection usually was turned off at the meter except when baptisms were planned so that the monthly billing was saved. The city water department did not charge churches for turning the water on and off, although a small fee was assessed against businesses and households for the same service. However, once the water was on, it had to remain on for at least a month with a minimum monthly charge of $1.25, whether any water was used or not. Of course, the bill could be higher if enough was consumed, but the basic charge allowed a generous amount of liquid. Few families and no church ever paid more than the minimum rate.

Usually, each church had about four or five baptisms a year and anywhere up to a dozen people would be dunked each time. The same water was used for two or three ceremonies during the warm half of the year, but with the winter, there was danger of freezing because as soon as the heat was turned off the temperature inside the churches lie close to that outside. In consequence, sometime in the fall the fonts would be drained and scrubbed. It cannot be said that any yearning soul truly was denied salvation during the winter because of lack of baptismal water, but the ministers certainly did not petition as intensely for confessions of faith as during the warm months because even one conversion meant reconnecting the water. Of course, once the first came forward, the expense was committed anyway so for the month anyway the old fervor returned to the pleas of "Won't you come?"

Regardless of pleas and subsequent expressions of renewed faith, winter baptisms were not popular. Most of the pools were about four feet deep, eight long, and four wide, thus holding just short of 1000 gallons of water which had to run about four hours in order to fill, with the water coming straight from the north pole. On one notable occasion, the decorum of the immersion was rocked a bit by an ejaculatory cry of "She-IT, Rev THAT'S COLD".

Of course, numerous other special events resulted from the Church activities. There were the usual ceremonies of promotion wherein the Beginner's Sunday School class would be promoted from the sand pile to the Primary Class, and the Primaries would go into Secondary and so on. At Christmas and Easter some sort of pageant would be offered using most of the kids in Sunday School in one role or another, and sometimes in two or three.

Usually, several weddings would occur during the year and the Church would be decorated with flowers for each one, often from someone's yard. The entire congregation would be invited to attend any Church wedding and just about everyone would turn out if the bride happened to be a popular girl, and no one would miss if the groom also was from the church.

There also were the sorrowful times when the Church was used for funerals. It was particularly tragic on those few occasions when some child fell victim to disease or to accident. The grief of the congregation would be genuine and without reservation and the group would be wrung out emotionally for a long time. Many petty factions then would find that their differences really were not worth the efforts required to sustain them, and for a time at least a peace would replace the bickering.

Peace was an illusionary goal with universal appeal. Chamberlain of Great Britain secured "peace in our time" by making an agreement with Hitler of

Germany at Munich in 1938. The upcoming World's Fair in New York City made things in Munich seem to be far away and of no consequence. None of it mattered much to us in Woodton.

CHAPTER XII

After a couple of months, it had become clear that the pool hall job wasn't working out very well. Mr. Williams insisted that his help be very prompt when starting to work—his idea of prompt was to be at least ten minutes early, and start as soon as you got there—but the clock meant nothing at quitting time. It was not that unusual to be required to work an hour or more past the stated time. No one ever complained because we were reminded several times each day that, "lotsa folks would like yer job." In truth, nothing else was available and with hard times directing every life style, quitting would have been an indelible black mark on my reputation.

Even so, the extra time at the job was interfering with my studies and Dad didn't like that. But worse, the main objective was not being met, namely making money. The entire thrust of this exercise was to make enough money that I could buy an aviation magazine and have maybe 50 cents a week to spend or save, and of course, I was expected to save most of it. The magazine cost 25 cents a month (or $2.50 for a year's subscription), so this entire effort was launched to gain about $2.50 a month after any savings. This was an admirable amount for a boy in his early teens, but I actually was making hardly anything at all and Dad was beginning to suspect.

Everything would have been all right if I had just taken my wage of 10 cents a night and 20 cents on Saturday. However, I was influenced by several men who hung around the hall and shot pool for money. There was no dearth of ways to set up a game, winner take all, so much a point, or so much for each ball dropped and so on. Some of these schemes were very involved and not too honest if you didn't watch the rules. These hustlers couldn't make any money off each other so they waited around until a new face appeared in the doorway. This happened two or three times a night; because, like I said, Woodton lay at the crossings of two highways and two railroads.

Sometimes a newcomer would lose anywhere from two to three dollars before leaving. These were rare finds, because usually 15 or 20 cents was about as much as anyone could stand to lose in one night. One time a new fellow showed up who talked funny. First, he said his name was Johnson

Tom, not Tom Johnson, his last name was Tom. Also he said, "crick" for "creek", and "youse" for "y'all".

One of the hustlers invited him into a game, and he agreed. He didn't know anything about pool at all, he didn't even know to put chalk on the cue tip. Johnson Tom lost $3.15 in a couple of hours and left. He returned a week later and let it be known he was a traveling salesman and this was his new territory. He lost $4.10 and left. Next week, he came back and after losing about two dollars, stated that he had heard of a new way to bet, a penny for the first ball, two cents for the next, then four, eight, sixteen, and so on doubling the money for each ball dropped. Johnson Tom wanted to know if anybody wanted to bet that way. One of the local hot sticks took him up and even allowed Johnson Tom to take the first shot, seeing as how he wasn't very good. Well, Jonhson Tom ran the table, 15 balls in a row and won $327.68 (figure it out). Our local hustler didn't catch onto what was happening to him until the eleventh ball, when the amount was up to $20.48. Our guy really did have to hustle then to cough up the final money, because no one in Woodton welshed on debts, not even pool sharks.

Anyway, Mr. Williams suggested I might make a little more money by playing the customers. This was quite illegal because the laws forbade gambling of any sort and were even more specific about participation by minors. Even my working in the pool hall was on the ragged edge of illegality, but honest work was acceptable even if the place itself was shady. Anyway, he suggested 7 cents a game, but failed to mention that my 10 cents a night ceased and that the winner always paid the house 5 cents a game for the use of the table, which I should have known but somehow it got by me. I had to win five games a night to break even with my straight salary, but I played only when customers needed an opponent. On a real good night for me, I might make 15 cents, but usually it was only four or five cents. And of course, he wouldn't let me go back to my straight wage anymore. To compound a bad situation, I actually had to borrow a quarter one night from Mr. Williams because I went into the hole playing pool.

So, I was locked into a semi-slavery situation, Chief Robinson was growing impatient because I didn't yet have a light for my bicycle; Dad thought I was blowing a lot of money because I never had any, and the mores of the town and times would not countenance quitting a job.

I writhed in this uncompromising arrangement for three or four weeks. I couldn't buy the aviation magazine, but I was able to browse each copy because it was carried in one of the drugstores and at the single newsstand in town. I could read for seven or eight minutes at each place and with no more than two visits to each I could get the gist of each issue. Trouble was, I wanted to buy one magazine and browse a second, so my aviation documentation was one half of what I wanted it to be.

During one of these browsing sessions, I noticed that the classified section in the back announced that an air show would be held in Memphis in two months, and that somebody was looking for a "teen-aged boy to help with an air show flying exhibition. Send experience to Box M, care of this magazine."

My letter, neatly handwritten on lined tablet paper —I thought that looked better somehow— rather than on notebook paper, was on its way that night. At first I couldn't decide whether to lie about my aviation experience, close to zero because I didn't think fly powered models would count much, or to just say I was interested. I decided to tell it straight:

Dear Box M,

    I saw your advertisement in the XXXX magazine for a teen-aged boy to help at the Memphis air show. I am your boy.
    I don't have any aviation experience at all, but I have been reading about airplanes since I was eight years old, and know a lot about them like why they stall.
    I will work hard and you will not have to tell me twice.

Yours truly,

Gaylord Crawford
801 Cherry Street
Woodton, Arkansas

As soon as I got off at 10:00 (supposed to be 9:00), I ran the two blocks to the train station to mail my letter. With great satisfaction, much anticipation, but no real hope, I dropped it into the slot marked U.S. MAIL on the eastbound Rail Rocket. I waited until it puffed away and then hurried home because my side trip had consumed about 45 minutes more than normal, and Mother was about to call the police.

CHAPTER XIII

About two weeks went by and I continued my drudge at the pool hall. My skill had improved marginally so the amount of money I retained also increased very slightly, maybe 10 or 15 cents a week. One night in walks Johnson Tom! This was quite a surprise because he had not been around since winning the big money. Everyone said he was afraid to show his face, but as I soon found out, he was just looking for bigger fish to fry.

Johnson Tom walks right over to me and without a trace of the funny accent, says, "Did you write this?" He had my letter to Box M! My complete surprise masked all rational response, "Y-y-yess-ir" was all I could stammer, which I guess was good enough.

Johnson Tom said, "Thought you did. I've got a Ford tri-motor airplane, gonna hop passengers at Memphis. Need to practice the system before that. Can you help me this Sunday at Bonair?" Now, I needed to ask Dad, but the enormity of the offer dulled my judgment considerably, so I agreed.

Again, my work caught Dad in a dilemma. He recognized the need to make money, and still considered the pool hall as only marginally acceptable. He knew I was into and onto aviation and that I could think of little else. He didn't like the thought of my going off to Memphis for three or four days, even though it was less than 40 miles away. I reminded him that he had left home at a younger age, and that I could camp out if I couldn't find a home to stay in. Actually, Dad was crossways with his own convictions, he believed that life was not easy and that everyone should become aware of that fact early. He also believed that honest labor was the subject and source of genuine pride. No matter how he turned it, my proposed actions met all the tests, the hang-up lie in the irresponsibility of those who would spend good money shooting pool, or going to air shows. He finally relented on the basis that the world was full of irresponsible people and he couldn't worry about all of them. Also, he had become turned on by airplanes because of my enthusiasm, and would have liked to have "watched" (not "gone to") the air show himself. My participation gave him a legitimate reason both to go and to watch, just to see what I was doing you understand. So the air show was approved, no matter how reluctantly, and by what circuitous route of reasoning.

I still wasn't home free because I had agreed to help out at Bonair on Sunday. After three or four days, I introduced the idea that my presence was needed to hop passengers on Sundays before the big air show itself. Well, Dad began to have some more concerns, but not wanting to go back on his word, he finally asked to talk to Johnson Tom, which he did. The talk inverted some thoughts for Dad. He found out that Johnson Tom had been flying for almost ten years, indeed had been trained in the Army Air Corps where he had served as a lieutenant. While in the army, he had been an instructor pilot for a short time and had been a test pilot later on. He had flown the mail, and also passengers for an airline that had gone broke. All of that was good. The bad part was that Dad was sure that Johnson Tom was little more than a crook. As I found out later, he was an honest crook. He never cheated anyone in the deliberate sense, he just set up events so that others cheated themselves, usually by taking advantage of natural greed. He would quote prices such as "ninety cents apiece or six for five-fifty, and I can let you have a dozen for eleven-fifty."

After considerable agonizing, Dad finally agreed. The only problem remaining was that I had to get to Bonair on my own where Johnson Tom was going to hop the passengers. It turned out that I could ride the bus to within five miles for 50 cents, or I could ride a train to within eight miles for 42 cents, but I could take my bicycle on the train and ride the rest of the way. I decided on the train, but it didn't occur to me that the destination was a whistle stop and that the train crew didn't like it that some baggage (my bicycle) had to be unloaded. But it all happened, and once off the train, I found I really had little idea where the actual flying field was.

I thought that I at least knew the way to Bonair and started pedaling down the graveled road in that direction. A graveled road is not good bicycle country, if you have never tried it, so it was pretty rough going, but still better and faster than walking by a considerable amount. After about a mile, I came up on a boy about my age who told me I was going toward town but he knew nothing about any airplane. So I kept on and after an hour and a half of hard riding, I figured I was maybe a couple of miles from town, when I passed from behind this line of trees on the side of the road and looked into a large field.

There it was! A Ford tri-motor. No one was about, but there just couldn't be two of them here in the same area on the same day, so I knew I had arrived. I walked my bicycle over the rough ground to the plane and then moved all around it, looking at every detail.

I didn't know it then, but she was a big 5-AT-C, with a wingspan of 77 feet 10 inches. She weighed 7500 pounds empty, and 13, 500 pounds fully loaded. She normally carried a maximum of 277 gallons of gasoline, and 34 gallons of engine oil. Some examples of this model could carry 355 gallons of fuel. She had a top speed of 150 miles per hour, and with 1700 rpm on her three engines cruised at 120 mph. She could climb at 1050 feet per minute immediately after take off and could rise to an absolute ceiling of 20,500 feet, but it would take more than an hour to get there. Not many did, I suspect. When new, she had been a beaut, and was said to have been owned by a Romanian prince. She now was about nine years old and had seen better days.

I looked the tired queen over. The corrugated skin was dirty and a lot of mud had been thrown up on the bottom of the body and on the lower sides of the wings and horizontal stabilizer. The right engine had lost a lot of oil in the past, and the nacelle was covered with a grimy black gunk. The two main tires did not have matching treads. The center engine was a Pratt & Whitney Hornet of 450 hp, whereas the side ones were P & W Wasps of 420 hp. Not very encouraging.

I found a note stuck in the crack of the door.

> Gaylord, get this ship cleaned up so it looks decent by tomorrow. Drain some gasoline out of the wing tanks to scrub off some of the grease.
>
> Johnson Tom

The Boy Scout motto notwithstanding, I wasn't prepared for this, but it looked like I didn't have much choice or time either. Inside the plane, I found a small stepladder, an old bucket, and a tattered cardboard box that contained a lot of rags. Also, there was another small but wooden box with a pair of pliers, a crescent wrench, a couple of open end wrenches, a screw driver and a ball-peen hammer.

I decided that the right side where the passenger's door was should be cleaned first. That way, the actual and impending passengers would form the best mental image, not knowing unless they really looked that the left side was just as crummy as ever. Unfortunately, the right engine nacelle was filthy, particularly on its left side where it could be seen easily from the cabin windows.

Johnson Tom said to drain some gasoline from the tanks, but how do you do this on a Ford tri-motor? From past reading about the airplane, I knew the main tanks were in the wings inboard of the side engines, and another was in the top of the body inside the center section of the wing. Although I had never thought about it before, it now occurred to me that here just had to be a way to drain the tanks. On the bottom of the wings, just inboard of the engines were several rectangular sections, maybe 10 by 10 inches, that looked like they might be removable. By standing on the top of the step ladder, I was able to undo a couple of fasteners with the screwdriver, and sure enough the thing popped open, hinged at the front edge, to reveal what looked like the bottom of a fuel tank. More encouragingly, there was a petcock and some copper tubing mounted on the bottom leading off in both directions into the wing somewhere. Upon being turned, the petcock dribbled a clear liquid that was indeed gasoline.

With rags, gasoline, and determination, I cleaned up the nacelle. In about an hour, it looked like new. It wasn't hard work really, most of the old stuff yielded readily to gasoline as a solvent. It was just dirty, and COLD. The gasoline evaporating from the skin felt like ice water.

Next, I tackled the right landing gear struts, wheel, tire, and mud guard. This cleaned up quickly, and other than chipped and peeling paint, looked pretty good. After that I worked on the right side of the body, starting at the door and working backward toward the tail. I figured passengers would be more likely to get close to the after parts of the body and the tail than they would to the engines. Periodically I had to get more gasoline to rinse out the rags as well as to wash the metal skin. By about three o'clock, the right side was looking respectable from nose to tail. The mud was still on the bottom of the wing and body but I had removed it from the stabilizer. Over all, the left side was not as dirty as the right so I decided to work on the inside.

Here there were 13 wicker seats, seven on the left and six on the right. Up front behind a door were two seats for the pilot and co-pilot. Somehow, I hoped the co-pilot was going to be me.

About all I could do was wipe down everything with gasoline. After an hour I had finished inside and it at least was clean. A seat here and there had a broken wicker cane, but nothing looked too bad. The odor of gasoline was pretty stiff, though. By opening a window in the cockpit, also a couple in the cabin, and leaving the door open, the fumes dissipated in an hour or so.

With everything as clean as I could make it at the time without different scrubbing materials, I looked around some more. There was a little torchier light at each seat, but I couldn't make these turn on. Later, I learned later that the fuse was removed, and most of them didn't have bulbs in them, anyway.

Just about the time I was finishing the cabin, up rolls a Pontiac coupe with a rumble seat, wire spoke wheels, a spare tire mounted on each front fender, and a rear view mirror mounted on each spare. A young woman, maybe twenty years old was driving and Johnson Tom was riding on the passenger side. She and he exchanged a long kiss, and as he gets out he says, "Stick around, Mary, I'll give you a free ride." She giggled and said she really should be going but she stayed anyway.

Johnson Tom comes striding up and takes a look and says, "You got this side looking pretty good, but you're gonna hafta do the rest of it before the Memphis show."

With that, he walks around the plane, looks at each engine, climbs on the ladder and checks the oil, and finds the loose inspection door where I had obtained the gasoline. He asked me to get the screwdriver, and after moving the ladder in place he tightens it up. "Now Gaylord, let me tell you about airplanes. Airplanes are the finest products of man's mind, but they are treacherous sons-of-bitches. Always stay on top of an airplane, never let the bastard get on top of you. When I tell you something has to be tightened up, or loosened, or replaced, don't ever argue with me. The very best anybody can do is hardly good enough because these machines are mean and will kill you if you let 'em. But I love 'em. Now let me show you how we crank the engines."

First, we climbed into the cockpit to check that the three ignition switches were all off. "Don't trust anybody about ignition switches. Always check 'em yourself", was the wisdom offered here. Then we pulled each engine through by hand. "Wanna make sure no oil or gasoline has drained into the lower cylinders" explained Johnson Tom. "If it has, we'll have to get it out by removing the spark plugs outta the lower cylinders." Fortunately, the engines moved easily through a couple of turns of each prop. That isn't quite right. The engines turned with equal difficulty throughout the two turns, because a radial of over 400 horsepower is not easy to turn by hand at all.

The side engines were not too hard, just a matter of stretching way up and catching the prop when it was horizontal, and swinging all of the weight on it while pulling the blade down to vertical. Then with the shoulder against it, the blade is pushed on around and upward until the prop is horizontal again, but one-half turn farther than before. The center engine was something else. That propeller was about ten feet in the air so we couldn't reach it at all. Johnson Tom produced a pair of heavy canvas caps that had ropes attached to them. Using the ladder, we managed to work one cap on each blade tip, then by pulling down on one rope, the prop turned slowly until it was vertical. Then by pulling on the other rope, the engine was turned another quarter-turn until the propeller was horizontal again. As I said, there was no gasoline or oil in the lower cylinders. That time.

Johnson Tom then removed a large crank from the rear of the cabin somewhere and set the stepladder up on the left side of the left engine. He mounted the crank on a shaft protruding a couple of inches from the side of the nacelle. Then he showed me a similar shaft on the right side of the other two engines. At the same time he showed me a priming pump on the outboard side of either side engine and said that a similar one was in the cockpit for the center engine. He unscrewed a lock on the handle of the pump for the left engine and opened a little petcock that admitted gasoline to it and gave it four slow strokes. He carefully relocked the pump handle and turned off the petcock.

"Gaylord, you crank this sonnava bitch —er 'scuse me, Mary— this God damned thing —er 'scuse me— as fast as you can. When I give you the sign —like this— you take off the crank, move the ladder out of the way of the prop and then pull this knob. That'll make the engine turn over a couple of times. After the engine starts, move to the center engine, then the right. Oh yeah, keep clear of the goddamned props. Got that? —Er, 'scuse me, Mary."

Well, not really, but he climbed into the cockpit and signaled me to start cranking. Boy! Was I in for a surprise? This was an inertia starter, the kind where one must spin up a little flywheel to about 12,000 rpm. Kind of like a hand cranked grindstone, but much more refined. I could hardly turn the crank at all at first, but it gradually speeded up and by throwing my weight at it I got it up to about a turn and a half a second. I later found out Johnson Tom was connecting the booster magneto to the engine being started. When he had this done, and I was up to speed, he gave me the sign. I pulled out the crank, scrambled down the ladder and moved it out where it was clear. I then ran back and pulled the knob. The most God-awful screeching noise came from the engine as the propeller began to move. I was completely flabbergasted that the engine turned over about twice, coughed out a huge billow of smoke and actually started running.

We repeated all this twice more, and with all mills turning, Johnson Tom throttled back to just a tick-over speed, about 325 rpm, with the engines making nice liquid noises like galoomp galoompity ga-loomp..., with an occasional backfire. He got out and urged Mary and me into the cabin. He followed, shut and carefully latched the door. She was ushered into the co-pilot's seat on the right, and Johnson Tom sat in the left or "love" seat. I sort of just stood there, watching. He showed her how to fasten her seat belt, and with a lot of giggles on her part he checked to see that it was snug across her lap. He turned to me and said, "Sit down back there somewhere and buckle up." I sat on the right as far up front as I could so I could see him in the cockpit. The right engine was just a few feet away, as big as life, and twice as noisy.

He eased open the three throttles, with the liquid sounds of the engines melding into an authoritative bellow as the speed increased. We inched forward and turned toward the downwind end of the field. A loud rumbling noise came from the rear of the cabin that could be heard over the bark of the engines. It took me a few seconds to figure it out, that was the tail wheel bumping over the ground. At the end of the field he stopped and ran up each engine, checked the rpm of each engine on each of its two magnetos, both individually and together, and when he was satisfied, turned into the wind, what little there was because it was late and everything was calm. He oozed the throttles forward slowly, the sound of the engines again changed from an erratic barking and occasional backfiring to a smooth and deep growl.

Slowly at first, then more rapidly the big Ford moved forward, crushing the grass and weeds under the wheels as it bumped over the rough ground. The speed increased, and the tail lifted from the ground. The rumbling noise in the tail ceased as the tail came up, leaving me pleased as punch that my analysis was correct. Although dirty, the wings were bathed by the air, and spiritually at least were cleaned, first gently then more vigorously so that the dead but promising looking metal of an airplane at rest exercised the parameters of the physical laws to overcome its inexorable conflict with gravity. As flight became an impending event, the wheels ceased rolling over each local perturbation of the ground and began to float from crest to crest until at last, after just a few seconds really, the man-made machine transferred to its occupants the freedom of flight, known to birds and insects for eons, but to man for just an eye blink in time. Like all other freedoms, the flight of man is volatile and perishable, and is maintained only with a constant input of energy, judgement and desire.

Quickly the craft gained altitude until at about 500 feet the throttles were cut back and level flight assumed. Carefully, Johnson Tom adjusted the throttles to synchronize the engines to the same speed, during which the sounds changed from a rapid wow-wow-wow to a slower wwoow-oo-wowww-ooo-wwow and then the dissonance ceased completely. This was much more difficult to do than it sounds because the tachometers for the side engines (along with the oil pressure and temperature gauges) were located on one of the engine mounting struts outside but where all could be seen from the cockpit. Johnson Tom would lean over and look out at the tach on the right and adjust that engine to the speed he wanted, then throttle back the center engine to get its sound out of it while bringing up the left engine by watching its tach out the left window and also listening to the sound. The tachs just got the engines close to the same speed, the sound was the final tuning. When the two side engines were synched, he then brought in the center one. He did it all very quickly. It only took about 12-15 seconds when everything went right.

Like I said, there wasn't much wind in the late afternoon so the air was smooth even at this low altitude. With the eyes closed, the ride was as motionless as sitting in a living room chair. Much noisier, naturally, or unnaturally I should say. Even so, it was a comfortable at-peace-with-the-world-everything-working-together-harmoniously type of noise, or so it seemed to me, and still does.

Opening my eyes, I was surprised to see that the wheels rotated slowly. Like most Fords, this one had mudguards over the wheels, and the different paths followed by the air in passing through the wheel assemblies usually caused them to turn all through a flight.

We flew toward and then over the town as Johnson Tom cruised back and forth at about 500 feet. This was lower than the legal limits, but if anyone had asked about it he could say that the altimeter was reading 1000 feet, not adding that he had set it there himself. He revved up and throttled back each engine in turn to make the most noise and racket that he could to attract the most attention. After 15 minutes of this, and with no part of the town or the immediate environs spared, Johnson Tom turned back to our field and synched up the engines again. In just a few minutes we were there and began to descend as the throttles were eased back slowly, ever so slowly, the smooth roar again changing to a wow-wow-wow as the engines began to run at slightly different speeds. We banked toward the field and when lined up, he eased back on the throttles some more, and the engines responded with contented grumbles and an occasional backfire.

The ground approached more and more closely and we skimmed over the fence and the Ford kissed the earth, main wheels first, with the tail high but lowering gradually as the speed dropped. The Ford progressively changed from a graceful and functionally beautiful thing of flight into a rumbling, awkward and dirty machine trundling over bumpy ground. We taxied back and he shut off the engines.

That was my first flight. I have flown hundreds of times since, both alone and with others, and I never fail to feel the emotion temporarily at least, or being unbound. I don't know if Mary had ever flow before, but she thought it was "just delicious." She thought it was funny too, judging by her giggles.

"Let's put your bicycle in the wing, then you'll stay with me in the hotel tonight." With that, Johnson Tom found a crank maybe six feet long somewhere in the airplane, and engaged a short shaft protruding down from the wing several feet outboard of the right engine. As he cranked, part of the lower surface swung downward along a hinge arranged on the inboard end to reveal a storage space for luggage. The bicycle wouldn't quite fit, but after removing the front wheel and turning the handlebars at right angles, we could almost crank the bin shut. It wasn't likely anyone would figure out how to open it but we took the crank with us anyway and piled into Mary's car, him in front with her and her giggles and me in the rumble seat, and we took off toward town.

Once there, Johnson Tom had Mary stop at the Planter's Hotel where he and I went up two flights of stairs to a room. He gave me a quarter and said "Find yourself a hamburger somewhere and try to not attract too much attention at the desk. I'll see you later." He placed the key on the bed and left.

I waited a few minutes and skinned out the door. This was Saturday night and I wanted to see what there was to be seen. For a quarter, I got two hamburgers and a coke. I also had fifty cents Dad had given me, so I took in a movie for a dime and got another hamburger when it let out. I got back to the hotel at eleven and was able to get by the desk without being seen and went up.

Johnson Tom was not there, in fact he didn't show up until six the next morning. He knocked on the door and I sleepily staggered over and let him in. "Let's go, let's go, we want to be ready to fly at nine." I washed up and dressed, and he shaved and changed into a uniform. It had a pale blue jacket with embroidered epaulets, darker blue boot trousers, black leather boots and Sam Browne belt. A pair of golden wings were embroidered over the left pocket and he had two hats. One was a regular helmet and goggles except that the helmet was snow white. The other was a military type of billed cap with a propeller embroidered on the peak. My eyes bugged out and he laughed and said "Just show business. You have got to make 'em think you are pure class. You are going to need some new clothes before Memphis, you look kinda rag tag." I had never thought about it, but along side him, I guess I did look pretty crummy. He was gorgeous.

Wearing his military cap and carrying his helmet conspicuously, we walked briskly to one of the restaurants, hesitated out front while he looked at the sky, grandly pointing at nothing at all while pretending to talk to me. He shaded his eyes and looked all around slowly as though he were seeking something rare and mysterious. Come to think of it, nothing at all is pretty rare.

When he had been observed by all, we went into the restaurant and sat at a table near the front, with him facing toward the window looking out on the street. Carefully, he arranged the helmet and goggles where it could be seen easily from the street. A waitress came skipping over, such an august personage must not be kept waiting. Using a British accent and a voice just loud enough to be heard but not overdoing it —just right for the effect— he said, "Bring my young man here a ham omelet with hotcakes. He hasn't mended too well since his parachute didn't open properly." Well, you would have thought everyone there was a jackrabbit, the ears sprang up and focused our way. Much more quietly so no one could hear, but pointing to me so everyone could see, he added "I'll take the same. With coffee. Bring him milk."

Boy! Were we ever served in style? For the other folks, the waitress came out with three or four orders of plates stacked on her left arm and carrying another in her right hand. Then she would serve the sausage and scrambled eggs to the oatmeal and poached eggs, and generally get it all mixed up. Two of them brought out our order, the prettiest served him, I was left with second best. But that was alright because second best was a long way better than anyone else got that morning.

Slowly, leisurely, oh so slowly, we ate, he having a second and a third cup of coffee. He broke out a newspaper, not just any old newspaper you might know, but a copy of the New York Times. I can't imagine where he got it, but he carefully read the inside pages so the front page was visible from the street to anyone who cared to look. Lots cared, and the sidewalk was jammed with the lookers. Ordinarily the restaurant owner would have hinted that a table not be held up that long, but a number of the sidewalkers came in for coffee and he didn't want to scare away the cause of the good business.

After an hour of this, we got up to leave with me remembering just in time to limp, not too much, but just a little. He made a big thing about tipping each of the waitresses a dime, and we left. Again, slowly, we walked up the street, crossed over and walked back on the other side. After about four blocks we were pretty much out of the downtown section so we slowly returned to the hotel. Inside, he asked the desk clerk if we could get somebody to run us out to the "airfield". On any regular day, this was just a cow pasture, but today it was upgraded.

Somebody in the lobby heard, as somebody was supposed to, and volunteered, as somebody was supposed to do. So we, actually he, checked out of the hotel and we got into the car that was offered. He grandly climbed into the back seat and sat in the precise center, erect and with arms folded and with his white helmet and goggle on, pushed up like aviators did, not down over his eyes. I sat in front, as was my place. Our benefactor made short work of the two or three miles to the field, expecting a ride I am sure. He is still waiting.

At the airfield, Johnson Tom had me get out the ladder and set it up, then he checked the oil again, being very careful about his uniform. Then he worked my bicycle around so he could close the wing storage bin completely. He put the tools and everything except the ladder and the two cranks in the bin under the left wing, and cranked it shut. He kept worrying about soiling his clothes but he did those things where he trusted no one, like checking the oil and the fuel, or where I was not big enough to reach.

"Now, Gaylord, there is supposed to be a gasoline truck here any minute. I want you to check and see just how much is pumped in. I'll be up on the wing handling the hose, so you will have to watch the pump on the truck. While we are waiting, let me tell you about the tickets. I don't want you handling any money. Everyone who wants to ride will have to have a ticket. I arranged to have these sold at the movie house in town. Now, you tear the ticket in two and keep half, and give the other half to the passenger. I'm going to pay you by the ticket, so don't lose any of your halves" I wished I had known before, because I didn't have a good way to keep up with a lot of half tickets. Johnson Tom continued, "Now, while I am up with one load, you get the next group ready. Line 'em up so they will march right onto the plane and sit down. Put the grownups and the heavyweights in front if you can. I'll turn the plane away from the crowd so we won't hafta shut down the right engine."

About that time, the gasoline truck comes up and we loaded on 203 gallons, the driver and I both agreed that was the amount. Johnson Tom addressed the driver, "Okay, when I'm ready for more, I'll fly over your station and jazz the engines. You come outside and wave to me that you understand, then you come right on out to the field. Okay?" It was okay, and the truck drove away.

He unrolled a coil of cotton-braided line and had me untie a bundle of stakes about four feet long with pointed ends. He had me pound these into the ground about 15 feet apart, and we strung the rope along the top, making a little barrier that was supposed to hold back the crowd. The Ford was parked about 50 or so feet beyond so the passengers would not have too far to go before boarding or changing their minds. Even at this early time, we already had a full load of people with tickets, but Johnson Tom delayed using one pretense after another until we had at least thirty people waiting in line to go up.

We went through the ritual of starting the engines, only I had to pull the props through by hand by myself, because he mustn't get his uniform dirty. Everything started all right, but the right engine needed two attempts at the crank before it caught. I laid the ladder flat on the ground and went to the cabin door. I took up 13 tickets, stuffing my half in my shirt pocket, and got everyone on. I moved up and down the cabin to see that all belts were fastened, and got out to assemble the next group.

Everything went smoothly all day. We actually made 24 flights, and filled every seat, for a total of 312 passengers. At two bucks a head, I had never seen so much money, actually I didn't see it then because the movie house was holding it. He didn't have to, but he explained the finances. "Now Gaylord, let me explain. I paid $5,000 for this airplane, and gave the owner $1,000 cash and a promise to pay the rest in six months. We flew almost six hours today, and normally that would have been about 360 gallons of fuel and 18 of oil. Takeoffs take more, so we used over 400 gallons of gasoline and 25 of oil. At 15 cents for the gas, we used up about seventy bucks of fuel and oil. I had to pay the owner of this field twenty-five bucks, and 15 cents to the theater to sell each ticket and handle the money. That right engine is going to need rings in another 30 hours or so, and that is gonna be three-four hundred bucks. So your see, it just looks like big money, but it takes big money to make it. If I'm lucky, I'll just about get the sonnava bitch paid off in time. Okay?" It had to be. Johnson Tom paid me a penny a passenger, and threw in 13 cents, so I made $3.25. I had made more in one day than in five or six weeks at the pool hall.

After a couple of weekends of practice, the Memphis airshow was looked to be fairly tame as far as passengers were concerned. Johnson Tom agreed he would fly over to Woodton and take Dad and me to the airport in Memphis. Mother was invited too, but she declined because she didn't really want to fly. She never seemed to worry when I did, but she preferred one foot on the ground for herself.

That's how it worked out. Johnson Tom came over on Friday evening before the show, and picked us up, us being Dad and me. It was almost dark when we boarded, but Johnson Tom just turned on the landing lights and opened the throttles and off we went. The Memphis airport was a lighted field as befitted a city of that size, so we just circled in a left-hand pattern until the tower gave us a green light and we turned onto the runway. This was the first time I had ever landed on a concrete runway, and I was surprised to hear the tires go "erk" as each touched onto the surface and spun up almost instantly to rolling speed. I still get a kick out of hearing airplane tires go "erk".

I could hardly believe the number of airplanes. There must have been several hundred, although the ability to estimate this sort of thing is not my best talent. There were a lot, anyway. Anybody can estimate a lot, so I know that is accurate. Most of them had flown in for the show, but a few dozen were based there, and had to share the grass parking areas with the visitors. There were men with white bands around their left sleeves who were directing the movement of airplanes on the ground. Some were pretty good at it but a couple almost caused a collision or two. Johnson Tom leaned out the window on his side and yelled down, "I'm based here, I park over on the strip there by that Beech Staggerwing." The guy on the ground didn't know a Beech Staggerwing from a trench mortar, but he says "Oh sure, just drive it on over". "Drive" it! Nobody drives an airplane, they fly them, or pilot them or taxi them, but they don't drive them. Johnson Tom says "Get a good look at him. He doesn't know an airplane has wings. That might be useful, never can tell."

So we taxied on down past the Staggerwing, and Johnson Tom says, "There's a better spot down here at the end, we'll see if we can park there. So he swung into a nice spot and began to shut down the engines. A plane director with an armband came up and said, "Hey, that spot is reserved." Johnson Tom said "Who for?" and the fellow on the ground says "A pilot named Johnson, supposed to be here tonight." Quick as a flash, Johnson Tom says "That's me, got here early, that other fellow back there told me to come on down here" With that Johnson Tom waved at the first man who had told him to drive down, and in the dusk the man waved back. "Well, okay, but I thought you were flying a Spartan Executive" "Changed my mind, I decided to bring this one instead." So the ground director made out a slip of paper that assigned the slot to Tom Johnson, flying a Ford Tri-motor.

As it turned out, a pilot flying a Spartan Executive did show up, but his name wasn't Johnson, Johnson couldn't come and this other fellow was a substitute. He was assigned a parking spot way off in a corner. I heard him complaining about it when I went to the john, but I didn't let on.

Dad decided he would find a rooming house for the night, which surprisingly he did. I slept in the airplane. I don't know what arrangements Johnson Tom had, but I am sure he had some special ones.

The airshow was pretty well run, these little events I mentioned can happen anywhere. It was a two-day affair, and there were several times in the morning and in the afternoon for hopping passengers. Each passenger hopper, and there were a dozen or more, would taxi up to a place where all of those waiting to fly were lined up.

By now, the Ford really shone, because I had found time to scrub it all over with linseed oil and hot water. About the only real problem was that the right engine was using oil, and throwing it all over the nacelle. We had to check the oil about twice as often as the other two, because it used so much more. And of course I had to wipe it all off, but it wasn't too hard now because the ship was clean.

There were two plans for a ride, the rider could take the next plane to come up for a fixed amount, or he or she could wait for a particular plane for more money, an extra dollar I think it was. The basic ride was five dollars, which was pretty steep, but there were a lot of people there, and a bunch had never ridden in a plane before and had come to have a good time.

The air show was different from what I expected. I thought it would be like the one I had seen when I was six, where all the people were able to get close to the airplanes, and just look around. No one got close to the planes unless they had a pass, which stated what their business was. Of course, Johnson Tom and I had a pass, and he got one for Dad also. We had to wear them where they could be seen. We wandered around as much as we liked, but there were a lot of policemen on duty who checked passes and asked questions to make sure everyone was where they were supposed to be. My pass was checked often, no one believed, at first anyway that a kid my age had anything to do with any of the airplanes.

There was a regular program during which various planes flew according to a schedule, and an announcer with a public address system that squealed off and on at first until they got it adjusted, kept the crowd informed about what was coming up and how it was going while it was on. All of the flying was for some sort of display of skill, individual planes doing aerobatics, three planes doing the same thing but in formation tied together by light ropes about fifty feet long attached to the wingtips, a midget plane race in which about eight or nine racers had a thirty minute race with the winner being the one completing the most laps around the course laid out on the field.

There was a farmer dressed in overalls who somehow got by the cops and wandered out on the flight line, looking in the airplanes and touching each one. Finally a cop saw him and chased him back into the edge of the crowd. Just about then, as a plane was about to take off, a man went running out to the plane waving his arms to get the pilot's attention, which he did, so the pilot waited up. The two of them conferred through the window for a few seconds, and the pilot got out of the plane and ran back to the area where the announcer and program director were, and they all had a little talk for a minute or two. While they were, this farmer fellow wanders back on the flight line, walking right past a policeman who was looking the other way. The crowd yelled at the cop and waved and pointed their fingers but that man was deaf or blind or something because the farmer got into the airplane and started playing with the controls. You could see the rudder move back and forth as far as it would go, and the elevators flapped up and down and the ailerons on the wings did the same thing. First thing you knew, he hit the throttle and that airplane started running around in circles, and of course the pilot notices it now and both he and the cop go running out and start chasing it as though a man could catch an airplane by running after it.

Well, that airplane got into the air with the most ragged takeoff I had ever seen weaving back and forth and I could just see that farmer fellow killing himself and maybe us too because I didn't believe he could get down without crashing bad. The announcer took up the case and began to tell the people there was no telling where it was going to hit so there was no sense running because one place was as safe as another. Meanwhile the airplane did all sorts of loops and rolls and made a pass by the crowd flying upside down. After about eight or nine minutes of this it came around and made a skittery landing on one wheel with the tail high in the air and spun around on one wheel in a ground loop. It just happened it stopped right next to where the pilot and cop were standing and they went running over to the plane and the cop dragged the farmer out to the plane and put handcuffs on him.

The pilot said something to the cop, kind of private like right in his ear, and the cop began to jump up and down and he broke his nightstick hitting it on the ground. The pilot found the key somewhere and released the cuffs on the farmer, who took off his overalls and stood there in a flying suit! He was an expert pilot and had won competitions for aerobatic flying. Everyone laughed and said they knew it all along. The cop didn't know it though and he had a broken billy club to show for it. I didn't know it either, but I claimed I did when everybody talked about it. In fact, I embroidered it up a little, people could see my pass pinned on my shirt and some of them asked if I had known about the farmer act. I said sure, his younger brother went to school with me. "Well, he sure fooled me," one man said. "Yessir, he fools a lot of people," I replied.

One featured part of the program was a batman, who had a framework of tubing attached to his shoulders that could be folded behind him or could be extended out to either side. In the extended position, the tubing supported some fabric that formed a wing of sorts. Between his legs and attached to each was some more cloth so that when he spread his legs wide apart, there was a stabilizing surface which acted like the tail on an airplane. He also wore a parachute and had a smoke bomb and his act was to go up and jump out with the wings folded. As he fell he released smoke from the bomb he carried, and flew around a little by extending the wings. Mostly though he just came down, but there was a little bit of control offered by all that paraphernalia. At the last minute, he would open his chute and land safely.

While he was getting ready for his first flight, he was donning the framework and with that on he was pulling on his parachute harness. His movements were considerably restricted by the framework, so he was having a tough time with the harness although he seemed to know what he was doing. A policeman there (a different one though from the one who broke his night stick on the ground) started to help him by pulling on the harness. In his eagerness to help, the policeman accidentally grabbed hold of the "D" ring of the ripcord and the chute spilled out on the ground. Boy! The batman ripped into that cop and called him just about every name I had ever heard, and laced him up one side and down the other. Naturally the cop was really sorry and tried to apologize, but the batman would have none of it. "You can help by telling the announcer that I will be delayed because of your stupidity and to bring up the next act, I'll tell 'im when I'm ready. Move!"

So the cop moved and the batman wriggled out of his parachute harness and the framework and spread the parachute out and repacked it right there. I was intrigued by how quickly he did it and how sure he was in all the things he did. He knew that chute up and down and got it all back together in just a few minutes. Then he re-rigged himself and when he was through he asked me to go to the announcer and tell him the batman was ready, and ask when he would go on. So I did, and the announcer looked at his schedule and said, "I'll put him on right after the tri-motor loop." He gave me a copy of the program and I took it back to the batman who looked at it and saw he had about 15 more minutes before he had to get in the airplane that would take him up.

Meanwhile, I was wondering about the tri-motor loop. Who was going to loop a tri-motor? Our Ford was the only one at the show, so I went sailing back to the parking spot and found Johnson Tom getting ready to go up. He was going to loop our tri- motor. Well, he hadn't said anything about it because he wasn't sure until we got here that he really was on the program, and, no, I couldn't go with him.

It was time to get started so we cranked up, he having pulled the engines through by hand himself before I had gotten there. Slowly, he taxied out of the parking spot and down in front of the people and the announcer, who began to play it up "Now, ladee-ee-ez and gent-tul-men, you now will see the most death defying demonstration of flying skill and daring yet to be seen by any audience." According to the announcer, every performance by every flyer at the show was the most death defying ever seen. "Pilot Johnson Tom, yes that's right, his LAST name is Tom, pilot Johnson Tom will perform a loop in the Ford tri-motor that you see taxiing in front of the stands now...." He kept on and continued to play it up as the Ford moved slowly down to the end of the runway. Many people began to look elsewhere, and some began to leave to get ice cream or whatever, because they already had seen dozens of loops and there was nothing thrilling or new about them by now. I began to feel sorry for Johnson Tom because I knew he liked to look big and important and nobody was even going to watch.

Johnson Tom ran up each engine and checked the magnetos as he taxied to the end, so that when he got there, he opened up and turned onto the runway in one smooth sweeping motion. The Ford got the tail up quickly, almost immediately it seemed to me, and with it held very high he kept it on the ground long past the normal lift off point until he got even with the announcer, and then with lugubrious ease the nose lifted and the Ford nosed upward and still more upward and then straight up and past vertical and over on its back and the noise of the engines suddenly ceased as Johnson Tom throttled back —the first time I ever heard him chop a throttle suddenly— and the Ford continued on around and still more and then was diving vertically and you could hear the wind whistling through and around parts of the airplane, and then he began to pull up and still more and the loop was completed with the wheels maybe five feet from the ground, then he opened the engines and eased down and touched the ground first with the left wheel and after rocking the plane over the other way, then with the right wheel. I was stunned by what I had seen. A Ford tri-motor looped from takeoff! Just to show it wasn't a fluke, he then flew around the field at about 20 feet and lined up with the runway again. He lowered down until the wheels were running along as if in a takeoff. Again he held it down until he reached the announcer's stand again, and once again he pulled the Ford up and over in the most ponderous loop you have ever seen. This time when he pulled out, again at about five feet, he touched both wheels on and without opening the throttle and gently rolled out in a landing. What a stunt! The people thought so too, and when he taxied back by the crowd as each performer did to take their applause, many folks stood up as they clapped their hands. The entire display from opening the throttles the first time to the end of the landing roll had taken less than five minutes.

That surprised the batman a little, and he wasn't even in his plane much less at altitude ready to jump. It surprised everyone except Johnson Tom, but it surely did build up the image of the Ford. When passenger-hopping time came again, we were filled every flight with passengers who had paid the extra dollar just to ride in the Ford that had done the loops.

The loops helped but even before that we were assured of a full airplane as often as we could make a round trip, and for as long as we wanted to fly in the allotted times. It took longer to taxi out because the field was so big, and longer to get back because we sometimes had to wait for the plane in front to load and get out of the way, but we did pretty good. We made eighteen flights on Saturday, and nineteen on Sunday and took in $1206 on Saturday and an even thirteen hundred on Sunday. Johnson Tom paid me twenty-five dollars for the two days.

All in all it was a great air show, and Dad thought so too. Late Sunday afternoon about six Dad and I got in the Ford and Johnson Tom flew up back to Woodton. We agreed he would pick me up again on Saturday.

X X X X

War broke out in Europe but it interested me most because of the airplanes. I knew every single model of every airplane on both sides that had been described in the magazines, and I was considered an authority on war planes.

CHAPTER XIV

We had a Boy Scout troop camp just about every summer. A lot of planning went into this because we had to have shelter, and transportation, not to mention food. It was not too hard to get the local commandant of the national guard to let us borrow a lot of eight-man tents as well as a field kitchen and enough folding cots for everybody, and to assign some trucks to haul the heavy gear, not to mention all of us. In addition to the drivers, a couple of guardsmen would be asked to go along and supervise the setting up of the tents. Since this was quite unofficial, the guard personnel could not be ordered to help, but there was never any trouble getting volunteers.

A full time cook and a couple of assistants were hired for the duration, which usually was two weeks. The Scoutmaster had to arrange for an adult man to spell him at the camp because someone had to be there at all times to be responsible and to be in charge. A general program of activities had to be laid out and the group leaders given special instructions, and so on. After all this was in the works even if not yet delivered, the cost was worked out. The Scout treasury paid for a good part of the camp because like I said we usually had a little wad from the take on Scouts' Day and from small donations given at Christmas time and the wills of people who had died. With this big contribution set aside, the remaining costs were divided by the number who said they were going so the fee per Scout could be estimated. If it was thought to be too high so that not many would respond, then a begging trip was made through the businesses in town. The two banks always were good for competitive donations —if the other one gave twenty five, maybe we can give twenty-six— that sort of thing. Almost any business would donate two or three dollars so sometimes it was possible to subsidize almost all of the total cost. The tab for the boys usually was not too bad, but even so, a lot could not afford to go.

The campsite always had to be on the banks of a river or a lake. We had several of each in the vicinity so the next step would be to get permission to use the ground. This usually was little problem because the troop had a good reputation for not being destructive. The place selected most often was a lake with the interesting name of "Old River". The name was quite accurate and descriptive because many years before, a hundred maybe, the lake had been the channel of the St. Francis river. This river, like many others in this country, meanders back and forth in a snaky path that generally runs in some overall direction —in this case north to south- but at any particular point it could be moving in just about any direction including north for our case. During high water, the river often floods the general area completely so that the kinks and bends are obscured by the masses of transient waters that sweep toward the sea, finding new and presumably better and faster paths for the transport of fluid, so that after receding it is found that a number of sweeping bends have been detached from the river by cutoffs that have created new channels. The old river beds still remain and hold lots of water and these isolated elements maybe three to ten miles long then are lakes, and almost any river that does not flow through solid rock will have dozens and dozens of them on both sides. Because most of them are curved in shape, very common names are "Crescent Lake", "Horseshoe Lake", "Rainbow Lake", or "Hook Lake." Somehow ours was special and was called "Old River", like I said.

The Scouts were happily unaware of these labors behind the scenes. On the Friday afternoon before camp was to start the entourage would assemble everything so as to be ready to go by night fall, or not later than midnight at the worst. Everyone then would go home to "get a good night's rest" before starting out first thing in the morning, be here at 6:00 am, everybody got that, yessir, okay see you in the morning. A few would show up at 6:00 am, but most were more casual about it, so we would shove off by ten o'clock, usually.

The trip to Old River was not too long, about an hour, everybody taking it a little slow because the heavy army trucks had a lot of gears to go through every time we stopped or slowed down. Also the guardsmen were required to stop at all railroad tracks before crossing them, so we moved steadily along but certainly were not racing anyone. Once there, there was a quick assembly to get everyone under control, because these same everyones wanted to dive in and go swimming or go fishing right away. But first it was absolutely necessary to set up the tents and the field kitchen, if we wanted to eat, and everyone did. The guardsmen really helped out, not so much from the muscle they applied but from the supervision and assistance in getting everything up and working. Somehow we always got the tents erected, the cots set up inside, and the kitchen fired up. It was touch and go for a while a couple of times, but we always got through before nightfall.

As I said, the arrangements always included someone to cook for the troop, because it was no fun eating raw or burned dough and meat for a couple of weeks. Besides that, we were there to swim and fish, and do a little leather craft, and maybe practice archery and life saving, and do a couple of million other things that the Scoutmaster thought up. A lot of us passed our swimming or lifesaving badges in summer camp. There was a lot of organization to all of this, and we were herded from one activity to another, with something very strenuous just before the evening meal. Then, with a good supper tucked away in most of us anyway, followed by an hour or so in front of the campfire —there always was a campfire even if it had been a hundred degrees during the day, which it sometimes was— most of us were ready to conk out. There wasn't too much resistance to lights out when "Taps" sounded at nine o'clock. That is about the way it was, generally a lot of structured fun.

One incident merits retelling, if only to show how unskilled some of us were. A lot of the Scouts liked to fish, and for this there were a number of wooden flat bottomed john boats. Just about all boats were wooden then. These could be paddled, but also they could be propelled by an outboard motor. At least two, maybe three, of the Scouts actually brought outboard motors with them so they could go up or down the river —we insisted on calling it a river— to the select fishing spots. Now in those days outboard motors were not very big by the standards of today. I don't really know how big they got, but a large one in our league was five horsepower. Also outboard motors were not the highly refined and docile engines of today. It almost was easier to paddle sometimes than to try to start one of those things.

Two Scouts, one with a motor, were going to go a couple of miles up the river to a very choice location. One of them was pretty big, really a lot of beef. The one with the motor was a little scrawny fellow, and they did make an interesting looking pair. The heavy one is sitting right at the front with his legs hanging over the edge in the water. The motor owner is about two-thirds way back, and doing things to the motor before starting it. Because of the weight distribution, the boat was floating nose down by a considerable amount, with no more than a couple inches of freeboard left in the front. The heavy weight is looking at his tackle and not paying any attention, the flyweight gets through with his preparations and starts to crank the engine.

This was long before the recoil starter days, each time a starting attempt was made one had to rewind the starting rope around a grooved section on the flywheel, which was right out in the open.

The boat had been shoved off, and was floating aimlessly as the starting exercise began. Flub-flub-flub. Rewind. Flub-flub-flub-flub. Rewind. Flub-flub- flub. On and on, with adjustments of throttle and spark advance after every three or four tries. Rewind. Flub-flub-flub. Rewind. Flub-flub-flub-rrrrrowrr-rrrrr-galoooomp. That damned little motor suddenly caught when the throttle was wide open and it had driven the boat forward so suddenly that it scooped up a hill of water over the bow and simply drove it under, boat, Scouts, tackle and motor. Everything was fished out of the lake and dried out, but that was the only time the motor ran or even hit during the entire camp.

Except for a number of minor incidents like that the camps went pretty smoothly. The biggest minor worry was constipation. Boys in their early teens sometimes forget about bowel movements, although to hear them talk, you would think that it was foremost in their minds. It was not unusual for a boy to go without going for close to a week. I suppose mothers must be attuned to this. Mine always gave me castor oil about three times a year for no other reason than to make me hate orange juice, because she always mixed the two together. Other mothers did the same thing, apparently, because my friends sometimes spoke of having to take castor oil that night. A real winner to look forward to all day! But I have strayed, back at the camp, mothers' concerns and attentions were happily left behind, and constipation could have been a problem except that the Scout Master checked everybody every day with the question "Been to Egypt?" Of course, you could lie about it, and most did the first day or two of delayed movement, but usually by the third day some mild laxative would be administered to everyone on general principles. So all together, most of us got through camp with no more than our regular irregularity.

There always was the problem of the food snitches. The general rule was that we could have all we wanted to eat, but that we had to eat all we took. There was no real difficulty with that, and we usually mopped out plates clean. But boys get hungry along about eight or nine o'clock in the evening, and in our camps at least, the kitchen would have been closed shortly after supper. A teen-aged boy who is hungry defies all adult comprehension. First, he is HUNGRY, and it makes no difference that he just packed away two adults' worth during the regular meal just two hours ago, he now is famished.

We knew we were going to be hungry later, even if the Scoutmaster didn't, so we always tried to stash enough at supper to provide a snack in a couple of hours. It didn't amount to much, five or six slices of bread, and enough meat for two or three sandwiches, and maybe some butter and jelly. The hard part was hiding the extra food while we sneaked it out, so we always wore a loose shirt or something with pockets. We learned the hard way that you don't stuff edibles into pockets that still contain a few fishing worms left over from the day. It was a lot harder to sneak out anything to drink, so we usually had to do later with just water. There was plenty of water, so we didn't have to finagle that.

Of course, these extra rations decimated the food budget, so the cooks always were complaining they were running out of a lot of things when we still had several days to go. It took an emergency dole of money one year to take care of an extra trip to the wholesale grocery house, not to mention arranging for the national guard truck to carry the stuff out to camp. After that, the Scout Master put a stop to it by having us appear for the evening meal dressed only in our shorts or our bathing trunks. With no place to hide anything, the consumption of the selected items dropped dramatically. In subsequent years, arrangements were made for a bedtime snack, and that kept things under control, more or less.

Snitching at meals was honest stealing, everybody did it. But you always could count on a couple who would try to sneak into the kitchen tent after taps and heist the makings of a few sandwiches. We never knew just who it was that was doing this, at least I didn't and everyone I talked to denied knowing who was guilty. Nonetheless, the cook kept complaining that the kitchen had been disturbed again during the night and that this or that had been taken.

One night, we had all hit the sack and most of us were asleep, I was anyway, when a couple of shots split the night, followed by a screetchy yell like someone was hurt. We came pouring out of the tents and there stood the Scout Master blowing smoke out of the barrel of a six shooter. He yelled, "He ran down the road that-a-way." So we started down the road that-a-way when the Scout Master called us to wait so he could get out in front and when he did we all galloped down the road in the dark with him leading the way by the light of the only flashlight in the party. After maybe a hundred and fifty feet he yells out "I think I can see him lying in the road up there." Sure enough, in about another thirty or forty feet, there was somebody stretched out with a big splotchy something all over the back of his shirt. We found out right off it was Billy Nail, one of the patrol leaders and he was clutching a can of peaches!

The Scout Master quickly said, "Billy Nail has been shot, rig a stretcher, don't shine any light on him it may be too painful for him." This was what we had passed all those merit badges for, so everybody went streaming back to camp to collect up blankets and first air kits and all the emergency stuff anyone could think of. We began to talk about Billy Nail. Why, I wouldn't have suspected him in a million years, why he was the one stealing the food all along, but how could one person eat all the food the cook said was missing, why he probably was selling it, that's it did you hear, Billy Nail was selling the food he was stealing out of the kitchen after taps, but Billy Nail, I wouldn't have thought he would do such a thing, and him being a patrol leader, and almost an Eagle, what do you think they will do to him, why he'll be kicked out of the troop, poor Billy Nail.....

About twenty stretchers were fabricated out of blankets and tree limbs, boat paddles, fishing poles, in fact just about anything that made any pretense at all of being a pole or stick about seven feet long. The Scout Master selected the best of the lot and rebuilt it with the pieces and contributions of two or three more. Meanwhile, Billy Nail was moaning and groaning something awful and we eased him on the stretcher, and began to carry him back to camp. "Somebody oughta call a doctor, how about the sheriff, do you think we will have to carry him back to town tonight?" The Scout Master tried to calm everybody down, saying "Billy Nail was a pretty good Scout, and I want all of you to remember him for the good things, and not for this thing tonight, because I know he didn't mean any harm." So we got him into the Scout Master's tent and got him as comfortable as possible in the dark, us gauging the comfort by the amount of groaning he was doing. Thinking back, he really must have been uncomfortable.

The Scout Master said he would go for an ambulance in his car, and that we were not to disturb Billy at all while he was gone. In fact, he was going to tie the tent flap shut and no one was to enter while he was gone.

So he takes off, and in a very short time it seemed to me here comes the ambulance. Out jumps the driver and the Scout Master and Billy Nail's father, and they load him in the back and zoom off, throwing a lot of gravel all over as the ambulance spun the wheels. The Scout Master comes back in an hour and says that Billy had died.

It just happened that was our last night out anyway, so the next day we packed up real quiet like, talking in hushed tones about nothing but the events of last night, and that Billy really was a good Scout and we didn't think he would hurt a fly. So we got in the trucks and cars that came and went back to town. Mother and Dad were shocked at the news and made a flurry of calls and then didn't want to talk about it any more.

That was Saturday about noon, and our next regular Scout meeting was the following Monday, and at the proper time I went to the meeting. The whole troop was there, everybody, even some who had not attended in a year. We dragged through the regular procedure of roll call, and when the role keeper came to Billy Nail's name, he choked up and asked the Scout Master if it should be stricken from the list. We all choked up too, because nothing like this had ever happened to any of us before. None of us felt ashamed as the tears streamed down our faces. The Scout Master said not just yet, we should remember Billy by leaving his space vacant in the line up. So his patrol shifted position enough to allow for Billy, every one crying and sobbing.

Right in the middle of this scene the lights went out. We all yelled and screamed and shouted such inane things as "Who turned off the lights?", and "Somebody oughta pay the bill." The lights came back on in about fifteen seconds, and somebody said we had paid the bill just in time and stuff like that, and we all laughed. We were laughing and talking when somebody remembered Billy Nail again, it just didn't seem like he could really be gone it looked like he was standing right there. HE WAS. He was standing in his regular place in his patrol, in full uniform.

Well, the discipline broke completely and we all crowded around and shook his hand and pelted him on the back and asked the same question over and over again "What happened?" "We thought you were dead." The Scout Master came in the room and told us it was all a big joke and boy had we looked silly making all those stretchers. I think we all looked even more silly just then, we had really been taken in. Some began to say they had known it all along and that they had not been fooled a minute. I guess if everybody there really subscribed to the Boy Scout law about being truthful, then I was the only one fooled. I'm telling you, I thought he was dead.

CHAPTER XV

Without really working at it, we fell into a routine by which Johnson Tom would decide where we would hop passengers and make all of the arrangements during the week. He would make sure the Ford was as conspicuous as possible both in the air and on the ground while he drummed up the action for the weekend. He would carefully select a few people and fly them around during the week, giving them a longer ride than normal so they would talk it up to the rest of the town. On Saturday, he would fly to Woodton and pick me up and we would arrive at the site by mid-afternoon. He usually had acquired a girl friend by this time. I always stayed at the local hotel and sometimes he did too, but usually he didn't.

He had decided that someone was going to walk into a propeller while loading passengers, so he scrounged some electric inertia starters for the engines. Actually, he got them one at a time, and we installed them ourselves. It wasn't much to it really, each electric starter just replaced the hand cranked one, and was mounted on the back of the engine by six bolts arranged in a circle. Mostly it was a matter of getting at it among the magnetos and exhaust pipes and wires. Then you had to watch that everything fitted together smoothly and without being forced. We had to rig up the electrical wiring and circuits to each starter motor, but again it was fairly simple to do.

The right engine was done first so he could shut it down while passengers were crowding into the door. The center engine got the next one because it was so high off the ground, and finally after a long time, the left. The engines still could be cranked up by hand, all the electric motor did was spin up that little flywheel for you. Otherwise it worked the same as before, you had to pull the props through to check for oil or gasoline in the lower cylinders, and the side engines still had to be primed at the nacelles, but starting at least became easy, as long as the battery held up.

Johnson Tom always flew at about 500 feet or less. He had flown attack planes for much of his army career, and in that business and in a real war, staying alive resulted from surprising the enemy troops and this was accomplished by flying as low as possible. He said that an entire squadron would fly a two and half-hour mission and never get up over a hundred feet. It really must have been exciting to those on the ground to have the noise of 15 or 16 planes of a squadron come booming up and then disappear over the opposite horizon all within a few seconds. He never got over it so Johnson Tom wasted no time or gasoline climbing to altitude, he just flew.

He flew with exquisite feeling for the subject. He always pampered the engines by oozing the throttles open and closed. He never ramracked an engine, in particular he didn't like to see power reduced suddenly on an air cooled power plant unless you were really in trouble. "Ease the throttles and let the temperature adjust gradually. It's not as bad with liquid cooling, because the coolant and all the thermostats keep the temperature stabilized but an air-cooled engine will change temperature all over the place when you suddenly pull back." In fact, the only time I ever heard him chop a throttle suddenly was when he looped the Ford at the Memphis air show.

Along those same lines, he always brought the plane in under power. "Two reasons," was his explanation. "If I need to go around because of a bad approach, I want those babies to open up without a lot of coughing and backfiring. If they have cooled down after a long glide they can't develop full power until they have warmed up again and that may take 15 seconds or more, meanwhile you are wondering why you are not going up. Second reason is I want to fly above absolute stall speed, so I usually fly onto the ground with the tail high. A three-point landing looks nice, but you actually have little control as it settles on. If I have to I can drag it in nose high under power like they do in the navy and set down several miles an hour less than in a full power off three-point landing. Those engines are to use, Boy, but don't ever abuse one, or I'll kick your ass."

Johnson Tom also was silky smooth at the controls and got an awful lot out of an airplane. One of the rare times that we were flying at 1500 feet, I forget why now but it must have been important, he said "Let me show you how to get another four or five miles an hour out or the plane. Now suppose you want to fly at 1500 feet at a slightly higher speed but at the same throttle settings as now. First, you ease it up about two hundred feet above 1500, and trim up and synch up, you may have to do both two or three times to get it right. Now when she is flying smoothly at that altitude, you wind in a little nose down trim —not much— you want to pick up maybe seven or eight miles an hour while losing that two hundred feet. With just a little of the extra altitude still left, like fifty feet, ease back on the trim gentle like so that when you are done you will be right at 1500 feet without gaining or losing any altitude. If you do it right, you will find you are maintaining several, maybe five miles an hour more than before you started. Now, you can only do it once, some people think you can keep on adding five miles an hour each time for any number of repeats, but if you could you could fly at any speed you wanted to, and that violates the laws of physics." That was a long speech for Johnson Tom, but he had shown me how to put the plane "on the step". It is a well-known trick today, and all the better pilots use it, but at that time there was no name for it and only a few very good pilots were aware of it. But Johnson Tom was a very good pilot, and I should add, getting a Ford on the step was a lot harder to do than on modern airplanes, because the elevator trim crank was over the door on the wall behind the pilot's head. It was kind of awkward reaching up and back to turn the crank while flying at the same time.

The Ford was harder to fly than modern aircraft in all ways. It had no trim tabs for the rudder or for the ailerons. If the plane tended to turn slightly in level flight, as it often did, the pilot could run the engines at slightly different speeds, with the accompanying annoying sound, or over a period of time minute adjustments could be made to the pitches of the propellers. This was no small task, and was done on the ground between flights and required that at least one propeller be removed from its engine. We did that once, but didn't really improve things much. Finally, Johnson Tom riveted a small piece of sheet aluminum to the trailing edge of the rudder, and with successive small bends, succeeded in getting the plane to fly straight. Wing heaviness was cured by burning gasoline from first one tank and then another. Not too bad but not too good either. The Ford always needed a little corrective pressure on the control wheel to hold a wing up.

Johnson Tom didn't say anything, but I could tell he was worried about that right engine. Whenever we had a good smooth field to fly out of or when we were not full, he would take off with the right engine opened up only to cruising speed. The take off roll was a little longer, and he had to overcome the asymmetrical thrust by applying a lot of left rudder, but it worked out all right. He was saving it as much as he could.

When we were flying cross-country like that, I always flew in the co-pilot's seat on the right side. As you might guess, he began to let me fly a few minutes at a time. The first time he let me fly the Ford, his instructions set all records for brevity. "You know this is the control wheel, pull it toward you or push it away to nose the plane up or down. Those are the rudder pedals, push the right one and the nose moves right. You know all that. Move each control slowly until you see how it affects the plane. Don't make any sudden moves, and just play around with it. If in doubt, just let go, it can fly better than you can. Better climb up to about a thousand feet to give yerself a little room."

So that was about it, and because of my reading and watching there really weren't many surprises. The biggest one was that the engines slowed down when the airplane was nosed up. I knew increased speed and windmilling would make them speed up when nosed down, but it had not occurred to me that nosing up would slow them down.

As my skill and his confidence in me grew, he would let me fly everything between the takeoff and the landing. After a few weeks, I was flying the airplane just about all the time we were in the air going cross-country. After a little air work, he began to let me taxi it on the ground. Of course on the first two or three times, I overcontrolled it and did a lot of swerving and S'ing, then I began to get the hang of it and pretty soon I could move it across the ground as straight as an arrow.

Sometimes, he would let me sit in the left seat in the air, then when we taxied up he would be at the door and would get out while I shut down the engines. Lots of times, he let me start the engines while sitting in the left seat. One time he stayed out of sight in the cabin and I got in and started up and taxied out to the end of the runway, and he quickly slipped into the seat and took off. As soon as we broke ground, he ducked down and let me climb out right by the crowd, and to ham it up I waved out the window as I—actually we—went by.

Of course the eyes of all the kids bugged out of their heads when I started the engines or taxied away from the loading area, so before long I found I held a similar stature among the kids and even some of the adults too. I didn't know whether to be modest and sort of off-hand say it wasn't really much to it, or to lay it on and make out it was really hard to learn and only those with special gifts and unusual talents could ever hope to be able to taxi an airplane much less fly one. Usually, I laid on how hard it was.

Without him ever saying I could I began to taxi at enough speed to get the tail up, if we had a way to go and there was enough room that is. He didn't say anything so I knew I was doing it alright. One time when we were at the end of the field at the end or the day and ready to leave for home, he said, "Just take off and climb up to a thousand. So I did."

Most of this was after we got the electric starters, he wouldn't have worked up the sweat on the hand-cranked jobs. That uniform you know. Wearing that uniform made Johnson Tom a giant among the adults, and particularly among the women. But he really didn't need it. He was a pretty big guy all around without it. My Dad was right about the man making the clothes, because a lot of men couldn't have gotten away with wearing clothes like that.

None of this hurt anybody, and it helped my image considerably. Johnson Tom was great for helping images, and he didn't mind me looking good. He realized that anything that made me look good made him look even better, because I worked for him and anybody would know I had learned it from him. A lot of bosses never catch on to that at all.

Now, I must admit not everyone agrees with what I just said, and some people might allow it was dishonest. I suppose it depends on just where you want to shade the truth. As far as I am concerned, if somebody wants to think I am just one notch below God, I really don't see any reason to set them straight. I have been blamed for so many things that went wrong where I had nothing to do with it at all, that I will accept any credit that comes my way, whether deserved or not. On balance, the undeserved blame outstrips the unmerited praise by a considerable spread, so far at least.

We flew mostly without navigational aides, usually with automobile road maps, although he used airways charts when we actually flew along them. After taking off, we just went "that-a-way", he would say. "We're heading for Holly Grove, that's southwest of here, find it on the map and get up there." It was strictly pilotage all the way, compass courses meant nothing because you could see on the map you wanted to fly to the right of Maryannna and a little to the left of Moro to get there. It was easier just to fly it than it was to figure out a compass course. At night it was the same way, except in some ways it was easier, because all the little towns are lit up and usually — exceptions exist— it is easier to spot a town at night than it is in the daytime through all the haze. We never got lost even once, or even came close. Several times we circled around looking for the field that was not too obvious, but we always knew we were just north of Arkadelphia or wherever, we just weren't sure which of those fields down there was supposed to be the one we wanted.

We had incredibly good luck with the weather, a lot more than our fair share. We flew almost every weekend, arriving on the scene on Saturday afternoon and taking passengers on Sunday. A couple of times, the weather was bad on Saturday, but cleared up by Sunday. A few times, it was cloudy on Sunday, but it only rained so we couldn't fly maybe twice. Even in the cross-country work coming and going, we had few occasions when we were delayed more than two or three hours.

So the passenger traffic did pretty well, weather permitting, and like I said, it was usually pretty good. Ordinarily, we could make 20-25 hops on a good Sunday, and one time we made 28. It wasn't always a sellout, but the airplane was being paid off and I was making five dollars on some weekends.

After about nine or ten weeks, the traffic began to dwindle away a bit. One day, Johnson Tom hit on a publicity stunt to scare up a little business. We would get a monkey and let it make parachute jumps. With a lot of ballyhoo before, this should drag the people to the field and some of them surely would take a ride.

It took a couple of weeks to find a monkey. I don't know where he came from, but one Saturday afternoon Johnson Tom had this little chimpanzee with him when he landed to pick me up. "Gaylord, this is Monk. Monk is going to make a couple of parachute jumps tomorrow" He then showed me a little chute that had been made out of a regular parachute that was too old and wouldn't pass inspection anymore. I don't know how he did these things, but Johnson Tom always seemed to be able to get anything like that with no trouble at all.

Monk complicated things right off. We were going to leave him in the plane overnight, but he would have none of that. We put him in the cabin and closed the door and were latching it when he jumped off the roof of the Ford right onto my shoulders. Monk had run through the cabin and had climbed out one of the open windows in the cockpit and onto the top of the plane. We closed the window, and tried again. Monk promptly opened the door and jumped on my shoulders again. One more try. We held the door latch this time so Monk began to screech and hammer on the door and jump up and down. We couldn't be sure but it looked like he would tear the cabin apart, so we decided to take him into town with us.

The hotel clerk was downright unfriendly, "Hell no, that ape ain't gonna spend the night in the hotel room. No telling what the little bastard would tear up." We tried coming back later when more people were in the lobby and sneaking him past the desk, but Monk began to scream just as we thought we had it made. The clerk threatened to call the cops so some other plan was needed. Finally, I held him in the lobby while the clerk scowled at me and Johnson Tom went to the room and cleaned up, and then he took Monk with him when he went out. He showed up at six the next morning with Monk on his shoulder, so I guess no one minded too much wherever it was he stayed.

After the usual strut around town, followed by breakfast and being transported to the field, this time by the girl friend, we got the plane ready and waited. During this time, Johnson Tom explained that after a couple of hours of passenger flights, or whenever it got slow, we would go up and drop Monk out. First though, we would remove the door then we would fly over town and while Johnson Tom throttled back, I would talk up the monkey jump through the megaphone. We then would circle slowly but purposefully back toward the field while I got Monk ready. When I tossed him out, his parachute would be opened automatically by a cotton line about fifty feet long that was tied to his rip cord on one end and to the plane on the other. We would only be about 300 feet up so he wouldn't drift too far while descending. If everything went right, he should land on the upwind end of the field, meanwhile we would circle and land and then taxi up as close as possible to where Monk came down. I would repack the chute while we taxied back to the crowd, and we would be ready for the new faces. When things slowed up again, we would do it again.

Good plan! But plans of mice and men are known to go astray.

Well, we had a few flights, and things got a little slow, so Johnson Tom decided the time was now. We put Monk in his harness in front of the small crowd, maybe twenty people, and he didn't seem to be interested one way or the other. We removed the door by knocking the pins out of the hinges— which took about a minute and looked like it had been done often enough before— I put it in the plane, and we took off. Over town and at about 500 feet, Johnson Tom throttled back into a glide while I shouted through the megaphone, "Come see the monkey jump with a parachute." Johnson Tom would rev up climb back and circle around and we would repeat. After nine or ten passes, I began to shout the time, "Big monkey jump in 15 minutes, at the airfield, just east of town."

You could see people piling out of the houses and some got into cars and started toward the field. Other than a couple of fender bending collisions from too many people trying to turn onto the main road at the same time and place, we encouraged about 50 people to come to the field with no trouble at all.

We circled around until most of them got there, it was only about three miles so it didn't take very long even for the stragglers, and those who couldn't make up their minds until they saw everybody else going and didn't want to miss anything. I urged them alone with the megaphone, and as soon as most of the cars were parked along side the road and everyone was walking toward the field, we figured we were about ready. We made one more pass as I urged them to hurry with the megaphone, and then a couple more circles over the field and we were really ready. Johnson Tom headed toward a spot beyond the upwind end of the field and flew over it so the right side with the door faced toward the crowd below. I tied the end of the rip cord rope onto a seat by the door, and when Johnson Tom throttled back the engines to indicate the spot, I tossed Monk out.

The line snapped tight, and the chute popped out of its pack. Just like that, Monk was dangling below his chute and wondering what happened. He didn't have long to think about it because he was on the ground in about 20 seconds, having drifted downwind maybe 500 feet. Meanwhile, Johnson Tom made a diving three-quarter turn to the right and was all lined up and ready to touch down, headed right where Monk was about to land.

It worked out just about perfectly. The Ford ran out and stopped within a few feet and a few seconds of Monk's landing. I hopped out and started toward him, and Monk came flying to me and grabbed me around the neck and wouldn't let go. I mean, he wouldn't let go! Then, he began to jabber. I was about deafened by Monk hanging onto me as tightly as he could and telling me all about it in a loud voice about an inch from my ear.

I couldn't handle Monk and fold the chute, so Johnson Tom had to come out of the cockpit and help. This delayed our return to the crowd by several minutes and put some tarnish on the overall effect. It wasn't too bad though, because we flew eight full trips before the backlog was worked down.

Along about one o'clock, the gasoline truck showed up and we knocked off and refueled. After 159 gallons, everything was topped off and Johnson Tom grandly paid the driver in cash, $23.85, and gave him a fifteen-cent tip.

After one flight, not too much business was in sight, so Johnson Tom decided to lay on another monkey jump. We flew over town again and repeated the procedure of the morning, and actually generating more reaction than before, probably because a lot of people were in church earlier.

When the new trade had pretty much arrived at the field, we began to circle and get into position for the jump. So I tied the line to the seat, picked up Monk and adjusted his harness. Everything went well until I started toward the door. You could just hear the click in his little brain. He grabbed me around the neck and began to gabble in my ear while I tried to disengage first one of his hands and then the other. Meanwhile, we missed the jump point and Johnson Tom throttled back and yelled "What the hell's the matter?" I couldn't answer because I was struggling with Monk, I was able to hold one hand while unwrapping the other, then by holding both his hands with one of mine, I got one foot loose and then the other. With an unnamed wrestling hold, I held him and stepped to the door and threw him out, or so I thought.

As soon as he was free from me, Monk reacted like a self-opening umbrella. His arms and legs spread out in a flash and he caught onto the doorframe, spread-eagled like a large X, but head down and facing out.

Now we had a situation. Monk was frozen in the door, looking at the world in a way that made him even more frightened. "Toss that ape out" yelled Johnson Tom as we passed the jump point again. But let me tell you, your problems have been as naught compared with getting a chimp to let go in these circumstances. I could get one of his hands free easy enough if I used both of mine, but then I either could just sit there and hang on, making no further progress, or I could try and hold on with one of my hands and then attempt to loosen Monk's other hand, but leaving both feet clamped on, and his tail around my neck.

Let me say right here, I know chimpanzees don't have tails. We called Monk a chimp, and he had a tail. I don't really know what kind he was but he was a monkey of some sort. It really makes no difference, he was not going to be put out again, and his tail gave him quite an advantage.

"Get your ass up here and fly this thing while I get him out", yelled Johnson Tom. I managed to get free of Monk by putting each of his hands on the doorframe and unwinding his tail from my neck. I scrambled forward and into the right seat and took the controls while Johnson Tom unbuckled and started off. "Don't try anything fancy, just circle around. Remember, if I fall out of this sonnavabitch, you'll hafta land it all by yourself."

So I circled back once and then a second time, following which Johnson Tom came running back to the cockpit with blood all over his hand. "That little bastard bit me," he wailed, "I spanked his ass, and he bit me," he repeated. He never did say how he got him dislodged, but I can guess it was simply because Johnson Tom was a lot bigger. But Monk made his mark on the way out the door, so I would say it was a draw.

We had flown out a couple of miles while he was getting Monk out and settling into his seat again so he made a diving turn to try and land and stop rolling near Monk. The whole thing was a disaster. Monk drifted about a mile off the field and landed in a tree. That wasn't too bad for Monk, but we found out later the parachute became tangled in the branches and was torn in several places.

We couldn't do anything just looking down at Monk so we flew back to the field and hopped three or four loads and then Johnson Tom sent me to get Monk. It took almost three hours to find him and get back, so it was late. "We'll hafta figure out a better way," was all Johnson Tom would say. We flew home, but it had not been a good day all around.

To make up, we agreed that next week we would take up passengers on Saturday and Sunday, and he would come for me early on Saturday morning so we could get a good start.

When Johnson Tom dropped in at Woodton with the Ford tri-motor next Saturday, I was surprised to see he still had Monk. He also had a new girl friend with him in the Ford, Johnson Tom that is, not Monk. Just as you might suspect, she lived in the town where we were going to fly later that day, and naturally as eating pie she had a car, so our ground transportation problems were taken care of. Naturally, neither Johnson Tom nor Monk stayed at the hotel that night.

Monk had been conditioned to the airplane all week by staying in it all day and even a couple of nights. He flew with Johnson Tom when he buzzed the town to work up the show, and he had worn his parachute harness and the parachute most of the time. So by now, he was quite at home and would scamper in and out at will. He showed no signs that he remembered the past weekend at all.

We did the usual breakfast bit, and Monk helped by sitting in the chair and eating bananas. After a time, the girl friend showed up in the car and took us to the field and we started hopping passengers. Things were quite lively for a while, sometimes Monk would go in the airplane, sitting in the co-pilot's seat wearing a helmet and goggles that Johnson Tom had gotten for him. Other times, he would he would stay on the ground with me, sitting on my shoulder and looking in my hair while I tried to reconcile my ticket halves with the number of passengers that had boarded.

Along about 10:30 business was still good, but Johnson Tom decided that we had to let Monk jump soon because the advanced publicity was doing its work, but not exactly as it was intended, because some of the crowd was getting noisy about it and demanding that it be done. We made a big display of putting on Monk's harness, and buckling on the parachute, as well as removing the door. We took off and circled around the field two or three times and headed for the jump point. As we approached and with about 15 seconds to go, I tied the rope to the chair and started to throw him out. CLICK! The little brain went into survivable mode and he threw his arms around me and hung on. Of course, we missed the drop point as I tried to break his holds, which I finally did, but he grabbed the door frame with both hands and feet, spread-eagled as before, but right side up this time. I was trying to loosen one of his hands when bla-t-t-ttt he defecated all over the back end of the cabin. Yuk! Gooey, messy, and **stinking**!

I wrung his hand loose and with him hanging out the door by both his feet, then by just one, I stepped on his toes until he let go. He missed the damned field by five miles. Just as soon as he dropped away, I hurried back to the cockpit and shouted to Johnson Tom, "We can't go back yet. Monk shit all over the airplane. It's a real mess back there." Johnson Tom gave me the controls and went back to look. He was back in just a second completely exasperated, "Goddamned that ape, you'd think we were mean to him or somethin'. We'll land and taxi to the far side of the field. Later we'll tell 'em it was time for a special inspection so we'll pretend to be working on something while it is being cleaned up." I knew "it" would be cleaned up by me, because Johnson Tom couldn't risk getting his uniform dirty.

So we landed and ran out to the end of the field, and parked as far away as we could, and I went at it. We drained some gasoline from the wing, which was a little tricky because the ladder was back with the crowd. Johnson Tom held me on his shoulders, after I had removed my shoes that is, and I was able to reach up and open the inspection door and got the rags drenched, and some on me too. With a lot of rags, a lot of gasoline, even more determination and with one hand holding my nose, visibly at least, it was clean after 15 minutes or so. But the smell! God! What a bruise for the nose.

We went back and hopped a load, during which Johnson Tom spotted Monk a couple of miles away sitting on a barn with the parachute hanging over the edge. He also found a field about a half mile from there that looked like it could take the Ford. So when we got back we took another load but the odor was pretty bad. When we got back with the second group, there wasn't much business left, because the comments of the first bunch pretty well scared off the third. We decided to go after Monk while we were waiting for new bodies and also hopefully for the cabin to air out. So we took off, leaving all the windows open, and a breezy flight it was too, and after a few minutes we got to the field near Monk. Johnson Tom got my bicycle out of the wing bin, and sent me after Monk.

I found him in no time at all and coaxed him down with an apple. Most people don't know it, but chimpanzees, Monk anyway, like apples about as much as they like bananas. I rolled up his parachute, and put him on my shoulder and we pedaled back. Oddly enough, no one had gathered around the Ford at all, I guess we had them all over at the other field, or maybe they didn't care. Anyway, we had almost no business waiting at all, so we took off, and circled over town while I regaled the place with the megaphone again, promising another parachute jump by Monk. We circled back to the field and found a small crowd beginning to assemble from my bally hoo.

I hopped out to organize the first of two or three loads before Monk's act, or that was the intent. Instead, I jumped right into the arms of the local sheriff who was accompanied by an exceptionally pretty but very serious looking woman about 30 or so.

"Hold 'er there, Boy. You and yer friend are under arrest." He clamps a handcuff on my wrist and says, "Go tell the other guy to come out here." There was a brief period of sorting out the mechanics of carrying out this order. I was under arrest and handcuffed. The sheriff didn't want to board the airplane, and the woman just stood there looking pretty and serious. After a minute or two, the sheriff unlocked my cuffs and said, "Go get the other feller. Don't try to run off, cuz we got yer number."

"What the hell we being arrested for?" was Johnson Tom's reaction. "I haven't done anything that bad. You say there's a woman with him. Damn, hope she's not pregnant, no that can't be, he arrested you too. What the hell did you do?" He shut off the engines and completely baffled, we hurried down the sloping floor of the cabin to the door.

"Howdy," drawls the sheriff, "I'm the sheriff hereabouts, and this here is Mrs. Wasserman, she's the president of the humane society in town and you two are under arrest for cruelty to animals." I was trying to think what animals I had been cruel to, decided quickly that Mrs. Wasserman couldn't know about the clothespin on the cat's tail, anyway Johnson Tom hadn't been in on that.

Mrs. Wasserman clarified things at once. "You are cruel and inhumane to that monkey of yours letting him fall out of that airplane like that. Lock them up sheriff." About then Monk comes shuffling out of the cabin, crawls up on my shoulder and begins to look in my hair. He didn't look too upset.

Quick as a flash, Johnson Tom gave her a big smile and said off hand like, "Why, Mrs. Wasserman, you can't be talking about Monk here. He loves to jump out in his parachute. He won't leave us alone unless he gets to make two or three jumps every week. Here, we were just going to go up and let him do it right now, why don't you come along and see for yourself?"

Mrs. Wasserman clearly was a little unsettled by this. It was obvious we were guilty of "letting" Monk jump because so many people had seen it. But Monk was placidly looking in my hair, and Johnson Tom had denied the charge with a counter offer. She had her duty to perform, but in all fairness, she should check her evidence. In fact, the arrest would not stand up unless the evidence was pretty good, but she didn't know about flying on the airplane. The sheriff didn't help. He had no intentions of flying in any airplane. With reservations, but much self-admonishment about duty, she agreed.

Johnson Tom gives her a great big smile and offers her his arm and grandly escorts her to the door, helping her in. "My goodness, what is that odor?" she asked. Nothing if not adaptable, Johnson Tom rips out, "Oh, that is a new airplane smell. All new airplanes smell just like that!" "It really must be new," she responded. "Oh, yes ma'am, this airplane is brand new, it's not even broken in yet." The Ford was nine years old, had over seven thousand hours on the airframe, and had had nine overhauls of four different sets of engines. That much we knew from the logbooks. We couldn't be sure everything was recorded because there was a full year when nothing was written at all. "Yes, ma'am, she's really new." Johnson Tom laid it on.

We took off the door, cranked up the engines again, with the electric starters working just fine, and we took off. We circled over the field, with me wondering how we were going to stay out of jail. I was sure that if I was put in jail, I wouldn't get any more merit badges, no matter how many times the

Court of Honor met. What a mess, and doubly so if Monk delivered again.

So I snapped on Monk's chute and tied the rope to the seat and prepared for the battle. But surprise of surprises, as I approached the door, Monk took a running jump and went out on his own! Actually, he did a backward flip throwing his head back and baring his teeth toward me as he rotated in the air. The line snapped taut, the chute opened and Monk drifted downward toward the field. Johnson Tom made the diving turn and we rolled up to Monk just as he touched down. It couldn't have been better.

For some reason, that damned chimp had decided at that moment that he did like it. We never had any more trouble with him after that, he seemed to delight in finding new ways to jump out the door each time, backward, somersaults, spread-eagled, doubled in a ball, cartwheel out the door. He really was innovative.

But back to this time; after landing we gathered up Monk and gave him a banana, rolled up his parachute, and got into the plane. Monk promptly conked out and went to sleep. Mrs. Wasserman didn't know what to do. She finally decided that Johnson Tom should pay a fine of five dollars because with inspired perception, she said," I'm sure your were inhumane to the monkey before he got to like it. "She also decided that I should attend a meeting of the humane society with her that night.

She rode back into town with the sheriff, then came back with her own car, and stayed until we had taken up the last passenger and put the Ford away in anticipation of tomorrow. Johnson Tom's girlfriend had disappeared when she saw we were in some sort of trouble, so Mrs. Wasserman gave both of us a ride back into town, and we agreed that I would clean up and she would pick me up at six thirty.

This she did, explaining the meeting was in the next town about 20 miles away. We drove at a moderate speed with her telling me about Christian duty. After about fifteen minutes of this, she started talking about the humane club. They took in stray animals and kept them a week or so while trying to find the owner, or failing that, a new owner. Usually they were unsuccessful, so the animals then were put to sleep. I was wondering what the animals thought about this when she got off on her husband. He had vanished "into thin air" without a trace. That had been four years ago and after becoming reconciled that he was truly vanished, but still not legally dead, she not having any children decided that her duty lies in helping animals. She helped a good many, her activities saw about 5 to 10 a week being put to sleep.

We arrived at the next town and went to the place of the meeting, but it was deserted. No one was there, no lights on, nothing. We sat and waited until it was well past starting time, and no one had showed up, so she decided we should go back. She fretted over getting the date mixed up but she didn't think so because she and Mrs. Adams, the chairman of the chapter in this town, and she had exchanged letters about it just this past week. There just had to be some misunderstanding and she would give Mrs. Adams a chance to explain because Mrs. Wasserman was sure she —Mrs. Wasserman— was not to blame. I didn't really care, because I didn't want to go to a meeting where they talked about the number of animals put to sleep. I learned later, several years later, that that was not the subject of such meetings, but I didn't know it then.

When we arrived back at her town, it was dark, and she suddenly said, "Have you had anything to eat? Why, you must be starved." So we drove to her house, which was just beyond the built up part of town, by itself off the road under some trees. We went in and she fixed me just about the biggest supper I ever had, only she called it dinner. Maybe that was why she got the time of the meeting wrong, because at home Mother always fixed us dinner at noon, and it was the big meal, and supper was sort of light. So it fell right in line that someone as mixed up about time as Mrs. Wasserman would feed me a meal like that at supper, she thinking it was noon, probably.

Anyway, she whipped up a couple of pork chops, mashed potatoes, green peas, hot buttered biscuits, a piece of chocolate pie, and milk. Before I dived in, she said a blessing that lasted about six or seven minutes, leaning heavy into asking forgiveness for our sins. I was really hungry by then so I had seconds on everything except pie. There was only one piece of that.

It was about eleven o'clock when I was finished eating and she had done the dishes. She said, "we'll have to get you back." So, we went out and found it was raining. We got into the car, getting a little wet while doing it. She inserted the key and pushed on the starter pedal —cars all had starter pedals or buttons on the floor in those days— and it cranked and cranked, but showed no interest in running at all. After a few minutes of this, it was coming down like pouring water out of a boot on a flat rock, and it looked like the car wasn't going to budge. She said, "Well, you will just have to stay here." So we ran back to the house, and got pretty wet while she fumbled for the key and got the door unlocked. Finally, we got inside, and I was chilled to the bone and my teeth were chattering.

"You'll sleep in here, get out of those wet clothes and I'll hang them up to dry." This was before the days of clothes dryers, so she had to rig up a clothesline somewhere, or maybe she already had one inside already. But with the high humidity, there was little chance anything would be dry by morning.

Everything I had on was wet, so I pitched my clothes outside the door and crawled into the bed raw and snuggled under the covers. Even though it was summer, there were a couple of blankets and a quilt on the bed and they really felt good. I dozed off and Mrs. Wasserman entered the room carrying a tray with milk and cookies. She offered a long blessing with an unusually long sign-off about being forgiven for our sins. I ate the cookies and drank the milk. She carried out the tray, and returned in a few minutes and fluffed up my pillow. To my shock, she crawled into the bed with me, and in a few seconds it was all over. In that short time, she had taken hold of my dong, which erected instantly, slipped it into her as she crawled onto me, and after a half dozen pumps maybe, I ejaculated. I don't know, maybe she got through at the same time, but without a word she got up and left. My surprise was so complete and my pleasure so swift that I lie wondering if I had dreamed it. Gradually sleep overcame me again and I dreamed she returned and repeated the sequence. I awoke to find she had returned and we were repeating. Things were not so fast this time, and she stayed a few moments after we were through and then left. She returned again in an hour, and left after a while and returned, left, returned stayed quite a time while we repeated twice. We both slept like logs until 5:30, when she suddenly awakened and said, "We must get you to the hotel." Quickly, she brought my clothes, which were clammy and cold, and she applied makeup while I dressed. Within fifteen minutes, we were driving toward town, the car starting with no trouble at all. She let me out a block away and I hurried inside and got to the room and had just covered up in the bed when Johnson Tom arrived. Even in that short time, I really was fast asleep and could hardly stagger out of the bed.

Other than that, it was a regular day, about like the others. We flew 24 loads, and Monk jumped three times. We agreed to a two day week end next time, and Johnson Tom would come for me late on Friday afternoon.

CHAPTER XVI

On the Friday afternoon following our arrest, I was getting ready for an early start like we had agreed, packing my small suitcase with toilet articles and a change of clothing. As usual, I was going to ride my bicycle out to the field where Johnson Tom would land and pick me up. I was within a couple of minutes of leaving when the phone rang. It was Johnson Tom.

"Last Sunday after I dropped you off, that damned right engine stopped. Had to fly on to Memphis on two. Needed a zero time overhaul and it won't be ready for another week. I'll pick you up at the pool hall in an hour." I didn't even have time to ask any questions before he hung up. So I finished my preparations, left a note for Mother, and rode off on my bicycle.

The pool hall was the same as ever. I didn't want to hang around because Mr. Williams would want to put me back to work —without pay of course— so I sort of stayed outside out of sight. After a while, up drives a wooden sided station wagon with the back completely loaded with something, and of course it was driven by Johnson Tom. "Get your ass in," was his greeting. "Bought ten thousand bedspreads, all seconds. Paid a thousand dollars for 'em. Got three hundred of 'em in the back. We're gonna sell all of 'em this weekend."

Well, I never thought I would be wondering how anyone would sell 10,000 bedspreads, much less over a weekend. I ventured a question, "How you gonna sell 10,000 bedspreads?" "How in hell do I know? Too good a deal to turn down at a dime apiece. They hafta be worth more than that. Throw you bicycle up on top and let's stop at the hotel."

While we were driving the short distance to the hotel, he told me more about the engine, "Now I know why they flew those tri-motors with co-pilots, somebody had to stand on the damned rudder pedal if a side engine failed. One man couldn't do it for more'n a hundred miles before he would be worn out." Fortunately, the trip to Memphis was only forty miles, even so it had been a physical workout for Johnson Tom to fly the plane alone like that. "That god damned prop kept windmilling, and that caused some of the damage to the engine. If I had had a little altitude, I probably could have stopped the prop by pulling up into a power off stall until the airstream was so slow it couldn't turn the engine any more. Once stopped, it probably wouldn't have started turning again." This was a slight admission that he should fly at higher altitudes cross country. The way to Memphis was table-top flat, and true to his style Johnson Tom always flew it at about two hundred, sometimes even lower. He had not had enough altitude to stall the plane to stop the propeller, and he didn't have enough reserve performance to climb much higher before he got there. Also, opening the throttles for a climb would have made the tendency to yaw to the right even worse, and he had all he could handle as it was.

It wasn't really a surprise to me. During the last three or four week ends, I had noticed we flew a little higher, maybe a hundred feet more than he had at earlier times.

By then we were at the hotel. Johnson Tom stopped and gets out and asks the desk clerk for Mr. Jergens, the owner. Johnson Tom had stayed here a number of times, and knew Mr Jergens. So did I, everyone in Woodton did. It was late in the afternoon and Mr. Jergens had left for the day. So Johnson Tom asked the evening clerk to call Mr. Jergens and tell him that he could have fifty bedspreads for fifty cents apiece. The clerk didn't want to, but a buck changed his mind. While he was making the call, we went back to the car and unloaded fifty spreads, and carried them into the lobby. It wasn't easy, three hundred bedspreads really fill up even a station wagon, and they were jammed in tight. Each was folded neatly and had a paper band about two inches wide fastened around it to add a little class and maybe to keep it from unfolding. The clerk came over and said, "Mr. Jergens will be over in fifteen minutes." "Figured he would," replied Johnson Tom.

Sure enough, in less than fifteen minutes, Mr. Jergens drove up and looked at the spreads, opened up about nine or ten to see where each was flawed and gave Johnson Tom twenty-five dollars. He saw the back of the station wagon still loaded down and asked if there were any more. Johnson Tom said, "Yeah, but they're all sold, you got the last ones. By the way, what's the name of the hotel owner over in Brink?" "Why, that is Joe Smithson, know him well." "Thanks," replied Johnson Tom, "I'm supposed to deliver fifty spreads to him tonight, and I forgot his name."

We left, and as soon as we were in the station wagon, he said, "The price was too low, we'll try seventy five cents in Brink."

We drove to the hotel in Brink and went in and Johnson Tom asked for Mr. Smithson. As we practically knew already, the night clerk said he wasn't there, and wouldn't be back until Monday morning. "Could you call 'im for me and tell 'im I have the fifty bed spreads for him at six bits apiece." Again it took a little money to grease the way, but this guy was an amateur, he made the call for a quarter. We went out to the car, laid out fifty more spreads and carried them into the lobby. The clerk came over and said Mr. Smithson would be right over, and sure enough in just a few minutes, a car drove up and a man who introduced himself as Joe Smithson got out and shook hands. After an inspection of three spreads, he gave Johnson Tom thirty-seven dollars and fifty cents. The name of the hotel owner in the next town was obtained as before, and we took off. "The price was still too low, we'll try a buck." This procedure was repeated at each town in turn until the owners began to dicker when the price got up to a dollar and seventy five cents. It looked like the spreads were really worth about $1.65 to $1.75 each in the market we were serving.

So we continued along like that all afternoon and into the night. Along the way, we sold 300 spreads for $332.50, but held out twenty five to use as samples the next day, so we actually delivered 275, and collected $300. The last hotel owner wouldn't pay us for the spreads not yet in his hands, taking the attitude that since he was a crook, why shouldn't we be. That's not the way most hotel owners are, I should say, but that was why we hadn't delivered them all, and why we had not been paid in full. Johnson Tom now had a third of his money back in a little over an afternoon, and still had 9700 spreads left to sell.

It now was about ten thirty and by that time we had arrived where we had been arrested only last week. "We'll knock off here. Let's see if the hotel has any rooms." It didn't, so we were faced with a sleepless and uncomfortable night. Johnson Tom made a call from the single phone booth and came out and said, "I found a place, but it can only take me. Call that humane society woman and see if she'll put you up." He got into the station wagon and disappeared into the night, with my bicycle on top.

Mrs. Wasserman purred into the phone, "You dear boy, you know I'll be right over to get you. We don't want to waste any time." In about ten minutes, she drove up and said, "Get in," and drove into the dark alley behind the hotel. "Here, now," she exclaimed. So, we here'd and now'ed right there. She had on a dress that buttoned all the way up the front and nothing else. It was all over in about a minute, she sat up and buttoned up and said, "Put your head on my lap so no one will see you." She then drove back to her place, avoiding the downtown area and taking the back streets with the poorer lights. We turned off the road into her lane, and she stopped the car, turned off the headlights and said, "Again." So, after a here, now, and again, we arrived at the house.

She then turned out the biggest supper I had ever seen, even bigger than last time. She was still mixed up about the time because she still called it dinner. I couldn't help noticing how pretty she was even if she was an old woman of thirty.

After a long blessing with the usual intonements about being forgiven for our sins, we tore into the meal. She told me more about herself. Mr. Wasserman was her third husband. She had married initially when she was 18 to a man about 40. He was quite well-off and bought her just about anything she wanted. After a couple of months, he unobligingly died in the middle of the night of a heart arrest. So, not yet 19, she was a wealthy widow.

She played it cool for a couple of years, fending off the young bucks that were after her bucks as well as her. At twenty, she had met a guy who had inherited some money of his own and after a very short courtship, they were married. Things went well for a couple of months, then he began to lose weight and became very irritable. Doctors could find nothing wrong with him except that he was run down. Finally, he hanged himself and again she was a widow, and now more wealthy than before. Mr. Wasserman was number three. He had no money, but he was a big strapping man and was as good looking as she was pretty, so they made a very handsome couple. He had disappeared after six months, and that was four years ago. Mrs. Wasserman just knew that he was alive somewhere, and would show up some day.

It was an interesting but wearing night. She fed me a big breakfast "to keep up your strength", and delivered me to the hotel. Johnson Tom also was delivered about the same time, but by a different girl than last week. This one was named Rachel. The two women looked at each other and left.

The station wagon was parked behind the hotel, I never did figure that out, and we continued our tour of hotels. When we got to Little Rock, he sold over 4000 bed spreads at about a dozen hotels and took in over $6,500. We didn't actually sell them all that week-end, but Johnson Tom did the following week. He grossed about $16,000, and paid off the note on the Ford, and gave me fifty dollars besides.

The overhaul shop did a good job and got the engine ready in 10 days. So we had missed only one weekend and then settled back into the routine.

Monk was becoming a true virtuoso in creating new exiting displays as he jumped from the Ford. He got so he would hand me the rope to fasten onto the seat, and when I made the end fast, he would yank on it a couple of times to test the truth of the tie, as though he knew that it was significant. Then he would back up to the left side of the cabin opposite the door, and wait for Johnson Tom to throttle back the engines. Monk would take a running start and go through the door in some new inimitable way. He seemed to enjoy it best when he could somersault backward after leaving the door. Of course, we played it up with the crowd so his jump truly was the high point of the day, because Monk had so much fun and the crowd could see just enough of it to want him to jump over and over again. We were not in business to have Monk make parachute jumps, but to sell rides in the airplane, so to the extent that Monk increased rides, to the same extent was he allowed to jump. Two, sometimes three a day was what seemed to be the point of maximum yield.

One day, after Monk had made maybe fifty jumps in all, we went up in the middle of the afternoon, and made the preparations as Johnson Tom circled to the jump point. Monk made his usual run to the door, but instead of jumping outward as he always had, he sprang upward in a swan dive like exit but with his feet widely spread, and his knees bent. Technique was not Monk's strong point, just exuberance.

Instinctively, I knew it was wrong, but before I could assemble any thoughts, I heard and felt the thump. I rushed to the door and looked back, and there was Monk, caught on the brace that ran from the lower side of the horizontal stabilizer down to the body near its lower edge. He was caught in an unnatural way, as though important things were mangled inside his body, and to make things worse, his parachute had been partially broken open by the impact and was beginning to stream out to the rear of the plane. All at once it did and in just an eyeblink it popped open, but instead of pulling Monk free, the parachute streamed out on one side of the brace with the lines passing around the front so that Monk was dangling on the other end.

The chute opened with a snap that shook the plane and shredded the canopy at the same time. With the tension of the lines thus relieved, the weight of Monk's body pulled the remnants of the shroud lines slowly from the brace. With me looking into his eyes as he grimaced in pain, he stretched out his arms toward me as the lines paid out to the end and then poor Monk fell away, turning and spinning slowly for the six seconds it took for him to fall the 300 feet to the ground. I watched him hit in a field, and there was no movement.

I was shaken from my daze by Johnson Tom's shout, "What th' hell was that bump?" I staggered to the cockpit, bursting into tears and blurted out, "Monk was just killed, he fell to the ground in that field." Johnson Tom put the Ford over in a steep bank so he could look and even though the chute had been shredded by the slip stream, there were enough remnants of it still attached to the shroud lines to show where Monk had fallen in a lot of weeds. Johnson Tom asked, "What happened, did he hit the stabilizer brace?" I nodded and he said, "I've got to get this thing on the ground, the stabilizer may be coming off right now." So he throttled back to reduce airspeed and circled toward the field and very gently let the plane down with as little movement of the elevators as possible. "We'll tell 'em we have to make a required inspection", said Johnson Tom as we taxied back. So he got out of the cockpit and made an announcement and started to get my bicycle out of the wing and somebody said, "It looked like the monkey's parachute didn't open," Johnson Tom bluffed it through, "Naw, it opened all right, it was just low that's all. The chimp got out of his harness and ran down the road, and my assistant here is going to go and get him."

Then to me he says, private-like, "Wrap him in his chute and try to bring him back."

I pedaled down the road, it was only about a mile to where Monk had hit, and laying my bicycle down off the road where it was out of sight, I went into the field to look for him in chest-high weeds. It took a long time, I walked up and down trying not to leave any part unsearched, and was about to believe that I was in the wrong field when a car drives up and Johnson Tom gets out but dressed in a pair of coveralls he used when we had to work on the plane. "Gaylord, move a little that way," he indicated with a shout. As he came out through he weeds we both got to Monk at the same time.'

There wasn't too much left. Monk was smashed to where you wouldn't know it was a chimpanzee almost. "I think we had better bury him right here," he said. "There's not any point trying to pick 'im up." So we did, but first I pedaled back to the plane to get the small spade that we had added to our tool kit. I noticed everybody was gone even though it was still time to fly some more. "Yeah, I sent 'em home before I came looking for you. The stabilizer brace is bent and will have to be replaced."

We were quiet while we walked slowly back to the plane. I couldn't help crying. Johnson Tom was upset too but he didn't cry. Maybe he had while I was gone. "I can repair the brace enough to fly back, but it will have to be replaced before I can get the airworthiness certificate validated again. Do you want to go back home on the train, or do you want to fly back with me tomorrow?" I chose to fly back because I would get home about the same time, anyway, and I wanted to see how he was going to fix the Ford.

Nothing was said as we started to work on the plane. Johnson Tom actually did all the work, but there really wasn't that much to it. He removed the brace completely from the plane by removing some bolts that secured it to the body on one end and to a kind of ball joint on the stabilizer end. "We'll get a blacksmith shop to make a copy of this out of steel tomorrow. It won't be pretty, and it will be heavy, but it will do until I can get it to Memphis for permanent repairs. Trouble is, they haven't made any models of this airplane since 1932, and I don't know where in hell I'll find another brace. Here, you better call your folks so they won't be worried."

We did all that and he got me back to Woodton late on Monday. I had missed a day at school, and I had about a million chiggers and five ticks from stomping through all those weeds.

As it turned out, the Ford was out of action for four weeks. Johnson Tom couldn't find another brace, so he finally had to have one made. Again, it wasn't that hard to do, the big part was in finding the same material that was used originally, and in getting it approved by the airworthiness inspector. He finally got it done, and while he was doing it, I had to catch up on some of my Scout work. Dad was beginning to push me because it had been almost twelve months since I had passed my Star requirements seven months after First Class, but it took a year to get my Life. Both he and I wanted me to go for Eagle. Also, I had to look for a job.

CHAPTER XVII

With the tri-motor out of action, my source of money dried up and I soon found I needed a temporary job if I was to preserve my savings. With Dad's approval, given without much fuss this time, I went back to the pool hall and asked Mr. Williams about employment.

"Why, Gaylord, you jest up and left me before, after all I did for you, you just plain left me in the lurch, you can't expect to come back whenever it just suits you. I got feelin's too you know...." This continued for several minutes, becoming a real tirade while he got his jollies off telling me just how low down and no account I was. I just listened him out, I figured when he was through he would let me work there again, in particular because he wasn't paying me anything. It almost turned out that way, but not quite. "I tell you what, you show up on...." this statement was interrupted by the telephone ringing and after the usual "Hallo, Dick's pool room." He listened for a minute and said, "Now, I thank you kindly, Mrs. Taylor, and when can Johnnie start? Yes, ma'am, that will be fine. Bye, now."

He turned back to me and said, "Like I was saying, you don't just show up and want to come back to me after leaving me like that, that just don't set right with me. Now that was Mrs. Taylor, fine woman, now she has been wanting me to let her boy Johnnie work here for near on to six months, but I haven't done it because I told her he would have to change his ways a little first, which she just now told me he has done, so Johnnie is gonna start here tomorrow. That's the way it is Gaylord, you can't just up and leave...." Fortunately, the phone rang again so I was able to slip out before he could return to his lecture.

Jobs were scarce, and I couldn't think of another opportunity right off. The drug stores hired boys to deliver prescriptions to homes, but it was necessary to have a driver's license to qualify. Although I had been driving since I was fourteen on back roads and away from the main traffic, and others did too, it was illegal. The police wouldn't bother you as long as you got into no trouble or didn't drive like you were about to get into some. An awful lot depended on whether you were thought to be a "good" boy or not, a good boy could do things that questionable ones could not, as long as no complaints resulted. The status of good was voided instantly when problems started. The drug stores couldn't depend upon such hazy definitions, they needed someone who could go anywhere in town anytime without worrying whether the police would stop them. I wasn't yet old enough to get my driver's license, so these limited opportunities had to wait.

The grocery stores had stock boys, but all of these jobs were filled and had a long list of applicants. The owners never felt they had to hire in the order of application, but as they saw the plight of the individual. The son of a needy family was much more likely to get the next opening than one from a family with more means. That let me out, we weren't rich by a long shot, but many had a lot less than we did.

I was mulling my fate when I happened to pass one of the drug stores and noticed a member of my patrol inside playing the pinball machine. This was Jim Dody, so I wandered inside and said, "Hidy, Jim." and he returns my hidy, and I watch him play the machine for awhile. He was really pretty good at it, and he ran up large scores regularly. These machines rewarded the player with free games so that a good player could literally play all day with little more than the initial five-cent coin.

Most people didn't win anything so these pinball machines were a lucrative addition to any store, and in some cases were said to make more money than the rest of the store combined. Of course, not much money was coming in when an ace like Jim Dody was hogging the machine, so most of the store owners who had pinball machines would pay off on the games if someone else wanted to play. The rules varied with the establishment, but the usual arrangement was that you could play up to about ten free games, any left unplayed at that time would be paid off at the rate of a nickel for two games. For an odd number, a nickel would be given for the last game, so that with five games left, the player would receive fifteen cents. This scheme was intended to encourage other players, because, like I said, most people did not win any free games or very many if they did, so it was the new blood at the table that kept the cash dropping into the hopper.

In reality, all of this was supposed to be for the adults, because playing pinball was considered to be gambling, and minors were not supposed to be exposed to gambling in any form. As you might guess, there was a fair distance between what we were supposed to see and what we saw, and this is just one such example.

Most storeowners would let the teen-aged kids play the machines if no adults were in the store or, if some were there and none wanted to play. Absent such adults, a kid's nickel was as good as any one's.

The problem arose when a kid began to get good. Most kids had a lot more time to spend than anything else so on an afternoon after school, a pinball whiz could tie up a machine for the rest of the day. The dilemma of the store-owner was that he couldn't just all at once forbid a kid from playing, because the owner was party to some fairly serious law breaking by letting him play in the first place. The kids knew that and could easily find ways to get back at the owner. It was extremely rare, in fact it happened only once, but one kid broke a window at night and told the owner he knew who did it. The owner thought he did too, but there was nothing to make an arrest on, so the owner knew he either had to stop all the kids or let that particular one play. So most of the owners paid the kids not to play any more and accepted this as being one of the expenses of doing business, while hoping not too many kids would get too good. I should add, this was before the tilt feature was made as sensitive as it is today. The tables could be jiggled quite a bit before the game was cancelled.

So Jim Dody had been playing for quite a while and Mr. Ferguson, the owner, considered me as potential fresh meat. He was about to run Jim off, after paying off of course, so he could encourage me to take the plunge into pinball addiction. I really had not played them much before, maybe five or six games total, but he had just paid Jim a dollar to stop playing. A dollar! That had to be forty games that Jim had won. Jim verified my count. "Yeah, I been taking in a buck, sometimes two every week now for a couple of months. This ain't the only machine I use. I try to keep spread out so no body turns me in".

I wondered if I could do the same thing and sat down to take stock. I began by counting up in my head all the places with pinball machines, then I had to get a pencil and paper so I wouldn't lose count. There was hardly a business in town other than women's shops that didn't have a pinball machine, and a lot of them had two, some even had three. For my purposes, extra machines didn't help, so I tried to tabulate only the locations of machines, period, without worrying about how many they had. I just couldn't believe what I had learned. According to my list, and I knew I had missed a lot, there were more than forty locations with machines. Some of these places were not the best to test your luck, because the clientele was pretty rough, but after the pool hall, I figured I was ready for almost anything.

Without revealing what I had just found out, I sought out Jim Dody again, and real casual-like asked how long it had taken him to get good playing the machines. "Oh, not too long, I didn't really think about it, I just found out I had a knack for them and after a couple of weeks I was winning money regular." How many games was that, would you say?" was the next very casual question. "Hell, I don't know.." we were beginning to use the forbidden words now in conversations among our peers, but the words didn't come out right because we weren't men enough to carry it off, but we thought we sounded tough. "Hell, I guess a hunnert games maybe."

Assuming he was half way right and no games were won during the training period, that would be five dollars committed to the prospect that I could make money playing pinball machines. I had the five dollars, that wasn't the problem, the hurdle was whether I would be wise in doing it, and what was the likelihood that I might not pull it off. Then I got to thinking about Johnson Tom. He had paid five thousand dollars for the Ford, knowing only that he had the ability to use it to take in several hundred dollars a week. He had spent a thousand dollars on those bedspreads, knowing only that they were worth a lot more than that. It seemed like the adults did this sort of thing all the time.

The more I thought about it, the more it seemed to me that businesses in general were just grown up examples of what I was thinking, but with a more acceptable reputation, maybe. What would be wrong with a kid trying it? Somehow, I had to talk to Dad about it, but I knew he would veto any suggestion of making money by gambling.

So finally I asked Dad, "What's it called when somebody goes into business, I mean how does anyone get into a business?" "Well, they have to think pretty strongly that they can sell whatever it is they want to make and then they have to find out what it will cost to start up the machinery or whatever it is, and then they invest the money by getting the machinery or whatever it is, and they start with a lot of advertising, and then they hope the customers will buy enough to make it all worth while."

Invest. That was the word. What did invest mean? I looked it up. "to use money for the purchase of stocks, property, etc with the expectation of future profit or income."

I went back to Dad. "Were all these businesses in town once small?" "Son, at one time the biggest business in the world was just one person wondering if he or she had enough money to risk to try to set up a business that might make them a lot of money." Risk! Then I realized that "invest" just means "risk".

"Don't they know whether they will make money or not?" "Absolutely not. If they did, the world would be full of successful businesses, because no one would try one that wouldn't make money. In actual fact, most businesses don't make it." That was a surprise to me, but I had picked up a clue. Businesses were started by someone who had some money from somewhere—WHERE?—who bought some stuff to start a business, hoping they would make a lot more money. Two new questions popped up. "What is gambling, and where did that money come from that people used to start a business?"

Dad answered the second question first, "Oh, they saved it, or inherited it from a rich uncle. Somebody had to save it. Now for gambling, that's where you risk something of value, money usually, hoping to win some more." My next question was loaded, "Dad, what's the difference between gambling and starting a business?" Dad looked surprised, "When you come right down to it, none. Outright gambling is not as respectable as starting a business, but in the end, there is no difference at all."

So I could take five dollars that I had saved and invest it in stocks, property, etc with the expectation of making a future income. Everything fitted perfectly, except that I would be investing in some etc, what ever that might be, rather than stocks, whatever those were. What would I be investing in?

I thought about it for a while, and finally hit on the word SKILL. I would invest my five dollars in a skill. But first, back to Dad. Were businesses ever started on skills alone? "Sure, all doctors have is a skill and a knowledge most people don't have, same thing with baseball players, musicians, and dancers. A lot of jobs are gotten because the person developed some skill." Dad didn't question me about all my questions, but he knew I was up to something. Everything now fitted. I would go into the business of playing pinball machines for money.

First, I had to plan my route. I didn't want to go in any one place too often, yet I wanted to be seen there enough that I wouldn't seem to be a stranger. If I just went in and started to play the machines, I might be run off, so I always had to buy something first. If it was a restaurant, I had to buy a doughnut or something to eat. I really had no real business in a beer joint, but I could buy some chewing gum or make some small purchase. Beer joints sold a lot of chewing gum because the customers thought this masked the beer from their breaths, so it wasn't too far out for a teen-ager to buy gum in one of them.

I figured that I could go to at most three places in one afternoon after school, and to four or five on Saturdays. That was better than nineteen locations, so I picked out the best 19 of the 40 or more places I knew about and worked out my program and spending budget. A nickel for a purchase at each of them used up ninety five cents of my five dollars of capital before I played my first game, but that was the plan.

So the first week I made the rounds and established my presence, 95 cents gone, and I had a drawer full of chewing gum. The second week I started over and played five cents in a machine at each location. I actually won eight games in one of the beer joints and was paid off because a police car drove up and Chief Robinson came in. He looked a little surprised to see me but just said "Hi, there Gaylord." I answered "Hi," and sweated a little to see if he was going to send his regards to my parents. He didn't, so I left.

Down 95 cents, won 20 cents, net 75 cents, less the 95 cents from last week, so I now had a dollar and seventy cents in my training. Third week, I broke even. I actually won as much as I spent. Even though it was not in my budget. I bought a doughnut and a cup of coffee to celebrate, I didn't feel quite right about it, but I added the cost of the refreshments to my total investment so that the amount now was a dollar eighty-five. Next week, I won ninety cents, so I was still 95 cents down. That was only a paid game or two in each location, I believe five was the most that I paid for anywhere, so no one was getting too upset about anything.

The only problem lies in those places where no other customers were in so the owner would just let me play out my games rather than pay. This took more time, but of course, my skill was improving all the time.

One Saturday, it was raining, and no customers were about so the owner saw no reason to pay me off. I continued playing and in about an hour I had won the maximum number of games that the machine would give, an even one hundred. I didn't want to play there any more, because I was doing this strictly for the money, and I could go no further on this particular machine.

So, I asked Big Red the owner for my money. He first was surprised, then evasive, then threatening. No one before had ever won a hundred games, so he claimed I had rigged the machine. Naturally, I denied it because there was no way that I could do such a thing. I knew nothing of the workings of these devices, and couldn't have altered any part of the inherent process if I had wanted to. Everyone jiggled and beat on the sides trying to make the ball roll where they wanted it, but that was discouraged by the crude and sometimes unpredictable tilt mechanisms. But Red insisted that I had not played fairly.

"Tell ya what, you win another hunnert games and I'll pay you for both." I asked if he was going to furnish the coin, "Hell, no you smart-assed kid, I made you a fair proposition. If you think yer good enough, you show how you got a hunnert games outta this here pinball machine while I watch." He was betting double or nothing, and all I had to do was risk five cents. I figured I could win another hundred games in another fifteen minutes.

So I plugged in a nickel and started. As luck would have it, and with Big Red standing right there, I won a hundred games on that one coin. Well, Red now owed me for two hundred games, that would be five dollars, if I could get him to pay me. It really was a combination of knowing the playing characteristics of that particular machine and some luck.

Well, Big Red had seen nothing like that before, so he began to crawfish,

"You jiggled it too much, it should have tilted back there." I argued that since it didn't, it was ok, but Big Red wasn't going to give in easily, "You show me that wasn't a fluke. You show me how many games you can win with a quarter's worth of nickels. Here, I'll furnish the nickels, but you hafta pay me back."

Big Red shoves in a five center, and I didn't do so good that time, I only got ten games. I could see the smirk on Big Red's face as I inserted the second coin. He was sure his suspicions were about to be corroborated, but that time I won sixty games, so now he was down two hundred and seventy games. Next coin, only thirty games. With an expression that showed he didn't know whether to laugh or to cry, he said with a guffaw, "See I knew nobody could win a hunnert games and do it legal like." Legal like or not, he owed me for three hundred games. I won fifty games on each of the last two try's so I now should be paid off for four hundred games, or ten dollars in all.

Big Red really began to squirm, he wasn't going to let go of ten dollars if he could help it, he knew he couldn't go to the police, but the code of the business world demanded that he pay me off. The word could get around if he didn't, and he knew it. There wasn't much credit in those days, everything being cash on the barrelhead, but he knew his deliveries would be slow and he would get the less choice selections of meat and the beer bottles with the dented caps, so he was in a spot.

Another customer came in while all this was going on, but neither Big Red nor I had noticed him. He stood back a little but he could see the play. When Red began to make excuses, this customer came into the scene. It turned out he was huge, I would guess he was six five and probably weighed close to three hundred pounds, but there was no fat of any consequence on him. He was just big, and looked it. He held a cup and a saucer left on the counter by an earlier customer, not yet cleaned off by Big Red. This was in itself an indication of his agitation, because whatever Big Red lacked in other admirable personal characteristics, cleanliness was not among them. Ordinarily, he kept the place straightened up and shining.

Anyway, the big fellow sort of slammed the cup and saucer down on the glass top of the pin ball machine and said, "Sonnava gun, I might've busted that glass. Sorry there Red. Say, I think you oughta pay 'im, whatta ya say?"

MONKEYS AND MERIT BADGES

The message was clear, so Big Red says quick like, "Oh, sure, Bull, I was gonna pay 'im. I don't know why you thought I wasn't." "I don't know either Big Red, I just sort of thought you might be thinkin' that."

Big Red goes behind the counter to wait on Bull, who just wants a cup of coffee, then Big Red comes back. He wasn't ready to give in yet. "Tell ya what, Kid, I got a Model "A" Ford a-settin' in the back. I still owe seven fifty on it (he meant seven dollars and fifty cents), I'll let you have it if we call it square, and if you don't come back." Now, this was about as unexpected as anything could be. Not in a million years that morning would I have thought that I would even be in grasping distance of buying a car by that afternoon.

Essentially, the deal being offered was that if I would take over the payments of two dollars a month, I could have the car, if the bank didn't mind. In effect, I was giving Big Red ten dollars for what he had in it, and was taking on the obligation of paying off seven fifty to the bank. Incidentally, there were a lot of bank loans in those days for ten or fifteen dollars being paid off at a dollar or two a month, so there was nothing unusual about this sort of thing. I asked Big Red what the car had cost him. " Oh, I paid twenty dollars for it," was his reply. I knew you could get a Model A Ford for twenty or twenty five dollars, so Big Red was telling it reasonably straight. I would have to talk to Dad.

"You can get a Model "A" for seven fifty? What would you do, take out a note at the bank?" I didn't know the details. "What does Chief Robinson think about this? It's one thing to drive our car around town a little bit without a license, everybody your age is doing that, but if you owned a car, I think the Chief would want to see a license. Let's see, you'll be sixteen in about three months. Maybe the Chief wouldn't mind if the car wasn't driven any more than ours has been. Maybe you had better talk to him."

So I hunted up the Chief. "Now, Gaylord, I am an officer of the law, and I'm sworn to uphold the law. What you are asking me is would I would let you drive around in a car I knew you owned even though you are a minor, when I also knew you didn't have a driver's license. Now, just what do you think my answer has to be?" I knew already.

The Chief changed the subject. "Hear yer gittin' close to earning your

Eagle Scout badge, is that right?"

"Yessir, almost," was all I could answer because all I could think of was that Model "A".

The Chief droned on, "Heard you was making close to straight A's out there at that high school, is that right?"

Again, I could think of nothing but the car, but managed a weak, "Yessir."

The Chief kept on, "Maybe I would like to know just what the high school kids are learning these days..." so he asked me a lot of questions about the shape and colors of stop signs and other road markers, and why we didn't park too close to a fire hydrant. Then he asked me if I knew what happened to bridges sometimes in the winter, and I said they sometimes iced over, and he said what would a good citizen do if he or she saw or was involved in an accident and I said call the police and try to help out if anyone was hurt. Then he says, "Gaylord, can you read that there sign over there on the wall, and I did, and he says, "Gaylord, I don't do this very often, but I'm gonna give you a kind of a learner's permit. Now, I want you to understand, it's good only here in town, so stay off the highways. And you can't carry anyone with you unless they have a good driver's license. Also, I don't ever want to see you skylarking around in any car, I want you to be going somewhere on some real business, not just circlin' the block trying to impress some girl. An' Gaylord, this learner's permit is automatically void if you ever have an accident or get a ticket for any reason, and if your grades don't stay hiked up there. "Spec you better let me look at your report card, no you are almost an Eagle Scout, you come and tell me if any grade is not up to snuff. And speaking of Eagle Scouts, I'm expectin' you to get that there badge." He filled out a mimeographed form which said it was a learner's permit. Where it said "date of birth," he filled it in one year early, and it said in hand writing "must be renewed on ..." and he had listed my real birthday. The last words were "Void if Chief Robinson says so."

As I left, he said, "Sorry you asked me that question, Gaylord, but you know I can't tell you can drive your own car when you don't have a driver's license." I didn't appreciate it at the time, but I know now he was a good cop.

When I got home, the Model "A" was parked in front of the house! There was a note under the windshield wiper,

Gaylord,

I talked to the bank, they said it was ok if you took over the payments. Just sign this paper, and bring it back to me.

Big Red

I looked at the paper, it was something from the Bank of Arkansas downtown, and it had a lot of fine print, but it had some blanks that were filled in with a typewriter. I really didn't know what to make of it, so I waited until Dad got home. "This is a note to the bank, it says you owe the bank seven dollars and fifty cents, and that you are going to pay them two dollars a month for four months, and that you will still owe them fifty cents besides that. It has been co-signed by Big Red." I said, "if I owe seven fifty, why am I going to pay them eight fifty?"

"That's for the interest and for the service fee to write this up. You don't have a credit rating, so the interest rate is higher than if you had borrowed money before and paid it off on time."

"What's it mean that Big Red is co-signer?"

"If you fail to pay, he will have to, and I'm pretty sure he would get title to the car if that happened. The best thing for him would be for you to default—that means you failed to make the payment—on the last one due. He would get to keep the car even though you had almost paid it out."

I didn't know about all this. It looked like I was getting into something I didn't know about. So Dad says, "I'm not going to tell you what to do. But think about this, is the price a good one, Can you expect to pay back the money, and if you failed, can you take the loss? In this case, it would be the money you had already paid, and the further use of the car. Also, Gaylord, I talked to Chief Robinson, and I know what he did. He went out on a limb there for you, and I don't want you to let him down."

I thought about it for awhile, if the tri-motor got fixed up, I could pay off the note easily. If it didn't, I could pay for it if I stayed in the pinball business. If both of these failed, I almost could pay it off with my savings, about seven dollars. Of course, I had other things in mind for the money I had saved, but I was considering the worst case, or so I thought.

I decided to sign. I took the paper down to Big Red and signed it in front of him and he said he would take it down to the bank and he gave me the keys. I went sailing home to take a ride in my car. My very own car.

Now, a Model "A" Ford required a little technique to start. Everything was manual, that is the spark advance and choke, so it was up to the driver to know just how to adjust these things. The spark advance was a lever on the left side of the steering wheel, in much the same position as a turn signal on modern cars, except that it had a friction adjustment of sorts that caused the lever to stay in the position where it was placed. Like I said, that was the spark advance, and up meant retard, and down was advance. On the other side of the wheel post was a similar lever, with a corresponding friction arrangement, and this was the hand throttle. Like the spark, the throttle was advanced when pulled down. There also was a throttle on the floor, but it always was called the "accelerator". Either one could be used to control the speed, but the accelerator didn't have a friction adjustment. So when you took your foot off, the engine slowed immediately.

Over towards the right, about midway, was a knob-ended rod mounted at about 45^0 that disappeared into the firewall down near the feet below. This assembly could be pulled out maybe an inch and a half, and it returned to its normal position by gravity. This was the choke.

To start, the ignition was turned on by the key right in the middle of the instrument panel which itself was in the center of the car, not in front of the driver. The spark was retarded to a position where experience indicated was best for a day with temperature and humidity about like this, the left hand reached through the right side of the steering wheel and pulled down on the hand throttle to feed a little gas, and the right hand went over to the middle just under the dash to pull out the choke. The starter button on the floor was pressed with the foot, and if every thing was done skillfully, which is not the same thing as being done properly, because everyone of these little beasts had its own little private variation on the proper way, but if everything worked right, the thing would start right up with a noise and vibration that only a Model "A" owner will remember and love.

Quickly, the spark was adjusted to the position thought best as indicated by past encounters of the third kind, and the hand throttle was eased back to normal position while the throttling function was taken over by the right foot on the floor accelerator pedal.

I knew all about starting Model "A" Fords, or thought I did. The Ford didn't though, it wouldn't start. It turned over vigorously enough, but it wouldn't even hit. Everything looked fairly normal under the hood, but looking under the hood never started any car.

While I was looking (just in case this might be the exception), little Jimmie Downs, maybe five, who lived a couple of doors away came up and said, "Gaylord, why did the man push the car here with the truck?"
"What man, Jimmie, tell me about it?"
"Oh, a man in a truck pushed this car, and a man sat in this car and made it go straight." A number of thoughts formed from innocent and isolated pieces that had found residence in the backwaters of my brain. I didn't know what to tell Dad.

"Well, Son, looks to me like you should talk to Big Red," was Dad's comment. So I confronted Big Red, who kind of passed it off, "Oh, yeah Gaylord, I forgot to tell you, it has been a little hard to start here lately, but you ought to be able to fix that up without any trouble at all."

The bank was no help either, "Gaylord, we really don't care what you borrowed the money for, all we care is that you pay us on time. If the car won't run, you will have to work that out with Big Red Williams. By the way, is your name really Gaylord Throckmorton Montmorency?" He had to read it off the note, he couldn't even remember what it was, but he remembered to ask about it.

I was thinking about getting a merit badge in Automobiling, which stressed maintenance and repair, and it looked like I was going to earn it. It turned out I did. The car had a burned out spark coil, which I replaced, and then it would at least run but not very well. Over the next two or three weeks, I tuned the engine, but could not do a very good job because one cylinder refused to hit properly. No, that is not right, it would not fire at all. Finally, Dad brought home a compression gauge which he borrowed, and we found that number two cylinder had no compression at all. None. I pulled the head off, and found that the exhaust valve spring was broken and the valve wouldn't close. While I was at it, I reground all the valves, and replaced several valve springs and two valves. So far, I had not driven the car one inch.

While working on the engine, the left rear tire went flat, and I found that the spare tire mounted on the rear was flat also, and very likely to remain that way. It had no tube in it and on the lower side of the tire where it wouldn't be noticed unless you took it off was a slit about three inches long in the tire casing. The one that went flat wasn't much better than the spare, so I needed one tire for sure, if I could get by without a spare. Upon closer inspection of the rolling wheels, I decided I needed two. Dad thought I needed three, and the fourth was on the "maybe it will last until payday" list. I got two of the tires, with plans for the third, if I could swing it.

With the worst of the tires replaced, I started the engine to take a ride, got about a car length, when a water hose burst. A closer look showed all of the hoses were paying interest on time. All were replaced with another three weeks gone while I assembled the money and the parts.

With new hoses at last, I started the engine to take a ride. I had just gotten it going when Mother called me from the house and I went inside for a minute and left the engine running, and when I got back outside I found the engine boiling over. I got it turned off and after it cooled off I restarted it several times and it would start to boil within five or six minutes. I checked everything I knew but my skills were too limited to find the trouble.

Probably the water pump was the most common opinion I got, so I obtained a used one and replaced the water pump. The car still boiled over within five minutes of starting, if anything it was worse. I received the advice it might be the radiator, so I pulled the radiator, and had it rodded out. It was a little dirty, but not nearly as bad as the symptoms of the car indicated. Put back the radiator, still boiled over. We now are in the third month, and I have not moved the car more than 30 feet from its original position in front of the house. Mother was beginning to get upset about this car in front of the house with all he parts removed. She was urging me to get it fixed or move it or something. I needed no urging, I was working as the limit of my resources in time and money to buy and replace all these parts, not to mentions the various repairs.

I was late on my bank payment on the third month, and the bank sent me a stiff warning that if it happened again, they would ask the co-signer to make the payment. I really had to scrape to make that payment, because my work was mostly on the car and it wasn't bringing in any money.

Fourth month. The engine would boil over within ten minutes of starting up cold, and would boil out a gallon of water in about fifteen minutes. Clearly not a roadworthy car. I couldn't use a car that wouldn't run as evidence of my Automobiling skills, but I was baffled. I had read everything I could find on the subject, which was not all that much, because this was long before the days when all sorts of do-it-yourself books were around.

I was describing the symptoms to somebody, and a third party overhearing said, "That has got to be a leaking head gasket. Pull off the head and see if you can find a place where a combustion chamber is leaking into a water cavity. It will be a fine line, maybe as thick as a pencil mark." That did it. After pulling the head, I found a thin line just like the man said connecting one cylinder and a water chamber. After replacing the head and the gasket, it ran normally. I had not retightened the head bolts the first time I had removed the head to work on the valves, and this caused the problem.

I was tightening up the head after running the engine when I suddenly remembered I had to make the payment on the note. Two dollars. I went skipping into the house, and found to my dismay and horror that I had only a dollar and a half, and worse, the note was due three days ago. Where had the time gone? I was scrounging around in my clothes drawers to see if somehow I had overlooked a few coins and came up dry. I didn't know whether to go to Dad or not, I knew the bank would offer me no leniency because of the overdue payment last time. While I was trying to think out my next step, the door bell rang and there stood Big Red!

"Gaylord, you just missed your payment at the bank again and they told me I had to pay up as co-signer, so I did and here's the receipt. I came to get the car like we agreed." He turned around and walked over to the Model "A", got in and turned the key which I had left in the ignition, and it started up as sweet as pie, and he drove off. It ran like a top. I had not driven it more than a hundred feet.

When I told Dad, he thought about it for a while and said, "Gaylord, your enthusiasm for a project of the moment caused you to lose touch with the world around you. Your lesson here is that the world keeps on turning and the clock keeps on ticking even when you are distracted by something. The other lesson I thought you would learn but in an easier way was that when it comes to automobiles and a lot of other things, it's not the initial cost that counts, it's the upkeep."

Things were not quite over with the Model "A". A couple of days later, I got a letter from Mr. Spooner, the President of the Bank. Mr. Spooner was a very kindly man who had lots of friends, and he had three earned doctorates and probably a dozen honorary ones. In the letter, he said I should come to see him.

Not knowing just what was up, I went down town to his office. I was shown in, and he came right to the point. "Gaylord, you defaulted on a note to this bank, and it will affect your credit rating for a long time if we don't do something about it, because we are required by law to fill out a report to the banking commission about these things. You are in the Scout troop and we can't have our Scouts going around with a bad credit rating, particularly when they are in line to make Eagle so this is what we are going to do. I want you to sign this note for ten dollars; that means we are lending you ten dollars this time, you are to pay it back two dollars a month for five months, and the interest and fee are going to be fifty cents. I can set that anywhere I want to, and I think that is about right. Now, you are going to deposit the ten dollars you have just borrowed in a savings account in this bank, and you are going to receive two per cent interest. That's not enough to pay the interest on the note, but it will help. Now each month, you draw out two dollars and pay off that much of this note. Notice that this is dated a couple of days before your last note was due, so on paper we loaned you this money before you defaulted. As soon as you pay this off, you are going to do it again, but next time it will be for fifteen dollars. With two good loans paid off like that, it will wipe out any black marks from your first loan here, and we can give you a good reference if you need to borrow money anywhere else. Now get out of here, Gaylord, I've got a lot of work to do."

It seemed to me that a lot of people thought being an Eagle Scout was pretty special, so I decided that maybe I had better get on with it.

X X X X X

The "phony war" ended in Europe when Germany suddenly overran Belgium in May of 1940, with Belgium surrendering on May 28. The withdrawal of the British armies and some of the French from Dunkirk peaked on May 30, followed by the surrender of France on June 22.

In the United States, the army conducted maneuvers and the Congress authorized a military draft. Blindfolded, Secretary of War Henry L. Simpson drew numbers from a hat on October 29 to start the proceedings, and the first draftees were entering service by mid November.

CHAPTER XVIII

Like I said, I already had passed my Star and Life badges, and Eagle was next. Each of these ranks were gained by an increasing number of merit badges from a list of 108 covering subjects from Agriculture to Zoology. Backing up to Star, the Scout needed three months of satisfactory service as a First Class, and any five merit badges from the list. To make Life, he had to have three months of satisfactory service as Star, and he needed five more badges for 10 in all. Five of these ware mandatory these being in First Aid, Physical Development or Athletics, Personal Health, Public Health, and Life Saving or Pioneering, or Safety. For Eagle, he needed six satisfactory months in as a Life and 21 badges, 13 being required and 8 elective. The required ones included the five mandatory ones already won in making Life, but he had to pick up the remaining two from the triplet of Life Saving, Pioneering or Safety so that he had all three. Then he also had to pass the requirements of Cooking, Camping, Civics, Bird Study, Pathfinding, and Swimming. He could pick any that he wished for the remaining eight. The two required badges of Pioneering and Pathfinding offer a fair sample of what the Scout was up against when completing some of these requirements.

Take Pathfinding. Among a lot of other things he had to do, the Scout could choose between making a boat that could support two Scouts and their gear or 200 pounds, or show how to load a pack animal for a trip in the wilderness. Lacking a real pack animal, and absolutely nobody had ever even seen a pack animal much less had the use of one, the Scout could demonstrate how to load a dummy animal made of saw horses or something similar. Boats always had interested me, and I had no problem keeping my passions for pack animals under control, so a boat it was to be. Besides, no other Scout in Woodton had ever made a boat.

At first, my thoughts visualized a craft with a sleek pointed prow and gently curving lines, varnished decks, polished brass gleaming in the sun, cutting through the water at high speed. This ideal was hard to dismiss, but as I began to think about it and to understand what was involved in the construction of a boat, realism began to set in as I slowly sorted out the difference between "desirements" and "requirements". In time, I realized that my objective was to come up with something that would merely float, would support 200 pounds while doing it, and could be paddled some reasonable but undefined distance. Anything beyond that would be to the good so to speak, but not needed in winning the badge.

It was necessary to build this boat from a knowledge and technology base of zero. While thinking of the form of the boat, I realized that I had no idea just how big it had to be. I touched base with Dad, who stated simply, "Son, anything that floats has to sink into the water enough to move aside or displace a volume of water equal to its own weight. A gallon of water weighs eight pounds, you want to hold up 200. Your boat will displace 200 divided by 8, or 25 gallons of water. Think you can take it from there?"

That was a good start! I found a five-gallon can and imagined five of these as being the amount my boat would sink into the water. It really wasn't too big, so I decided that maybe six feet long might be about right. A very simple structure began to coalesce in my mind. Two boards, six feet long and sawed off at a 45° angle on one end would form the sides. A piece of corrugated galvanized roofing iron —or "tin", as we called it— would become the bottom and ends.

I mentioned my design to Skinny, who became enthusiastic. Next day, he was at my house with two boards laid over the handlebars and seat of his bicycle. He had walked his bike with this load on it the mile and a half from his house to mine, and said he had a piece of roofing tin but I would have to help him carry it. So we rode double on his bike to his house, got the metal sheet, walked and carried it back to my place, fighting it all the way because it was four feet by eight feet and a stiff wind was blowing. Then I rode him double on my bike to his house for his bicycle, and we both rode back to mine.

The boards turned out to be 8 feet long and 10 inches wide, a little longer than needed, but otherwise perfect. The roofing tin also was 8 feet long and it was to be folded up around the ends, but it was obvious that the metal would not wrap up to cover the ends unless the boards were shortened, but the question was how much could be cut off to use all the length of the sheet metal and still have the longest possible boat.

I was taking first year algebra, and wondering why. While thinking about the boat during an algebra session in school, I suddenly realized this was like some of the problems that filled the algebra book. I could hardly wait to try my luck with my own problem.

I sketched out a profile showing the side of the boat with a 45° on one end and cut square on the other, like this:

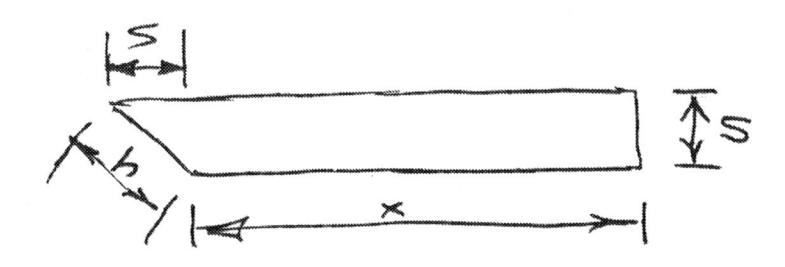

After a number of false starts and followed by a series of attempts that begin to show I was on the right track, I formulated an equation. The length of the sheet iron was eight feet, as was the sum of the three lengths representing the ends and the flat bottom. Haltingly, and not too sure where this would come out, I wrote

Length of iron = h + x + s = 8 feet = 96 inches and s = 10 inches

So far, so good. From geometry, which I also was taking, I knew the hypotenuse of an isosceles right triangle is the square root of 2 (or 1.414), times the length of the legs. In my sketch the legs were the same as the width of the board, or 10 inches, the hypotenuse would be the sloping end and that would be 10 x 1.414, or 14.14 inches.

So, quickly because I could see it was going right.

Length of iron = 14.14 + x + 10 = 96

x = 96 - 14.14 - 10

= 71.86 inches

How about that? I couldn't wait to write down how long the boat would be, but I could see the answer

Length of boat = x + 10

= 81.86 inches

I was genuinely thrilled. I thought a $30°$ might be more rakish and faster looking, so I calculated it too. After the initial experience, the answer just fell out. Again using geometry, the hypotenuse of a $30°$-$60°$-$90°$ triangle is twice the short leg, which was 10 inches, and the long leg is square root of 3 (or 1.732..) times the short leg. The equations of the boat then were

Length of iron = 96 = 2s + x + s

= 20 + x + 10

x = 96 - 30

= 66 inches

and

Length of boat = s$\sqrt{3}$ + x

= 17.3 + 66

= 83.3 inches

Son of a gun! Later, much later, I learned this is called a "parametric study" in which dimensions that will be fixed in the ultimate design are altered to see what the effect will be on the final form and performance.

That little problem opened my eyes to algebra, and thereafter it took on a new meaning. I can say that from that day to this there seldom has been a day that I have not used algebra for something. It has been the second most useful thing I have ever learned, being exceeded only by reading.

I now had two choices, the 30° form would be racier, but the floor of the boat would be only 66 inches long compared with a full 72 inches for the 45° angle. Also the racy-looking boat would sink minutely farther into the water, and might have slightly more drag because of this, and it would go aground sooner for the same reason. A little reluctantly because I was getting further away from the original idealistic concept, I chose the 45° design and proceeded to build.

I had to bend the corrugated iron up 90° at the stern, ten inches from the end, and make a 45° bend 14 inches —plus a smidgen— from the other. This roofing tin was 16 gauge galvanized iron and corrugated like I said. The whole thought behind corrugated iron is that it will resist being bent like that. I am here to tell you, it does its job superbly.

I knew that somehow the corrugations would have to be removed in the vicinity of the bends. It took awhile, quite awhile, but I found I could flatten them out by pounding them against the concrete street with the flat end of an ax. The neighbors cringed for a couple of afternoons as I bent the reluctant iron into shape. Actually, it had to be reshaped a couple of times because the bend lines had to run straight across from side to side so the iron would fit snugly against the boards at the corners. That, I found, is not easy to do. To make tight joints, I nailed the iron to the boards with galvanized roofing nails spaced about an inch apart. Quite a pile of nails, not even considering the ones that bent and became unusable.

At last, after a week or so, my craft was ready, so I got my patrol together and we agreed to take a hike to Crow Creek on the next Saturday and to camp out that night. Crow Creek was five miles away, and we hiked there often, so we knew exactly where we were going and how to prepare. However, all prior events had been without a boat, and the logistics of this additional equipment became manifest on Saturday morning.

I guess I have mentioned it before, but let me remind you a fair amount of gear is needed for an overnight hike; food, cooking utensils, blankets, hatchets, and knives, not to mention again the mandatory first aid kits. Each Scout must be self-sustaining, and all of this stuff is about the limit of what a boy can be expected to carry for five miles. It wasn't the weight as much as the unruliness of the pack; a blanket just does not roll up into a knapsack no matter what the Handbook says, unless there is nothing else in there with it. Something has to hang on the outside, and this usually turned out to be the cooking and eating utensils. Invariably this gear is made of aluminum, or metal anyway, and it clanged and banged together as one walked, so you could hear a bunch of Scouts on a hike a quarter of a mile away just from all the clatter. That aside, we also had to carry the boat on this trip.

Now I never weighed it, but I would judge the boat was at least 50 or 60 pounds and all together not too tote-able. We doubled up the pack loads of four guys, and the four without packs carried the boat with one at each corner. After about six blocks, it was decided that it might carry better if inverted, because the hands then could get a grip on the wooden sides. That was a little better; but eight of nine blocks later, we sat down to rest and decided we had to find a better way.

While we rested, Skinny took off and returned with his bicycle. We found that the boat could be balanced on the seat and handlebars, and the entire lash-up then could be balanced and pushed along by two Scouts. It took about a minute to realize that all packs could go inside the boat without adding any noticeable burden, so we then began to make time.

One minor problem lies ahead, but we did not think to cross that bridge before we got to it. Our path to Crow Creek led eastward out of town along the railroad right-of-way. After a mile or so, a county road angled in from the north and then paralleled the tracks for several miles farther than we were going. A drainage ditch separated the two, this ditch being a full ten feet across and as deep. I looked at this spot recently, and my memory of it is correct. The way across was and still is won by a single 2 by 12-inch plank spanning the ditch, although I am pretty sure the one used today is not the same plank. We had crossed this ditch using this plank lots of times and it always was a little thrilling, but this time proved to be really sporty.

As you can see, our task was to move a bicycle loaded with a boat across 10 feet of plank nominally a foot wide, but actually a little less because of dressing and trimming losses. We practiced this on the ground using a couple of lines scratched in the dirt, and after a little experimentation, we thought two Scouts could manage it. One would back across while he held the boat on the handlebars, with his legs straddling but toward the front of the front wheel. The second Scout would straddle the rear wheel and follow along while holding the boat on the seat. Neither had more than four inches on either side for his feet if the wheel was centered, which it seldom was.

We inched this monstrosity across, with a lot of "OOPS" and three or four almosts, but somehow it was done, mainly because God looks after utter fools. Try it sometime, and you can get an idea of how dumb growing kids can be, in case you need any examples.

With the big load safely across, two of the unencumbered Scouts lost their balance and fell into the ditch, getting wet in the slimy water at the bottom and skinning a leg and a hand. The first aid kits were whipped open and all wounds were mopped with Mercurochrome and bandaged.

Once across it still was about three or four miles, but all smooth sailing until we got to Crow Creek. We tried two or three other ways to carry the boat, one being to place a couple of wrist-sized trees trimmed to a good length under the boat fore and aft and with a Scout at the ends of each. This worked fairly well, but the bicycle arrangement was better. The best way of all came up the road behind us in the form of a tractor drawing a four-wheeled flat bed trailer. Upon being invited, we piled on the boat, bicycle, packs, Scouts and all. But first we had a little conference about accepting a ride when we were on a hike. A Scout is supposed to hike when on a hike. We decided that this was a special case because no one was working on a merit badge or award that required hiking, and we did have an unusual amount of luggage. So it was agreed that it was alright to ride, but we still felt a little guilty about it.

We fairly flew down the graveled road at about 15 miles an hour. That may not seem like much, but the trailer was a steel tired vehicle, and of course without springs. If you haven't tried it, a springless trailer on a gravel road is about the best shaker in the whole world and will absolute homogenize your guts.

Our plans for camping and boating matured as we approached the creek. Again we conferred and agreed that the creek itself was not the best launching spot, but that a nearby gravel pit (where gravel had been extracted long ago) would be better. So we selected a good place at the gravel pit with a clear bank, while others made camp. In this case that was just throwing the blankets on the ground and taking a nap.

But I had work to do. A couple of others who wanted a ride in the boat helped shove it in. To my dismay and shame, and the whooping amusement of the others, it began to fill rapidly with water. The two boards did not have enough excess buoyancy to hold up the roofing iron, not to mention all the nails so it would have sunk had we not pulled it out. Obviously, two Scouts and their gear, or 200 pounds, would not get very far in this contrivance.

Skinny just happened to have along a pot of tar that he had found somewhere, and he suggested that we melt it and pour it inside at the junctures of the wood and metal to seal out the water.

This was a very straightforward idea, except we didn't yet have a fire. No problem, fire making was s skill emphasized from the first day and we often had competitions whereby the contestants would build fires under a string stretched tightly about 18 inches above the ground. The first fire to burn the string in two won. So we were pretty good at making fires, but we were honor bound to make fires with no more than two matches. We usually took more along just in case, but no fire could use more than two.

This time, as luck would have it, whoever was making the fire used two matches without success. We really gave him the razz about being such a tenderfoot, but since he really was, he was halfway exonerated.

But we still needed that fire, and the regulation two matches had been used up. As usual, we had plenty more, but the rules and honor required that particular fire now could never be built. After a solemn conference accompanied by a modicum of guilt all around, we decided that someone else could build a fire in another location and not violate the fire code. So, he yielded his place to a Scout with more experience who then exercised his skills.

Would you believe it? Number two flubbed it, also. More razzing, but with a little less spirit this time. A third site was selected a few feet away, not as choice as the first two but not bad. Same thing. Incredibly, seven Scouts in six more locations muffed it in turn. We all agreed the code had been stretched far enough, and the sixteenth match had to do it or we would just have to go without a fire for cooking or for tar for the boat.

Carefully, oh so carefully, we selected with infinite care the dry tinder and the small branches as well as the larger sticks, paying particular attention to the rule, "If it doesn't crack, throw it back." This referred to test for dry wood, when breaking it in two it should make a cracking sound, otherwise it is too green for a fire, or a young one anyway. We constructed the wood cage with excruciating care, and when no one could improve upon the nuances of the lay of each stick, the final match was struck and offered to the base. The tinder caught, blazed up with vigor, and as quickly died down and with an emanation of smoke, went out. Amid our groans and self encroachments, it suddenly blazed up and licked through the wood, igniting first one piece and then another. In two or three minutes the fire was healthy and self-sustaining. With rousing cheers, we in our several ways began to cook, or to melt tar.

I was too distracted by the boat to eat or even think about eating right then. I stirred up the fire and put the tar pot on. It took about an hour to coax it into melting, with the odor distracting from the camp cooking which offered little enough enticement anyway.

After a time, the tar melted enough to pour and after applying it inside along the seams, we launched. Things looked better this time, with only a hair-line leak, so tentatively I stepped into the boat and sat down. So far, so good. Another Scout stepped in and sat down also. Just about then I realized that we had no paddles nor had I even thought of any. As though it were planned that way, I said with confidence, "Let's paddle with our hands to the other side."

So we paddled that way, and slow work it was too. The boat was about as steerable as a tree branch, and no faster, but we managed to get the 75 feet or so to the other side and turn around. About half way back, I felt the water. We were seated right on the corrugated bottom, so both of us got wet about the same time. Actually, there was a little bit of water all along from the cracks along the edges, but now it was rising fast. Furiously we began to paddle, urging the reluctant boat to higher speed. The prize goes to the swift and the water, being the swifter, won over us with a licentious gurgle as the boat sank about ten feet out from our side. Perhaps the racy bow would have helped, but not enough I am sure and slopping wet from the waist down we dragged it out.

We tried to fix it before it got dark, but we didn't even get all the way across that time before it sank. Next day we scraped out all the tar, re-melted the lot, hammered in all the nails with the butt end of a hatchet, and re-poured. All the way over, half back, and down we went. I suppose we re-caulked four or five more times before we had to start for home. Never, by even the most generous stretch of the generosity, could it be said that the boat floated safely with just two Scouts, much less their gear.

By that time the boat had been named "The Rock", a little undeservedly because it did float a little before sinking. "Titanic" also was proposed, but "Rock" won out and we abandoned it on the bank and went home.

My chagrin increased when I got home, because I found I had left Thomas Jefferson behind. Dad drove me out to the spot in the car, but I couldn't find him. Dad looked at the Rock, but didn't say anything. Others did though, it remained there to be seen by all on subsequent hiking trips, a permanent monument to my ignorance. I never lived it down.

A full fifteen years later, I was in the vicinity and wondered if I could locate the old gravel pit. It had grown up a lot in weeds and pine trees, but it was there. The remains of the Rock were there too, the side planks almost rotted away, and with the corrugated iron completely rusted but still intact. Like so many endeavors of mankind, the Rock was a total failure in the thing it was meant to do, but by still being there, it revealed an unplanned defiance in the battle with the elements, a tenacious characteristic it was not designed to have at all.

I also found Thomas Jefferson! My initials and the date were still visible on his back, and he seemed about the same. I left him there, and I still wonder if he recognized me. I also wonder if he is still there now.

Since I couldn't claim the boat as an accomplishment, I showed how to arrange a pack on a dummy pack animal. Not very exciting, but it got me the badge.

Another mandatory badge was for Pioneering, with one of the requirements being to build a crane that would lift 200 pounds. The crane didn't interest me as much as the boat, but I dug in and started.

Again, the problem was a total lack of information. There was a book in the high school library entitled "The Boy's Own Book of Engineering", author unknown to me now, but he did a good job, which described in some detail just how a boy could make a railroad with wooden tracks, a clamshell bucket dredge, and a scow to float it on when making a pond deeper. I had read and reread this book several times and found it captured my thoughts completely, but the boy in the book had one big advantage, he had all the materials in the world. It was nothing for him to assemble twenty planks, or fifty 2 x 4's.

Such riches were beyond me, it was the limit of my resources to scrounge up just one board, although a couple of 2 x 4's were not too hard. Almost any building job always had a few lying around. but of course the 2 x 4's would be knotty, and the lone plank would be warped. Our friend in the book actually inspected his lumber at the yard and rejected those pieces that were not up to his standards. Only grade "A" for him.

From this background, it seemed to me that the vertical member or mast was the critical element. The boom that extended out and supported the lifting tackle didn't appear to be too much problem, a 2 x 4 would probably do, and certainly so if doubled, should one not be strong enough. I sketched out what I thought was a suitable design, like this:

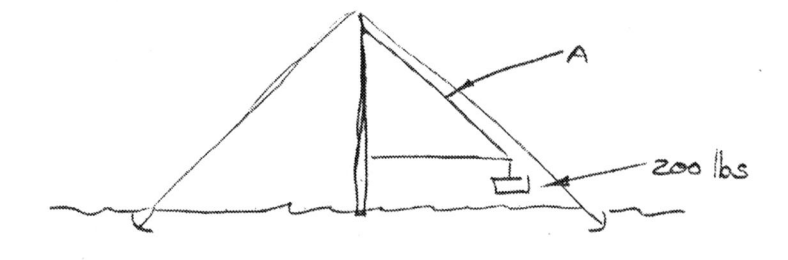

Using my algebra and trigonometry, I discovered that the rope labeled "A" would need to sustain a load of 282 pounds if the boom were straight out for maximum reach and if the rope were at 45°. I figured a safety margin was needed and arbitrarily decided that 350 pounds would be about right.

All that was the easy part. The mast either had to be self-supporting or it had to be braced or "guyed" as I found the proper term to be. To be self-respecting, the boom would have to swing in a full circle, so the mast would need guys in four directions. Allowing the guys to clear the boom meant that these be at a slightly flatter angle so that each would intersect the ground at about the same distance from the mast as the height of the mast itself, plus just a little more. Again using algebra and trig, I learned that each of these guys also would have to sustain a load of about 350 pounds if the same safety factor were to apply. That meant each guy would have to be fastened to something that would hold fast when being pulled by 350 pounds. So it turned out that holding up the 200 pound load was the least of the problems, because I needed four of these anchoring points.

Dad showed me how the utility company used metal anchors that were placed in a hole several feet deep, and then "busted" with a rod-like tool that expanded then into the undisturbed soil around the bottom of the hole. When done properly, these anchors would hold several thousand pounds.

The crane was to be used and useful around a camp, because just about anything a Scout did or made was more or less useful around a camp. So everything needed to make it had to be in the woods or had to be carried to camp, with the carrying on somebody's back, probably mine. These earth anchors that Dad showed me weighed like buckets of lead, and were carried to the site on a utility company truck, so a better solution was needed.

Dad said that they used to bury a log for earth anchors, but the logs rotted away and left the structure un-guyed and un-braced, so logs weren't used any more. I figured I wouldn't need mine until the logs rotted away, so I tried burying a log. I had to dig a hole about three feet deep and about as long because I planned to use a piece of fire wood for the log. Now that is a bit of digging, especially for a teen-aged boy with nothing but the official Boy Scout belt-spade for the tool. It took me about three hours to get a hole barely big enough and I sat down in collapse, because that was only one of four. Clearly, I needed a better plan.

While this was going on, we took a hike and just for the heck of it we camped along the railroad right-of-way. We had never done this before, and our spot was on a hill that had been cut away to allow the tracks to go through on an even grade, and from our campsite we looked right down at the rails perhaps fifty feet below. When it suited our purposes, and it did often, we could remain completely out of sight from below just by backing away from the edge of the cut. It was a lovely camping spot, the only problem was that it was a major climbing effort getting our stuff up to the top. The approved route was right up the side of the cut, using weeds and small saplings for handholds, but this was heavy going even when unburdened with a pack. With a pack almost everyone had to go a long way around that avoided most of the steep parts, but which added three or four hundred feet to the distance.

Right at the edge of the cut was a dead tree, fifty feet high, and in sound condition. The side of the cut dropped away almost vertically from the trunk. There was my mast, and self-supporting. All it needed was to have the branches lopped off, which was done in a few minutes because everybody got into the act. Although a merit badge was supposed to be a solo effort, removing the branches was alright because everyone needed firewood and it wasn't my fault if someone needing wood got in there and chopped off all the limbs before I used the tree as a mast.

We got enough wood for twenty camps, and in fact did burn from this same supply over a period of a year. When the wood was all removed, there was the mast, straight and tall, and just waiting for the boom to make it into a crane. The boom was made of a tree limb that had a good crotch in the right place so that the total length was about what I needed. The crotch was laid against the tree trunk and it was kept from slipping down the trunk by a lash up of rope tied to the boom and to the tree. Using all the remaining ropes in camp, I quickly guyed the boom so it was supported level, and a line was dropped from the end of the boom to the ground below. Several of us went tumbling down to test it by swinging on it. It didn't take long to find that this arrangement would support four or five Scouts with ease, because that many of us would swing on it at the same time. I could barely wait to clean up the design.

When I got home, I arranged to borrow a double-sheaved block and tackle from the utility company, as well as some scraps of galvanized wire to use for the boom guy, and some other odds and ends, and we took another hike the following Saturday. I re-rigged the boom, making it look a little less like a project by a committee, and attached the block and tackle at the free end of the boom, with the hauling end of the rope tackle up at the top. When it was all done, we lowered the free block with the hook on it and tied all the Scouts' gear into one big bloody lump and hoisted it and two Scouts to the top. The rest of the Scouts scaled the side of the cut and most of them got to the top just about the same time as the bundle and the other two.

With clear conscience I presented myself to the Court of Honor for the merit badge, and described my crane project. My reviewer was not too impressed with the use of a tree as a mast, so I had to be heard by another that night. The second man thought it was alright, but deferred to the first. It was decided that I should present to a third, but there wasn't enough time that night, so a time was set for an afternoon the next week.

The third reviewer was a civil engineer who worked for the highway department. He listened to my description of the crane in its final form and then asked, "Gaylord, why did you decide to use a tree? Why didn't you use a guyed mast?"

I hadn't anticipated this question at all, but I described my calculations and how difficult it was to come up with an anchor that would hold over 350 pounds.

"Who helped you with the calculations?"

"No one, " I answered, "I just used what I had learned in algebra and in trigonometry."

"Show me how you came up with your load for the anchors." So I went through my work from memory because I had not thought to bring any of it. When I finished, he said, "Gaylord, I hadn't realized just how hard it is to make that crane. I think you did a fine job, and there is nothing wrong with using a tree for a mast. They do it all the time in the logging business. Don't worry, you'll get your badge." And I did.

That crane was used regularly after that. It remained in place for years, being modified and changed and sometimes improved, but still basically the same structure I had contrived. Fifteen years later, on the same trip when I found the Rock, I also found the crane, or what was left of it. The mast was there, not so sound as when we used it, with rot showing here and there. The boom was gone, but the wire that I had rigged to support it was still fastened to the top of the mast, dangling down and swinging in the breeze.

X X X X X

Most of these hiking and camping trips involved several Scouts. Like I said, much of the time in camp would be spent in pursuing or in using some skill of Scouting. After supper was eaten, and after a few songs sometimes, we always got around to talking about girls. Actually, it was more basic than that, we talked about screwing girls.

These discussions were tests of manhood, because nothing ever could be phrased in the form of a question, but must be offered as gospel from the personal knowledge and vast experience of the speaker. Every word was soaked up and the slightest hint that the speaker was just winging it or guessing brought the scorn of the group heaped upon his ears. Gleefully, someone would say, "Why, Jimmie Jones doesn't even know how to DO it, listen to him talk." These were difficult conversations because, if nothing was said, then this would be detected after a while, and the loudest talker would say loudly, "What's the matter, David Worth, haven't you had any yet?"

So there was a lot of talk. It was incredible, how many and how often some of the boys were winning, or so they said. It was difficult to say who was really talking and who was just talking in these sessions, because some of the exploits sounded reasonable, but it did not seem that someone whose voice was changing would be so successful. Some of the claims were pretty far out. "Why, I was just walking by and she called me in and we went out on her back porch and I screwed her right there in broad daylight." Just about everyone claimed at least one event in broad daylight, but most said they were getting it most of the time at night in the back seat of a car, usually on the golf course. Of my own knowledge, none of us had a driver's license, although some of us were driving without one, but certainly not very much at night. If only ten percent of the strokes on the golf course were counted, it would have been parked solid with cars every night.

At first, I didn't know how often was often and had no reason to doubt the claims of performance, but found the prowess was a little hard to accept. After my experiences with Mrs. Wasserman, I realized that the frequency was exaggerated by factors of twenty or more to one, if you accept that there had been a conquest in the first place.

The objects of these copulations were usually girls no one else knew, from some town thirty or forty miles away. The reason for this was simple self-preservation. If one talked too much about screwing Barbara Williams on the bench by the swimming pool, the word would be passed around that Barbara was good for a make, and sooner or later her father would hear and start investigating. It didn't happen often, but these were the days when statutory rape and shotgun weddings were thought about seriously. No one wanted to receive a rape charge even if only fifteen, because in those times, the popular fiction for public pronouncements was that the girls were completely innocent and nice girls didn't do that. In private, some were learning how, but each was careful not to give away any sign that she was not nice.

In these confused days of developing puberty, we thought a nice girl would turn to stone or something if she even heard some of the words we were using with increasing frequency. There were not many stone girls walking around, and we knew some of the nice girls had heard some of the words and one or two even used a couple. But the sure knowledge that nice girls didn't do anything was the source of a great amount of mental confusion and anguish. If you went out with a nice girl, you knew she didn't, so that was that. If she wasn't a nice girl, then she would be expecting to be ravished and any failure to do so would mark you as an ignorant kid or a bumbling one at best. As an example, Mary Axworthy was a nice girl, except that it was said that she had, after all you had heard it around a campfire when one of the braggarts was a little bold in saying who did. You hadn't really believed him at the time but it might be convenient if he had been telling the truth.

So everyone tried to discover signs that would reveal the big secret, her toes pointed out when she walked if she had, or she would stare you down if she chose. All of these signs obviously were fallible, so we gradually accepted the fact that it doesn't show unless she gets pregnant.

Compounding this turbulent collection of thoughts was the fact that we all knew or thought we knew where procreation started. That meant by demonstrable product our mothers were members of the segment that did, but all of them were known to be nice girls even if a little beyond being girls. The slightest hint otherwise brought the challenge "Are you saying something about my mother?"

Boys have a hard time accepting the fact that their mothers did, just as fathers have trouble knowing that their little daughters are going to. Fathers also have a hard time explaining things to their sons because the boy's mother is the object of participation.

The qualms of fathers aside, these same analyses and conclusions had to be applied to our sisters, although the water was not quite so muddy here because everybody knew that Jim Atkins' sister did, because the entire football team had consummated the act with her on the same night or so it was said. So some sisters did, but they were known not to be nice girls.

Obviously these questions were being sorted out in each of our minds. To help our thought processes we adopted the same mental blinders used by society for other matters. We merely changed the verb to indicate the degree of waywardness that accompanied the act. If a girl was "cut" or "laid" she was barely fallen at all and could claim some remnant of being nice if she didn't repeat the performance, or not too often anyway. When she started screwing she had crossed the line but still might reclaim her status if she stopped. She had fallen to the final depravity when she started fucking, and she was no longer nice or could ever hope to be again.

I've noticed the same sort of thing is used in other evaluations of moral performance, a little white lie is told to further the purposes of the speaker without hurting anyone, a fib is a little worse, but may have a minor amount of justification, but not much, a lie is downright hurtful even if not meant to be, and a god damned lie is issued with ill intent. But all are lies. So we exchanged our white lies, fibs, and lies but few god damned lies about our performances and the objects thereof. I should add that Mrs. Wasserman was never mentioned by me at all for the simple reason that no one would have believed it, particularly that she drove from her town to Woodton fairly often to see me on the nights when the Scouts met. It's funny how the truth sometimes is harder to accept than a lie.

When we had exercised the limit of credibility about our own adventures, we bragged about the manhood of someone known to all but not in the family of any of us, typically the football coach. This was easier ground because we no longer were defending our own stature, but exalting that of another. I doubt that this gentleman had any idea of the exploits attributed to him. According to the rumors, he had applied his thrust to each and every unmarried female teacher in both the elementary and high schools. He also was a cutter of the swath not to mention women in the adjacent towns, where he had missed a few but he was going back.

He had been caught in the act several times by the football team —these guys really got around— while getting one of the sexier and better-looking teachers to conjugate her verbs. The location of the discovery in every single case was right in the big middle of the football field at midnight. You would think he would catch on and find a spot and time subject to fewer inspections, but he never did. He was caught regularly, or so they said.

I suppose this series of events have their counterparts everywhere, in other countries and societies as well as our own. So, there was nothing at all unusual, and in the context, nothing particularly vulgar about any of it. This may seem consistent to the fact that away from home anyway we were beginning to punctuate our conversations with all the obscenities we could think of. But that is part of growing up; it just takes a while to get it out of the system.

One thing happened though that may have been a little unusual. Two of the Scouts in the troop had really bragged it up about how they had visited a whorehouse when on one of the trips the school band made. We all thought they were lying. Then we decided maybe they weren't when they both turned up with the clap.

CHAPTER XIX

We flew the Ford for a couple of months after Monk's death, and business was slow. So Johnson Tom thought maybe we should have another monkey. I really don't know where you would go if you wanted a monkey, but Johnson Tom had a knack for that sort of thing and after about three weeks of looking he found one. I don't know who thinks up names like this, but this new monkey was called Profanity.

Unless it was mine, never was a name more inaptly chosen. Profanity was a sweet little female, she never caused any trouble at all. If we told her to sit, she sat, when we said to come with us, she scrambled up on one of our shoulders for a ride. She just was no problem, and after Monk's robust personality, Profanity was a little dull.

Maybe it was the times, or maybe people were not excited anymore about taking a ride in an airplane, but Profanity never filled the airplane after a parachute jump like Monk did. Since the Ford was paid off, the operation was still quite profitable, but on some Sundays we wouldn't fly more than a dozen loads.

So we continued our old routine, but we were really going a long way sometimes to find new territory, We went into eastern Texas, and Louisiana, and did a lot of flying to get there.

One time I was taking off and Johnson Tom was guarding the throttles. We always did that, whoever was not flying held the throttles forward so that they wouldn't vibrate closed or a backfire wouldn't slam one of them shut. The Ford wasn't one of them, but some airplanes are vicious about backfires shutting the throttles.

I really wasn't thinking about anything in particular and was up to about 125 feet when suddenly he pulled back the right throttle and I was caught with an asymmetrical thrust and an underpowered airplane. We had a handbook issued by The Airplane Division of the Ford Motor Company that said with any one engine out their tri-motor would climb "very satisfactorily" and could be flown straight or turned in either direction. They kept on laying it on by saying it could be taken off on the two outer engines with the center one off. They also said that under two-engine operation there was a need for careful handling and conservative judgment on the part of the pilot. That part they got right, I won't say they were wrong about the other things, exactly, but on that Ford at least a side engine failure really got your attention.

Now the first thing you think you want is more power. Since we were just off the ground, the other two engines were wide open anyway, and there was no more power to apply. So mostly I just stood on the left rudder to hold it straight as I nursed the Ford up to a couple of hundred feet in that very satisfactory climb they talked about. In about two minutes we were there and about two miles from the field. Johnson Tom just sat there with his hand holding the right throttle back and saying nothing, so I decided to make a wide turn to the left, away from the throttled engine and circle back and land. So I did, and had an exciting time of it too, because the Ford didn't have enough reserve power to make much of a turn and to maintain altitude.

When I was about half way around, I had lost 75 feet, and the field was about a mile and a half away on my left, and I was going downwind. There wasn't much, only about ten miles an hour, but I knew if I tried to fly straight while I regained altitude we would be miles downwind from the field and it would take a long time to beat back. So I deliberately continued my turn, giving up altitude to keep the field close by. When the turn was completed, the field was a half-mile in front, and I was down to fifty feet. It was just luck there were no trees in the way so I held it straight and flew it right over the fence and cut the rest of the power and settled on. The Ford ran out and stopped.

I leaned back exhausted. Johnson Tom lit into me. "Why did you continue to turn when you were so low?" I explained my reasoning, and he said, "Okay, then you did it deliberately, then that's all right. I thought you just didn't have a plan. Your only mistake was that you should have gone farther out and gotten a little more altitude before starting to turn back. How much altitude did you lose on the turn?" I replied it was a little over 150 feet. Then Johnson Tom came right back at me, "We were empty, how much would you have lost if we had had a load?" I didn't know, twice as much, maybe. "Right, what would you have done if you couldn't have maintained altitude flying straight ahead because of the load?" I would look out ahead for a landing spot. "What if you were over trees, and there was no place?" I didn't know, try to hold off as long as possible and stall it onto the tree tops as slow as possible. "Okay, you passed. Now, take this sonnavabitch off again, and let's go home."

So I taxied to the end of the field and opened up and had just broken ground when Johnson Tom pulls the left throttle. Son of a gun! Again I wasn't really thinking about anything, but came to enough to climb to three hundred feet before starting a turn to the right this time. When we were on the ground and stopped again, Johnson Tom said, "Okay, let's go home." So I taxied back to the downwind end of the field and opened up and had just broken off and was up to about 15 feet when he pulls the center engine!

Now the Ford manual was pretty much right about losing power on the middle engine, I'll have to give them credit. That center engine didn't carry its share of the load, and a lot of people thought the Ford should have had only two engines, only bigger. Anyway, we continued to climb pretty well, but of course at a considerably reduced rate.

I got it up to 500 feet and said to Johnson Tom, "I think we could go on this way." He says, "You're right," so he opens the center throttle and I synched up all the engines, and flew home.

After that, he pulled a throttle on me regularly. I got so I could handle the Ford on any two engines, and a couple of times he pulled two engines at the same time. The Ford is not a flying machine with just one engine going, particularly if it's a side engine.

Like I said, business was slow, so one week end we agreed that we would work both Saturday and Sunday next time. I was out at the field in Woodton at eight in the morning. He was already there, so we immediately took off and he surprised me by going back to Memphis, and when we get there, he takes me to a doctor who gives me a physical examination. "They've changed the rules, and you have to pass a physical before you can handle tickets." I thought that was a mighty funny rule, but I passed the physical all right or I guess I did, because I continued to handle the tickets just like I had before.

But not that day. As soon as the doctor got through with me, we went to the airport to go hop passengers I thought, but instead Johnson Tom took me out to a two-place open-cockpit Waco biplane. We went up and out over a cleared area a few miles south of the Memphis airport, over Mississippi actually, where he showed me how to spin an airplane and to recover. That was a wild airplane ride. In an hour and a half, we did twelve spins, six each way. After the demonstration in each direction I put it in the spin and recovered each of the ten times, getting better after each one. Then we got in the Ford and flew way down in lower Mississippi to carry passengers the next day.

On our way back, Johnson Tom said, "Gaylord, I am going to be away for about two months. I've been in the reserve since I was in the Air Corps and I have been called in for some refresher training. I should be back in time for your sixteenth birthday, so look for me then." He dropped me off at Woodton and flew off in the Ford. I decided that I would use the time to concentrate on finishing the requirements for my Eagle badge. I figured I would have it all done in about three months.

Then Dad came home and said that it just happened that way, but it was decided to have the annual Father-son banquet on my birthday. If I could get ready in time, I could receive my Eagle badge on the same night. Also, the annual Scouts' day where we ruled the town would be one week earlier.

I mentioned Scouts' Day a while back, and said that was when we raised some money, but I didn't say how. Well, it was all arranged between the Scoutmaster and the town officials that for one day, the Scouts would rule the town. Naturally, we got an excused absence from school, and there always was a surge in application for membership just before the big day.

We selected a mayor and a police chief from the senior members of the troop, and a judge, but almost everyone else was a cop. We assumed control at eight o'clock in the morning, and the Scout cops would swarm out into the downtown section and would arrest just about anyone for just about anything. The one arrested would be taken to court and would be declared guilty forever unless the individual wanted to remove the smear from his good name by paying a fine. A fat man would be hauled in for overloading the sidewalk, with a fine of ten cents. Jaywalking was a common offense, fine a nickel, littering the sidewalk with a cigarette butt cost a nickel, and a cigar butt rated a dime. Of course, the town's people were in the spirit of the thing, and it was great sport to see just how ridiculous an offense could be, and there would be an additional fine at the end of the day for the transgression judged the most atrocious, as well as one for the person receiving the most arrests during the day, and so on. With about twenty five Scout cops scouring the streets, and with the very generous cooperation of a lot of people, we could take in $150 without much effort. That was a pretty good pile of money in those days, and it went a long way toward covering the costs of the summer camps.

The banquet put some pressure on, so I had to work hard on the three or four merit badges that were not yet completed. While doing this, I tallied up those I already had to be sure that I would not be short, that would certainly be embarrassing after all the fuss. Rudolph McCrary, a fellow in my class, was going to get his on the same night, and I guess he was doing the same thing.

I had started getting merit badges back when I was still working on First Class, working on the required ones first. I had acquired these in the following order: Swimming, First Aid, Safety, Personal Health, Public Health, Physical Development, Pioneering, Pathfinding, Cooking, Camping, Bird Study, Life Saving, and Civics. Interspersed between and along with these I had picked up electives in Art, Automobiling, Aviation, Bookbinding, and Electricity. I was still working on Handicraft, Horsemanship, and Reading, and it looked like the last of these would be done about a month before my birthday, and that would make up the 21 needed. I also was almost through with Chemistry, Mechanical Drawing, and Machinery, and was hoping to complete them too so I would have more than the bare minimum. I didn't make it with this last three, but I did get them at the next Court after I made Eagle.

Making Eagle was important, and represented the culmination of a long time and a lot of work. But equally important, I wanted to get my driver' license as early as possible on my birthday, because Dad said he would let me have the car for the day if I was licensed. So I also had to study the rules of the road for that examination.

All of these things proceeded along, it is amazing just how much progress can be made when the time to do something is limited, and you really want to get it done. Finally, my birthday arrived, as everyone except me was sure it would do. Bright and early, well early anyway, because I am not too bright when I first wake up, I arose and wolfed down breakfast, and Dad drove me to the police station for my driver's test.

There were several people already there. I had to wait my turn, which was number six because that many of the others were brighter and earlier than I was. The examiner on duty really didn't care that it was my birthday, because it was the sixteenth birthday for almost everyone there. I read the chart on the wall, and took a little written examination which asked such stuff as how far must you park from a fire hydrant. When all of us had been through the written part, he started the driving tests. Each in turn went out to their automobile and he rode around asking each driver to stop, and turn and backup and park. Each of the boys ahead of me were flunked in turn! The girls all passed. I began to sweat.

My turn. We get into Dad's car and I drive the examiner around like he wants me to and when we get back he says, "Ordinarily, I always flunk 16 year old boys on their initial tests, just to knock some sense in their heads. Now I notice that you had that special slip from Chief Crawford, so I am going to pass you, with the firm understanding that you are about the worst driver I ever let through." No matter, I had passed! I now could drive legally and without worrying if I was going to be stopped, unless I was really doing something wrong, that is.

I hurried home, to learn from Mother that Johnson Tom had called and said he would be at the field where he always picked me up by one o'clock. That was only ten minutes away. Yes, I could take the car, since it was my birthday, but don't think this is going to be a habit.

Johnson Tom was landing just as I drove up. He taxied up and got out and he was in uniform, a real one this time. I didn't know much about military rank, but later I found he was wearing major's oak leaves, and of course pilot's wings. He whistled when he saw me in the car and looked pleased when I told him I had just gotten my license.

"Gaylord, it looks like this country is going to get itself into a war in spite of everything, or those in higher places think so anyway, and I have been called back for at least a year. I can't keep the Ford so I have sold it to a guy in Tulsa, and I have special permission and leave to take it there now. I thought it would be nice if you had a last flight in the old bird."

Well, I sort of choked up on that. Without really thinking about it, I had sort of thought that it would still be around to hop passengers for another hundred years, with me taking up the tickets. But Johnson Tom urges me inside and has me sit in the left seat, and I taxi out. At the end of the field, he turns to me and says, "Gaylord, I want you to take it around the field by yourself. You have been ready for quite some time, but you weren't old enough until today. Just do what you have been doing and everything will be fine. Your parents know all about this, and they are parked right over there with your uncle." Before I can think of an answer, he gets out of his seat and walks to the rear, steps out and latches the door. He runs around the rear of the plane and came into view in my window and gives me a wave.

So I opened up the Ford, took off and flew it around the field. It really wasn't much to it, about like the times before when Johnson Tom had been in the back of the plane. I made a good takeoff and a good landing, When I got back, he said, "Now, if you want to you can take it over to Wider and back, but don't waste any time, I've got to get on my way." Wider was a little town about ten miles away, so I took off and flew there, circled twice, and flew back. By now I was feeling right smug and pleased with myself.

Johnson Tom shook hands with me and said, "Well Gaylord, I don't know when I'll see you again, but there's one thing you can be proud of, there is not another person in the whole world who ever soloed on a Ford tri-motor, particularly on their sixteenth birthday. Oh, here's your medical certificate and log book. You have to sign each page." He handed me a regular flight log book with a lot of time in the Ford signed off by him as the instructor, and also the solo flight. The medical certificate surprised me, but then I saw it was dated the day we went to the doctor in Memphis.

Johnson Tom flew away in the Ford and I never saw it again. I learned about a year later the guy in Tulsa cracked it up on the first flight. He wasn't hurt, but the Ford was washed out completely.

X X X X X

Dad and I went to the father and son banquet with me driving and during the ceremonies Rudolph McCrary and I got our Eagle badges. I hate to say it, but at the time it was a little disappointing. I had been working on it so long it didn't seem possible that it now was mine. I didn't feel any different but down deep inside I hoped that I had truly earned it, or if I hadn't maybe I wouldn't disgrace it while I worked up to it. In time, earning my Eagle became one of my proudest achievements.

The banquet was over at about nine, and I drove Dad home. He said I could take the car and go out with the other boys. I was driving toward town and was stopped at a traffic sign right at the edge of downtown, when I saw Mrs. Wasserman. She saw me at the same time, and waved me over. She knew this was my birthday, and she had driven over to give me a special present, which she did.

I got home just a few minutes after midnight, put the car away, and thought about the events of the last eighteen hours. By almost anybody's standards, my sixteenth birthday was a pretty good day, and just about the best I ever had.

CHAPTER XX

PEARL HARBOR! Shock, unbelieving, rage! None of these words could describe the feelings. The enormity of the event exhausted the ability of the inner mind to express itself even to itself, and the same ineffectual words were repeated over and over and over. Each person tried to find the combinations of spoken sounds to transmit to others the depths of despair, the heights of anger, the widths and lengths of the emotional stirrings of the mental process. No matter what words were found, each was but the most minute tip of the emotional iceberg contained within each breast.

Bastards! That was the kindest thing that could be used to describe a people who would launch a sneak attack, and on Sunday morning too when those being attacked were all in Church. Surely God would not forget nor forgive such a treacherous act.

Although the attack occurred just before noon, our time, that is central standard time, the fact was not known for several hours. We heard about it when it was announced timidly in mid-afternoon by a radio announcer in Memphis who was not sure it wasn't a joke, and said so. It must be a joke, no one would have the nerve to attack the United States, after all we had the best damn navy in the world.

Soon the radios, no matter what station might be the source, began to blatt out the news, repeating and repeating again what had been repeated just a minute or two before. The simple fact was that the news services had no further news after the initial story. No one knew what to believe, because some of that information had been proven to be false, or disclaimed at any rate.

By next morning, more reliable information had come in on the wire services, including the dramatic photographs of the eight battleships burning, all damaged badly or sunk. By now there was little doubt that the essential theme was true, but the details were elusive and contradictory. And the information was so slow in arriving!

What did they say? Our navy sunk? It was not enough to bomb our naval base, but they sank some of our ships too. Why, we are helpless, the Japs will be invading California tomorrow. We are sitting ducks. Somebody ought to be held responsible for all this. Everyone was talking, mostly without rationale, repeating themselves as new listeners came and went.

Great Britain had agreed previously that it would declare war on Japan if the United States became involved in a war with that country. Britain acted with unique haste, actually declaring a state of war between the British Commonwealth and Japan before the United States. That doesn't mean we dragged our feet too much, we declared war on December 8, just after Clark Field in the Philippines was struck, barely 10 hours after Pearl Harbor. Germany and Italy declared war on the new Allied powers on December 11. The war in Europe truly had become World War II.

While still reeling from the trauma of Pearl Harbor, news arrived about Midway Island. "Where is Midway Island? Did you know it belonged to us? I never heard of it, did you?" But they are holding out, the damned Japs won't take Midway Island, wherever it is." Then Guam was invaded by 6000 Japanese on the 10th, and capitulating on the 12th. Meanwhile, four hundred United States Marines inspired the country by holding onto Wake Island, sinking two Japanese destroyers, and killing more than 700 before being overrun by a bigger force on the 22nd. These events seemed to overlap one another, the mind could hardly comprehend the happening of today before its sequel of tomorrow brought more bad news and blurred the image of the two into one. Meanwhile, the consequences mounted, each reinforcing the one before. There seemed to be no good news at all, except that Midway was hanging on.

Bad news or not, there really was no need to worry, everyone knew that the Japanese really couldn't fight, and that all they knew how to make were little paper umbrellas, and silk covered wire framed toy airplanes powered with rubber bands. Once we get on our feet, we'll have this thing wrapped up in a couple of months. Meanwhile, until we do, we'll just have to put up with rationing of gasoline and tires, and some foods like sugar. It'll only be a few months, there's a war on, you know.

Normally, the recruiting office in the post office building saw no more than two or three potential enlistees a day, and maybe a tenth of these were interested enough to come back for more information. On Monday afternoon following Pearl Harbor, the entire football team went down to enlist. All of them were big men on the campus or BMOC's because of their association with the team, but this joint act raised their stature even more. This kind of patriotic reaction was repeated all over the country, the mental processes of young men being saturated with the heady news bulletins. Others who were about to be drafted decided that they could get the best deal by signing up early.

The recruiting offices received orders to hold up for a day or two until the army and navy could turn itself around from a peace time organization to one that was going to have to fight a war. They had to gear up to accepting thousands a day into receiving stations and assigning them to basic training, rather than the few dozen of just last week. The services knew even if the eager enlistees didn't that every single one had to be fed and housed and kept busy until all of the talent could be sorted out and compared with the needs of all the new military organizations being formed, and that every one would need training.

So the football team was held up by a combination of circumstances, giving the coach enough time to sit them all down for a little talk. Some were too young, being only ninth and tenth graders. Most of the juniors were only seventeen and even those seniors already eighteen needed their parents' permission to enlist, a fact that had escaped the notice of most of them. The principle also talked to the team and tried to get across the point that it was more important for everyone to complete their high school education than it was to go running off to a war. Some listened, some didn't.

Those who were too young came out best because they had put it on the line only to have the line withdrawn. They were heroes without having been tested; it was the seniors who felt the whimsical reactions of the collective mindset. Most were eighteen or would be before the spring semester was over. Those who chose to remain in school until after graduation somehow were made of slightly lesser stuff, maybe not as manly as they might have been. This was a hard burden to bear, but since more stayed than joined, they as a group were able to reestablish themselves and subdue this weak but nagging challenge to their manhood.

I was neither fish nor fowl in all of this. I was not yet seventeen at the time of the attack, so I was too young to join even with my parents' permission. I would still be barely seventeen at graduation, and though the law permitted seventeen year olds to enlist with parental consent, the services tended to discourage this unless in the last half of the seventeenth year. So it looked like I might be a civilian for almost a year after graduation. This was not the happiest prospect because it would be difficult to get a job if it was known that I would be leaving in a few months for military services. Also people would ask unfairly if I were classified 4-F for physical disability, or maybe might be a draft dodger.

During this time of high emotionalism and unclear thoughts, Dad talked it over with me and his words were inspired. "Son, everyone complains about this country going to hell, and about all the politicians driving it there, but I want you to remember one thing, no matter how confused the reasoning for being in the jam we're in or where we might be going, when this country needs you to serve, I want you to go and do the best damned job you can. For every one of those rights and privileges that we enjoy there is at least one responsibility, and you will not be much of a man if you don't carry your responsibilities while enjoying your rights. I had hoped my time in World War I would help guarantee there would never be another war, and I had hoped you would never have to go to war at all. Making war is the most asinine project that man has ever come up with. But no matter how stupid war is, your duty is to go and I know you will see it that way too. You will have to make the decision when you want to join up, but as soon as you graduate, not before, I'll give you permission whenever you are ready. Another thing, if you should not be accepted because of some physical defect we don't know about, you can hold up your head because you stood up and were counted. That's the important part, being counted. Don't ever sneer at someone who was turned down in the physical examination, because it could be you. Also, Son, I can't tell you how to think, but let me tell you what I think about the Japanese. I don't consider them cowardly or sneaks because they hit us with a surprise attack. War is a dirty business, and there aren't any rules except to get them before they get you. The only smart way to fight a war is to hit 'em while they aren't looking, it is just plain dumb to shoot it out with another guy, because you can get killed that way, and your Mother and I don't want you killed in this mess."

More bad news followed. Mac Arthur was ordered to leave Corregidor in Manila Bay on March 12. But shortly afterward the first breath of fresh air arrived. It was reported that the Doolittle raiders had bombed Tokyo! That's showing 'em! They had flown B-25 land bombers from the deck of the aircraft carrier USS Hornet, being carried to within 700 miles of Japan before taking off. Actually, the raid had occurred on April 18, but the planning had begun on March 1, not quite three months after Pearl Harbor. All the planes were lost, some landing in the sea, others in China, and two in Japan itself. The raid caused little damage in Japan or to its war effort, but its effect upon the United States was electrifying. There was a feeling of being uplifted, things can go right, we can win, it will be harder than we thought, but we can do it!!

More bad news. The island fortress of Corregidor finally fell to the Japanese on May 5. The defenders had no choice, it was reported that their island received a continuous bombardment of 16,000 shells on May 4 alone, in the end they simply had nothing left. Then Midway was lost.

It was clear we were in for a long fight, and I knew I had to go to war. I had no real idea of what being in a war would be like, there were many photographs in the newspapers and Life magazine, and in the newsreels at the movie theater, but it was difficult to imagine myself in the middle of it. But I knew I would have to go.

Meanwhile, school moved even more slowly than normally. The work was not hard, but it dragged so. While sweating through the course work of this final semester of my senior year, I had to get ready for graduation. First, the administration had each of us tally up the courses we had taken all through high school and calculate the cumulative grade point as a check against the one already recorded.

I found that at the end of four years of high school, I would have accumulated 17 credits where 16 were needed to graduate. I had or would have two years of algebra, courses in plane and solid geometry as well as trigonometry, two years of Latin and two of French, a year of chemistry and one of physics, four years of English composition grammar and literature, two years of history, one of music, and several non-curricular activities which yielded parts of a credit each. Had I taken a different set of options, I could have had courses in shop work, or in several on-the-job training programs, not to mention two years of Spanish or four years of Latin. Woodton High was a good school, and I'll put it up against any other at the time, and it still looks pretty good even today.

I had a good "A-" average, pretty good but not good enough to be valedictorian. In fact, I was 5th in a class of '85.

I almost made a "D" in the last half of that year. We were studying Shakespeare in English Literature. It is all a matter of personal taste, but I never have been able to relate to Shakespeare and it is not from being indifferent. I have read and seen a number of his plays, and have tried, but it just doesn't seem to be my thing.

The beginnings of this incapability began to become evident in English Lit. We studied Shakespeare for an entire six weeks of pure agony; I hated to read the plays, and I never got the point even with the most intense concentration. I simply did not relate. My grade was going downhill like a rock, in fact it already was a "D" and it might go to an F for the six weeks. Worse, there was no way to redeem it except by an absolutely impossible route. We could raise our six weeks grade by one letter by reading and reporting on three Shakespearean plays outside the regular assignments. Already I was choking on Shakespeare in class, and the solution to my problem was to choke on him at home as well. To get a "B", I would have to read and report on six of those wretched works.

Suddenly, someone in class told me about Charles and Mary Lamb's "Tales of Shakespeare." In one comprehensive volume these inspired authors had reviewed all or most anyway of William's writings, summarizing and analyzing each so that some of them actually began to make sense. I avidly read Charles and Mary and reported on enough to get up to a "B" and was on my way to an "A".

My benefactor, I forget who it was now, blabbed it all around about the Lambs, so almost all of the poor grades began to be buoyed up by the extra work being turned in. After a few days of this sudden rain of reports, all with a certain sameness, Mrs. Brown our lit teacher began to smell a rat.

Using methods known only to teachers, she choked the information out of someone outside of class, then next day she announced that she had heard some of us were getting our information from the Lamb couple. She said that wasn't fair to those who were getting the good stuff from the real source, so she went around the room and asked each of us individually if he or she were using Charles and Mary. Some admitted, others equally guilty did not, in fact most didn't. When she got to me I had a terrible choice to make, knowing that at best I would have a "D" and maybe even an "F". But as an Eagle Scout I had to admit it. A Scout is truthful, and an Eagle even more so. I really don't know if I would have owned up had I not been an Eagle. I like to think that I would have, but I really don't know..

When she had interrogated all of us, she said, "Well, I have never had anything like this before. I am going to disallow all outside work from anyone for extra credit, I know that's not fair either but that is the way it is going to be. For those who admitted using the Lamb reference I will raise your grade by one letter." So I got a "C", and even with that my grade averaged out to a "B+" for the semester, and ordinarily that would have gotten me out of the final examination in that course. But not this time, and Mrs. Brown called me into her office to tell me why.

"Technically, you qualify to be excused because you do have a 'B+' for the semester, but you know you didn't really make it. Anyway it always is the teacher's choice to excuse or not to excuse, and I choose that you will be examined. Now, I have never done this before, but I also choose that you be examined on Shakespeare only. I know you got out of all your other exams, so with nothing to distract you and with Charles and Mary to give you guidance, I think you should do very well. I'm doing this because I know you tried, and I really want you to like Shakespeare, and someday I think you will."

I really studied all the plays we had read, using Charles and Mary to outline each one and I absolutely aced the exam, and knew it while I was doing it. I wrote on the bottom of the paper, "Thank you, Mrs. Brown; I really am going to try and like Shakespeare." When I got it back, she had written, "I know you will Gaylord, some things just take time." It is still taking time, and I haven't gotten there yet. But thank you again, Mrs. Brown, because I am still trying.

I made an "A" on the test and wound up with a "B+" for the semester. She wouldn't give me an "A" because she said I hadn't earned it, and she was right.

The school year finally ended, the class voted not to have a yearbook to conserve paper. We had our class picnic and senior prom and ordered our gowns and mortar board hats and endured the ceremonies of the baccalaureate sermon, the valedictorian address; "Honored faculty, beloved parents, and fellow students, I stand before you tonight, not as your valedictorian but as the voice of youth saying to those mature ears which grace your magnificent demeanors, we stand ready to assume the mantle of responsibility and to serve. We shall not let you down...." You have heard it a thousand times.

Finally, it was over. The guys all exchanged hand-shakes, and hugs and kisses with the girls some of whom revealed that they might, and stood around for a while before going home or to the parties.

When we got home, I found I had left my lock on my locker. I went back to get it and entered the now vacant building. The janitors were sweeping the floors, I collected my lock and looked inside my empty locker, realizing suddenly it no longer was mine. I walked up and down the cavernous halls when a feeling of illness and disorientation began to overcome me. I didn't belong here anymore! My place was outside, I must leave! I ran to the door and left and I have never been back.

I went home and said, "Dad, I'm ready to join up."
"Thought you would be, we'll go down tomorrow." So we did, and at 17 years, 3 months, I enlisted.

Five of us were sworn in by the sergeant and put on a bus for Little Rock, where we would report to Camp Robinson. When I got off the bus at Little Rock, a sergeant there handed me a telegram and said, "Crawford, you have emergency leave of five days. Your mother just died of a stroke." My immediate reaction, before the shock set in, was a feeling of dismay that no one would ever again call me Gaylord Throckmorton Montmorency Crawford.